DEBT

of

WOLVES

LINNEA K. WARREN

This novel is a work of fiction.

ISBN: 9798874467043

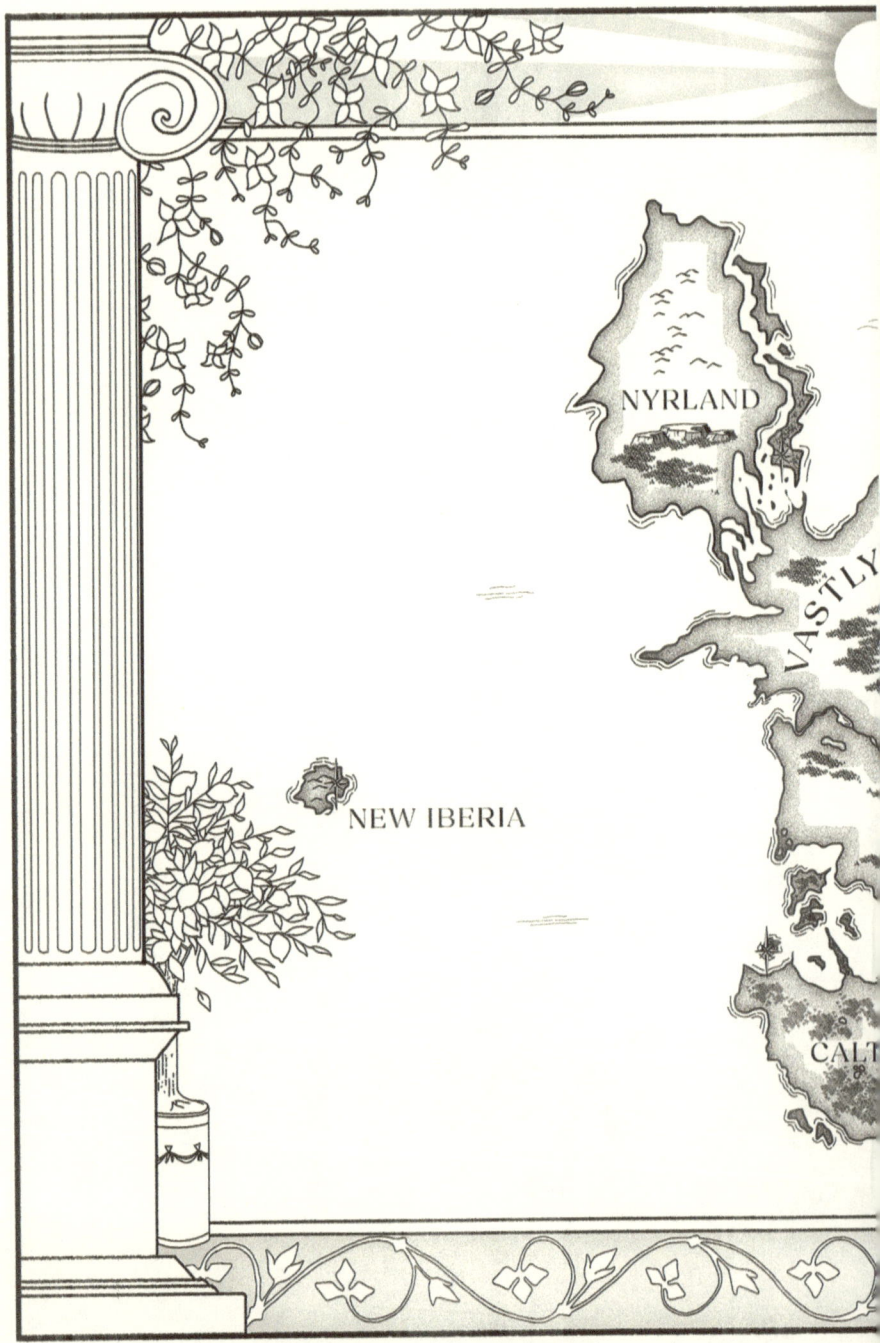

NYRLAND

VASTLY

NEW IBERIA

CALT

AVEN

ND

THE CENTRAL TERRITORIES

ERRA

TYRNNTH

N

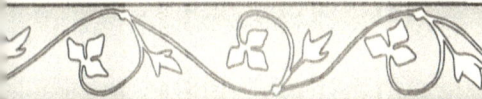

To those who read to know
that they are, in fact, not alone:

You are not, my friend.

PROLOGUE

"You see that?" Max said, nodding toward the screen. "Tyrnnth sunk that boat off the coast."

Steven straightened and glanced at the screen.

"I heard they sank from engine failure."

The coffee shop quieted as the newscaster went on, images of a boat flashing across the screen, as well as a young woman.

"Reporters suggest New Iberia may be involved, Emmaline Shrouder, the King of New Iberia's Second, now missing. Some claim she may have been on board the Centrallian vessel when it sank."

"Steven."

The prizefighter turned, Max leveling him with a look.

"Yes?"

"I need you to know something," Max said, regarding him. "This could all change very quickly and I don't want you to be caught off guard."

Steven's brows drew together. "What do you mean?"

The aged trainer made a contemplative noise and scrubbed his jaw. "I've seen war. This is— this could be the start, and I don't want you to be surprised when it hits."

"No," Steven said, smiling. "The Central Territories? Tyrnnth isn't even a sixteenth of our size."

"They know that. Don't think it will stop them."

Steven's smile disappeared as Max leaned forward, dropping his voice. "When it gets dark, remember that is when light is brightest."

"Max—"

"No matter what happens, do not lose hope," Max pressed. "Can you promise me, kid?"

Steven turned away, watching children pile out of a bus, a mother with a stroller. A man with aging parents.

War couldn't hit Central.

"I don't— I don't know." Steven looked up to watch a video of the young King of New Iberia shield his face from a hoard of reporters and flashing cameras.

Even if the downed boat and missing woman were connected, it wouldn't affect Steven.

Over the last nineteen years of his existence, Central hadn't shown signs of falling prey to the outbreak of wars around the world.

The Central Territories were far too large, too distant.

Steven would be fine, and Max was wrong.

1

There was a king in the infirmary.

In and out of consciousness, Steven watched as the man made his rounds, his suit perfectly pressed underneath his olive trench coat.

They had met once.

It seemed like a lifetime ago.

The reality of war had been a distant thunderhead; imminent, but not quite real. Jay had been alive, and Steven had been declining King Bardolph's offer to move to a foreign land to gain citizenship for a Blood Challenge.

With Jay's status as a registered Central Territorian convict, he had been destined for the front.

The choice had been easy for Steven.

Though the concept of a war ending in one fight had tugged on his sleeve at the time, he had made his choice.

It hadn't made a difference.

Jay's body was somewhere in a field beyond enemy lines, his body to burn with the rest of their unit when Tyrnnth's fires reached them.

When Steven opened his eyes again, the king was at the foot of his bed, looking over a clipboard attached to the frame.

"Ah, you're awake," King Bardolph said, settling the clipboard back. "How are you feeling, Mr. Castellen?"

Steven's focus caught on shifting curtains, bright, golden sunlight filtering into the room.

They needed to close the windows.

If Tyrnnth advanced and diffused gas, it would be a matter of moments before everyone would be choking on their own blood.

Everyone but Steven, who would be able to do nothing but watch.

"Steven?"

The prizefighter started. "What?"

"I asked how you were," King Bardolph said. "When you didn't reply, I offered my condolences for the loss of your unit and brother."

Steven worked his jaw. "You just want me to come to New Iberia so I can fatten myself up for slaughter. And make *you* look good in the process."

Nurses turned and paper sheets crinkled as soldiers shifted.

The king leaned forward, grasping the frame behind Steven's head.

"You're not the only one coming back with losses, Mr. Castellen," King Bardolph said, his voice low and hazel eyes burning. "The only difference is, you can make a *much* bigger difference now."

Steven's lips tightened. "You're a little close."

"Uncomfortable?" The corner's of the king's eyes crinkled. "Trust me, with war, it only gets worse."

Steven exhaled when the king stepped away, straightening his coat. "I must assume your answer is no."

"I haven't had time to think about it."

King Bardolph huffed a laugh.

The curtains behind Steven swelled, a breeze snaking over his skin. He instinctively flinched, the New Iberian king tracking the movement, his eyes on the curtain as he adjusted his suit cuff.

"I was told something rather interesting before arriving to this base," King Bardolph said, sliding the window closed. He stepped back in a smooth motion. "I would have let you be, but I heard you can breathe Tyrnnth's poison. This is a rare thing for anyone not born of their country, and I had to inquire your services again upon hearing it."

When Steven didn't reply, King Bardolph sighed.

"Did you know I attended several of your fights years ago?"

Steven gripped his sheet. "What?"

"New Iberia hosted a tournament that year," the king said simply. "Mr. Castellen, have you watched any footage of Tyrnnth's Blood Challenges?"

"They're banned."

"From watching?"

Steven nodded.

"Of course," King Bardolph said, running his tongue over his teeth. He looked toward the infirmary door. "I believe your War Leader is concerned for country morale."

"Yes," Steven said. He didn't need to watch the footage to know the Blood Challenges were horrifying.

The rumors were enough.

The king met Steven's gaze. "Regardless, whatever you and Grand Leader Hawthorne are made of, I have decided it's the same thing."

Steven's brows drew together as King Bardolph went on.

"Though Hawthorne wields his strength with cruelty, you, Steven— you are precise, thoughtful," he said. "Furthermore, if you can breathe Tyrnnth's poison, you will be unaffected by the smog in the capital."

"I don't think—" Steven began.

Didn't think what?

He *could* breathe Tyrnnth's poison. Whether or not he could win a fight against Luther—

"I don't think I can take him."

"You say that despite never having watched a Blood Challenge."

Steven shut his mouth.

"I wouldn't reach out if I didn't think you stood a chance," King Bardolph said. "From the moment I watched you beat men several times your size, with little effort, I figured I would eventually reach out to offer a position amongst my assassins."

"Assassins?"

The king's lips thinned as he adjusted his suit cuff again.

"Yes. But my— I don't have a proper teacher. And," King Bardolph said, dropping his hands, "one could end the war much quicker this way."

"Right," Steven said.

"Have these last few minutes cleared anything up for you?"

Steven ran his hands over his face. "So, I would live in New Iberia until I gain citizenship, then ship off to fight Luther?"

"Yes. I will assign training, studies, and if I actually grow to enjoy your company, I may invite you in on some scheming," the king said. "Though that is yet to be seen. But you would not remain idle. Our enemy does not rest, and neither shall we."

Our enemy.

New Iberia had a grudge against Tyrnnth, the enemy War Leader having had nearly the entire immediate royal family wiped out several years ago.

The twenty-year-old man with scars on his hands before Steven had been the only one left alive.

The prizefighter looked down at his sheet-covered body to the collection of shrapnel and bullets on his bedside table.

All of that had come out of his body.

It was a shock he wasn't dead.

"You are well, by the way," King Bardolph said. "Your chart says you can leave anytime."

"I'm surprised."

"I'm not. You are not normal, Steven," the king said, eyes

narrowing. "I'm not sure what's wrong with you, but in these times, it is just right."

King Bardolph glanced at his watch. "Time to go. Will you be joining or staying?"

Steven sighed through his nose and met King Bardolph's gaze, the challenge in them.

"You think I have a chance against the dictator?"

"I think you're the only one who does."

Steven shut his eyes and leaned his head back.

His brother was dead.

His childhood best friend, Grace, either dead or working her life away in a slave camp.

Steven's parents, dead— for awhile.

His trainer, dead.

He had nothing else to live for.

2

With a curse under Steven's breath, he rolled out of bed. He rubbed the heel of his palm into his eyes, as if he could erase the image of his brother getting shot in the back.

It never worked.

Steven cracked open his door to find light gilding the steps.

He hadn't left any lights on.

It was second nature to strap a knife to his hip.

Just in case.

As he glided down the stairs, he heard a mug set down onto the table. Steven fastened his robe tighter.

One of the usual visitors.

Again.

"Hello," Steven said tiredly, stepping into the kitchen. A woman sat at the table to his left, mug in hand.

He reached the cupboard in three strides.

"A male friend. That, I haven't seen in an age," the young woman said, her voice accented.

"And *he's* not here." Steven filled a glass of water, his voice hoarse from sleeping. He looked to the woman, her blonde hair draped over a shoulder as she studied him.

His eyes flicked to her hands, noting calluses and scars.

"Are you an ex? Or someone interested?" Steven grabbed the

seat adjacent to hers.

The woman huffed. "How often do *visitors* come along?"

"Enough to warrant me not being surprised to find you."

"He's changed quite a bit then."

"So, an ex."

The woman raised a golden, arched brow. "Guilty."

Steven leaned back in his chair, the wood groaning.

"What's your name?" he asked.

"Natalia." The woman lifted her chin. "And you are?"

"Steven."

"Well met." Natalia offered a smile, though a coldness shone in her eyes. High cheekbones, a straight nose—

"You seem familiar," he said. He wouldn't be surprised if he had passed her on the New Iberian capital's streets after three months. Though Evynmare sprawled across the island's entire northeastern coast, Steven had nearly navigated its entirety.

"I used to visit." Natalia shrugged.

Steven took a sip of his water. "Where are you from?"

"Vastlynd. You don't have a New Iberian accent either."

Steven nodded. "I'm from Central."

Natalia angled her head. "Are you a refugee? I didn't realize New Iberia was taking any, despite the alliance."

Steven shook his head. She hadn't recognized him, then. Or didn't bother to watch the news.

"I'm here under the king's blessing to gain New Iberian citizenship for the Blood Challenge against Tyrnnth's dictator."

Natalia leaned back, tapping a nail on her mug.

"Ah, yes. I heard they were outlawed in Central," she said, blowing out a breath.

"A stupid law." Steven shook his head. "We need it most."

Natalia pursed her lips, continuing to study him. Steven ignored her and gazed toward the still-dark windows. Sunup was a little ways off, an approaching autumn stealing more and more light each day.

DEBT OF WOLVES

"Why did they ban them?" Natalia asked.

Steven looked at her. "For morale. Luther ripping his opponents to literal shreds wasn't helping. Don't you watch the news?"

"I try not to." Natalia winced, looking at her tea.

Steven smiled. "I wish I didn't."

Luther Hawthorne was a beast.

But Steven could be, too.

"Do you play the piano at all, Steven?"

His brows furrowed, hesitating. "I— yes."

"Great. I want to hear a song before I go." Natalia leaned back in her chair. Steven huffed a laugh, the woman clearly convinced he would oblige her.

He'd likely never see her again, anyways.

Steven rose and stalked to the piano beside the stairs, taking a seat at the worn bench.

"Any requests?" he asked the wallpaper, rolling his stiff wrists.

"Nope."

Easy enough. Steven inhaled, and began.

The cottage filled with sound, each key and chord out of tune in a way Steven found endearing.

He didn't know what he was playing, though he figured it would satisfy the woman's request.

The song began thoughtful, meandering. His fingers drifted over the keys, allowing the song to escalate before drawing to a close. As the last note faded, he opened his eyes.

Natalia was leaned against the wall, her eyes fixed on his hands.

"Who taught you?" she asked quietly.

Steven gripped his hands in his lap. "My mother."

It had been an age since he had heard her play. He never would again. Natalia's lips tightened as she nodded.

She departed after leaving her mug to dry, Steven left to wonder why she had been dumped.

Perhaps she had dumped Steven's friend, in this case.

8

Steven stood at the glass door afterward, watching the sky lighten above the turning orchard, more orange and yellow leaves strewn about the ground than the day prior.

Steven was another day closer to ending Luther Hawthorne's life, and the war with it.

He blew out a breath and curled up on the couch, willing time to pass and his nightmares to stay at bay.

3

Farran had arrived.

Steven knew from the scent of breakfast tea and whisper of pages.

The prizefighter opened his eyes, light streaming through the windows lining the unlit fireplace, Farran seated in the armchair opposite to him.

"Good morning," Farran said pleasantly, closing his book. "Was there a spider in the attic again?"

Steven leaned on an elbow.

"No," Steven ground out. "You had another guest."

Never mind Steven would have never known, if not for his nightmares to wake him.

Farran huffed a laugh and ran a hand through his golden hair.

"Dare I ask whom this time?"

Steven laid his head on the couch pillow, eyeing a crack in the wood beam above.

The interaction had happened hours ago, but he couldn't seem to remember—

Steven sat up, snapping his fingers. *"Natalia."*

Farran spewed his tea.

"Surely not," he breathed, reaching for his handkerchief. "What did she look like?"

"I'm assuming things didn't end well."

Farran wiped his mouth, giving Steven an exasperated look. The man's face had paled since Steven had uttered the woman's name.

The prizefighter tried his best not to smile, for Farran's sake.

"Blonde, tall. Blue eyes."

"And what did she want?"

Steven scoffed as he looked at Farran. "They all come here looking for you. Honestly, I'm not sure how you haven't been assassinated yet."

Farran shook his head. "Believe me, if Natalia wanted me dead, it would have happened long ago." He cradled his mug, steam dancing in a gilded ray.

"You must not know who she is," he went on. "Natalia Hawthorne is Luther's wife and assassin. If she were here last night, it would have been to kill you."

Steven shook his head. "I almost want to believe you, but it is impossible to picture you with an assassin."

"I am serious, Steven," Farran said, exasperated. "And we courted before she was sold as a peace treaty to Tyrnnth, and thus, before Luther turned her into a weapon."

Steven chewed on a lip and ran a hand through his dirty blonde hair, fingers snagging on tangles.

"Should I be worried?"

"Not at all." Farran brought his mug to his face. "The time for worrying is over. For whatever reason, Natalia left you alive."

⸺

Despite the sun, the autumn air was brisk.

Steam rippled off Steven as he assaulted the punching bag hanging off the stand in the cottage driveway, his breath curls of smoke.

Farran was to attend a peace conference tomorrow. Five

months into the war between the Central Territories and Tyrnnth, the neutral country of Vastlynd was stepping in to offer an opportunity for some sort of civil conversation.

Steven admired King Ridgeway's attempt.

That was as far as his admiration for the King of Vastlynd went.

The only reason the man's country remained neutral and untouched was due to him selling his own daughter off to the Tyrnnthian dictator.

A living treaty.

Steven had looked into the history after Farran had left, confirming the woman's identity.

Natalia was indeed a trained killer, and appeared quite loyal to her husband and new country.

It was a wonder Steven wasn't dead.

Maybe he hadn't appeared much of a threat.

Steven had never been to Vastlynd, the large country bordering on Central Territories' northern border.

The conference was to be held in King Ridgeway's palace amongst the snow-capped peaks above Zephyr, the capital city of Vastlynd.

Steven sent another punch at the bag, sweat stinging his eyes. Another strike, and another—

If the peace conference didn't end in a truce, Steven would declare his Blood Challenge.

He did not miss the irony.

Tyrnnth's dictator had been spewing propaganda before Steven's training this morning. Tyrnnth's War Leader, Ares, had also appeared, going on about how they were saving the world.

Steven hadn't forgotten the time he had crossed paths with the War Leader at the front.

Ares was nothing short of a sharp-tongued liar and killer.

Steven blocked out the memory as cranes began calling overhead.

He halted, panting as he watched their formations draw close, rattling bugles filling the air.

While his world had changed with war, theirs had not.

The sun still rose, the cold still stole the breath out of his lungs, and there were still birds.

He wasn't sure if the same rang true in his own country.

Steven continued his session after the cranes passed, his mind drifting back to the peace conference.

Farran had invited him.

Steven would somehow have to remain civil, even if he came face to face with Luther Hawthorne and Ares Valeryn.

The King of New Iberia had made good on his word to fill the prizefighter's idle time with studying. Several books and documentaries later, Steven knew more about Tyrnnth's political history and creed.

While the information had been meant to prepare Steven, it had instead further terrified him.

It would not be unlike Tyrnnth to burn Steven's country to the ground and bury the bodies in the trenches, despite their leaders calling it salvation.

It did not sound like salvation to Steven.

He threw his head back, hair shifting from his brow. When he closed his eyes, he saw the front, gunfire ringing in his ears, the ground shaking as artillery rained—

Steven drew in a sharp breath and renewed his assault.

4

Steven adjusted his tie as he ascended the snow-coated, Vastlynd palace steps. With the capital in the valley shining like a river of stars, he knew he would be stepping out often to enjoy the view, as well as the cold.

Voices streamed through the tall, open doorway as Farran and Steven entered, a crowd milling about the large entryway. Though beautiful, Steven found the painted ceiling and crystal-laden chandeliers frivolous.

With war on the other side of Vastlynd's border, he couldn't help but find all the finery a waste.

It would all burn the same when Tyrnnth decided Central was not enough for them.

Because if they could so easily conquer the Central Territories, surely they wouldn't stop there.

If Luther and his father, Ares, were convinced they were saving the world by burning it and starting it anew, perhaps they would extend that kindness to Vastlynd next.

Steven and Farran passed glittering gowns and pressed suits as they climbed the grand stairs and entered the ballroom. Floor to ceiling windows lined the walls, showcasing a light snowfall against a black sky.

A servant with a tray of pastries passed, Steven's mouth

watering at the sight and scent. Another servant with stuffed pork rolls—

Farran caught Steven's wrist.

"In Vastlynd, the king eats first," Farran said quietly.

"I'm starved." Steven shook off his friend's grasp, adjusting his suit cuffs. "And too hot. When's this thing supposed to start, anyways?"

Farran offered a polite smile. "Be glad you were not born into court life. I doubt you would last very long."

"I am glad." Steven couldn't imagine. "They'd probably pay me to live somewhere else."

Farran laughed broadly, shaking his head. "It's quite possible."

The room quieted, the men looking toward the dais with the rest of the room.

King Ridgeway had arrived.

The man looked to be in his late forties, bearing ash brown hair streaked with gray, a few lines on his face. A ruggedly handsome man, Steven supposed.

He now had no doubt he had met the king's daughter.

Though King Ridgeway's eyes were darker, his straight nose and lips bore a resemblance to Natalia's.

Sold. This man had *sold* his daughter to Tyrnnth. Steven clenched his jaw as the king smiled at the crowd.

"Welcome, all," King Ridgeway said. "We gather for the hope of peace amongst our nations. Please, enjoy the food, company, and music as the leaders gather for a discussion. There will be dancing afterward, regardless of the outcome."

Steven didn't pay attention to the rest of the king's spiel, becoming distracted as a tray of molasses cookies strode by.

The crackers on the plane just hadn't cut it for him.

King Ridgeway raised a glass of wine as he wrapped up, Steven accepting his own from a servant.

"To the future," King Ridgeway said. The room parroted and drank with the king, the crowd lost to Steven's pause before following suit.

Farran clapped a hand on Steven's shoulder as King Ridgeway descended the dais, the orchestra starting an exuberant piece.

"Here we go," Farran said, dropping his hand.

Steven followed his friend, snatching a pork roll as they passed a refreshment table. Steven stuffed the soft, hearty pastry down his throat before Farran could stop him.

"You're not even enjoying it." Farran said, frowning over a shoulder.

"Wanna bet?" Steven's words were barely discernible. Farran exited the ballroom and approached an oak door down the hall.

"Are you sure they'll take my presence as a peaceful gesture?" Steven asked, brushing crumbs away from his suit.

"You're not a Blood Challenger yet," Farran said. "Tonight, you are simply Steven Castellen, my server."

"Honored."

Farran set his hand on the knob, hazel eyes pinning Steven.

"King Ridgeway will send you out if you do not show proper respect for each leader," Farran warned. "This includes the ones you hate, as well as the ones you know a bit *too* well."

"Yes, sir." Steven offered a stiff salute, his eyes catching on the light glinting off the medals Farran bore.

He was dressed in his finery tonight, his chest adorned in military decorations from a war Steven knew little about, and one his friend never mentioned.

Farran gave Steven a pointed look. The prizefighter sighed and dropped his salute.

"Yes, Your Majesty," Steven said, bowing at the waist. When he straightened, the King of New Iberia was smiling.

"Perfect. Now next time, don't roll your eyes."

The king opened the door and Steven followed him in.

The prizefighter's smile died as he took in Ares Valeryn's assessing gaze and adder's smile.

Despite the three months since Steven's last interaction with

Tyrnnth's War Leader, Steven regularly saw Ares in his nightmares.

Ares had been there the day everything went to hell on the front.

The War Leader had promised to dump Jay's body into the trench with the rest of their downed unit.

Steven took an uneven breath, turning his attention toward the other Tyrnnthian seated beside Ares.

Luther Hawthorne was watchful and quiet. The dictator was a beast of a man, muscular even beneath a wool, herringbone suit. His silvery blonde hair was tousled, his face angular, though not in a way that made him look cruel, as the look appeared on that of his father's.

"Grand Leader Hawthorne, a pleasure to make your acquaintance again," Farran said, taking his seat. He nodded to Ares. "War Leader Valeryn, you look well."

Mismatching last names, despite the relation. Steven had found it strange until he had learned the dictator had changed it to match his mother's surname.

Perhaps even Luther didn't wish to associate with his father.

Steven stood behind and to the right of Farran's chair, a servant awaiting orders.

Ares' glacial gaze slid from Farran to Steven, his lip curling back.

"Why is this foreign foot soldier with you?"

Luther eyed Steven, his expression unreadable.

"Because he is my friend, and tonight, my server," Farran said plainly, his hands clasped on the table before him. The New Iberian king turned, his expression softening.

"Mr. Castellen, could you please fetch some water?"

"Yes, Your Majesty."

Steven turned and crossed the room. When he reached the refreshment table, he picked up a carafe and filled a glass.

He should have brought poison.

At least then he could have been more than a server.

He was the world's greatest prizefighter, Luther's ruin, and here he was, pouring a glass of water before his enemies . . .

A hand settled on his shoulder, rooting him in place.

"You know, I am not actually that thirsty," Farran said quietly. "I would like for you to wait outside, please."

"I can behave."

"Steven, I—"

The prizefighter turned, his mind catching up to register what his eyes already beheld, a familiar honey-brown gaze watching back.

"Grace."

Steven hadn't seen her since the draft, her safe house destroyed after Steven had volunteered for the front.

"I thought you were dead," he whispered.

"I would like you to wait outside," Farran insisted. Steven's eyes drifted to Grace's wrists.

Manacles.

Steven looked to Luther and Ares. The dictator sipped from his glass while Ares offered a smile.

"We have servants, too," Ares said.

Steven's grip tightened on the glass and he wondered if the room could see it shaking.

Ares went on with a gesture of his pale hand. "I caught a spy in our shipyard searching for this particular slave. I thought it may be in our best interest to bring her along tonight."

"Let me take care of this," Farran insisted.

"I am not leaving this room," Steven said.

"What is the meaning of this?"

Everyone turned toward the door as King Ridgeway entered, the king's eyes burning holes through Steven.

"If you speak to King Bardolph in such a tone again, I'll have you thrown out, boy." King Ridgeway braced his palms at the head of the long table. "Am I clear?"

"Crystal, Your Majesty," Steven replied.

The Vastlynd King took a seat, Farran following suit. Steven positioned himself beside Farran, watching as Grace mirrored the prizefighter.

She wouldn't look at him, her eyes on the wall. He noted her collarbones jutting above her mist-gray gown.

Tyrnnth had starved her and dressed her in their colors.

Steven ground his jaw.

Grace's eyes were clear, though. She looked over and met his gaze long enough to give him a small smile.

She was alive. It would have to be enough for now.

Grace's eyes slid to Farran, her gaze thoughtful.

"The princes will be here soon," King Ridgeway said, Steven drawn back to reality.

"They run on island time," Ares crooned, leaning back.

Never mind that Tyrnnth and New Iberia were island kingdoms themselves.

Steven kept his mouth shut.

He cast a glance to Farran, noting how he regarded Ares before flicking his eyes to Grace.

The oak door swung open, two men entering.

Both Calterran princes were tan and dark-haired. The older of the two was tall and broad, bearing a beard and long, unkempt hair, the ends bleached from the sun.

The younger was lean, hair shoulder-length, and bore a five o'clock shadow on his face. While his eyes were dark and somber, his older brother's seemed alight with an inner fire.

The chair creaked as the brute sat at Farran's side, the lithe one claiming the chair beside Luther.

Grace shifted on her feet, chains clinking.

The brute's attention snapped to it, his eyes narrowing as he regarded her. To Grace's credit, she held her chin high and didn't balk.

"Prince Zakkai Mililani, Prince Memphis Makani, welcome," King Ridgeway said. The brute nodded to the first name, the lither to the second.

"I didn't realize we would be bringing slaves to the *peace* meeting," Zakkai rumbled, cutting a glance to Luther.

"A pleasure to see you, too, Prince," Luther replied, his voice edged in steel, and to Steven's surprise, much quieter than he expected.

Memphis huffed, the chain hanging from his nose to his ear shifting. Luther cut the younger prince a glance that had Zakkai leaning his tattooed forearms on the table.

"You rip that out, your throat will be next."

King Ridgeway sighed. "With that, let's get started."

———

King Ridgeway grew impatient as the meeting proceeded, and Steven somehow managed to curb his urge to beat his enemies in the head with a chair.

There was little progress, if any. Tyrnnth was set on conquering and Calterra refused to offer an opinion.

Before the meeting drew to a close, Zakkai stood and braced his hands on the table, addressing Luther.

"One more thing," the prince said. Steven watched his gaze shift upward, the fire in his eyes growing brighter.

"I want her."

Steven's heart stopped, Grace's eyes pinned on the wall.

Ares blew out a breath as no one deigned to reply for a moment, the prince's request fully registering.

"Don't you have enough?" Ares sniped.

"Enough what?" Steven wasn't permitted to speak, but he had to.

"Castellen," Farran warned.

Steven stepped forward, Zakkai turning toward him. The brute was at least a foot and a half taller than Steven, but the prizefighter could take him if he really wanted to.

Though he would likely break a bone.

Or several.

"What do you want with her," Steven bit out.

Calterra's heir smiled.

"Stand down, Steven," Farran said, his voice distant despite being beside him.

"Answer me." Steven took another step.

He hadn't anticipated the slap. The prince had struck so fast, Steven hadn't time to react. His cheek stung, his eyes watering from the impact. As his vision cleared, he realized he had been wrong.

It had not been the prince, but Farran, now before Steven and a hands-breadth away.

"Stand down."

A roiling, uneasy feeling swept through Steven as he stepped back, Farran's eyes guttering.

The king somehow managed to seat himself gracefully, turned away as Steven's face grew hot.

His best friend had slapped him in front of his enemies.

A few beats of silence passed before Zakkai spoke.

"She's your friend."

"Yes," Steven said quietly, watching Farran shut his eyes. The king cursed softly, propping his head on a hand.

Zakkai smiled, drawing Steven's attention.

"You don't have to worry about her. I'm sure she'll make lots of friends with the other women in my harem."

The screaming in Steven's head wouldn't quiet, even as the orchestra played some of his favorite pieces. Even as people wished him luck and told him how much they loved watching his fights.

He couldn't feel much past rage and shame.

After Zakkai had mentioned his *harem,* Farran had physically dragged Steven from the room.

The king had known the prizefighter couldn't stand another second in that room. Not without drawing blood.

Farran had escorted Steven outside.

"My deepest, sincerest apologies," Farran had began, his voice pained, and nearly believable. "I am—"

"You *slapped* me," Steven spat. Farran stilled, tendrils of breath drifting towards the black sky.

"I know. And I am so, desperately sorry."

Steven shook his head and turned toward the sparkling capital beneath the mountains.

"I have to maintain a certain image. I know I could have handled it better, but I reacted. Please forgive me, Steven."

Steven hadn't replied.

Leaned against the pillar in the corner of the ballroom, he considered the fact that he no idea what it was like to be king,.

Perhaps it was a great deal worse than what he thought if it could allow for someone like Farran Bardolph to crack every now and again.

The symphony closed, the crowd parting as the ballroom doors opened to allow the royalty in.

Farran entered first, a gold crown atop his golden hair. On his arm, a raven-haired woman dressed in a black silk gown. Deep olive skin, jade eyes, a diadem atop her head—

She was royalty, but Steven had never seen her before.

Zakkai and Memphis followed, Ares and Luther on their heels, murmurs rising.

The band started up again, ushering in a sense of normalcy, even as enemies prowled the floor.

Farran began dancing with the strange, beautiful woman, the pair graceful as they swept across the ballroom. The crowd seemed to take it as a sign none of them would be harmed tonight, and joined.

Steven turned to find the Central Territorian War Leader stalking up to him. The man's russet-brown hair went past his shoulders, red and black tattoos peeking above the neckline of his suit.

Steven had met Jaxin Brown before he had chosen the front with Jay. Jaxin's sole duty was to run the country in wartime, whilst the President remained tucked away.

Jaxin stopped before Steven, offering a nod.

"You weren't at the meeting," Steven noted.

"I forgot my crown," Jaxin drawled.

Steven huffed a laugh. Jaxin was far from royalty, the War Leader having grown up in a Nyrland village before immigrating to Central.

"Who's dancing with King Bardolph?" Steven asked, nodding towards the pair. Jaxin regarded the woman, taking a sip of wine.

"Her Majesty, Adira Theron," Jaxin replied. "Empress of Nyrland."

From what Steven knew, Nyrland was a wild, untamed empire just northwest of King Ridgeway's country. Though the territory was vast, it bore a meager population.

"She looks a bit young to be an empress," Steven said.

"Empress Theron didn't have a choice. The children of the other chieftains had been dead for years. When she turned eighteen, she was the only one left for the position."

"And now she's trying to woo the King of New Iberia."

"She's seen the game played." Jaxin shrugged. "But so has King Bardolph."

The men toasted to the end of the war before Steven found himself at the edge of the dance floor. Adira had disappeared, Grace now dancing with the young New Iberian king.

Farran returned the smile Grace offered, her wrists free of blood-stained steel.

It had been over three months since Steven had seen her. If he didn't come up with a plan to smuggle her out tonight, the chains would return to her wrists as soon as the party was over.

Farran caught Steven's gaze, the king leaning in to say something to Grace as he motioned for Steven to approach. The prizefighter weaved through dancers, relieved when Grace turned and smiled.

A physical weight seemed to fall off his shoulders at the sight.

"I didn't realize they would let you out," Steven said, meeting Grace's eyes. He hoped she could read everything in them.

I'm sorry I didn't try harder.

He had written her off as another dead friend, the only effort at finding her put forward at the beginning of his stay in New Iberia.

Farran had asked about Grace, remembering seeing her at the edge of the pit during Steven's fight at a tournament New Iberia had hosted *years* ago.

The king had sent a hunting party, following Tyrnnth's trail until ending up silenced at Central's eastern shore.

The shipyard Ares had mentioned, Steven now knew.

If Farran hadn't sent his men to find Grace, Ares would have never brought her as a taunt.

Farran had spared her.

Steven could save her.

His weapons were a mere brisk walk away.

"Luther and Ares wouldn't have let me out, actually," Grace said, looking at Farran. "King Bardolph bought me."

"What?" Steven blurted, looking to Farran for an explanation.

The king smiled tightly. "I have my methods."

If Luther and Ares had brought Grace to use against Farran . . .

"What was the cost?" Steven asked.

"People shouldn't have prices," Farran replied sharply. He withdrew his arm from Grace's back, his eyes softening as he looked at her. "If you'll excuse me, I'm going to leave you two to catch up."

Farran nodded to Steven before disappearing into the crowd.

"You're worried about him," Grace said, accepting Steven's hand. They began to dance, Steven still reeling.

"I never realized how complicated everything could be." Steven shook his head and attempted to smile. "It doesn't matter, I'm just glad you're here. I thought you were dead, and then I thought you were going to be someone's *slave* . . . "

"And I'm not." Grace smiled. "Hooray."

"You haven't changed much, have you?"

Steven felt lighter than he had in months.

Hope. There was hope in the midst of this.

Grace was proof.

———

Steven leaned his elbows onto the balcony banister, the party muffled behind the windows at his back. Before him, the capital cast the falling snow in silver.

He savored the cold air in his lungs and on his skin, snowflakes like small kisses on his cheek.

He had danced for hours, savoring the calm before reality and war set back in.

Because it would, and it would hit like a brick wall.

Steven hadn't seen the empress for the rest of the evening. He had caught himself scanning the room only to find her presence lacking.

How hard would she try to gain Farran's favor? If the country was as small as Steven imagined, Nyrland had much to gain from an alliance with New Iberia.

His shoes pressed into the snow as he wandered to the far end of the balcony, admiring the city below.

Vastlynd was snow-coated evergreens, jagged mountains, sprawling wilderness— it made Central appear tame, subdued.

He hoped to return someday.

"Enjoying the party?"

Steven turned to find a woman sitting on the rail, dress draped over the banister as she leaned against the wall.

He had found the empress. "What are you doing out here?"

"Getting fresh air, same as you, I take it," the empress said, her eyes flicking over his outfit before settling on her nails.

Steven nodded, leaning against the rail.

"And are you enjoying your evening?"

The empress smiled, something cutting and cruel about it. "No."

Steven smiled back. "And why's that?"

The woman slid from her perch, light gilding her dark hair in red-gold hues. "I am not fond of people and I hate dancing."

"Shame." Steven slid his hands into his pockets.

"So I've been told."

The orchestra began a new piece on the other side of the glass. Before Steven could think better of it, he offered a hand.

"Despite your distaste for people and dancing, I've been wanting to ask regardless."

The empress stared at Steven's hand, her eyes snagging on his calluses and scars.

"Who are you?" she asked, eyes flicking up.

"Steven."

The woman didn't need to know he was a professional fighter, and for some reason, he didn't want her to.

He also didn't want her to know he was Farran's pet, being groomed for a fight that may very well end in his own death.

For now, he was Steven, a random, well-dressed stranger, feeling bold enough to ask an attractive woman for a dance.

She watched him for a moment before taking his hand.

"And you are?" Steven said, as if he didn't know already. The empress tilted her head back and smirked.

"Adira," she said. "Now pipe down, so I can at least enjoy the music while I suffer through this."

26

Steven obliged.

Snow continued to fall as they swept across the balcony, their Vastlynder waltz flawless.

They moved as if in question and answer.

A full moon to the tide, Spring's response to Winter.

Steven lifted his hand, the empress turning in the gilded light, her eyes on his as her breath clouded between them. He drew her back in, his hand splaying over her the small of her back as they swept into the final chorus.

Steven was grateful for the dance lessons Max Fitzgerald had coerced the prizefighter to attend.

As the song's last note faded, Steven took a moment to catch his breath, searching Adira's eyes for some sign she may have felt anything he had over the last four minutes.

Her chin lifted, not balking from his attention.

"It's not so bad dancing with someone who actually knows how to."

"Not bad at all."

Adira's focus shifted toward the windows, Steven following her line of sight to find Luther and Ares conversing with Prince Zakkai.

Calterra's heir nodded to something Ares said, Memphis stalking toward them. The younger prince crinkled his nose as Luther spoke, though Zakkai merely listened as he took a sip of wine.

"Friends of yours?" Adira drawled.

Steven shook his head. "Definitely not."

Perhaps Memphis was decent, but Steven would never get the chance to find out.

He had avoided the Tyrnnthians and Calterrans all evening, not trusting himself not to bash their heads into the floor.

Adira sighed, as if she could read his every thought.

"You?" Steven asked.

"I don't have friends." The empress withdrew her hands,

Steven now aware it had been well over a minute since the song had finished.

Adira turned away. "Thanks for the dance."

"Wait."

Adira turned toward him, raising an arched brow. "Yes?"

"You walked in with King Bardolph."

She leveled Steven a look. "Yes."

The prizefighter slid his hands into his pockets. "He won't tell me what the price was for the servant he bought today. Did you happen to overhear anything?"

"Oh, I know what he paid." Adira smiled, though it wasn't friendly. "The question is, why do you need to know?"

"He's my friend."

Adira scoffed and turned away. "So sentimental. His Majesty paid in cash and favors. I want trade connections, and Ares needed to fulfill a debt owed to me. It worked out for everyone today."

Adira walked away, Steven was left to wonder what he may have gotten Farran into.

———

Farran and Grace waited in a limousine.

Steven had been descending the palace steps when he found his watch missing and turned back on a heel.

As he strode for the ballroom, a whistle floated over the chatter of departing guests.

Jaxin stood at the meeting room door, a watch hooked on his finger. Steven followed the War Leader into the darkened room.

"What's this about?" Steven asked, snatching the watch. Jaxin shut the door and strode for the windows. In the dim light, it took Steven a moment to recognize the figure gazing at the city below.

King Ridgeway turned as Steven clasped on his watch, Jaxin halting at the king's side.

"We don't have much time, Caradoc's son is the suspicious

type," King Ridgeway said, his face drawn.

Jaxin nodded, his arms banding over his chest. "Well then, why don't you start, Your Majesty?"

"I'm sorry, what's this about?" Steven asked. He looked over his shoulder before finding the men regarding him, their faces unreadable.

"Steven," King Ridgeway said, "there's no easy way to say this, but you are my son and heir."

Farran had set him up. An attempt at a joke from a man who spent too much time reading books and drinking tea.

Steven laughed and looked to Jaxin, the War Leader's face cold.

The prizefighter's smile faltered. "You can't be serious."

"We are," Jaxin said, checking his watch. "The quicker you accept it, the more time we have for other topics."

Steven shook his head at the king— their physique seemed similar, the golden-tanned skin . . .

Though Steven knew Harrin hadn't been his father by blood, as the man had attempted to kill Steven the day he had found out, Steven's father-by-blood couldn't be the King of Vastlynd.

It was ridiculous.

Steven's mother had worked in a bakery her entire life and her history had never suggested crossing paths with royalty.

Why would they lie to him about this?

A thought gnawed on the edge of Steven's mind, reminding him that his older brother *had* burned the documents before Steven could see them.

"How certain are you?"

"Completely." The king shook his head. "And you went on to become so successful at such a young age. It has been something else to watch you grow into the man you are."

Steven took a step back, the king going on as Jaxin tapped his foot against the floor.

"Evelin would have spoken up like you had today."

Steven's mother.

His more recent memories of the once vibrant, kind-hearted woman consisted of a dark room, a deathbed, and a grave. The end of the line for her fight against an unnamed sickness that had wracked her body for nearly a decade.

Before her decline, Steven kept a few fond memories close.

His mother at the piano bench, his feet swinging as she taught him notes and chords. Her elegant hands kneading bread dough, a flour-dusted apron. Afternoons walking the beach in sunlight.

Steven opened his mouth to speak.

"We have more important matters to discuss," Jaxin cut in.

"How did this happen?" Steven had to ask anyways.

If Eric Ridgeway truly was Steven's father, the king could have rescued Steven's mother from their toxic environment, or even just helped with the medical bills.

And yet he hadn't.

With his endless resources and wealth, he could have found a cure for whatever sickness had torn Steven's mother apart.

"Evelin, Harrin and I used to work together," the king said. "When I heard of her health, I began to visit. I hadn't realized Harrin would attempt to kill you if he found out about your heritage."

Steven shook his head. Harrin had been a small-town mechanic his entire life, giving little opportunity to work with a *king*.

"We don't have time for this." Jaxin stepped forward. "In short, the world leaders conducted secret meetings with Ares heading them up. When the group didn't agree with his grandest idea yet, he killed off his naysayers." The War Leader's eyes darkened. "His Majesty here only made it out because he sold his daughter off to Ares' son."

"Don't forget the rest," King Ridgeway added.

Jaxin narrowed his eyes at the king. "Ares used to like his acquaintances before he started killing them off. Some would say they were all friends."

Jaxin looked at Steven. "In his supposed kindness, Ares gifted the women a shot that would pass on a set of genetic modifications to their children. From what we know, it made their kids unnaturally strong." The War Leader angled his head. "We think that's why you and your brother can breathe Tyrnnth's poison."

Ares had gifted strength?

Steven's entire career—

His enemy was to thank for all of his successes.

"One of the other adverse affects of the shot is it eventually kills its host," King Ridgeway said quietly.

Steven's knees felt unsteady.

Ares had killed Steven's mother.

He had caused the sickness that had her suffering for over a decade.

Jaxin took a step forward, Steven dragging his gaze from the window.

"You are the most suited to fight Luther, as his mother bore the same shot," Jaxin explained. "We wanted you to know. You've seen Luther rip his opponents to shreds, but he will not be able to do the same to you."

Steven blinked, seemingly enough response for Jaxin to continue.

"Along with this, we have a task for you."

5

"The cost of your friend was more than money. My spies gathered Adira Theron's presence in New Iberia is also a part of the deal," Jaxin said. "There is a rumor she may have ties to Tyrnnth."

"What do you want me to do about it?" Steven asked.

"Keep an eye on King Bardolph and the empress. Report to me and tell no one you are doing so. Understood?"

"To protect him?"

Jaxin slipped a paper into Steven's suit coat pocket.

"To protect your country, Steven." The War Leader raised a brow.

"And don't tell anyone about my involvement," King Ridgeway cut in. "It will harm the princess."

Natalia. Steven had a sister.

They had met, talked, and Steven hadn't a clue who she was.

"It would be best not to tell anyone of your heritage until after the Blood Challenge," Jaxin said, glancing at his watch. "The world powers are unsteady right now, and someone might find a way to use you in an attempt to tip it in their favor."

"Or kill me," Steven said.

The War Leader offered a bitter smile. "You've got the right idea."

Footsteps issued, Steven turning toward the door.

It seemed Farran had grown tired of waiting.

When Steven glanced toward the windows, hallway light flooding the room, the Jaxin and King Ridgeway were gone.

"Steven, are you in here?" Farran called.

"Yes." Steven cleared his throat, walking to the door.

The fools hadn't even asked if he was *good* at lying.

They would find out soon, he supposed.

Farran peered into the room as Steven stepped into the hall.

"I trust you found your watch," Farran said. Steven held up a wrist as Farran followed the prizefighter down the hall.

"Was it a woman?" Farran asked, his voice low. "We were just leaving, and I believe you had all evening—"

"No," Steven cut in, gaining a sidelong glance from his friend. Steven blew out a breath.

"No," Farran repeated slowly, gliding down the stairs.

Steven grimaced. Farran would know how to tell when someone lied, trained in courtly schemes since he was a boy.

"I was just admiring the view," Steven said, striding across the entryway, Farran's footsteps echoing beside his.

He didn't look to see if Farran believed the lie.

The hotel was relatively close to the palace, though the walk long enough for the cold to seep through every shift in Steven's clothes.

Morning sunlight crested over mountains as a breeze swept by, Steven dipping his chin into the sherpa lining of his jacket.

While autumn still ruled in New Iberia, winter had already sunk its teeth into Vastlynd.

The Tyrnnthians were descending the outer palace steps when Steven reached them.

Luther's jaw tightened as his guards formed a circle around them, their gazes pinned on Steven. The dictator stuffed his hands into his overcoat pockets.

"Can I help you, Mr. Castellen?"

"In a way, yes," Steven said, cocking his head. He held a fist over his heart and raised his chin. "Grand Leader Hawthorne, I hereby declare my Blood Challenge against you."

Though still and watchful, Luther's eyes seemed to storm. Steven noted Ares smiling, though the prizefighter wouldn't look at him.

"Are you willing to endure the Culling?" Luther asked. "There are too many challengers and our laws demand it take place first."

Steven had never heard of such a thing.

"What does it entail?"

"Outliving your competitors," Luther said, shrugging. "The odds are ruled by dice."

Terribly vague.

"I am willing," Steven bit out, as if he had a choice.

He had yet to lower his hand, still waiting for Luther to accept what he couldn't deny.

The dictator nodded once. "The Culling begins two days after Tybauch's caves floods, so the tides will decide when I see you again."

Also vague.

"Alright."

"I accept your Blood Challenge," Luther said, offering a pale hand. Steven shook it, finding the dictator's skin as cold as the gusts around them, his gray eyes frank.

"We are agreed then," Luther said, stuffing his hand into a pocket. "I will see you at the Culling sometime this winter. I'm sure King Bardolph will keep you informed on when it shall begin."

"I'm sure."

A Culling. The sound of it made Steven's stomach turn.

He could outlive his competitors.

Steven had already outlived most of his countrymen, the

thought more sobering than encouraging.

Though at the rate Tyrnnth was conquering Central, Steven wasn't sure if there would be much left to save if he managed to win the Blood Challenge.

Steven finally looked at Ares. "What are you smiling about?"

The War Leader shrugged, his teeth and hair nearly as white as the snow around them.

"Nothing, Mr. Castellen. I just think I will enjoy watching you perform at this event." Ares' pale eyes sparked. "I've heard you've always been one to put on a good show."

⁂

Grace was in the hotel lobby when Steven returned, two cups of coffee on the low-lying table before her.

Steven shucked off his jacket as he neared the plush chairs overlooking the mountains, nearly level with the building itself.

"Good morning, Grace," he said, marveling that it was possible he could say it at all.

She was alive, she was free.

Grace smiled. "Is it a good morning?"

Steven dropped into the chair beside hers. "I'm not sure yet."

Where he had expected relief and some sort of toxic excitement for declaring his Blood Challenge, he only found dread.

Steven reached for a to-go cup. "You didn't have to."

Grace raised a soft brow as Steven leaned back.

"She didn't."

Steven turned to find Farran approaching, dressed in slacks and a cable-knit sweater. Steven frowned at the cup.

"I almost drank out of this."

He passed the cup to Farran, the king sliding into a seat. "We weren't sure when you'd return."

Grace reached for the other cup. "And how did it go?"

"I have to go through a Culling first, whatever that is."

The sky was so pale blue now, the snow blinding in the sunlight.

As if the clouds had only converged for Steven's meeting with the Tyrnnthians earlier.

Steven didn't notice Farran was talking until Grace idly tapped the prizefighter's leg with a foot. Steven looked at Farran as he finished.

"The amount of people needed to warrant one would have to be quite substantial," Farran said, his face drawn.

Had he paled?

That usually wasn't good.

Grace leaned forward. "I'm sorry, what is a Culling?"

"Danger, death and dice or something." Steven scrubbed his face with his hands. "And tides."

Grace made a noise that Steven assumed meant she didn't know anymore than before his brilliant explanation.

He dropped his hands and looked to Farran. "Is this Tyrnnth's attempt to draw the war out?"

"No, the next Blood Challenges still ensue with the Crow Moon in the spring. A Culling can only take place mid-winter." The king frowned. "You may have to take on an entirely different gauntlet of training now."

Steven groaned. More training. He was *always* training.

Though an outlet, it ran him ragged. He was tired of preparing. He wanted Luther dead and the war over *now*.

"You didn't tell me this might happen," Steven said. "It would have been nice to include this in your prescribed studies."

Farran shook his head. "There would have to be over sixty people challenging Luther. I can't imagine where they'd be coming from with Blood Challenges outlawed in Central."

"I know where they're from," Grace said, cradling her cup. "I worked at the dock after Tyrnnth emptied our safe house. Since I could speak and understand Tyrnnthian, they kept me to work as a translator. I brought food to the officers regularly."

Steven inwardly winced.

He had yet to ask about her time as a captive.

"They mentioned mines and something about planting rumors. It didn't make sense to me then, but now it does," Grace went on. "Tyrnnth is setting you guys up to kill each other."

Great.

Steven turned to the king. "Grace sure has lovely insight, what terrible things do you know about the Culling?"

Farran dragged his gaze from Grace and surveyed the room.

"Perhaps it shall be a conversation for another time."

Steven looked over a shoulder to find strangers with phones unabashedly taking photos, people drawing nearer to hear them.

It seemed a world-famous prizefighter, New Iberia's king, and a newly freed slave had been recognized.

Steven sighed and turned. "Well, Grace. I don't know what you want to do, but I'm sure you're welcome to join us. I'll be training most of the time, but I rest on the weekends. I'm not sure what His Majesty does all day. Paperwork?"

"I keep him in check," Farran said. "I've been told Steven is a nuisance to my staff and locals."

"It only makes sense," Grace said.

Steven smirked. "You want to know what kind of *nuisance* I deal with at the king's weekend home day and night?"

Farran was up and out of his seat in a moment. "I think it's time we go. Don't you think, Steven?"

Grace smiled. "I might tag along for now."

———

Steven had been running through the forested park beside the New Iberian castle when he happened upon Adira Theron.

He noted her were legs more muscled than he assumed, her slightly up-tilted eyes and olive skin showcasing her heritage.

This eighteen-year-old was an *empress.*

What sort of trade agreement did she hope to make? Surely there wasn't anything important enough here worth leaving her seat of power for.

Steven slowed, his breath coming in fast and hard after cresting the hill behind him. Adira angled her head, her ponytail reminding Steven of a warrior's helm.

He had felt calluses when they had danced. Perhaps she was more of a force to be reckoned with than she seemed.

Perhaps now would be a good time to investigate.

"Miss Adira," Steven greeted.

The empress nodded and blew past them.

Perhaps not, then.

Steven had little to report to War Leader Brown.

Farran resumed his meetings, the conflict across the sea keeping him busy enough that he missed half the meals Steven and Grace spent together.

Grace had managed to secure an apartment and job, despite Farran offering a room in the castle.

If she felt bad about leaving her country behind to live a safe life in New Iberia, she didn't let on.

Steven had felt the bite of guilt soon after leaving Central, remembering *why* he left only slightly helping dissipate its gnaw.

If this went the way he wanted, he would cause far more damage in one fight than months at the front.

Steven wondered what his former trainer, Max Fitzgerald, would have made of his decision. What would his mother and Jay make of it?

Steven supposed it didn't matter, as they were all dead.

Steven had completed a private training session when he found Jaxin Brown leaned against a villa lining the street.

"I see New Iberia has been treating you well."

Steven wiped the sweat from his brow, waiting for a car to pass before joining the War Leader. The street was moderately busy, people bustling about, bikes and small vehicles winding through.

Blustery clouds raced above, promising rain.

"What's the occasion?" Steven asked, walking beside Jaxin as they headed toward the coast.

"I thought I'd check on you in person." A breeze blew the War Leader's russet hair past his shoulders. In a t-shirt, Steven could make out more of the tattoo on Jaxin's neck, spotting a beak and feathers.

"Anything to report?" Jaxin asked.

Steven blew out a breath, looking toward the horizon. "Farran has meetings with his council everyday and tons of paperwork. Nothing out of the ordinary."

Steven's attention turned to a second story balcony as a woman stepped out to pull in a line of laundry.

"And the empress?" Jaxin asked.

Steven shrugged. "I saw her once. Farran never mentions her."

Jaxin surveyed the street, citizens preparing for rain as a heavy sheet hit the west side of Evynmare.

They would be sodden in less than a minute.

"I received word Her Majesty, Ms. Theron, will be meeting with King Bardolph this evening. I want you to catch a glimpse."

Steven frowned. "Do you know what it's about?"

"Trade, but I don't buy it."

Steven ran a hand down his neck. "When?"

Jaxin glanced at his watch, slinging on his leather jacket.

"You have an hour."

Steven hailed a cab to the castle.

Grace had been in the midst of preparing dinner when Steven and Jaxin dropped onto her doorstep, drenched from the downpour.

Jaxin had stepped in to help Grace, to Steven's surprise.

The prizefighter had been out the door soon after, Jaxin and Grace conversing over the sizzle of a pan and the steady chop of a knife.

Steven strode for the king's study, tray in hand, glancing up long enough to note the king's personal guard not on duty, but rather, two men Steven had never seen before.

He curled his shoulders in and hid his face beneath his servant's cap as he approached.

He did not stop as he made for the door, one of the armed men stepping forward.

"Their Majesties are in a meeting."

"I am well aware. I was sent by the king himself."

Steven stepped around the guard and slipped in, Farran's raised voice covering the sound of the door shutting.

"We have plenty of resources ourselves, Empress."

Adira stood before the king's desk, Farran's line of sight blocked as she leaned toward him.

"Correct me if I'm wrong, but New Iberia is an island of farmland and vineyards," she said. "You have *much* to gain from Nyrland."

"With all due respect, Your Majesty, we have other allies that offer us the same resources."

Steven blew out a breath.

It was just a trade meeting.

"Yes, but for how long? The Central Territories used to offer plenty," Adira said, her voice low. Steven silently set the tray down. "How long until your other allies fall?"

"Is that a threat, Ms. Theron?" Farran's chair groaned as he stood. Steven hid his face, though he had yet to be seen.

"It's *Empress* Theron to you."

"Let me remind you—"

Okay, he'd seen enough. Steven strode for the door, bowing his shoulders further, altering his gait—

"Excuse me?"

Oh, Farran had seen him.

And the king was *pissed*.

Adira slammed a palm onto his desk. "You said this meeting was *confidential*. You can't even keep your servants in check—"

Steven slipped out the door as Farran rounded his desk.

"Wait!"

Steven did no such thing.

He hurried for the stairs, not trusting the king to halt the elevator.

As Steven's feet hit the top step, the study doors opened. By the time Steven heard Farran calling, the prizefighter had already disappeared into a room down another hall.

His heart hammered as he shucked off his uniform and donned casuals, eyes on the door.

He would tell Farran about it later. Maybe.

There was nothing wrong in worrying for a friend meeting with a potential enemy. Steven ran a hand through his hair and stuffed the uniform into the closet, telling himself he had done the right thing.

The storm had cleared by the time Steven hit the night-darkened capital streets, inhaling the scent of coastal, night-blooming flowers.

Despite the autumnal temperatures on Castle Hill, the lower altitude of the city below allowed the native flowers to bloom until the eve of winter.

When November rolled in, and the shift of wind with it, even the warm capital would succumb to snow.

Steven stuffed his hands into his pockets as he neared Grace's villa. Stopping just outside the door, he watched a hanging planter shift as the wind picked up, the floral scent twining with the salt of the sea.

He knocked once and let himself in.

Jaxin was leaned back in an armchair, his attention on Steven as he entered and shut the door.

"Report, Castellen," Jaxin said.

"All's well." Steven kicked off his shoes and threw his jean jacket over the back of the couch before taking a seat.

"What did they discuss?" Jaxin asked.

"The Empress wants to trade. She said Farran's allies may not last long, and Nyrland could supply what he might be lacking soon."

Grace appeared from the hall. "She threatened him?"

"I guess it could be." Steven shrugged. Grace's brows knit together as she claimed the seat beside him.

"Tell me exactly what you heard and saw," Jaxin said.

Steven did.

The War Leader stared at the ceiling, Grace stared at the coffee table. Steven followed her line of sight to find a book she had found at a garage sale last weekend.

With Farran.

Jaxin rose from his seat and crossed the room to the entryway.

"What do you think, War Leader?" Steven asked, rising.

Jaxin donned his jacket. "I know Empress Theron can't be trusted. I'm sure His Majesty knows this already."

"Is he in danger?" Grace asked, joining Steven's side.

Jaxin sighed. "He should be fine."

The War Leader took in the coolly-lit city beyond the paned kitchen windows, his fingers idly adjusting the cuffs of his jacket.

"When all of the chieftain's children disappeared, Adira Theron was the only one to return," Jaxin said. "I don't trust her."

6

There was someone in Steven's suite.

He could feel it as he neared, his footsteps slowing on the plush, red carpet. He glanced over a shoulder before setting his hand on the knob, leaning in to listen.

No voices or footsteps, at least that he could hear.

He unlocked the door and pushed it open, revealing his guest as she sat in his favorite chair.

"Steven," Adira said. "I've been waiting for you."

"How did you get in?" he asked, slipping in to shut the door behind him. She didn't rise, one leg crossed over the other, sitting as though Steven's chair was some sort of throne.

"I picked the lock."

"And why are you here?"

"You are a Blood Challenger, are you not?"

Steven ran a hand down his neck. "I will be after the Culling."

Adira drummed her fingers on the armrest, watching Steven as he approached, halting a few feet away.

"You made it past my guards," Adira noted.

"Pardon?"

She huffed a laugh as she rose. "You're different than I imagined."

Steven's eyes narrowed. "What do you mean?"

Adira angled her head, her smile lupine. "I hadn't realized how many manners of the king would rub off on the famous, spoiled prizefighter by now."

Steven leaned against the armchair beside him. "I see."

"You do not deny my previous accusation."

What had she said? Ah, her *guards*—

"Maybe I have better things to do than argue with a spoiled chieftain's daughter."

The words felt sour, Steven's stomach twisting. Something in Adira's eyes guttered, but she didn't lower her chin. Steven waited for the verbal blow, but none came. He cleared his throat and looked away.

The chieftain and chieftess, Steven had learned, had been the previous emperor and empress of Nyrland.

They were both dead.

"I wasn't even here last night," Steven said.

It wasn't a lie, though it wasn't the entire truth, either. He didn't wait to see if she bought his claim and strode for his small kitchen.

"Coffee?" he offered, if only because he needed it, and couldn't stand Adira's silence.

"You must not plan on sleeping tonight."

"You say this as if you don't plan on killing me."

"If I wanted you dead, you would be already," Adira said, taking a seat at the bar. "I don't play with prey."

"Good. I don't either." Steven leaned against the back counter. What else could she want? He opened his mouth to ask.

"I want to train with you," Adira said.

"What?" Steven's fingers tightened on the counter behind him. "Why?"

She definitely wanted him dead, then.

And she wanted to make it look like an accident.

The empress shrugged. "I'm here for trade agreements. No one is *agreeing* and I need an outlet. Something I can do that I'm good at."

Steven smiled. "I guess you're in luck, because I'd like to find out just how good you are."

"We are agreed then?" she asked.

Steven stuck out a hand, Adira shaking it once.

"We are."

He hoped it was a good idea.

Steven's training doubled after Adira joined in.

He spent rest days reading books Farran had assigned him to read, wandering Evynmare with Grace, and visiting the king.

When Steven had told Farran the foreign empress had asked to join his training regimen, the king had blanched.

"Is she pleasant?" Farran asked.

Not really. Steven told the king as much.

Adira put up with Steven, though sometimes he swore he glimpsed something warmer.

With the few times their paths crossed, even Grace had yet to draw something kind from Adira.

Steven didn't mind the empress though.

Everyday, the news grew bleaker. Tyrnnth had advanced further north, burning and butchering along the way.

While Steven grew stronger, his country grew weaker.

When he was alone in his darkened room, silence heavy and shadows drawn, sometimes he would gaze east, hoping all of his effort would be enough.

And prayed, against all odds, Central could hold on long enough to see him try.

7

"Downtown brown?" Farran asked, picking up the box hair dye. "How is this different from what I already have?"

Grace cleared off her bathroom sink, pursing her lips as she watched him through the mirror.

"Your hair is a coppery gold," she said. "This will make it a light, ashy brown."

Farran smiled and set the box down. "I don't think this will be enough to make me look unrecognizable."

"I wasn't sure if anything darker would wash out," Grace said, biting a lip.

"We should have bought a wig."

"Too late now." Grace opened the box. "Are you sure you want me to do this?"

Farran looked at his reflection and sighed, turning his head. "I guess it would help to have people second guess whether or not I'm amongst them. Prior to being stabbed, my assassin would have to do a double-take."

"Oh, please," Grace said. She neared and ran her hands through his hair.

She had a party to attend tonight, as per request from her job as a barista at the cafe on the corner. When she had revealed her lack of a date, Farran had volunteered.

Of course he would.

She spent most nights in his bedroom, reading beside him on the bed, or in his small personal library.

They drank tea, listened to records and talked.

Or didn't talk at all.

The silence that sometimes drew between them was never awkward, and Farran was thankful for a friend that allowed it.

Silence is only awkward if you make it awkward, she had told him once.

He breathed easier when she was near him.

Sometimes.

Other times, he breathed far too fast, heart racing.

Farran was forever grateful for the moment he had caught her in the castle kitchens after dark, soon after she had arrived to New Iberia.

She had nightmares, like him. Though she hadn't shared what about, Farran had invited her to his room for tea.

She agreed, and he still remembered what she wore and the way her hair draped over her shoulder in the elevator.

The way she smiled at him.

Their time together had been a reprieve. The war put on hold, no world beyond his room and the delightful woman who had deigned to accept his invitation to tea at midnight.

He had continued to invite her, to all manners of spending time together, and for some reason, she continued to say yes.

If Farran was especially fortunate, she would fall asleep reading a book beside him, or allow him to set her novel aside and draw her in.

"Just for a little while," she always said.

He always woke her before dawn, as she had requested. It seemed she didn't want to spend a true night with him.

Farran wasn't sure when she would allow it, though he imagined he would have to marry her for something like that.

He hummed, leaning into her touch as she continued to run her fingers through his hair.

"Seems clean enough," Grace said, withdrawing.

"Oh." Farran opened his eyes. "Is that what that was?"

Grace barked a laugh, stepping back. "Your shirt, please."

Farran stilled. "What?"

Grace angled her head. "Your shirt. I imagine you don't want dye on your pretty, white button-down?"

Farran should laugh. She was attempting a joke, and it would be polite to indulge her. Instead, he swallowed and let his hands drift to the top button, but no further.

"What is it, Fare?"

He surveyed the space. "It is quite bright in here, love."

Understanding flashed across her face and she stepped forward, cupping his face in her hands. "Your scars don't scare me. I think you're beautiful, with or without them."

She ran her hands down his chest, over his heart. "Scars just mean you're alive. That you've survived."

She meant it. He could see that in her eyes.

Farran sighed and nodded. "Okay."

His shirt set aside, Farran turned toward the sink and waited for Grace to begin her dyeing process.

Though his back was laden with whip scars and marred flesh, his chest repulsed him the most, the flesh covered in mismatched lacerations and rippling burns.

Something in his chest broke when Grace ran her hands over him and murmured, "You're perfect."

His eyes grew hot as he shut them.

"I'm really not, love," he said quietly.

He was not perfect in so many ways, he nearly laughed.

Though Grace had seen his scars in the dark, there was truly nothing to hide in the light.

He had been tortured when he was seventeen, in his father's war.

When the enemy had found the king's son on the trench floor, they had dragged him behind their lines and tortured him.

It had been days.

They had burned and cut and whipped him until he couldn't breathe, until his body had given out, bones and muscle showing as his body shut down.

Those were the scars Farran bore.

His father had killed an entire battalion just to have him back, and Farran would never forget the rage in his father's eyes.

Caradoc Bardolph had never been the same since then, and neither had his heir.

Farran had never spoken of it to anyone, and wasn't sure when he would be able to tell Grace, despite her acceptance of him and the marks of hate on his body.

She saw them much differently, and he hoped he could see them the way she did someday.

He heard Grace open the sink faucet, the sound of a chair scraping across the floor.

"Take a seat," Grace said. Farran did, draping his elbows over the counter and leaning his head down. Grace began to work her hands in his hair and he melted into the counter.

Farran sighed, savoring her proximity to him.

"You're safe now," she said quietly.

For a moment, he nearly believed her.

8

Steven hated rock climbing.

Adira had insisted it was a needed skill.

Upon agreeing to the task, Steven regretted it at first glance of the cliffside they were to descend and scale, a briny sea breeze whipping hair from his brow.

With the few sessions he had spent with the empress, he had spent most of them shaking and swearing.

His muscles and tendons straining, his mind reeled each time he glimpsed the sea beneath.

The Culling was to be held on Tybauch, a tunnel-riddled Tyrnnthian island surrounded by cliffs.

A perfect prison.

If he could master the climbing, he could use the bars of the prison to free himself. At the very least, he would have more options of travel than the tunnels.

Steven hadn't seen Jaxin since their last meeting, and had little to report to the War Leader anyways.

Neither empress nor king deigned to speak of politics.

Steven noticed Farran and Grace gravitating towards each other over the last few weeks. Though Farran hedged the subject, Steven knew something had shifted.

He hoped that whatever it was, everything would turn out well for them.

As it was, Grace hadn't revealed anything to Steven either, going so far as to call him a *busybody*.

With the training, studying and visiting, Steven woke one morning to the tides having risen in Tyrnnth.

The Culling would begin within two weeks.

"What's your country like?" Steven's voice was a rasp. He threw a punch, Adira dodging effortlessly.

"Distracting won't work," she breathed.

Steven smiled. "I know, princess."

He threw another punch, Adira's answering block solid.

"It's big, beautiful. Lots of woods," Adira said. A duck and strike. Steven nearly missed the block.

"That's it?"

Adira dropped to swipe a leg for his ankles, Steven pivoting out of the way.

"Nice," he breathed, wiping sweat from his eyes.

No trainers today; he had decided he would take a break from the masters for the rest of the week.

Adira was enough.

The empress had taken it upon herself to teach him Nyrlandish fighting techniques, training even New Iberia couldn't offer.

Adira's foot connected with Steven's face.

He hissed, a hint of an apology flashing in her eyes. He made for the water table.

"Where'd you learn that?" Steven asked, pouring two cups. Adira stopped at his side.

"An old friend."

Steven had not forgotten his first conversation with the empress. She claimed she didn't have friends. He wondered what

Adira considered him, after these weeks together.

As far as he could tell, she felt more than toleration.

He didn't give it much thought. They were fight partners, and that was as far as he would consider.

Jaxin and King Ridgeway's assumptions on the empress' connection to Tyrnnth seemed ill-made.

Though Adira had threatened Farran during the trade meeting, she was *always* dealing threats.

Farran and Adira hadn't held a meeting since, to Jaxin's approval.

"An old friend taught me, too. Grace's dad, actually," Steven said.

"He must be a good teacher." Adira finished her swig, dark eyes on the city below.

They were in Farran's personal open-air workout room, one of the uppermost levels of a tower jutting up from the castle. With Steven's rooms just a few levels down, the space had proven quite convenient.

"He was," Steven said, smiling.

Max Fitzgerald.

When Jay had been imprisoned for their father's murder, their mother since passed away, Max had taken Steven under his wing and allowed him a room in their manor.

When Steven became of age, he began attending the acclaimed trainer's classes.

No one would have guessed Steven would have excelled. By the time he was a senior in high school, he had already won two first place titles in worldwide competitions.

The media had paid attention to him since, and he had only improved in the year since then.

Until war had knocked the world out from under him.

If everything hadn't fallen apart, Steven would be halfway through his first semester of college.

He was certain his scholarship was null now.

So many things that had mattered, now didn't. And things that should have mattered— well, it was too late now, wasn't it?

All of his important things were buried six feet under the ground, or dumped in a trench. Other than his new and found friends.

War had changed everything.

Max and Steven had been at a national-level fight when Tyrnnth had attacked Central's shores. Without warning, vats of gas had broken open, poisoning cities, events, buildings—

The crowd, Steven's opponent, and Max had been dead in minutes.

And their deaths hadn't been clean.

Steven could still feel Max's blood on him as his trainer and the closest thing he had to a father had choked on his own blood in Steven's arms.

"I'm sorry for your loss," Adira said. Steven found her watching him.

"I'm sorry, too."

The empress tightened her ponytail and strode back to the ring, turning at the center to angle her head at him.

"Again?"

9

Farran led Grace up a winding staircase, starlight filtering through the windows.

"Why are we going to the training ring?" Grace asked, the hem of her dress in one hand, the other in Farran's.

He looked over a shoulder. "It's a surprise."

Farran opened the door, amber light glowing from the strands of bulbs hung over the circular, open-air room, Farran's record player set against the wall.

"We're going to dance, aren't we?" Grace stepped out and took in the space, as if searching for the punching bag Farran had already hefted down the stairs.

"You said there were too many people at the party last week," Farran said, shutting the door behind him. "It seems there isn't a crowd here tonight."

"Fare," Grace said, smiling at him.

He had yet to grow accustomed to this particular smile.

Farran stalked to the record player, procuring an album from the small collection he had brought.

"I have wanted to dance with you to this song for awhile," he said, setting the vinyl.

The record set into motion, music filling their corner of the world. He turned to Grace and paused. His lips parted as he took in her eyes, her dress. She angled her head, her honey-brown hair shifting.

"Are we staring or dancing tonight? I am fine with either."

A laugh broke through Farran. "I apologize. I hadn't had this opportunity last week."

It was true.

He had been recognized immediately at the party last week, ensuing an onslaught of interruptions, ogling, and offers to dance.

He had politely declined every offer but Grace's.

Farran took Grace's hands in his and pulled her in, music drifting as a breeze lured in decadent, night air.

The record played itself out. Farran took his time with their kiss, Grace's thumb brushing his jaw as she held his face.

Was it possible this was real?

The king felt he would open his eyes and watch his reality become dust on the wind.

Impossible to gather again from this height.

He rested his forehead against Grace's, his chest rising and falling unsteadily.

She smelled like vanilla. And nutmeg. An ever-changing scent, dependent on what she baked that morning.

"One more surprise," he murmured.

"Surely you'd have thought you'd run out of them by now."

Farran smiled and brushed his thumb over her wrist before letting go, stepping to one of the open windows to grab a rope, a ladder dropping into view.

"Oh no," Grace lamented.

Farran gave her a wicked grin. "It'll be worth it."

"I'm going to die."

"Nonsense, love," Farran said, tugging on the ladder. "I'll be right behind you."

"You plan on dying too, then."

Farran smiled and **Grace** sighed as she approached. She grabbed the rungs, meeting Farran's gaze when she was level with him.

"I'm not sure I like all of your surprises."

"You speak too soon."

Grace grabbed the next rung, Farran steadying the ladder, a hand on her back. He stepped up as she disappeared over the ledge and followed. When he reached the stone lip, he found Grace already fallen back onto the bed of blankets, laughing at the sky.

"It's beautiful," she whispered.

He forced himself to look up, a million twinkling lights looking back, galaxies bursting across the sky.

At the pinnacle of the world, the view was boundless.

Grace awoke to kisses along her jaw, so whisper soft, she was caught between staying in whatever dream this was, or waking to the summons.

A huff of breath on her cheek.

She had been caught pretending to sleep.

Grace opened her eyes to soft, purple sky, dawn-laden clouds drifting above. She shifted, finding Farran's head propped up on a hand.

"Good morning, love."

That voice. It was far too early to try and deal with—

Early.

Grace had stayed the night again, despite swearing it off. She rolled onto her back and covered her face with her hands.

"Is something the matter?"

Grace shook her head against the blankets, lowering her hands.

"I didn't get up in time."

"I'm sorry. I would have woken you sooner, but I slept in, as well."

She couldn't do this again.

Every time they were alone, they went farther than she, deep down and truly, wanted to go.

One of them would end up far more hurt than the other intended, and she desired much better for her dearest friend, and for herself.

Grace propped her head with a hand, mirroring the king. "There are some things we probably shouldn't do anymore."

Farran didn't balk. "And what were you thinking?"

"I want to be friends with you. Before anything else."

Farran reached for her before drawing back. "You certainly are my friend. I just— I guess I can't keep my hands off of you, as well. Can't there be both?"

Grace smiled. "No, not yet."

Farran nodded and shifted onto his back, his scarred, elegant hands clasping over his chest.

"It may be difficult for me to adjust. I apologize I haven't meant— I must have read you wrong."

"You didn't," Grace said quickly. "Not at all. I just haven't been honest with you."

"So, less hands," Farran said, smiling. "Is that all?"

"Would you like a list?"

Farran straightened. "Yes, please. Tell me every way I've muddled your brain, and spare no details."

Grace bit back her smile, shaking her head. "Farran."

He grabbed a wad of blankets and shoved it under his chest.

"Please?" he asked.

Grace laughed, shaking her head. "Why?"

"I would like to know, for later."

"For later."

"Whenever you revoke this 'no hands' thing," Farran said, his fingers providing air quotes for him.

Grace settled back onto the blankets and closed her eyes.

There was no guarantee she *would* revoke the rule.

Though they were entirely compatible, and she felt far more than fondness for him, there was something that nagged at her about him.

She did not know what it was, or what it meant.

Apart from that, they were moving too fast.

If Farran wanted her around long-term, she needed time to think about him in that regard, without his hands and body involved.

She wondered if he even thought about her like that.

Perhaps she was just a bit of fun, though he could have found far more willing women than herself for that.

Grace felt Farran lean over her.

"Does this mean no more kisses?"

She smiled, shook her head. "Friends don't kiss each other, Fare."

"You are quite serious about this," he said, his breath on her cheek.

This hopeless man had already eaten a mint.

"Okay," Grace said, opening her eyes to find Farran hovering over her, something like melancholy flashing in and out of his eyes.

Curiosity replaced it.

"Okay?" He shifted closer. "What does that mean?"

Grace lifted her chin. "One more kiss. And then that's it."

"Oh yes, of course." Farran grabbed her hand, his eyes on hers as he kissed the back of her hand.

"That's it?" Grace squeaked.

Farran smiled. "Of course not, love."

Grace screamed, Farran flipping her body onto his and rolling her onto the blankets. He leaned over her, his forehead against hers.

"There's no way in this wretched world I would waste my last kiss with you, Grace Fitzgerald."

As he began to kiss her, a piece of her believed he was right.

Maybe this was their last.

Grace hadn't meant to cry as Farran seemed to speak everything he wouldn't say in those moments on the rooftop before the world awoke.

10

Tyrnnth's ships had been spotted outside New Iberia's shores the day before Farran snapped into a state.

Steven had requested tea, under the pretense of missing Farran's company at the meals the king missed with the prizefighter and Grace.

Grace scarcely mentioned him, seeming to have delved deeper into work, picking up extra shifts and spending her downtime passed out on her couch at her villa.

Steven watched the king across the dining table, sunlight streaming through the cottage windows. The shadows beneath Farran's eyes deeper than Steven had last seen them.

Farran took a sip as he met Steven's gaze.

"May I ask what is on your mind, Steven?" Farran asked pleasantly.

Steven regarded his friend. "I'm thinking I should ask how you're doing, and make sure your response isn't canned."

"There is no need to worry for me."

"Is it Grace?" Steven leaned forward.

"No," Farran replied quietly. "I am glad she is here."

Steven tapped a finger against the wood.

"Is it the Culling?"

"I know what you are capable of."

Steven pursed his lips and Farran sipped his tea. The king met Steven's gaze and smiled.

"Steven. Please, what is it?"

Insufferable.

"Will you please tell me what's wrong? I know something happened," Steven insisted. Farran's smile dropped, his brows drawing together.

"Is this you asking, or the man you answer to?" Farran asked frankly.

Steven started, his pulse quickening.

"Look, Farran—"

A knock jarred the room, the men turning toward the sound.

Natalia let herself into the cottage.

"Good morning, Mrs. Hawthorne," Farran said, the words clipped. "And to what do we owe the pleasure of this visit?"

Steven's sister didn't look as though she were here to kill either of them, though Steven wondered if she would try.

"I have a target in town and someone sent *someone* to visit," Natalia said, shrugging. "The job should take the weekend."

Farran rose. "Natalia, we have talked about this."

Steven caught movement outside, turning to look as a slight, young woman wandered the orchard. Clad in a cornflower blue dress, a curtain of pale, golden hair hung to her slim waist.

"Why?" Farran asked. When Natalia didn't speak, Farran tore his gaze from the woman.

"You know why," Natalia breathed, her voice cold. Farran clenched his fists, though Natalia didn't speak again as she swept from the house.

Steven walked to the windows, the woman continuing to wander under the barren trees.

"Is this a girlfriend of yours?" Steven's attempt at humor fell flat. Farran came up beside him, hands in his pockets.

"This is bad," he murmured.

The stranger paused, turning her face up as a flock of birds

61

passed. She turned enough that Steven glimpsed her face.

Eyes the color of pale sage leaves, alabaster skin— as the birds disappeared, her eyes locked onto his.

A hand was on his shoulder, turning him away.

"You should probably go. I apologize, I hadn't any indication Natalia would bring a guest today," Farran said. Tremors travelled through the king's hand through Steven's sweater.

The prizefighter halted before the door.

"Are you okay?"

Farran withdrew his hand and slipped it into a pocket. Pasting a courtly smile on, he nodded.

No, Farran was not okay.

"I'll see you Monday," he said, and ushered Steven out the door.

———

Steven was at Grace's villa within the hour.

"Has Farran ever mentioned a sister to you?" The words were a rush, the door shutting behind Steven as he crossed the room. Grace sighed and looked up from her book.

"No," she said. "His family was killed."

"All of them?" Steven dropped onto the couch.

"Well, he has extended family ruling other cities."

Steven hummed, leaning his head back. A few moments passed, Grace shifting in her chair.

"I think he's being threatened," Steven said.

"It is war."

Leverage. If Farran had a sister in the hands of their enemy, the king would be an unfit ally . . .

Grace settled, adjusting the blanket over her lap. "Tell me why you think Fare is being threatened."

"I saw a girl today, at the cottage. Natalia brought her," Steven said carefully. "She looked seventeen, maybe eighteen."

"And you think this girl is Farran's sister?"

"She's got light green eyes, blonde hair . . . I don't know, they look like they could be siblings, and he was acting weird."

Steven set a hand against his mouth. "It just doesn't make sense for Tyrnnth to throw away his entire family. It's not like them *not* to play dirty. I think they kept his sister to use against him. A time of war seems like a good time to pull that chess piece out."

Grace drew her blanket closer. "That would be awful."

"We need to know if it's true."

"Why?"

"Because," Steven said, "if Tyrnnth can use Farran, they will."

Grace sat up. "And New Iberia would have to step out of the war."

Steven sighed through his nose, attempting to calm the skittering wave of anxiety underneath his skin. "I think we need to find out if it's true, and then decide whether or not to tell Jaxin."

───

Steven showered and dressed, another day of training in the books. With winter's fingers brushing frost onto New Iberia's upper elevations, darkness had already fallen.

Steven watched Grace enter his suite in the reflection of a window. He turned to find her dressed in brown slacks and a turtleneck.

"That's your getup? You look like you're ready to open the coffee shop for the old timers."

Grace almost smiled, uncertainty in her eyes.

"Are you ready?" Steven asked, rising.

She frowned. "No."

"Great, that makes two of us." He checked his watch. "Farran's guards should be switching shifts. Let's go."

———— ❧ ————

Farran was spending the weekend at the cottage, which meant Steven and Grace had one night before the king would be flitting about the castle again.

Steven picked the lock on the king's study doors, Adira's claim on the outdated security proving true. Within a minute, a click sounded and they eased into the dark room.

The glow of the capital reflected off the ceiling, allowing Steven to make it to Farran's desk with ease. He began picking the lock on a desk drawer as Grace opened the closet.

"Is it possible he would keep something this important in the vaults below the castle?" Grace asked.

"If he wanted others to know."

The lock clicked and Steven rolled out a drawer of files. He turned on his phone light and plucked through. Business reports, meeting minutes, trade agreements . . .

Steven shut the drawer and began unlocking the next.

"Any luck?" Grace asked from the closet.

Steven shut a drawer of pens and notepads. "No. You?"

"I found a box with papers. But I don't have—"

"C'mere."

Grace approached and knelt by his side, Steven angling his light into the shoebox.

A white and cobalt knit hat and matching scarf. Letters.

"These are from his family," he said quietly.

Grace nodded. "They are, that's his father's name."

Steven shook his head, setting more of the papers aside. "This is his keepsake box."

Grace looked up the moment he did, her face pained.

"We are terrible people," she whispered.

"I know."

Steven moved a stack of drawings, Grace reaching for a folder.

"This is his will."

Steven peered over Grace's shoulder as she opened the folder, his eyebrows raising as he read. It was definitely Farran's will, and the man had an unholy amount of money to his name.

Not to mention an entire kingdom.

If Farran were to die, it seemed New Iberia's next ruler would be appointed by his council.

But his cottage and orchard, truck, a large sum of money—

Grace looked at Steven. "It goes to you."

The prizefighter put a hand to his mouth and forced himself to keep reading.

"He wrote you in, too," Steven said, reaching to turn the paper over. "He must update this often."

Grace looked away.

"I found something." Steven jut a finger. "Look."

Grace leaned forward, brows drawing as she read. "There's no name on that account."

Steven nodded. "That's because he doesn't want everyone to know about it. I'm sure that's her."

He shut off the light as Grace finished jotting the number on her wrist, the contents of the box carefully packed away.

They rose and Grace's breath caught.

"Good evening," Farran drawled, a silhouette in an armchair. A coil formed in Steven's gut as Farran rose and slid his hands into his pockets, walking to the desk.

Shame felt like ice in Steven's veins and heat on his face, a curse word repeating in his brain.

This was bad.

Very bad.

The king held out a hand, Grace handing him the box.

Farran's eyes flicked to Steven's, distaste and ire in them.

"You could have asked," Farran said quietly and turned away. He placed the box into the closet, and before Steven or Grace could utter a word, the king was out the door.

It took a moment for Steven to move, to remember to cross

the room and find his suite. Grace peeled off.

He was a terrible person.

Quite possibly one of the worst.

But he had finished what he had set off to do.

As Steven leaned against his door, running a hand through his hair, one thought rose above the others.

Farran had a sister.

And Central had an ally they could no longer trust.

11

Steven didn't glimpse the King of New Iberia for two days.

On the morning of the third, Steven sat in the dining hall, watching snowflakes fall outside.

Castle Hill's first snow.

And Steven's reminder that the Culling drew close.

Adira strode in with a plate piled high with breakfast.

"Morning, princess," Steven said distantly.

It was usually their habit to eat before training. Though they weren't training today, she had showed up regardless.

Adira mumbled something by way of response.

"Wonderful to see you too," Steven continued, looking up. The empress' eyes narrowed as she sat.

"It's too early for that kind of energy," she said. Steven smirked and looked to his plate, wondering where his appetite had went. He had barely touched his stuffed, savory omelette.

"It's snowing," he said. Adira acknowledged him with a grunt before digging into her food. A couple minutes passed before she deigned to speak.

"The tides have risen. Expect the Culling to ensue sooner than you were told."

Steven groaned and leaned back, running his hands over his

face. He felt, more than saw, the empress smile.

"What's so funny about it?" Steven dropped his hands.

"You haven't had any coffee today."

Steven waved her off, giving his breakfast another good look before shoving it away.

"There's some more. Since it looks like you don't have enough already."

Adira hissed, leaning forward as the dining hall door opened. The empress settled as a servant approached.

"Mr. Castellen, His Majesty has requested your audience in his study," the servant said. He cast a look toward the empress. "As soon as you're finished here, I imagine."

"I'm finished, I'll be right there," Steven replied.

"Someone in trouble?" Adira held her mug to her face.

Steven scoffed and flicked his eyebrows up as he rose. "And aren't you smug about it."

Adira smiled. "It's just nice it isn't me for once."

———

Farran was at his desk when Steven entered the snow-bright study.

"Take a seat." The king gestured to the chair before him. Steven wiped his palms on his pants as he approached, the room stuffy with the fireplace roaring against the wall. The leather chair sounded too loud as Steven sat, Farran's eyes on the windows.

"Grace claimed you sought to learn whether or not I had a sister in Tyrnnth's captivity," the king said, drawing his attention to Steven.

Right to it, then.

"Yes."

Farran raised a brow. "Yet you wouldn't simply ask? Why."

"I don't know," Steven lied.

The king smiled in a way that wasn't the least bit friendly, leaning forward. "You wanted to know, so you could do what, exactly?"

He already knew. Somehow.

The king leaned back with a sigh.

"I do have a sister, and unfortunately, Tyrnnth does have her. When Tyrnnth massacred my family, they kept Faye alive to marry one of Ares' generals when she became of age." Farran scrubbed his face with his hands before dropping them. "Natalia and Luther have kept an eye on her for me."

The king looked to the fireplace. "Ares has been threatening me with her demise for weeks."

"Why hasn't Luther bothered you?"

Farran's eyes darkened as he looked at Steven. "Luther's father has enough pride and strength of will that Luther needn't do much. Make no mistake, Steven, Ares rules Tyrnnth. His son is simply a scapegoat."

"So if I kill Luther . . . " Steven drummed his fingers against the arm of his chair. Farran's lips thinned as Steven swore under his breath.

"It's unfortunate that Luther must fight the Blood Challenges. If Ares was dead and Luther was left to rule, things would improve dramatically." Farran sighed, his gaze settling on the fireplace again.

Steven crossed an ankle over a knee. "If that's the case, why don't we take Ares out?"

"His guards and network are too far-reaching."

"I think it's worth a try. If not, this is all for nothing."

"No," Farran said quietly. "The war ends if you win, and the sooner the better for that."

Steven rubbed his face with his hands. "But—"

"It would save a lot of unnecessary bloodshed, Steven."

"I know that," Steven scoffed. "But to kill Luther just to have *Ares* continue to reign . . . what if we took them out at the same time?"

"You won't find a willing assassin."

It sounded as if Farran had tried.

Leather groaned as the king rose. "Thank you for meeting me."

Steven looked up, noting Farran's shadowed eyes.

The prizefighter had yet to apologize for the intrusion days ago.

He swallowed and rose. "Thanks for the invite."

Steven walked to the door and turned at the threshold, the king staring out the window. The prizefighter opened his mouth, but Farran spoke first.

"The Culling begins in three days. Your flight leaves the day after tomorrow at nine o'clock sharp."

———⦿———

Steven dressed in sweats and a sweatshirt before dawn. Murmuring greetings to the kitchen staff, he headed out.

The air was crisp, the ground covered in a dusting of snow.

Steven stretched and breathed in the awakening day for two bone-chilling minutes before breaking into a run, his most favored route ahead of him.

Southwest of the castle would take him through the countryside. After a few miles, a left at Farran's cottage would cut through farmland and forest, the road opening up to the coast and back to the capital.

If Steven was feeling generous, he could pick up a coffee for Farran and hitch a ride up Castle Hill before the drink grew cold.

Steven had made many friends this way, the majority of citizens awake at this hour being elderly fishermen.

But Steven wasn't sure he felt generous yet.

As the sky lightened, asphalt gave way to gravel. After miles of rolling hills, Steven passed the cottage and began the long bend towards Evynmare, slowing as he crested a particularly steep hill. At the pinnacle, bare-limbed trees broke up frost-laden fields, a roiling, bitter ocean beyond.

After fifteen minutes of descent, Steven met the coast, a metal guard fence separating him from the cliff's edge.

The wind whipped against his face, his legs and arms pumping as he neared the city, salt clinging to his skin. Gulls cried overhead as he raced another mile, his feet meeting Evynmare's sidewalk.

Steven slowed as he approached Farran's favorite cafe. At this hour, they would have fresh chocolate croissants and warm raspberry pastries. Grace would be beaming, and likely throw in some extra goodies.

Steven took a turn before ever reaching it.

Perhaps an apology was needless if time could heal the rift.

Though time was the only thing that wasn't guaranteed for him.

Steven's thighs burned as the slope increased, the capital pooling beneath the glistening castle.

It would be several miles before Steven reached the top, and he *should* slow if he didn't want to strain something—

He nearly killed the newspaper boy.

"Hey!" Steven skittered off the sidewalk, the boy's eyes flaring as a stack of newspapers went flying.

"I'm sorry, Mr. Castellen," the boy squeaked, face reddening as he began picking up the papers.

"It's okay, I— let me help you." Steven blew out a breath and crossed the street to grab the farthest papers, not trusting the boy to not get ran over.

An elderly woman reached her bottom step and stooped to pick up an errant paper.

"Would you like a new one?" Steven offered.

Never mind every newspaper had been on the ground.

The woman's hand rose to her throat as she read. Steven looked at the paper in his hand.

Tyrnnthian War Ships Prowling Capital Coast

"They're here," she whispered. "They haven't finished Central and they're already here. Why?"

"I don't know," Steven lied.

Perhaps the threats on Faye's life were not enough pressure for the king.

A knock sounded at the door, Steven tightening the towel around his waist.

"Yes?" he called. He kicked his discarded clothes into a corner of his bathroom.

"It's me."

"Come in." Steven crossed the suite as she entered, the prizefighter disappearing behind his half-closed bedroom door. "Ms. Theron, how can I help you today?"

"I came to give you a proper education on the Culling."

Steven donned jeans and a t-shirt before grabbing a pair of socks, entering the living room to find Adira in his chair again.

Steven took the seat across from her.

"Do you know where the contestants are coming from?" Steven asked, pulling his socks on.

"A Culling calls for at least sixty Blood Challengers," she said. "I believe most of them are coming from Tyrnnth's mines."

"How do you know?"

"I don't." Adira raised a groomed brow. "I take it you don't want to kill your own countrymen."

Steven ran a hand through his damp hair and leaned back.

"No, not really."

Adira shrugged. "It makes sense they'd sign up. Declaring a Blood Challenge allows them a chance at freedom, as well as the opportunity to kill the man who enslaved them. Not to mention end the war, if they succeed."

Steven wondered what Jaxin made of it; banning Blood Challenges just to have his citizens competing regardless.

72

"There goes country morale." Steven tapped a finger against the armrest. "Do people ever sacrifice themselves when they recognize someone else is stronger?"

"Most believe a fight is the best way to prove such a thing." Adira pulled her hair up in a ponytail, Steven tracking the muscles in her forearms.

"And how do you know so much about this?"

Adira smiled. "Oh, Steven. Just say thanks and listen up. Your life depends on it."

<hr />

Adira perched on Steven's counter and spoke for an hour, every word out of her mouth worse than the last.

Inside Tybauch's tunnels, Steven would have to watch for flooding, hallucination-inducing algae, and pits where a fall meant death at the hands of starvation or worse.

"Worse?" Steven asked, exasperated.

"I'm getting there."

Steven wondered if knowing everything would do more harm than help, his stomach twisting as she went on.

"And that is why you stay well away from the southern caves," Adira said, her hands pinned under her thighs as she swung her legs.

Steven had since decided the empress enjoyed torturing him.

He narrowed his eyes and set down his mug. "I think I've heard enough."

"I haven't even gotten to the best part," Adira said.

Steven approached, bracing his hands on either side of her.

"If you tell me one more story, I'm going to vomit."

"Better now than later. The smell will attract the beasts."

Steven looked up at the ceiling and groaned. "Don't tell me. What, they release lions into the caves?"

"Tyrnnth has a sick sense of entertainment."

Steven stepped back. "Is that all?"

"One more thing, actually." The empress slipped from the counter, tilting her head as she looked up at him.

"I'm going with you."

"Grace," Steven called, not bothering to knock before throwing open her villa's cobalt door.

He'd taken his layers off on the walk down, the temperature rising with every step toward the coast.

After Adira's monologue, he needed the air.

He shucked off his shoes and tossed his overcoat, accidentally decapitating a flower in the process. He stooped to pick it up as Grace entered the room.

"How did you know?" she asked. Steven straightened, noting the wariness in his friend's gaze, as if the bright, yellow flowers he bore were some sort of joke.

Steven huffed a laugh. "Don't you like flowers? I figured it'd be nice."

Grace leaned against the wall. "So you don't know."

"No?" Steven said slowly, crossing the room to jut the bouquet toward her. "I think they're dying already."

"They are. Thank you, Steven." Grace took them to the kitchen, Steven perching on a stool. He pulled a plate of cinnamon rolls toward him.

"Now tell me what all this 'did you know' business is about."

Grace placed the flowers in a vase as Steven stole a pastry. As she set the vase on the counter, a glint caught his eye.

"What the hell is that." He grabbed Grace's hand.

"That is the 'did you know' business," she said tiredly. Steven inspected the elegant diamond ring, Grace half-dragged across the countertop.

"Who?"

Grace dropped the hand propped under her jaw, drawing the other back to herself.

"Farran."

Steven gaped, the corner of Grace's lip twitching upward.

"And you said yes."

"No?" Grace turned and wandered through the sunbeams streaming through the windows. "We're . . . pretending I said yes."

"Why?" Steven wondered why Farran had never mentioned it.

"He says it will keep me safe while I'm in Tyrnnth."

"Are you in the Culling, too?" Steven's heart was in his throat. Not *another* person to worry about—

"What? No. I'd die," Grace said. "I'm on the rescue team."

There wouldn't be much left of him to rescue if he was injured, in light of his conversation with Adira.

"I'd rather you not see what I look like if I'm injured there," Steven said. Never mind the entire event would be broadcasted.

"I knew you'd say that. And you already know that—"

"—you don't care. I know. I have to say it anyways." Steven waved a hand.

"That's right," Grace beamed. Steven smirked, looking at the brilliant diamond on her finger.

"You're more excited about volunteering for a hopeless rescue team than you are about being engaged to a *king*. A very nice king."

Grace groaned and dropped her head to the counter.

"Don't remind me."

"You could have said no."

Grace lifted her head. "I did!"

"I'm not convinced for some reason."

"*Steven.*"

"Sorry. What do you have to do now?"

Grace straightened, running her palm over the counter. "Media stuff. Telling our story and stuff."

"Ah, of course. Stuff. Do you want help practicing your lies?"

Steven and Grace spent an hour going over her story.

The citizens passing beneath Grace's veranda were far enough Steven hadn't worried about anyone overhearing them, faces turned toward the late afternoon sun as it bathed the city in gold.

Steven drew his overcoat around his shoulders as a breeze swept by. It felt colder than it looked, nearly all of the hanging planters brought inside.

Grace had still insisted on spending this conversation in the sun, as if she wanted to hold onto the last bit of warmth and light before winter truly set in.

"Have you had enough?" Steven asked. Grace kept her gaze on the ocean, boats pulling into the harbor.

"Do I sound convincing yet?"

No, she did not. Though Steven knew Grace could keep a secret, she could not lie.

"Just do your best."

Grace offered a small smile. "You didn't answer my question."

"I know. Please get this weird fake engagement thing over with as soon as possible. It's weird."

"I'll try." Grace slunk into her chair, the two of them quieting to watch the sun finish its descent into the ocean, a breeze picking up.

As stars began to show, Grace passed out in her chair. Steven rose and stretched, his breath fogging in the cold.

Another day done, another day closer to facing Luther.

Steven carefully lifted Grace and carried her inside.

Steven was at the front again.

Instead of being shot in the back, Jay was shot behind his legs.

Steven screamed as his brother crawled, dust and blood

clinging, artillery rattling his bones.

As Steven reached his brother, a bullet went though Jay's forehead.

Steven may have been screaming or sobbing when he looked up to find Adira leveling the gun at him.

He awoke just as she pulled the trigger.

Steven bolted upward in bed, chest heaving, sheets sweaty. After a minute, his heart slowed and eyes adjusted to the faint city light reflecting off the ceiling.

He dressed and exited his room.

It had snowed. A white blanket coated the royal grounds and forested park along Castle Hill.

The halls empty and dark, Steven found his way to the royal kitchen. His footsteps echoed along the tile floor as he made himself a cup of hot chocolate, going so far as to throw in a few marshmallows.

Mug in hand, Steven found himself on the floor of the glass elevator, the window cold at his back.

He sipped the warm, sweet beverage as he watched stars twinkle in the frigid, velvet black night.

He was to leave in a few hours.

His hands began to shake and he cursed.

He couldn't be afraid.

Fear would get him killed. It would have him dead several times over, in many different ways, before death truly came to greet him.

He couldn't afford to think like that.

And he *knew* that, but—

The elevator dinged, Steven throwing himself toward the doors a beat late.

He grimaced and settled against the window, the city shrinking.

With most of the staff home, there was only one person *this* could be at this hour.

Steven blinked back light as it filled the elevator.

"Oh," Farran said.

"Good evening, or morning." Steven lifted his mug. He opened his eyes enough to note the king's untucked shirt and mussed hair.

"It's midnight," Farran offered.

Steven stared at the king's feet as Farran stared at his reflection in the window.

The king turned on a heel. "I'll leave you to it, then."

"Wait," Steven said, causing Farran to pause. "You proposed."

Farran's eyes narrowed as he worked his jaw. Steven waited as his friend seems to collect his thoughts.

"Yes," Farran said, his voice quiet. "I told Grace it was so she'd be safe. But to be completely honest, I lied about my intent as soon as I gathered she was likely to say no."

"You just met her."

Farran looked up and sighed. "I know, but I feel as though I've known Grace for a lifetime. She just— it's *her*, for me. Does that make any sense?"

Steven nodded, though Farran continued to study the ceiling.

"I did it for several reasons. I want . . . I like her, and I'd like to have her— around." Steven watched Farran grasp for words. "And I want her safe. There's more, but . . . I don't want to talk about it."

Fair enough.

"Wouldn't her *importance* give Tyrnnth more reason to take her?"

Farran shook his head. "No, not my future wife. Though I've been aiding your country in this war, stealing my— bride . . . " Farran shook his head again, sliding his hands into his pockets. "I would rip them to pieces."

"Why don't you do that now?" Steven couldn't hide the edge of hysteria in his voice.

Farran had been holding out on Steven. On his entire country. The king ran a hand through his hair.

"Balance. I need to maintain my country. If New Iberia went

all-out, it would cost more than my people may be willing to give," Farran said quietly. "I'm already untested, my people and father's council watching my every move—"

"Well, while you and yours remain comfortable over here, this war will cost me everything," Steven snapped.

Farran wouldn't meet Steven's gaze, the king's eyes on the city below. Steven leaned his head back against the window.

Another time. If Steven lived through the Culling, they could have this conversation another time.

"So you're Grace's fiancé until she's done with the rescue team?" Steven asked.

Farran leaned against the threshold. "I believe everyone will be shocked when our engagement ends so suddenly."

Steven sipped from his mug. "Why did you think she'd say no?"

Farran pursed his lips, a few moments passing before he spoke. "I just knew." He shrugged. "Besides, I've done . . . I can't have her. In all honesty, she is far too good for me."

"Farran," Steven said, but the king shook his head, his eyes guttering. He wouldn't look away from the blackened horizon.

A thought settled into Steven like a stone.

"Tyrnnth threatened you," he said quietly. "Are you going to do what they asked?"

Farran gracefully entered the elevator and pulled a wire.

Cameras? Audio? Farran knelt before Steven, his eyes cold.

"There are warships just outside my capital and a knife at my sister's throat, even with Ares' general's ring on her finger," Farran said, his voice drawing thin. "What would you do, Steven?"

"What have you done?" Steven asked quietly.

"Nothing yet."

Steven opened his mouth, but Farran went on, rising.

"Survive the Culling, Steven. Your Blood Challenge won't be far behind."

Steven's jaw tightened, something in his chest doing the same.

Jaxin had to know Farran couldn't be trusted.

The Culling could last up to twelve days. Could Farran ruin everything in less than two weeks?

"Jaxin will kill you," Steven warned.

"I know."

"If I don't first."

Farran gave Steven a small, sad smile, though it was gone after a moment. "I cannot promise anything."

Steven sighed, regarding his friend.

"I know," Steven said, though he wasn't sure why.

12

Steven and Adira arrived to a hotel that evening.

The prizefighter opened the sliding glass door and stepped onto the balcony, waves crashing below.

The ocean inhaled before letting go, another crash sending salt into his face, his eyes shut as he breathed it in.

As his flight had entered Tyrnnth from the east, the country had looked crammed; multi-story homes with tin roofs crammed along curving, weaving streets. As they had drawn south, the crowded, dusty streets gave way to cobblestone and order.

Tyrnnth was far larger than Steven had assumed, and he had only seen a glimpse of it.

A knock at his door had him greeting Adira, the empress clad in a fine, black dress. She extended a slip of paper.

"Burle offers the best orchestra performances in the world. It would be a sin not to experience at least one."

Steven took the slip of paper, regarding Adira, her raven hair draped over a shoulder, the other side pinned up. Since he had last seen her, she had put rogue on her lips and darkened her lashes.

"I have nothing to wear."

Adira procured a bag. "I figured."

Steven dressed in the washroom.

When he stepped out, the empress was standing at the window, her face bathed in golden light as she gazed toward the setting sun.

She turned to him and ran her eyes up and down.

"You almost look presentable."

Steven ran his hands over the lapels of the fitted suit.

"All black," he mused. "This seems to be a theme for you."

"You'll blend in," she said, stepping forward. Steven offered his elbow, the empress threading hers through his.

Adira smiled. "We're going to be late, by the way."

"Are we?"

They walked through the lobby before Adira prodded him.

"Can you run?"

Steven's smile was answer enough, the empress dropping his arm to break into a sprint.

Adira's heels clicked against darkening, cobblestone streets, Steven impressed at her nimbleness in the delicate shoes. As they ran, she cast a wicked grin over a shoulder.

Delight.

Steven wondered if she saw the same look on his face.

Steven and Adira entered the concert hall as the first song was to begin. The lights dimmed, the crowd hushed as the conductor raised his baton for the first symphony.

Adira withdrew her hand as she sat, Steven settling beside her.

The hall was elegant, the musicians finely dressed.

When everything had gone to hell after the last Great War, one of the things that had returned in the rebirth of society had been music.

There had always been music, he supposed, but the music that had followed had been different. A mirror of a time long since passed.

Empires and kingdoms had returned, as well.

The tumultuous time had needed the stability of single rulers, though Steven wasn't sure what they needed now.

As he watched every musician's eyes on the conductor, he understood the importance of *one* ruler.

If the ruler was just right, perhaps a masterpiece could be made.

But life was messy, and not nearly as simple.

The violins entered with a crescendo, cellos following suite. The tone of woodwinds.

Music from another era.

Jay had been a musician. He had played guitar, and sang. Steven could still hear his voice; a soulful sound with rough edges.

Kind of like Jay himself.

Steven's heart constricted, swallowing as the swell of strings filled the room. A knitting of melodies and harmonies, layers upon layers of sound dancing in the air.

Steven looked at Adira as the song crested in an encompassing wave.

Her eyes were closed, the heart-breaking finale seeming to freeze her portrait in place.

As the song drew quiet, Adira opened her eyes, turning to find Steven still watching.

Was she crying?

Steven leaned in. "Soft-hearted worm."

As the crowd clapped, no one heard Adira hiss and Steven laugh.

The performance ended with Tyrnnth's national anthem.

When the final note faded, the crowd stood and clapped. No one seemed to notice Steven slide his hands into his pockets.

Yes, the music was beautiful.

No, he would not cheer for the anthem of his enemy.

The musicians were not at fault. Steven had stood for that. For all he knew, the dictator forced every concert to end with the piece.

The empress' heels clicked as they meandered back to the hotel. Despite the hour, the streets were still busy.

Adira paused by a window display, a delicate string of lights strewn across a swath of velvet. Steven's shoulder brushed hers as he stopped to stand beside her.

"I didn't realize Tyrnnth would be like this," he admitted. Inside the window, dozens of wood carvings sat, waiting for someone to admire them and take them home.

"This is the better part of the country," Adira said. "Everyone focuses on the east, the islands, and the mines."

Steven took a pointed look around the square. "And who profits from the mines?"

Adira turned, eyes narrowing.

"It is not *their* choice," she whispered, casting a look around them. "Some Tyrnnthians left when things began to turn, but most can't with the cost."

"Why not have citizens work the mines?"

"Locals work Tyservn."

"The island next to Tybauch."

Adira nodded, stepping closer as a group of men strode by, singing obnoxiously loud in Tyrnnthian's native tongue.

Steven watched her as she watched everything else.

"The fumes kill non-locals too quickly to send slaves to Tyservn, but the mines— anyone can work there. Ares must have had it in his head to save Tyrnnthian lives when he began conquering and shipping people here."

"You know an awful lot about this, Adira," Steven murmured, her face inches from his. She finally looked at him.

And then down her nose, somehow possible at this angle.

"I'm an empress. It is my job to know these things."

Steven raised his brows. "I see."

"How would you do it if you were in Luther's shoes?" Adira asked, stepping back, allowing Steven's heart to slow a fraction.

He shrugged. Steven had never paid enough attention in the classes that taught politics. Even with the books Farran assigned on the subjects of war and history . . .

Steven would have to learn it all before becoming King of Vastlynd.

When he didn't answer, Adira went on.

"I can tell you what would happen. Your mines are empty, as no one is willing to work them. Your steel production is down, as well as weapons production," Adira said, raising a brow. "In a world on its feet after the art of war has been changed, you no longer have enough weapons for your terrestrial armies."

Adira took a half step towards him.

"Now someone shows up on your shore, and you are unprepared. You reach out for another country, hope they pity you enough to step in, and pray it'll be enough."

"I still wouldn't have slaves," Steven said quietly.

Adira shrugged. "The world would be better for it."

She had finally agreed with him. He smiled.

"But," she said, Steven's smile faltering, "your country would fall."

"Then maybe it should." Steven offered his elbow. The empress regarded him for a moment before intertwining hers through.

Steven could have sworn she walked a fraction closer than before.

He took the cold air in his lungs, feeling every bit awake and alive.

The evening felt as though he wasn't to find himself on an island designed to kill him the next day.

And Adira . . .

Steven swallowed his dread as they walked.

He didn't want her to die. Whether or not the rumors of her

ties to Ares were true or not.

And he wasn't sure what that said about him.

———— ⌒☙☘⌒ ————

Steven held the hotel door for Adira and followed after her. The lights had dimmed since they had departed.

"So much for going to bed early," Steven said, his suit jacket slung over a shoulder. He reached into his pocket for his key as Adira leaned against the opposite wall.

"Now, Ms. Theron—" Steven began, the lock clicking.

"I'm here for my key."

He smirked and slipped in. "Oh, I'm sorry. What were you thinking?"

"Steven," Adira warned, following and shutting the door behind her. Steven hung his jacket on the back of a chair and loosened his tie.

"Do I get to keep the suit?"

Adira grabbed her key off the nightstand. "I hope you do."

Steven leaned back against the table, bracing his palms against it.

"Thank you for the evening," he said. Adira regarded him, her hand on the doorknob, faint amusement in her eyes.

It disappeared in a blink.

"Are you ready?" she asked.

"Are you?"

Adira stilled, her attention on the ceiling. Steven instinctively held his breath, listening for a threat.

The empress strode for the balcony and threw open the door, Steven on her heels.

"What is it?" he asked.

Adira leaned into the breeze, chilled air welcoming on his skin, the smell of salt and night filling his senses.

"Do you hear it?" she asked.

Steven leaned beside her. "Someone is playing piano in the lobby."

"Bartholomew's Sonnet," Adira said, her voice dropping.

Steven looked toward the slivers of moonlight dancing on the water, the lull of the tide below.

Between the sounds of the resting sea, and the thoughtful, wonderful notes, a request was out of his mouth before he could consider it.

"Do you want to dance?"

Adira looked at him, close enough Steven could feel her breath on his cheek.

"I hate dancing."

Steven looked at the grated floor. "Right, I—"

Adira took Steven's hands and stepped onto the balcony, the space nearly too small for both of them.

It was a beautiful song.

Steven held the empress near as the melody unfolded, notes and waves and moonlight and *her*—

He wasn't sure how long they danced before he let loose a long breath to pull away, looking into Adira's eyes.

Something flickered in them, though Steven couldn't identify what.

The pianist had finished minutes or hours ago, Steven wasn't sure.

"Thank you for the dance, Ms. Theron," he said, tucking a strand of hair behind her ear.

"I'll find you tomorrow," she said.

Steven angled his head. "Not if I find you first."

Adira huffed a dark laugh as she stepped away, freeing her hands from his.

"Good luck with that."

Steven smiled, Adira's eyes narrowing. "What?"

"Nothing," he said quietly.

She was insufferable, even after an orchestra and a dance in the moonlight. He stepped forward and cupped her face with his hands.

"May I?" he asked, quietly, as if he spoke too loud, someone would swat his hands away.

Adira's eyes shifted from his eyes to his mouth.

She was so close he could feel the warmth radiating off her body.

Her gaze flicked up, cold steel in them again.

"You really shouldn't."

Adira was out of reach and bidding Steven farewell before he could register what happened. He wasn't sure if he replied, though he must have. He usually did.

The air was cold and quiet after she shut the door.

Steven's heart hammered as he leaned against the window, watching the ocean undulate.

Fool.

They were friends, fight partners, nothing more.

As they should be.

Perhaps the evening had been the empress' attempt at distracting him from tomorrow. One last, decent night, before all hell broke loose.

Any good friend would have done the same.

Steven ran his hands over his face and groaned, standing in the night air until his bones chilled and fingers froze.

───※───

Through darkened windows, cameras flashed and people clamored as the limousine pulled up to Tyrnnth's palace.

Steven stepped into noise and chaos, turning to offer a hand to Adira. The empress watched him a moment before threading her arm through his. People screamed as she did.

Had his offer been perceived as more?

Steven nearly dropped her arm.

The crowd faded as they followed the Blood Challenger before them to the throne room.

Pale stone walls and arches lined the black marble floor, polished to a reflection, as if Luther Hawthorne desired to hold court over a dead, black lake. Floor-to-ceiling windows lined the room, offering a panorama of gray clouds over a frigid sea.

Luther was dressed in a maroon suit, a steel crown atop his head. Though he feigned arrogance as he lounged on his cut-stone throne, Steven noted his shoulders appeared tight.

Max had taught Steven to read his opponents.

Luther met Steven's gaze before directing his attention to the empress. A shadow passed over his eyes, but disappeared as he looked to the next Blood Challenger.

Adira disentangled her arm from Steven's as they neared the row of competitors before the dais. He halted beside a stranger, Adira at his right side.

When the procession ceased, Luther stood and the crowd behind Steven quieted. Cameras flashed, lighting the dictator's harsh face.

"Fate will now decide what the Culling will bring," he said, his voice echoing. Natalia and Ares ascended the dais, taking position beside Luther's throne.

Luther withdrew a pair of dice and approached a raised tray. As the dictator shook them, the sound reminded Steven of dry bones clacking against each other.

"For length of minimum stay." Luther released the dice, the room seeming to hold its breath as he peered down.

"Steven days."

Murmurs went through the crowd, contestants shifting as Natalia joined Luther's side.

A week. They could survive a week.

"For limit of Blood Challengers," Natalia said, not at all looking like the woman Steven had encountered twice now. Her face appeared sharper, her eyes colder.

She shook and released the dice, a muscle in Luther's jaw feathering.

"Two," the assassin announced.

Hushed voices rose amongst the contestants and crowd seated at their back, some outright gasping.

The odds couldn't have been worse.

Steven was glad he had an alliance with the one of the most skilled fighters he had encountered.

Since Jay, at least.

Natalia stepped back, replaced by Ares.

"For number of beasts," he announced.

Adira had told Steven the enemy War Leader had genetically manipulated each animal they would encounter; experimentations he had finished playing with.

The War Leader released the dice and smiled. "Twelve."

Voices rose and contestants swayed, cameras flashing as they captured the shock. Steven released a breath and looked toward Adira.

The empress' chin remained high, her eyes clear.

Steven wondered if she was the only one unafraid.

The rest of the ceremony consisted of rules and introductions.

When the line reached Steven, he straightened.

"Steven Castellen of the Central Territories."

Adira spoke next.

"Adira Theron, Empress of Nyrland."

Steady, strong. She was the embodiment of the two words, the rock in which the tide would break for.

It made him wonder what he looked like standing beside her.

More introductions ensued before Steven turned at a familiar voice.

"Memphis Makani, seventh prince of Calterra."

The prince's beard was neatly trimmed, his dark eyes focused. With his hands clasped before him and shoulders back, he almost appeared confident. If not for his locked knees and stiff posture, Steven would have believed it.

He was surprised to see the prince here.

Farran had heard rumors of Calterra meeting with Tyrnnth. Though Luther appeared indifferent, Ares' eyes had since narrowed.

More introductions droned on before Steven's heart stopped dead in his chest, a familiar voice pulling him back to the present.

It wasn't real, though.

It couldn't be.

"Cassius Jay Castellen," the voice said. "Slave of Tyrnnth and Central Territorian convict."

Steven turned, his dead brother staring back at him, a half smile on his face.

"Hailing from death at the front, and the deepest pit of hell in Tyrnnth's mines," the convict finished with a mock bow.

Jay was alive. It was *impossible*.

Steven had watched him die.

Jay's bloody, broken body on the front had been Steven's last memory of him. When the prizefighter had returned with a vehicle to retrieve him, Jay was dead, Ares toeing Jay's lifeless body with a boot.

But Jay was not dumped in the trench. He was here.

Steven breathed a curse, Jay's smile unfaltering.

Jay was *here*.

Steven's brother would face genetically-modified beasts, danger, and desperate men and women clawing for a way out—

Steven noted the thinness in Jay's body, the hollows of his cheeks pronounced. Steven had never seen him malnourished before.

Could he survive what was to come?

Slave. Jay said he had been a *slave* of Tyrnnth.

"That concludes the procession of competitors for the Culling," Luther announced, rising. "May the most clever and resilient live. I will be waiting on the other side, eager to fight two worthy opponents."

Luther eyed the competitors, his gaze snagging on Adira.

Jay was here. Adira was here.

Something in Steven's chest tightened.

He could only take one with him.

———⚮———

As soon as Luther took a step, a contestant turned and ran. No one reprimanded him. The dictator snapped his fingers as the contestant reached the door and a lance went through the contestant's chest.

Once dismissed, the crowd began to stir. Steven unabashedly shoved his way to his brother.

"Jay," Steven rasped, embracing him. Jay laughed and smacked Steven on the shoulder, squeezing tight. Steven shook his head, stepping back. "How?"

Jay's eyes darkened, though he remained smiling. "They tried to kill me, and I lived anyways. To spite the bastards, of course."

Steven surveyed Jay, noting his bloodied, chain-marred wrists.

They were so much worse than Grace's. It looked as if Jay had worn them for *months.*

"It's okay—"

"Okay?" Steven hadn't realized he'd grabbed his brother's arm. "This is—"

"Better than being dead." Jay withdrew his arm.

Steven looked up to find Jay's smile drop as he beheld something behind Steven. A glance over Steven's shoulder confirmed his brother had spotted his ally.

"Jay, this is Adira, she—"

"I know who she is," Jay said, the words clipped.

"Steven, a moment please," Adira said, tugging. Steven cast a glance over his shoulder as the empress pulled him away.

"How do you know my older brother?" Steven asked, his voice low.

"I don't. You said he was dead."

"He was. I don't— that's him. Right there." Steven pointed a finger. "How does he know you?"

"The news, I imagine." Adira shrugged. "Do you have a suggestion on how he would otherwise?"

"I do," Jay drawled. Steven turned to find Jay behind him, arms banded over his chest. "Someone had to take care of you after your parents were murdered."

"How dare you." Adira's voice was deathly quiet.

A bell peeled, a hissing sound filling the room.

"I'll see you on the other side, princess," Jay said. He turned and set a tattooed hand on Steven's shoulder. "Find me at the surface."

"Don't hurt her," Steven said. "Promise me."

Jay smiled. "I don't make promises I can't keep."

Before Steven could argue, his vision blurred and all went black.

13

Steven heard dripping and opened his eyes to darkness. He sat up, neck stiff and joints sore.

The Culling had begun.

Steven calmed his breathing. There was no telling how long he had been out, or where he was.

Up and out, that was what Adira had instructed him.

Only death awaited those in the caves.

The stone beneath his palms was wet and cold. He heard the faint sound of waves crashing.

After two minutes, his eyes adjusted and his nerves settled. He could see outlines of his surroundings as dim red lights lined the tunnel floor every few yards . . .

Forward. That led up.

Steven rose, boots scuffing. He held his breath.

Silence answered.

He softened his footfalls and crept forward.

After a few minutes, he noted faint, cool light in the tunnel. He quickened his pace, pebbles skittering. When he neared the corner, a scream pierced the air.

It had come from behind.

It wasn't Adira, it wasn't Jay.

Steven ran towards the light, the scream cutting off to leave a haunting silence in its place.

He cursed under his breath. How was he supposed to survive a week here? Someone hadn't even made it through the first fifteen minutes.

Steven rounded the corner to find an opening in the wall, the sea roiling on its other side. He whooshed out a breath and ran to it, inhaling fresh air.

The sun would set in a few hours.

He grimaced as he tried and failed to fit through the opening.

Eager to get to the surface, Steven hurried along the curving wall, savoring each glimpse of sky through the holes and cracks in the stone.

On the ride from the hotel to the palace, Adira had mentioned a bunker ladder within the heart of the island. Though the concept of a quick, easy way to the surface sounded appealing . . . he would have to travel *further* into choking darkness to find it.

He figured he shouldn't allow his rock climbing training to go to waste, anyways.

All he needed was a proper hole in the wall he could slip through.

───

It was two hours before Steven met a solid rock face. He would have to take a right at the last fork. He turned and treaded carefully, avoiding bits of slick, green algae.

Hallucinating-inducing algae, he had been told.

His heart had already stopped dead in his chest when he thought he had seen hands reaching from the crevices in the floor.

His head pounded with every step.

Steven peered through a gap in the wall to find it was already getting dark. When he looked forward, he found a figure heading his way.

Was it real? The stranger blurred as Steven attempted to focus.

The gait, the way the man carried himself—

"Jay?" Steven asked. He didn't dare speak too loud and attract whatever stalked the tunnels.

The man angled his head, his appearance a swirling mist. Dark hair, a broad-planed face. In the shadows, Steven swore the edges of the man's eyes crinkled as he smiled.

"So much for finding you at the surface," Steven said.

His smile dropped as the mist cleared.

A knife thrust for Steven's chest, the mirage clearing to reveal a stranger. Blood ran as Steven stepped back, the blade cutting through his jacket and shirt. He stumbled back and drew his knife.

They had all been allowed one personal item.

Steven was certain every contestant bore a weapon.

The men circled, Steven noting the limp in his opponent's gait.

Steven shot out, quick as an asp. The hilt of his knife jammed into the man's side. In another maneuver, Steven had disarmed the man, his knife clattering to the floor. The stranger cursed and lunged.

Steven didn't want to kill him. He was likely another Central Territorian, seeking a way out of Tyrnnth's mines and taking a chance at ending the war.

Steven let go of his knife as the man neared.

The stranger grabbed Steven's arm and twisted, making to slam him into the wall. Steven grasped the man's other arm and jerked, letting go as momentum sent the man careening down the tunnel.

Steven grimaced at the thud and silence in its wake.

Heart hammering, Steven wiped the sweat off his palms and picked up his knife. He needed to reach the fork and put distance between himself and the contestant.

Surely a beast had heard the commotion and was on the way.

Steven halted, his vision blurring and doubling again.

The stranger's body was still and bloody. Jay's face flashed in and out of focus, Steven raising a hand to his throat as he beheld the manacle scars that remained as the mirage flickered.

Steven fell to his knees.

He hadn't wanted to kill anyone. With the beasts, he figured he could outlive the others.

He shook his head, running a hand through his hair.

"You were never supposed to kill anyone, Steven."

The prizefighter's head snapped up.

Someone familiar sat against the dark, wet stone, an elbow leaned on one knee, the other resting on his leg.

The bald head and thinning eyebrows, the man's athletic build; everything seemed so familiar, yet *wrong*—

Despite the pressure in Steven's head, pain lashing down his neck and chest, he shook his head.

"Max," he breathed. "You're not supposed to be here."

There was something else to remember about Max. How did he get here? Wasn't he . . .

"Dead?" Max smiled. "If you stay here another minute, you'll be dead, too."

"It's the algae. You're not Max," Steven said quietly.

"What makes you so sure?" Max said. Tears filled Steven's eyes at the accent, the familiarity. "As I was saying kid, you never should have taken a life. But you killed at the front, and you're killing again now."

Steven rose and backed into the wall. He may have been shaking his head.

"I had to. I'm sorry," he breathed.

"Don't apologize to me, I'm already dead." Max shrugged. "You're going to do it again anyways."

Luther. Did he mean Luther, somehow?

Max's attention turned to the hall, lights flickering out. Or was that the algae again?

"Run," a voice whispered. Not Max's, but—

A mirage of Adira leaned against the wall, nodding to the side. She turned to smoke, her command lingering in the air.

"What?" Steven asked, his voice hoarse.

A rock skittered, Steven stilling. A huff of breath . . .

That was not a man.

Steven looked to where Adira had indicated. A slim cut in the rock, barely visible with the dying light—

Steven would have to hope and pray there was purchase on the other side to cling to, if he could even *make* it through the gap.

His heart thundered and head pounded as a growl reverberated off the walls, Steven's hair standing on end.

The creature's steps quickened, Steven following suit, throwing himself towards the gap.

With a shout, Steven squeezed his shoulders inward, dirt stuffing under his fingernails as he heaved himself through. Time slowed as he hoisted his legs out, teeth snapping on the other side of the hole. Steven slipped as teeth snapped, his fingernails breaking as he grappled for an edge.

Whatever had been at his heels was too large to follow.

After a few minutes clinging in fresh, open air, the prizefighter's head cleared.

Max hadn't been real, Adira hadn't been real. Jay wasn't dead.

Steven reminded himself these facts as he clung to the slick rock, waiting for his heart to calm. Blood slid from the wound on his chest, soaking his shirt and the waistband of his pants.

He hadn't realized the stranger had cut so deep.

Steven climbed, teeth gritted, until darkness bid him to collapse on a shallow alcove. Curling against the cold, wet stone, he fell asleep to screams and roars, left to wonder if they were real or not.

———— ❧ ————

Steven dreamt of Adira.

They danced in moonlight beside a black sea, and when Steven leaned in to kiss her, she didn't stop him.

He inhaled as something pierced his side. The empress pressed her body against his, one hand on the small of his back, the other wrapped around the hilt of the dagger piercing his new suit.

"Adira," he breathed.

She kissed him again, and despite it all, he kissed her back.

It lasted but a moment before the empress shoved the blade clean through his ribs.

Steven woke gasping for breath.

Groaning, Steven threw a rock from under his side over the cliff, listening for the splash. When it took longer than expected, he peered over the edge.

He had summited a third of Tybauch.

Steven looked towards the horizon, anchoring himself. After tending to the cut on his chest, he drank dewdrops clinging to the moss and continued his ascent.

The light grew and diminished by the time Steven couldn't muster the strength to continue.

Progress had been slow. When the prizefighter dared a look down, he could see the alcove he had slept on the night before.

The screams and roars had continued throughout the day. At one point, he heard a splash, as if death at the rocks was better than being eaten alive.

Steven was inclined to agree.

Limbs shaking and fingernails bloody, he heaved himself onto another alcove. He laid atop the plush moss, his breath ragged and heartbeat in his ears.

His heated skin soon cooled and he rolled under a root-laden overhang. Despite his layers, the cold persisted and he tucked himself further in.

Adira had said something about mastering the cold—

They had nearly finished a climbing session when a freezing

wind snapped up off the coast. Steven had shivered and rubbed his palms together, hanging above the ocean within his harness.

One glance at the empress told him she wasn't the least bit bothered, despite wearing even less than him.

"How are you not cold?" he asked. Adira's eyes remained northeast.

Toward Nyrland.

"I was told a story once. About a villager that fell in the ice," she said, her voice distant. "He had been there for hours by the time he was pulled out, alive and well."

"How?"

Nyrland's winters were frigid; surely her story wasn't anything more than a bedside tale, or at the very least, an exaggeration.

Adira smiled, looking toward Steven. "He pretended he was a seal."

He laughed, but Adira merely continued climbing. "When you are cold and wet and alone, you may just be desperate enough to try it, too. And you won't be laughing when it works."

Steven's body wracked with shivers, a hollow tone sounding as wind slammed into his side of the island.

It hadn't been this miserable the night before.

It wouldn't hurt to try Adira's mind game. Then he would find out if she had been pulling his leg or not.

He blew out a breath and imagined himself a snow leopard. Covered in thick, warm fur. In his . . . den.

Steven rolled his eyes.

This is stupid.

Another whip of wind worked through his layers, Steven curling inward. He again pretended to be an animal he definitely wasn't.

His trembling subsided the slightest.

Perhaps this would be worth being made fun of for later.

While waves crashed below, roots shifting and grazing his face, Steven's breath steadied and he fell asleep.

Dawn of the third day revealed the end of Steven's climb.

Craning his neck, the rock face was sheer.

He would have to reenter the tunnels.

He drank and assessed the scabbed-over line on his chest before shimmying to a nearby opening.

With one last look toward the horizon, Steven entered Tybauch's prison, slipping into a dark hall. He followed the orange-red lights lining the floor.

No screams or roars this morning.

The prizefighter attempted to quiet his steps, his body stiff and sore from climbing and sleeping in the cold.

Two or three minutes passed before the hair on his neck rose, Steven stilling as he listened.

A huff of breath sounded from around the bend.

Steven unsheathed his knife and crept forward until a man came into view, his body a statue. Before the stranger, milky white eyes and ebony claws gleamed.

The man was too lithe to be Jay, his hair too long—

The fanged beast took a step forward; a massive canine of some sort, nearly half its skull exposed to reveal ivory bone.

Memphis Makani was staring Death in the face.

The prizefighter prepared to slip away. Memphis would keep the animal occupied, ensuring Steven's escape.

He wouldn't have to kill Memphis if the beast did.

The prizefighter took a step back, swallowing dread and something far more bitter.

Something tugged on his heart and he paused, watching as the lupine beast lowered its face and pulled back a blackened lip.

Fangs, each nearly as long as Steven's forearm—

Memphis had a brother. Several, if he was the seventh. Steven couldn't help but think of Jay, who had sacrificed everything to keep him safe.

If Zakkai were here, which he *couldn't* be, as Calterra's Crown Prince and heir—

A wet sniff cut through the air, spit smacking to the floor. The creature took a step forward, but the prince wouldn't move.

Memphis would die without a fight if he stood a moment longer.

Steven cursed the prince under his breath and grabbed a rock. Before reconsidering, he hurled it. The rock cracked into the creature's exposed skull, the animal rearing back with a snarl.

"RUN," Steven ordered.

Memphis woke from his stupor and stumbled as he turned to run, the creature roaring.

"There's an opening here," Steven called, already running.

Once out, the prince would have to shimmy to the alcove. If he couldn't make it, falling would be a much better than being ripped apart by one of Ares' beloved, cursed pets.

"I can't climb." Memphis' voice was hoarse. Steven turned and noticed the blood on the prince's thigh, the limp in his gait.

Of course.

Behind Memphis, the beast appeared to be a wolf, covered in patches of black fur.

And it was *massive*. The length of its leg was easily as tall as a man.

Steven reached the opening, his mind screaming at him to *move* as his heart told him to wait. He watched the creature rush forward, it's maw open to reveal long, yellowed fangs.

Memphis was close now.

White eyes, *white eyes* . . .

Adira had told of such a beast.

Steven shoved his nerves down as Memphis neared. The prizefighter broke a stalactite free and raised it, his free hand pressing a finger to his lips.

Memphis' brows drew together, his face contorted. He made to look over a shoulder.

"*Don't,*" Steven snarled. Memphis obeyed and pushed harder.

As the prince made to hurtle past, Steven threw the stalactite and wrenched on the prince's arm. The prizefighter pressed a hand over Memphis' mouth as the prince made to shout.

The stalactite shattered down the hall, the sound echoing as the pieces scattered. Steven didn't breathe as he watched, in horror, as the wolf slowed, its ears twitching as it made to pass them.

At this angle, Steven could now see more of what Ares had done to the animal. He wondered if he was hallucinating again, or if Memphis could see it, too.

The furless patches of skin bore checkered black ink, stark against its pale, scarred skin.

Tattoos.

The wolf halted, ears twitching, its nose to the air.

Too soon. The wolf should have ran past.

They didn't have the time Steven thought he had bought. He dared a look at Memphis, finding the prince's eyes wide with terror. He met Steven's gaze and shook his head.

He wouldn't even *try* to climb out the hole.

The muscles beneath the ink shuddered, the wolf's jaw snapping as it turned to face them. As the beast lunged, Steven shoved Memphis aside and pulled his knife free.

Teeth snapped, Steven inhaling hot air and carrion.

How many lives had this creature claimed already?

If Jay or Adira . . .

Steven shut down the thoughts, stumbling over the uneven floor as the beast's head swiveled to him. He eyed the wolf's neck as it closed the distance, the wall looming at Steven's back.

Memphis shouted, the wolf turning toward the noise. Steven rushed the beast's throat, a strip of skin stretched taut.

Memphis screamed, Steven baring his teeth as he ran his knife across flesh, a snarl cutting through the prince's agony.

The wolf whipped its head, Steven pivoting from snapping jaws. The prizefighter struck again, drawing the blade deeper, his muscles and joints straining.

Steven nearly lost grip of his blood-slick knife as he pulled away.

But he had struck true.

As Steven backed away, narrowly missing another snap of teeth, the wolf snarled as it turned away, its legs already faltering.

After a few too-long seconds that seemed to last an eternity, Steven heard its body collapse down the tunnel.

Steven turned to Memphis. The dark-haired prince had blacked out, his body soaked with blood, his right arm hanging on by tendon and sinew.

Steven lurched, nausea roiling. He had seen much at the front, but never had to deal with injuries directly.

He would have to now.

How soon did the rescue teams respond? If everything was being broadcasted, surely they had seen what had happened to the prince.

Steven couldn't leave Memphis. What if the team didn't show in time?

With the scent of blood in the air, surely far worse things were already on the way.

Memphis' shout had saved Steven's life.

He surveyed the space, taking in the blood and carnage.

If they stayed in the alcove outside the opening, other beasts would come to clean up the mess, smell them, and wait for the prince and prizefighter to reenter the tunnels.

They would be stranded.

And with Jay waiting for Steven at the surface . . .

Steven looked at the ashen-faced prince, loosening an unsteady breath as he wiped his blade off.

<hr>

Steven hurried, Memphis dead weight on his back.

The prizefighter had hastily tied his ripped shirt over the prince's injury in an attempt to staunch the blood.

Teeth gritted, he had nearly vomited as he cut the remaining pieces tethering Memphis' arm to his body.

Steven told himself a missing arm was better than being dead.

He hoped Memphis would agree when he came to.

Steven lost track of time as he ran and stumbled upward, the tunnel turning inward. Even with small orange lights every few feet, Steven squinted against the shadows playing tricks on his vision.

When was the last time he had eaten?

He considered turning around and choosing a different path when he noted a faint blue light. He shifted Memphis' weight as he approached, the glow brighter with each step.

Steven lifted his head as he entered a cavern. Stories above, millions of pin-prick lights glittered.

He was standing in a cave of starlight.

He drank in the sight before allowing reality to resume. He desperately needed to rest, his body weak from the hours of carrying the youngest Calterran prince.

Steven was yet to figure if the effort had been worth it, as it was only a matter of time before the prince bled out, or another predator found them.

Then they'd both be dead.

He should have left the prince in the alcove.

Though, Memphis could have rolled off in his sleep . . .

Steven sighed and began to cross the cavern, the space reminding him of an ornate, glowing cathedral.

Each footstep echoed, small rocks skittering in the dark. He stilled as a scuff sounded across the space. He stopped and rested a hand on his knife as a man approached.

"Why do you have that man?"

"He needs help," Steven said. The stranger offered a shrewd smile.

"I see. I thought you were going to use him for live bait. Run, while he gets taken instead of you," the man said, flexing his fingers. Steven slowly lowered Memphis to the ground, the prince groaning.

This was not a friendly opponent, Steven had decided.

"Why waste your energy?"

"What do you want." Steven straightened, every muscle in his body tight as a bowstring.

The man crossed his arms. "You're the famous boxer."

Steven barely registered the movement against the wall. He shifted his feet, covering the hiss against stone.

"And you are?" Steven asked.

"Mallory, from the Eastern fight pits." The man widened his stance. "We've met before."

Steven had thought the stranger seemed familiar; the heavily-muscled arms and chest, the mustache. Steven had watched him fight during a national championship.

If Steven had been forty pounds heavier, he would have fought against him, too.

"It was hard to recognize you with the blood all over your face," Steven said, his jaw tensing as he noted the man's unmarred wrists. "You're not an ex-slave?"

The hissing grew closer, Mallory unaffected. Steven wondered if the man had some sort of hearing loss, or if Ares' genetic manipulations had given Steven a keener sense of hearing.

Mallory smiled as he shook his head. "I forged a birth certificate. Why waste my skill at the front when I can take out the entire war in one fight?"

Is this what Steven sounded like to other people? He vowed to never speak again.

"You should move on. Let us pass."

Mallory barked a laugh, his dark eyes narrowing. "Champion prizefighter, Steven Castellen, scared? I'll take that as a compliment."

"You don't want to fight me," Steven assured, his body tensing to sweep Memphis up. Whatever had lurked at the back of the room was near now.

Mallory stepped forward. "I sure as hell do, actually."

He whipped out a blade, his face pinching as he looked down.

"Tyrnnth's *ally?* You can't be serious," Mallory said.

Steven drew his knife, eyes flicking to movement in the dim light.

How many hours had Steven carried the prince? His arms felt as if they could snap. Sweat beaded at his forehead.

"Last chance," Steven said. Mallory opened his mouth as a rattle filled the room, reverberating Steven's bones. A chill ran down his spine as both men stilled.

Mallory's eyes widened, locking onto Steven's. In the glow behind the man, a serpent's head rose. In a flash, a pair of jaws snapped around Mallory's midsection.

Steven hauled Memphis up and ran.

Mallory's scream followed Steven as he raced for the opening in the right wall. His legs slammed into something, both prince and prizefighter sprawling to the ground.

Steven looked at solid-yet-not rock he had stumbled over and blanched. Steven had tripped over the serpent's body, nearly thirty feet away from its massive head. Steven fought to move as he watched the snake attempt to swallow Mallory whole.

The man was still alive.

If the snake did manage to swallow him, the fighter would die a slow, painful death.

Steven cursed and rose, depositing Memphis inside the hall before jumping over the serpent, making his way back to Mallory. The man's screams shifted, Steven's ears ringing.

The prizefighter's stomach dropped as he caught sight of the snake's head—

It had already swallowed Mallory's legs, the man's hands reaching past blood-streaked fangs.

This was a nightmare.

Steven would wake in his bed at the cottage, listen to the rustle of leaves outside, the smell of tea and pancakes wafting up the stairs . . .

Steven raised his knife, the serpent's ochre eyes zeroing in on him. The snake jerked, swallowing Mallory's chest.

"Kill me," Mallory screamed, his eyes on Steven's.

Something in Steven broke, reminding him of the day Jay had begged Steven the same mercy, not wanting to be left alive for Tyrnnth to play with.

It had happened anyways.

Steven couldn't kill the serpent. Not like this, not with a knife. He would be dead before he even tried.

He roared as he threw his knife and Mallory's sobs cut short.

A rattle and hiss filled the cavern, but all Steven could hear was Mallory's broken scream echoing in his head.

The prizefighter didn't look back as he flung Memphis over a shoulder and ran like hell.

14

Steven had made it to an outer wall by nightfall, cold wind kissing his brow as he leaned out the gap in the wall. There was a mossy knoll to the right, the only thing that had gone well that day.

Steven hefted Memphis and inched toward the outcrop, his body trembling by the time he set the prince down.

He closed his eyes for a moment and woke to a sea of brilliant starlight, the moonless night making it appear as though Steven could reach out and touch them.

The prince stirred, drawing Steven's attention.

"How do you feel?"

Memphis' eyelids fluttered, a sheen of sweat on his brow.

"Water?" Steven offered.

Memphis nodded weakly, Steven squeezing drops free from a wad of moss.

"You cut my arm off," Memphis whispered. Steven stilled.

"It would have been hard to travel with."

Memphis shook his head. "I should be dead. It's fine."

The prince passed out, Steven pressing the back of his hand to the man's brow. Infection had set in.

Steven braced his elbows on his knees, exhaling as he looked up.

A beautiful night for the end of a nightmare.

A cold one, too. Steven couldn't feel his fingers and his blood-soaked clothes were freezing.

He pushed away the awareness and focused on the sky, noting the reds and blues and yellows amidst the deep black.

The night sky always reminded him of his tattoo.

Sic itur ad astra.

He wasn't sure what it meant to him now.

Where it once represented willpower, striving toward his goals, and gaining glory— it felt hollow.

Fame and success meant nothing in this new world, where war haunted his past, present and future. Already, he was a different man than the one who had volunteered for the front.

Maybe someday, after it all, he wouldn't flinch at fireworks and gunshots and a cracking log in a too-quiet room.

But then again, maybe he would.

The sky above proved there was still beauty, even in the most horrific of circumstances.

Giving his life to the Blood Challenge would be his last shot at reaching those stars.

It was the only fight Steven had to win now.

Steven awoke to Memphis' labored breath.

A brief survey confirmed the infection had a firm hold on the prince, his skin pallid and hair matted to his sweaty forehead. Steven withdrew his hand and leaned back.

"The rescue team is on the way," Steven said.

Never mind they should have arrived already. How many hours had it been? Despite the darkness, dawn couldn't be far off.

Steven cut two strips of his shirt and rebound Memphis' shoulder and thigh dressings, tossing the old ones over the ledge.

If the rescue team didn't show within the hour, Steven was sure the prince would die.

He dabbed a moss wad onto the prince's forehead.

"It's a beautiful night," Steven said. "Lots of stars."

Memphis did not reply.

"More water," Steven went on. After several wads of moss, he wasn't sure if Memphis would swallow or drown, and gave up. He leaned back and closed his eyes.

There wasn't much more Steven could do.

It was sobering to know the prince would likely be dead the next time Steven awoke. He had nearly fallen asleep when, between Memphis' rasping breaths and the crashing waves below, a new sound materialized.

Rotors.

Steven jumped to his feet, the sound growing until flashing lights shone above, voices echoing.

"Down here!" Steven waved his arms until a flashlight blinded him and a man shouted back. Steven jumped back as rocks peppered the ledge.

"They're here," he said, dragging Memphis closer to the wall. The prince's head slumped against Steven's shoulder.

Zakkai's feet planted onto the knoll, his face grim.

"He's lost a lot of blood," Steven said. "And he's fevered."

Zakkai crouched before his brother. "I'm going to get you out of here. You're going to be okay."

Memphis didn't reply, Zakkai standing to his feet.

"Thank you, Castellen."

Steven rose, careful to leave Memphis undisturbed.

Zakkai pulled Steven into a rough embrace, his next words spoken rapidly, quietly.

"Tyrnnth has taken over a third of your country, and your largest draft disappeared overnight."

Steven didn't have time to reply before Zakkai stepped back, smiling grimly. "Good luck."

Steven nodded stiffly, his lips a thin line. "You too."

When fear was running highest, Central Territorian deaths

broadcasted for the world to see, Tyrnnth had launched another wave. Over a third— and an entire draft.

Steven's knees felt weak.

Zakkai scooped Memphis up, the former so much larger than the latter, Steven suspected Calterra's king had sired sons from different women.

It wouldn't surprise Steven, as Zakkai had a *harem*.

The prince nodded to the surface.

"Your lady friend is here. Tyrnnth wouldn't let them rescue a rogue son of Calterra, so she joined my team." Zakkai tugged on the rope, the line going taut as he began to ascend.

"Grace?" Steven shook his head, of course it was her. "Why wouldn't they save him?"

"Bad politics," Zakkai called, rising steadily.

Tyrnnth and Calterra were allies, then.

Steven hoped he hadn't made a mistake.

As light and rotors dimmed and quieted, Steven decided he had done the right thing.

If Memphis was resisting the alliance with Tyrnnth, Steven was thankful the man had been spared.

In a sick game where killing was expected, Steven was grateful he had been able to do just the opposite.

He wondered what else he could do to spit in Ares' face from this distance.

Steven was exhausted when dawn greeted him.

The Culling had to last a minimum of five more days, even if the survivors dwindled to the limit.

He hadn't figured out what to do about keeping both his brother and Adira alive, as the Culling couldn't end if there were more than two survivors . . .

Adira was still a puzzle to Steven.

If Adira had been raised by Ares, there was no telling how cunning she could be.

Steven leaned back, taking in the storm clouds on the horizon, a brisk wind snapping up.

Zakkai had left his jacket. Steven hadn't noticed until he had rolled over in the night.

Though three sizes too large, it was warm, the outer material rugged, the inside sherpa-lined. Steven drew it further around himself.

He needed to get to the surface.

Before his friends slaughtered each other.

———— ❧ ————

Steven came across a steel door.

His head spun as he halted, his empty stomach gnawing. He set his hands on the circular, rotating handle.

Anyone, or anything, could be on the other side.

Without his knife, Steven felt naked. If something were to happen now, all he had were his wits and fists.

He supposed it's all he would have against Luther, so surviving the rest of the Culling would be the real test.

Steven wrenched the handle, wincing as the door groaned. He slipped in and shut the door behind him.

Yellow lights lined a smooth, concrete hall.

Steven walked until he faced another hall jutting to the left. He held his breath as he listened, peering around the corner.

A red smear, a black doorway.

He'd continue straight, then.

Steven did not want to die here.

He hurried as quietly as possible, ignoring the pit in his stomach.

Some halls led to dead ends and fruitless doorways.

In an attempt to find the ladder to the surface, Steven had

wound up lost in a labyrinth.

He ran a hand over aged graffiti, mesmerized by the many names from a war long ago.

Through Farran's prescribed studies, Steven had learned Ares' great grandfather had been the one to write the treaty banning all methods of modern warfare.

The concept had sounded ideal, until reality set in.

Steven's mind flashed to blood-soaked trenches, gunshot wounds, and rotting men.

Though a country could no longer be wiped off the map in a single blow, Steven couldn't say things had changed for the better.

Slaughter was slaughter.

Instead of being incinerated in his home, he would now bleed and suffer before death.

At least he could do something about it, he supposed.

He could fight.

And there was hope.

Steven leaned against the wall, allowing his body to rest.

Ares claimed he was saving the world, and Steven's grandchildren would thank him someday.

Steven wasn't sure how *that* added up. There would be no grandchildren to inherit the land if everyone was shipped off to work until they died, or left to burn.

Steven inhaled deep, willing strength into his bones.

He needed to get to the surface and *breathe.*

Calluses scraping, he rubbed his face with dirty, blood-stained hands.

This war *had* to end, but not in the way Ares wanted.

Steven's body felt the shift before his brain did. He held his breath, hair rising on the back of his neck.

Something, or someone, was here.

He looked down the hall, searching for a door. Most had fallen off their hinges. If he could find an intact one, he could wait until whatever was tracking him passed.

And sleep. Already, he needed rest.

Steven's vision blurred as he aimed for another hall.

A shrill cry broke the silence, the sound unlike anything Steven had heard before. He cast a glance over his shoulder as he made to turn the corner.

Two sets of eyes stared back at him.

Steven's body locked. What the hell was he looking at?

Hyenas, they used to be hyenas.

Blood dripped from their maws, large, midnight eyes devouring him. Razor-thin claws clicked against stone, though their hairless, dark bodies did not move.

Clicking issued behind Steven and he turned to find two more creatures, eyes and bodies still.

Steven was beyond sufficient expletives.

His heart slowed, cold licking the soles of his feet.

Though he couldn't will his legs to move, he turned his head to find the other hyenas had neared, silent as death.

Steven was a dead man.

Those unholy, black eyes did not blink. Clicking issued from both sides, the cadence familiar.

Between the drops of blood falling between blackened fangs and his too-loud heartbeat, Steven could have sworn he heard morse code.

Ares had way too much time on his hands.

The thought jarred Steven, blood rushing back into his body.

He *needed* to move.

The prizefighter ground his jaw, whipping his head to see that the other pair of hyenas had neared ten feet.

Which meant the other pair—

Black teeth flashed.

Steven's legs pumped, everything in surprising clarity. He passed gaping doorways, dodging rubble and debris. Claws clicked and frenzied cries issued at his back.

Way too close.

Steven ran harder, legs unfeeling. He reached the end of the hall and turned, nearly crashing into the wall. Stars burst in his vision, the floor lights sparser down this hall.

Claws slipped and the beasts slammed into the wall, Steven's ears buckling under their shrill cries.

What had Ares done to these animals?

And if he could do this to an animal, what could he do to a man?

Steven pushed harder, his heart in his throat.

If these creatures were intelligent, they would likely rip out the backs of his ankles before going for his neck.

Steven realized, too late, that there was no exit at the end of this hall, the failing lights having shrouded his view.

He should have taken a left.

This was it, then.

He was going to die. And it was going to hurt.

Steven would be ripped apart by mockeries of nature, made by Ares himself. It almost seemed a fitting end; in the end, was Steven not another of Ares' creatures?

If he ran into the wall hard enough, maybe he would black out and feel no pain when the hyenas ripped into him.

Yips and cries issued as Steven sprinted, the creatures gaining.

In the flickering light, he could have sworn he saw an outline— A door.

It was a miracle. Or a mirage. Steven threw himself into his legs, darkness swirling at the edges of his vision.

He was so close. He could make it.

He could—

Pain tore through Steven's calf. He careened, his jaw slamming into the floor. Stars danced and hot blood filled his mouth. Teeth gritted, he covered the back of his neck as his enemies surrounded him.

He had been so close.

And it had not been enough.

Frenzied yips joined the sound of cloth tearing, Steven's body yanked this way and that. His jacket sleeve gave way, flesh sundering beneath.

Steven may have been screaming. He watched his blood pool on the floor, the hyenas a swirling darkness around him.

His arms were jerked away from his neck.

Steven looked up and focused on the door ahead, as if it would open to the world he would walk into next.

Where would he go?

He should have talked to Grace about this. She knew where she was going. Steven didn't. He closed his eyes and began to pray, as if he couldn't feel his flesh being torn from his body.

Steven opened his eyes to a mirage. The door before him opened, a glint of steel flashing. His neck jerked, nerves exposed to fang and beast, and all went black.

15

Radiating pain, throbbing heat, darkness.

Steven had been broken and bruised before.

This was much worse.

He had somehow survived a mauling. The thought had him jarring upright, pain seizing his body.

He groaned and fell back, his head landing on something solid, yet soft. And warm. He opened his eyes to Adira looking down at him.

"Welcome back to the living," she crooned. Why was she smiling? He had nearly died, and it was not a smiling matter.

Perhaps he was dead, and the pain had followed him. Adira had already died, and was here to taunt him.

"Am I dead?" Steven asked.

Adira's smile became crooked. "You're well on your way."

Alive, then.

"How long have I been out?"

"Long enough for me to tie a tourniquet."

"I'm sitting up." Steven tried to, at the expense of his head spinning and pain gripping his body. He hissed as he straightened, his heartbeat pounding in his ears.

They were in a cylindrical chamber, a ladder to his left. The empress sat with her back to the wall, watching him. Her eyes drifted to his neck.

"How bad is it?" he asked.

"Not as bad as it could have been. Your arms took the brunt of it. That jacket saved your tendons from being torn out."

Steven let out a shaky breath. "I'll have to thank Zakkai later."

"What?"

"He gave me his jacket for sparing his brother," Steven said, his words growing quiet. He was starving, the pit in his stomach gnawing.

"You saved Memphis Makani?"

"I tried to. He's missing an arm now, though."

"That's better than being dead."

There was no telling if Memphis survived the rest of the day. Steven wouldn't know until the end of the Culling.

He looked down, the chamber stretching far below, lights darkening the deeper it went.

"This is the shortcut," he said.

Adira hummed, stretching her legs out over the drop.

Steven looked back to the empress. "You saved me."

"How will you pay back the ever growing debt?"

Steven managed a smile before a wave of pain overtook him. He doubled over, gritting his teeth until it passed.

Adira had tied the tourniquet above his calf. He surveyed her work, sighing through his nose.

If he lost even a *part* of his leg—

"Adira . . . "

"It's just until we reach the surface."

Steven looked up, yellow lights fading to white.

"We should go before infection sets in," Adira said.

Steven closed his eyes, attempting to master a wave of nausea. When he settled, he found Adira watching him.

"Thank you," he whispered.

"Don't thank me yet. There's no telling if you'll make it," Adira said, rising to her feet.

"How far?"

Adira offered a hand, Steven taking it. The world swayed as the empress gripped his torso with another hand. She took a step back and nodded to the ladder.

"After you," she said.

Steven lifted a brow at her. "I might fall."

"You won't."

Steven set his hand on a rung.

"Last chance," he said, unable to turn his head. Adira didn't respond, Steven huffing as he raised a leg.

Stars danced and he cursed.

"It'll hurt here, or it'll hurt there. Either way, you're going to be in pain," Adira said at his back. "Will it be here, with an infection, or at the top, without one?"

The climb was hell.

Steven took a break at every ledge, his head spinning and wounds bleeding as he panted through his teeth.

When they had reached the top, Steven had been too weak to open the hatch. After a vivid string of curses, he shifted to the end of the rung, Adira sidling next to him. Her eyes searched his own before roving his face, likely taking in the sheen of sweat.

"You have an infection," she said. Adira threw back the lid, a wave of cold, fresh air entering Steven's lungs.

He rolled onto the floor as Adira stalked off.

He wasn't sure how much time had passed when he felt the empress cut a line up his pant leg.

"On your stomach," she ordered.

"This is going to suck," he said hoarsely, obliging her request.

"Bite this," Adira said, offering Steven a rag.

As she scrubbed torn flesh, the bit muffled Steven's screams.

She didn't have anything for pain.

After cleaning and alcohol, the empress stitched him back together and wrapped her work in a bandage.

Steven, on his stomach, shifted to look at Adira. Her brows drawn, she finished sewing his pant leg. She flicked her eyes to him, smirking.

"I've seen worse," she said. "Give me your arm."

Steven removed the rag from his mouth and smiled at her.

"Always. So. Polite." A deep breath, an unbearable wave of pain.

"Oh, stuff it, Castellen."

Adira either noticed Steven was so tense he couldn't move, or truly wanted him to shut up, placing the rag back into his mouth.

She didn't seem to mind his suffering as she scoured his wounds and sewed his forearms.

Part of Steven wondered if he shouldn't let her help.

If Jay was right, and she was Ares' daughter, she could be his biggest threat here.

And yet . . .

He should have died.

"Why?" Steven asked aloud, the bit spat out on the floor.

Adira was nearly finished now.

She leaned back and surveyed the bandage on his forearm.

"What do you mean? We're allies." Adira pulled Steven's sleeve down. "I wasn't going to let you become kibble."

Steven nodded numbly, his gaze settling on the strip of windows behind the empress. Night was falling.

"I saw you in a hallucination," he said, though not sure why he did. Perhaps it was the fever speaking. "You showed me how to get out of a bad situation."

"Oh really?" Adira was nearly finished sewing his sleeve.

Somehow, she was much better at stitching skin than fabric.

"I saw my trainer, too." Steven's brows drew together. "He told me I shouldn't have killed anyone. Ever."

Adira tensed, nearly imperceptibly, but Steven went on.

"I had to on the front, it was my job. The contestant in the tunnel was an accident, but . . . what the hell is that about? Max is dead."

He wasn't sure why he was talking.

"Steven." He looked at the empress, her hand atop his arm, even as her work was finished. "It was just your head. If Max is dead, he's dead. I'm assuming you care about his opinion above everyone else's, I don't know. But I wouldn't think about it anymore. If he cared about you, he wouldn't guilt you about something you don't have a choice in and then leave you to die."

Steven nodded once, twice. "Right."

Adira rose. "I'm going to make a fire to keep the animals out."

Steven looked at the open doorway behind her.

Though they could descend into the hatch again, the thought didn't sit well with him.

Adira gathered wood from an alcove, Steven watching her weapon glint in the dim light. Her personal item, a sword of all things, remained strapped down her spine.

"Won't a fire attract other contestants?" he asked.

"It will be the last mistake they make if they approach us."

Steven's brows furrowed as he looked at the double-edged blade. There was still blood on it.

"How many— how many people have you killed?"

Adira made her fire, enough time passing that Steven assumed she hadn't heard him. Flames danced along the wall and on her face, Steven's eyes growing heavy from exhaustion and the dull roar of pain.

Adira wasn't looking at him when she finally answered.

"Don't ask questions you don't want the answers to."

———

The silence woke Steven. He eased onto his forearms, pain firing down his arms.

It was morning, and Adira was not here.

Rubbing his face, he collected his bearings and rose. He shuffled to the doorway, taking a deep breath as he surveyed the grass-laden hills.

Adira said Tybauch was beautiful in the summer, the land covered in wildflowers, the sky alive with sparrows and terns.

He stepped out of the bunker, the breeze ruffling his hair and cooling his skin.

"Adira?" he tried.

The empress was likely out hunting. Steven hoped her prey was game and not people, his blood running cold at the thought. He thought she had slept beside him last night, but couldn't recall for certain.

Steven crested a hill, the pinnacle offering an unobstructed view of his surroundings. The island of Tyservn was shrouded in mist, Tyrnnth too far to even spot.

Adira had spoken true; Tyservn was much too distant a swim.

No man, woman, or beast roamed, though perhaps they lurked just out of sight. There were plenty of bunkers to hide in.

The wind shifted, a faint chemical smell brushing his senses, reminding him of the front. Perhaps they made weapons and poison on Tyservn.

Steven slid to the bottom of the hill and headed back into the bunker, eager to rid his senses of the smog.

He halted as the hair on the back of his neck rose. He pivoted.

A muffled shout, a clatter—

Adira's sword was on the floor, her mouth trapped under a tattooed hand.

"Let her go," Steven snapped.

Jay rolled his eyes. "Steven, really—"

Adira thrashed, her eyes flaring in warning. Something slammed into the back of Steven's head, arms banding around his chest.

Steven jerked, a shout and thud following. Pivoting, he threw his shoulder back.

A fist met Steven's jaw, copper and something jagged in his mouth.

The last thing Steven saw was Adira lying beside him on the concrete floor, already out.

16

Eyes shut, Steven heard murmurs and crackling logs. Pain radiated from his wounds, his jaw.

Steven ran his tongue over his teeth and found one absent. He grimaced and opened his eyes to a starless, black sky.

He raised himself onto his elbows, taking in the ring of fires encircling a small camp.

"Sorry," Jay said. Steven turned his head to find his brother beside him, something glinting between his fingertips. Jay offered a grim smile. "I'm pretty sure I saw the tooth fairy get eaten yesterday."

"What the hell was that for?"

"I needed to explain some things, and we both know one of your party wouldn't have let me do so willingly," Jay said.

"You're not supposed to hit women."

"She would have decapitated me if I hadn't."

Steven blew out a breath. He would throttle his brother when he was physically capable.

"We're outside," Steven said. There were several people sleeping in the camp.

And not one at another's throat.

"Last night we holed up in a bunker and two of us were taken. It's less claustrophobic out here." Jay shifted, raising his dark eyes to the fire. "I have a theory, though. I don't think we'll be attacked if Her *Empressness* is here."

"We all taste the same," Steven countered.

"Sure. But whatever Ares did to these critters . . . " Jay shrugged. "I think they'll recognize Ares' adopted daughter and stay the hell away."

Jay wanted Adira alive, for safety or to sate his curiosity. That was good.

"How did . . . " Steven gestured toward the group.

"We declared Blood Challenges not knowing the Culling would happen," Jay said tiredly. "We decided we wouldn't play the way Ares wanted."

"Only two can walk out."

"No walking required." Jay picked up a stick, prodding the central fire. "Tomorrow, we'll figure out who's most qualified to face Luther. The rest will swim."

"Tyservn is too far," Steven pressed. When Jay didn't reply, Steven sighed and changed the subject. "How were the mines?"

Jay's eyes darkened. "Hell. All of us are from the lowest shaft."

"I'm sorry," Steven said. For allowing Jay to be taken prisoner, for not trying harder. "When Ares said you were dead, I—"

Jay looked at him. "It's not your fault, Steven. I played dead."

"Why?"

"I told you to shoot me and you didn't." Jay shrugged. "I knew you couldn't save me. I was surrounded and you still had a way out."

The scene played in Steven's head, the blood, smoke and soldiers—

"You were shot in the back. How are you able to walk?"

Jay smiled coldly. "Ares patched me up so he could experiment on me. When he saw I could breathe the gas, he decided I was worth the effort."

He turned toward the fire. "And then they used me until there wasn't anything left to play with."

Jay's fears had become his reality.

"How long?" Steven asked.

Jay leaned back. "I don't know, it was hard to tell."

A woman sat up at the edge of the fire, Jay's eyes flicking up. He nodded to the stranger. "Steven, this is Zahara. Zahara, Steven."

"A pleasure to meet you," Steven said. Zahara's brows drew together, looking to Jay.

"He has such nice manners. How am I supposed to believe you're related to him?"

Jay scoffed. "He's been influenced since I last seen him. Don't let the manners fool you. He's as insufferable as I am."

"You're really a famous boxer?" Zahara leaned forward, wrapping her arms around her knees.

"Not as famous as I thought if you don't know me," Steven said, earning a smile from Zahara.

"Insufferable," Jay muttered. She looked at him and raised her dark, arched brows.

"Are you going to finish your story?" she asked. "I'm invested now."

Jay sighed, making a face. "I guess." He looked toward Steven. "Anyways, I was pretty much dead when I was thrown into the mines. These guys are the only reason I lived through it."

Steven looked to Zahara, some form of gratitude on his mind when he opened his mouth to speak.

He barely registered the shadow before it materialized.

Adira had her sword at Zahara's throat. *"Start talking."*

The camp stirred and Jay rolled his eyes. "I just finished."

Adira snarled and pressed her blade further, Zahara's dark eyes glowering at Jay.

"I guess I can run my mouth some more, though I'd prefer this discussion without your weapon at my friend's throat."

"You're in no position to ask anything," Adira snapped.

Jay sighed. "We're a group of ex-slaves taking advantage of the pass out of the mines. The strongest will go on, the rest will escape."

Adira let out a bitter laugh. "There's no way out. You have to lose a limb, die, or kill everyone else."

"He's telling the truth," Steven said. "Jay wouldn't lie to me."

Adira's eyes slid to him. "And would you lie to me, Steven?"

"You would know if I was."

It was true. Adira saw through people in a way that unsettled him. He was grateful he lacked the ability, as the empress seemed plagued with a distrust for everyone.

"Adira," Steven tried.

She narrowed her eyes at Jay. "If someone lays a finger on me, they're dead."

"Fair enough," Jay said.

Adira dropped her blade. "Tell me the lies you were told."

"We heard a lot in the Slauvebach foothills."

Zahara frowned at her fingertips, a shallow, red line across her chestnut throat. Jay pretended not to notice.

"In the southern bay, there's a gully in the water with a set of stairs leading to it. If you don't believe me, you can see for yourself. We head there on day seven."

"Believing you can swim to Tyservn is a mistake many have made."

Jay's dark brows rose. "Good thing we won't be going that far."

Adira watched him for a moment. "You'll see who's strongest and the rest escape."

He nodded. Adira huffed and looked past him.

"That may not be necessary. There are three days left and plenty of beasts. They'll find a way to the surface soon enough, if they're not already here."

"I have a feeling they don't have a taste for empresses."

"Worried for me? That's cute." Adira smiled.

Jay bristled, but the camp settled after Adira took a seat, wiping her blade in the grass.

Zahara met Jay's eyes once before lying down, putting several feet between herself and the empress.

"You should get some sleep," Jay said. "We take watches and it's still my turn."

"Wake me next, if you still trust me," Steven said.

Jay smirked. "That remains to be seen."

Steven lied down, grass scratching his face, the ground colder than he had anticipated. Despite the pain, he was out within moments.

Steven's dreams were full of lightless tunnels and scraping claws. He did not turn as he felt something approach, even as it drew near.

Steven found he could not move, his feet leaden and glued to the blood-stained concrete. He tried to will his feet to shift, but all he could do was stare as flickering lights winked out one by one, each closer than the last.

When the last light had extinguished, Steven felt hot breath on his neck.

Carrion and decay.

A window appeared, Adira and Jay on the other side of the glass. She nodded as Steven's brother spoke. Farran walked in, a woman at his side.

Faye.

Steven's mouth wouldn't open to cry for help.

Nobody would look at him, glasses in hand as they enjoyed some sort of gathering without him.

Faye caught sight of Steven. He tried to move, tried to call her name—

There were more beasts now.

Faye stepped closer to the window, watching him.

Steven inhaled just as jaws snapped around his throat.

Steven didn't speak during breakfast.

He hadn't thought of Faye since before the Culling, and yet she had been in his dream.

She had let him die.

Though Jay had cast him glances, Steven hadn't met them.

After breakfast, Jay and his posse gathered to fight, a weighty chill and promise of snow in the air.

Zahara checked Steven's injuries as Jay set up a fight pit.

She had been conscripted into the war as a nurse.

Jay had mentioned she had tended to him after he had been found in the mines, one foot in the grave.

"When did this happen?" Zahara asked.

"Two days ago," Steven said. Zahara raised a brow as she continued to survey his wounds.

"You said they were hyenas?"

"Yeah."

Zahara looked up as she wrapped his calf. "Are you sure this happened two days ago?"

Steven frowned. "Give or take."

Zahara shook her head. "It looks as though it happened *weeks* ago. How did Empress Theron treat you?"

Steven huffed a laugh. "With expert care, apparently."

Zahara dusted off her hands. "Maybe they don't make med kits like they used to."

Steven offered a tight smile. "Yeah, maybe."

Afterward, he found himself seated at the edge of a makeshift fight pit, stretching his arms out in front of him, gauging the pain with the movement.

He had woken this morning without much of it.

If Zahara was to be believed, somehow his body had managed to complete weeks of healing overnight.

It should be impossible.

Adira prodded him. "Want a berry?"

"I thought those were bad."

"No."

Steven nabbed a few, watching as his brother drew a bracket in the sand, two men warming up in the pit.

"You just can't eat too many. It'll paralyze you for two hours." Adira threw the palmful back.

Steven huffed a laugh, propping his elbows on his knees. "You ought to feed your opponent now."

The taller and darker of the two men, Dalmar, faced the lither, pale-skinned Cyrus. His layers discarded, the latter had tattoos on nearly every surface of his arms.

"Who's going to win?" Steven bumped his shoulder into hers.

"The tall one," Adira said simply.

"Why?

"He's bigger."

Jay whistled and the fight began.

"Who do you think?" she asked, the men circling. Jay watched with a hand on his chin.

"Cyrus," Steven replied, watching as the man lunged. Dalmar pivoted, the movement a bit jerky.

"Which one is that?" Adira asked, leaning back.

"You didn't bother paying attention to introductions this morning?"

Cyrus swore as Dalmar landed a blow to his gut.

Adira shrugged. "Why bother? The likelihood of more than two people making it out of this alive is very slim."

Eyes turned toward them.

Steven leaned in. "That's not very nice, Adira."

Adira smiled in that unfriendly way of hers. "They're all thinking it anyways."

Cyrus knocked Dalmar out of the pit, whoops drawing Steven back to the present. When his gaze landed on Jay, the convict watched him back, something like unease in his eyes.

———❧———

The next fight was swift, the opponent knocked out within a minute. A man bearing tousled, ginger hair grimaced at his downed opponent.

"I didn't mean to hit him so hard," he admitted, his voice thick with a brusque, lilting accent. A Hymnlynder, Steven guessed.

Jay joined the victor's side and looked down.

"Remind me not to get on your bad side."

They dragged the unconscious man from the ring, Steven's brother dusting off his hands as he returned to the bracket. Steven watched him scrawl the name Sebastian.

"Zahara, Adira," Jay called.

"No thanks," Zahara said. Adira and the nurse looked at each other, the latter making a face. The empress nodded.

"That was easy," Jay mused, writing Adira's name. He rose and approached the ring, smirking at his brother.

"Can you fight?" Jay asked. Steven looked at Zahara. She pursed her lips, brows drawing upward.

"Though he has healed a bit, it obviously isn't a good idea."

"Nurse Rutheme doesn't approve." Jay crossed his arms. "Do you?"

Steven smiled back. "Scared?"

"Let's get this over with before it snows." Jay jerked his chin toward the pit. Indeed, the air felt heavier, the horizon line already blurring with snowfall.

Steven entered the pit, sand crunching underfoot.

Someone whistled and Jay burst forward. Steven blocked three strikes and pivoted.

"You missed a shot," Jay noted.

"I'm letting you warm up."

"So humble, as always." Jay lunged, Steven darting away,

ignoring the twinge in his calf.

Maybe Zahara had overestimated him.

Steven grit his teeth, steadying himself.

"C'mon, Steven," Adira called. He turned toward her, Jay landing a blow to his jaw. Stars wheeled as Steven blocked Jay's next strike.

Steven tasted blood.

He would no longer be holding back, either.

Steven landed two blows before Jay could shift away. Steven ducked out of Jay's fist and dropped, sweeping a leg for his ankles. Jay stumbled, his peers shouting as he neared the border.

Steven straightened, pain leeching into his calf and arms, sweat stinging his eyes.

Maybe he would lose.

Jay smiled. "Look who's winded for once." He advanced.

Jay had wrestled his entire school career, and had continued to in jail. If he managed to get Steven on the ground, the fight would end in a matter of seconds.

Steven dodged Jay's arms. Before the prizefighter could block, Jay's fist met his stomach.

Steven groaned and backed away, avoiding the urge to double over.

Jay let him.

"Don't go easy on me, brother," Steven warned. When Jay advanced, Steven dodged and feigned a strike. Jay fell for it, Steven swinging a foot for his jaw. The convict stumbled away, a slew of curses following.

"If you want to call it quits—" Steven began, light snow falling on his hot skin.

"Oh, please."

Jay lunged.

17

Grace's back met cold metal as she slid to the floor of the helicopter, allowing her eyes to shut for a moment.

They had lost the woman they pulled from the lake.

Grace had been rooting for her.

One moment, the young woman was stepping into the water to wash the blood from her face, the next, she was pulled under.

Grace watched as a sheet was laid over the contestant, hiding the half-moon bites covering her body.

Hilda.

That was her name.

She had been killed by leeches the size of sheep.

Grace shuddered and closed her eyes once more.

She wasn't sure how she'd sleep after this experience. She had seen a lot in the last half week, and knew there was only more to be seen.

Steven was still alive, and Jay—

Goodness, she had thought him *dead*. She prayed he'd survive. It had been years since she'd seen him.

The helicopter shuddered against an assault of wind and snow as it made its way back to the Calterran war vessel.

Zakkai had thrown a rescue team together for his brother, Memphis.

Grace had somehow managed to convince the prince to stick around for everyone else, not trusting Tyrnnth's rescue team to pull through.

For some reason, Zakkai had heeded her request.

The prince would pay for his disobedience when he came face to face with his father, King Vincere.

Calterra and Tyrnnth were allies.

Zakkai said his brother issuing a Blood Challenge had been an embarrassment for their entire county.

Grace hadn't asked where Zakkai aiding his brother's rescue put him, as well as aiding all of the other survivors now.

Not that there were many.

Most contestants died.

Grace hadn't slept in forty-eight hours, her hands pruned from washing, cleaning and wringing.

She was nearly asleep when someone settled beside her, clothes rustling and warmth radiating.

"You should strap yourself in," Zakkai said, his voice low. Grace grunted an acknowledgement.

This was a fine place to sleep, she had decided.

Someone sighed, probably Zakkai.

The next thing she knew, she was being lifted off the metal floor and placed into a chair, straps buckling.

Just as she succumbed to exhaustion, she could have sworn she felt a blanket settle over her.

18

Steven and Jay called a tie. With snowfall growing heavy, the entourage spent the rest of the day relocating to Adira's bunker, gathering food and firewood along the way.

Though the ex-slaves were afraid to be in a confined space, the bunker was the most ideal shelter with the snow to come.

As daylight faded, Steven threw his last bundle of dead grass onto the floor.

Adira approached as he finished adjusting everything. He raised his brows as she tossed a pelt over him.

"Oh, thanks—"

Adira crawled under and everyone's eyes snapped to them.

Steven swallowed, unsure of where to look.

"What are you doing?" Jay asked.

The empress leveled Jay a look. "I nearly froze last night."

"Heartbreaking."

Adira narrowed her eyes.

"I don't trust you," Jay went on.

"You don't need to, I'm not in your bed," Adira spat. Both empress and convict looked to Steven.

He shrugged. "It's fine."

Jay's eyes narrowed, arms banding.

Adira groused and put her back to the room.

"That really ain't a bad thing you got going on there," Sebastian offered.

It wasn't helpful, but Steven didn't say anything. Jay stalked off, tending to the fire before finding his own spot on the floor.

With warmth radiating beside Steven, the rise and fall of the pelt as Adira breathed, he drifted to sleep.

Jay was alive. Adira was alive.

It was all Steven needed at the moment.

Purple iris' danced upon the field, grass undulating in an ocean breeze. Steven caught sight of someone heading his way.

A crown of pale hair, a cold face with sage-green eyes.

"Faye." Steven took a step towards her.

The princess broke into a run, daisies crushing underneath.

Steven began to jog.

He had nearly reached her when she halted, eyes flaring at the ground. She fell to her knees.

There was a body. Steven cleared the grass, able to make out the bruised and bloody face—

Farran.

The sky bruised blue, black and red, akin to Farran's too-still face.

"No, no, no," Steven muttered, falling to his knees.

There was a tea kettle going off somewhere. Steven could barely stand it. There wasn't enough oxygen in his lungs.

He was sure his heart would burst with the effort to draw more in.

Steven clutched his chest, trying, trying, trying—

He woke to screaming.

Steven jolted, a body pinning him to the ground.

A hand pressed over his mouth and he blinked back darkness. Adira shook her head.

The screaming turned guttural, pleading.

Steven tried to rise, but Adira wouldn't allow it.

He glimpsed over her shoulder.

The fire had died, allowing him to see vague shapes, and nothing more. A deep-throated growl reverberated along the walls, Steven's body icing over.

"It's not Jay," Adira said, her words barely discernible above the screaming.

"Let me go," he rasped. Adira did, but a moment late.

Steven staggered to his feet as the screaming ceased, nearly taken out as a creature ran past, a body dragging in its wake.

Jay was shouting and tripping out the doorway. Steven grabbed his brother's elbow, holding him in place.

"Sebastian?" Steven asked.

"No, it took Cyrus." Jay swallowed, his eyes searching the dark, snow-laden horizon. "Help me build a fire. Watch shifts can't be spent alone anymore."

It had snowed a foot overnight. There would be no fighting today.

A day inside the bunker, warmed by fire and company, did sound appealing to Steven.

They still had no idea what had killed Cyrus.

Steven hoped they would never find out.

The group spent the morning milling inside, sharpening weapons and talking. Sebastian told a few half-hearted attempts at jokes, Zahara shared Calterran lore—

Nobody spoke of Cyrus.

Jay had covered the gore with grass, but Steven knew the group could see through it.

Steven also hadn't missed the ring of tracks surrounding the bunker. It seemed they had been stalked long before the beast had came to claim a life.

The hours left everyone restless, and by that afternoon, all but Steven, his brother, and Adira, had left to gather more food and firewood.

With two fires to burn each night, they couldn't chance running out of material to burn.

Steven had been content to stay behind and make sure his brother and ally didn't slit each other's throats.

"Tyrnnth is going to be disappointed you tamed their violent custom," Adira mused, sitting criss-cross on the floor. Steven mirrored her, Jay leaned against the wall with his legs stretched out before him.

The convict shrugged and stretched his arms above his head, light gilding his dark hair with reddish hues.

"Don't care," he replied.

Steven gave Jay a pointed look. "You wanted to talk."

"Yes." Jay clasped his hands together in his lap, eyes on Adira. "I want to know why an *empress* would issue a Blood Challenge."

"Why," Adira asked flatly.

Jay angled his head, offering a bitter smile. "I don't want to fight you unless I have to."

Adira's eyes sparked with challenge. "A wise decision."

Jay opened his mouth.

"Story, please," Steve interjected. "I'm curious, too."

It was true. Steven had wondered ever since she had revealed she would be attending the Culling.

"My friends opted out," Jay said. "It's just between us three now. I assume anyone left in the tunnels are dead by now."

"Yes, you are likely correct." Adira exhaled. She looked around the bunker, her voice dropping to a murmur. "I took the cameras down." She shook her head before meeting Steven's gaze. "Though I am Empress of Nyrland, the rumors are true. I was raised by Ares."

Steven was unsure he was hearing correctly. "What?"

Adira's eyes guttered before she steeled herself, straightening.

She wasn't kidding. And Steven had heard her right.

He had been sleeping next to the daughter of his enemy for *days* now—

"How?" Jay asked.

"Ares destroyed our capital and shot my parents as it burned. In the same night, he took the children of every chieftain and chieftess and pitted them against each other."

Steven watched as Adira ran her fingers over the grass on the floor.

"I lived, the others did not. When Ares saw how the memory of— of it all affected me, he removed it. Then he told me who I was. Or, who he wanted me to be." Adira looked up. "The lies in my mind wore off recently."

"So why are you here?" Jay asked.

Adira looked to Steven as she answered.

"I am here to murder Ares' son."

Steven watched her back.

"You're going to end a war out of spite," Jay said, disbelief dripping from each word.

Adira looked at Jay. "Blood for blood. Ares thinks I am his weapon, but I will be his undoing in the end."

"So what does he think you're doing now?" Steven asked.

Adira bit her lip and looked at the floor. "He thinks I'm here to take Tyrnnth for myself." She shook her head. "But I don't want it. I just want my people avenged, and to wash my hands of him."

"In what world would Ares be okay with you murdering his own son?" Jay asked.

Adira looked at him, her eyes darkening. "Ares has long thought his son too soft. Luther was raised by his mother. When he found out why his mother died— well, it doesn't matter. Ares prefers me. But what he doesn't know is that I plan to take them both out."

"To what end?" Steven asked quietly.

"What do you mean?"

"You kill Luther, you kill Ares. You go home," Steven said. "Would not someone just like them rise up to rule Tyrnnth after, now with reason to go to war with you?"

"There is no man worse than Ares," Adira said.

Jay made a face.

At least there was something they could agree on.

"I have one more question," Jay began. "You are willingly going to betray the man who raised you?"

"I have watched my parents die in my nightmares, waking and sleeping, enough, that it doesn't matter what Ares did for me anymore."

Something in Jay's eyes darkened.

He looked at Steven in silent question. The prizefighter sighed and directed his attention to Adira.

"Revenge can be quite the motive." He had issued his Blood Challenge to redeem a death. "I believe her."

Something in Adira's eyes guttered, but disappeared in a blink, Steven left to wonder if he had imagined it.

The hurried crunch of footsteps approached, Steven turning to watch Sebastian career into the doorway, cheeks flushed and eyes wide.

Jay was on his feet. "What is it?"

Zahara burst through the doorway, Dalmar beside her.

"They're gone," she breathed.

"Sam, Mika— they went over a hill. When we went to find them, there was only blood and tracks," Sebastian breathed, his voice hollow.

"We never heard a thing." Dalmar looked over a shoulder, his body shaking with shock, fear or cold, Steven couldn't tell.

Jay ground his jaw, looking toward the snow-laden hills.

"Should we go after them?" Sebastian asked.

Jay was silent for a moment too long. He sighed and shook his head, turning away. He went to the woodpile and began gathering.

"No," he said.

Because Steven knew it, too.

Jay's friends were already dead.

19

Adira was asleep at Steven's back, one of her arms grazing his spine as she rested it atop her sword.

He kept his eyes pinned on Jay, asleep across from him.

Jay had insisted on sleeping closest to the door.

Steven hadn't been able to rest due to it, even with two watchmen and twin fires blazing.

Eventually, he gave up keeping watch over and flipped over, daring to put his back to the room.

Adira's eyes opened, blinking back firelight.

"I was using that," she murmured.

"What are you talking about?" Steven whispered.

"Your back. It's warm."

Steven huffed under his breath. "I'm sure you'll survive."

Adira made a noise and made to flip over, Steven laying a hand atop her wrist.

"Do you want to talk?" he asked.

Adira raised a brow. "No."

"Back warmth taxes," he tried, unable to hide the smile that tugged on his lips. Adira drew her hand back to herself and sighed.

"Alright."

Steven drummed his fingers, looking at the metal of the

empress' weapon. "Tell me about the sword."

"I earn a question for every one you ask," Adira said.

"Deal."

Adira absently ran a hand over the metal.

"I named him *Addenox*. He was given to me by a mountain warlord for completing training."

Steven's brows rose. "Not true."

Adira's eyes met his, the corner of her lip lifting.

"I wish it were." She sighed, looking at the sword again. "The warlord's son made it for me in an attempt to earn my hand."

"I take it his attempt didn't work."

"No, but I wasn't about to give him the sword back either."

Steven smiled as Adira ran her hand through the grass.

"Warlords," Steven mused. "Do tell."

"I was trained by several. *Someone* insisted I learn from the best, or the worst, I guess you could say." Adira shrugged. Steven opened his mouth, but the empress beat him to it. "My turn."

"What do you want to know?" Steven propped his head on a hand, Adira pursing her lips as the sound of crackling logs filled the gap.

"Is it true Jay shot your father?"

Steven's mouth went dry. "It's not my story to tell."

"He just doesn't seem the type."

"I guess you would have had to be there."

Adira watched him before nodding, her gaze flicking to his chest. "Now tell me about your tattoo."

She had seen it countless times during training, never once showing interest until now.

"It's a long story," he said, idly running a hand over it. Adira looked at him until he sighed and lifted his shirt.

The piece was dark in the firelight, the colors muted. In a half-empty hourglass, starlight slipped through a bottleneck. On either side, a wing spread across his chest. Below the wings, a banner.

"The hourglass is filled with stars," Steven said. "And—"

"But why."

Steven looked up to find her staring at his chest. Naturally. He was showing her his tattoo.

He shook his head, running a finger over the banners. "It has to do with the phrase."

"Sic itur ad astra," she murmured. "Latin for . . . stars on wings?"

"Such is the path to the stars," he translated, tugging his shirt down.

"And what does it mean to you?" Adira asked, meeting his eyes.

Steven's lips thinned and he looked to the floor.

"I don't know anymore. It used to mean— well, my time here is limited. I wanted to make it all worth it." He paused, searching for the words. When he looked up, Adira was still watching him, her eyes softer.

"I got it as a reminder to keep striving and reaching, but the meaning is different now." Steven sighed. "And if you're about to ask me what it means to me *now,* I don't know."

The meaning had been marred by the man who had given Steven the means to succeed.

He shifted. "Do you have any tattoos?"

Adira set her hand on the hem of her shirt.

"That's enough of you two," Jay said, a hand on Steven's shoulder. "It's our watch."

Adira lowered her hand and glowered at Jay.

"You should see my tattoos, princess," he said. "Prison tattoos that look as good as mine are highly coveted."

Adira scoffed, turning her back to them. Steven rose and joined his brother at the wall, taking a seat on the floor.

"You should have been sleeping," Jay said, procuring a piece of wood from his pocket. Steven watched the set of fires dance at the doorway, smoke drifting out the window.

"I know why you did it," Steven said, his voice hollow.

"What?"

Steven looked to Jay, the convict watching him carefully.

"Harrin," Steven said quietly.

Jay's eyes darted to Adira, warning flashing.

"I always wondered why . . . " Steven didn't finish. Harrin had been abusive to both of them. Physically to Jay, verbally to Steven. The only reason Steven hadn't experienced both was because of his older brother.

Jay had always stood between them.

Harrin had still been Jay's father.

"I'm sorry," Steven said.

Jay loosened a breath, setting the edge of his knife to the wood.

"Some days, me too."

⁂

Steven and Jay talked of Grace, the tree house, school, their classmates— people and places likely destroyed by now.

Neither mentioned it.

"Remember when Grace stuffed a sock down Simon's throat?" Jay said, a wood shaving falling to the floor. He appeared to be making a bird.

"Hot, wet sock. It had been *roasting* that day," Steven lamented.

Jay shook his head, another shaving joining the floor. "Despicable, naughty Grace." He lifted his head. "Even though Ares used her as a bargaining chip, I'm glad she's okay."

"Me too." Steven sighed through his nose.

"What did King Bardolph pay?" Jay asked, resuming his carving. Steven glanced at the empress against the wall.

"A sum of money."

Steven stoked and fed the fires, dawn dusting the snowscape outside in deep blue hues.

It was their last day.

Adira was in a sour mood. Steven knew she would be the moment Jay had greeted her.

"Good morning, princess!"

Steven had barely reigned in his laugh as the empress rolled out of bed, snarling and weapon ready.

A crisp wind whipped Steven's hair from his brow as he stared at the horizon, the ocean stark gray beneath a brewing of clouds.

People would die today. If not from the swim, then from the creatures that had surfaced.

Steven wondered if there were any other contestants alive. If the Culling couldn't end until there were only two left . . .

He shook his head as Jay's friends began to pass.

Adira's shoulder brushed Steven's, drawing his attention. When he looked toward the bunker door, he found his brother thin-lipped. Steven grimaced and set his feet into motion.

Steven's breath fogged as he stepped into Jay and Adira's footprints, steadily approaching Tybauch's northeastern edge.

He glanced back at Sebastian, Zahara and Dalmar.

They were quiet today.

Jay hissed, Adira stepping to his side, her hair snapping in the wind. Steven jogged up to meet them.

The snow was blood-stained, ivory bones littered throughout, ravens taking flight.

"Keep your eyes open," Jay said hoarsely.

Steven looked at Adira, the empress appearing even more cold and distant than usual.

"What is it?" Sebastian asked.

"Don't look too close. I think— just keep moving." Jay shook his head. "We don't have time to go around."

Sebastian reached the hilltop and stilled, Zahara raising a hand to her throat beside him. Dalmar threw up.

Jay stalked down the hill. Steven forced himself into motion, refusing to look at the corpses.

People.

Ares had dumped *people* here, for the world to watch get torn to pieces. Steven's fists clenched in his pockets.

Soon enough, Steven would find a way to end Ares' reign.

If not for his sake, then for the rest of the world's.

The prizefighter looked to Adira. She moved effortlessly, even in the uneven terrain, carnage on both sides.

With her involved, perhaps he wouldn't have to kill Ares at all.

———

They reached the cliffside by noon.

Steven leaned against a rock, suppressing a shudder as he watched the roiling waves. A hollow tone filled the air as wind wove through the tunnels.

"We should go as soon as possible," Sebastian said, rubbing his palms together. He somehow appeared more pale, as if the day's events had leeched away any remaining color on his skin. Steven turned to find Jay watching the ocean, a hand propped under his chin.

Steven had asked about the ink on Jay's fingers, a letter beneath each callused knuckle.

LOVE WINS.

The convict had merely told Steven he'd tell him later.

Jay seemed to think they would survive the day.

"Boss?" Sebastian tried again.

"Yes." Jay's eyes shifted to Steven, raising a dark brow. Steven made a face, both brothers turning toward Adira.

"I have a feeling you're not going," Jay drawled. Adira smiled.

Jay ground his jaw before turning to Steven. "I don't want you to do the Blood Challenge."

"I've been fighting for years, Jay. I protect myself now."

Steven had grown out of the boy Jay remembered. Even with their time on the front, Jay had yet to accept the change.

Or refused to believe it.

"Look, lads," Sebastian said. "If you don't mind, we're going to start swimming while we have daylight."

"One of us will be behind you," Jay said.

"Best of luck to the lady." Sebastian turned away, Dalmar pushing brush aside to reach the stairs. Steven found Adira absent.

"Is there no way to convince you?" Jay asked.

"If we fight, it'll just make it harder for you to swim."

"So maybe."

Steven offered a grim smile, Jay sighing as he looked away. The prizefighter studied the tracks Adira had left, his eyes following them over the hill.

Something slammed into Steven's skull, ice biting his palms.

"*Stop—*" Steven snarled. Jay swept in and straddled Steven, entrapping his limbs. Steven grit his teeth as he struggled to break free. Jay tightened his hold.

"I have no intention of seeing you ripped to pieces by a psychopath." Jay drew back a fist.

Steven braced for impact, eyes shut tight. After a snarled curse, Steven opened his eyes to find a blade at Jay's throat.

Adira was back.

"Have a nice swim, jailbird," she crooned. Jay's eyes burned holes through her. He opened his mouth to speak as a guttural scream cleaved the air. He leapt up and stammered toward the cliffside.

Steven took Adira's outstretched hand and stood, nodding once. They stalked to Jay's side.

Sebastian raced upward, Dalmar caught in the grasp of some sort of primate. Steven's blood ran cold at the sight, Dalmar's screams quieting as he disappeared down a tunnel.

Steven shut his eyes.

This couldn't be real.

"It is real," Adira said. "Jay, Sebastian needs to jump while the beast is distracted. Zahara is already swimming."

Steven opened his eyes, his shoulders loosening a fraction as he spotted Zahara's arms arcing above the water. The current pulled back, jagged rocks beckoning—

Unholy hoots and hollers issued from below, a shiver snaking down Steven's spine. Dalmar's screaming had ceased.

Jay muttered to himself, running a hand through his dark hair. He paced the edge before stopping before Steven, tattooed hands on his brother's shoulders.

"You promise you want this?" Jay asked hoarsely.

Steven nodded. "Yes."

"You're insane." Jay wrapped Steven into a crushing hug. "Don't die."

Steven had opened his mouth to respond, but Jay was already racing down the steps, Steven's words lodged in his throat.

Jay knew how to act under pressure. He would be fine.

The beast hollered, the sound echoing over up the cliff, a spike of fear driving itself into Steven's chest.

How had this become his reality?

"Snap out of it," Adira said. "I can't have you in a panic."

He looked toward the empress, her arms crossed and expression frank. He resisted the urge to grab her shoulders and shake her.

"When you're panicked, you say what you're thinking out loud."

"No?"

"You do. Why would I lie about that."

Steven groaned and ran his palms over his face. "Good to know, I guess."

Perhaps he hadn't been wise to refuse Jay's offer to take his place in the Blood Challenge—

No.

Steven couldn't live with himself if Jay were killed in his place. If someone had to die, Steven wanted to be himself.

A hand set on his shoulder with surprising gentleness. Adira was watching him.

"There are two beasts heading this way," she said. "I need you to build some fires. Can you do that?"

Steven didn't watch as Jay and Sebastian leapt into the water. He did not watch as Adira dropped rocks onto the creature that had begun streaking up the cliff, Dalmar not enough to sate its appetite.

Steven did not glance at Jay's progress in the churning, wild sea, and did not inquire of who was alive and who wasn't.

Adira had given him a task, and he was glad for it. As he built and tended each fire, he listened to the empress sharpen her blade.

When Steven was finished with the third fire, he joined her side.

"They swam strong," she said. With the darkened winter sky, he couldn't see anything beyond dim white caps.

"Swam? Adira, are they dead?" Steven couldn't ignore the drop in his stomach.

"No, I just can't see them. If there is a boundary, I think they would have crossed it by now."

Steven listened to the surf crash, the smell of smoke in his lungs.

"Surely you know Tyrnnth won't save them," Adira said.

"We're hoping Calterra will. They saved Memphis."

"That's a lot to bet on hope," Adira mused.

"It's all we have left," Steven murmured, looking over a shoulder. "Have you seen the beasts?"

Adira smiled, a chill running down Steven's spine.

"They've been here for awhile." She pulled out a knife and offered it. "Courtesy of your brother. I swiped it before he could forget to give it to you."

Steven and Adira sat back to back between three fires.

The prizefighter passed the time feeding flames and attempting to think of anything but their situation.

He couldn't recall when Adira had placed her hand over his, but neither of them had pulled away.

"How do you know so much about this place?" Steven asked, his voice low. Adira shifted, her fingers tightening.

"I cannot discuss it," she said, her voice equally quiet.

"I want to know why you're not afraid."

Adira sighed and leaned her head against his shoulder.

"I am not afraid," she said, so quiet Steven could barely hear, "because it is not my first time here."

She turned and looked at him, firelight in her eyes.

"And the first time was so much worse."

"What were the odds?"

Adira's eyes darkened. "One survivor, three creatures for each contestant."

Steven's brows furrowed. "How many contestants?"

"Too many, and too young."

"But there hasn't been a Culling in two hundred years."

Adira gave him a small smile. "That's what you've been told." She sighed, looking upward. "Ares didn't want just anyone to be his puppet. They had to prove themselves."

"The chieftain's children—"

"Yes," she whispered. "This was where we went. The last one standing would rule Nyrland."

Steven wasn't sure what to say, so he didn't speak, his brows drawing together. Adira wouldn't look at him.

Did she kill them all herself?

Steven knew he hadn't voiced the thought aloud, but still watched as something impossibly hopeless flickered in and out of her eyes.

"No." Steven was shaking his head. "Adira—"

Snow crunched, the sound growing closer with every too-fast heartbeat in his chest.

Adira rose and offered a hand. Steven took it, calluses scraping, and joined her side.

They could talk when this was over.

If they lived.

It could be their reward for surviving; the complete truth. If she could trust him knowing her darkest secrets, perhaps Steven could trust her with his own.

Maybe he could finally tell someone who he truly was.

The weight of his unseen crown bore down on him the more he kept it to himself. He was the future King of Vastlynd, and he did not want to be.

Perhaps Adira knew what that feeling was like.

"Steven," she said, her voice deathly soft. Steven dared a look over his shoulder to find her eyes on his. "There is no need to be afraid when you are the one to fear."

Growls rumbled as wind guttered the fires. Steven's eyes snapped to the perimeter, scanning for whatever manner of nightmare would come to greet them.

Jay's knife was slippery in Steven's palm.

Adira's sword suddenly made a lot more sense.

The prizefighter and empress slowly turned, backs pressed.

"We hold them off until the rescue team arrives," she said. An unearthly gleam of eyes shined beyond the flames, huffs of breath rising above the sound of crunching snow and snapping logs.

A massive white bear stepped into the light. As its muscled body turned, it displayed bald patches and white-checkered tattoos, bearing the same pattern the wolf had borne. It growled, revealing blood-stained, brown canines.

Steven raised his knife and risked a glance over a shoulder to see what had Adira's attention.

A lioness, fur black as midnight, paced the edge of the fires.

"Did they team up?" Steven asked, watching as the bear neared a gap between the fires.

"I wouldn't be surprised if they share thoughts," Adira said.

"What?" He felt, rather than saw, Adira glance over her shoulder.

"We're switching."

Before Steven could argue, Adira pivoted, Steven turned to face the black feline.

Steven couldn't get a warning out in time.

The lion burst forward, teeth snapping. Steven shouted as she struck, blood spilling on the snow.

Steven stumbled, a hand to his side. Behind him, Adira shouted.

The ring was too small for them.

Steven backed toward the darkness, the lion following.

His blood shown in her tracks, another reminder his side was torn open. He couldn't tell how deep the wound was, but he couldn't feel his guts on the other side of his fingers.

A good sign, but it still hurt like hell. His steps were unsteady.

Would other beasts show, now that blood was in the air?

Steven could barely hear Adira shouting.

"Here, kitty, kitty," he drawled, the pain in his side stealing most of his breath, his fingers slick with blood.

The lioness' eyes glowed before winking out as she passed between the fires and into darkness with him.

If Steven jumped the cliff, he could swim until the team arrived. He glanced toward the edge, snow crunching as the cat quickened her pace.

"Where are you going?" Adira shouted. She grunted, the bear bellowing. Steven glanced to her.

Both bear and empress bled, the snow dark beneath their death dance. Adira's legs were braced, her jaw set as she held her sword upright. The bear roared and Adira swung her blade—

Brush raked bony hands over Steven's back.

He halted, releasing a breath. Waves roared beneath, awaiting his fall.

But he couldn't jump. Not with Adira fighting for her life, too.

Steven angled his brother's knife and dropped into position, distant firelight reflecting off the blade.

The lioness launched.

The first thing Steven felt was red, hot pain. He pivoted, slicing through the feline's flesh and fur, despite feeling and *listening* to his own bones crack.

The cat had her jaws around his forearm. Steven tried not to scream as he rolled, the cat holding firm. Another bone snapped.

Steven threw himself into another roll, the cat following. The beast growled, readjusting her grip. Searing pain shot through Steven's body, fraying his nerves.

He reigned in the dregs of his strength and *kicked*.

The lioness released her grip and hissed. Steven braced, nails breaking, and kicked again.

Snow shifted, the cat's claws digging for purchase.

The beast fell from sight, a crack echoing up the cliff.

Steven shakily rose to his feet, his torn forearm pressed to his side. He could hear his blood hissing as it hit the snow.

The adrenaline in his body spiked as he beheld Adira beneath the bear as it rose on its hind legs, its lips puled back in a roar.

"MOVE," Steven shouted, losing his footing as he ran. The bear began to fall, Steven launching his knife and hoping, hoping, *hoping—*

An enraged snarl ripped from the beast's throat.

Not in response to the knife in its side, but to the sword now driven through its neck. The bear reeled, thrashing and choking. Adira fell back to the crimson-stained snow, not bothering to watch the beast stagger into darkness.

Steven let loose the breath he had been holding.

He pushed the pain aside and gathered enough strength to

reach Adira's side, falling to his knees.

She looked at him, her breath labored, chest rising and falling in an unsteady pace. Steven ran a hand over her brow, moving stray hair aside.

"Are you okay?" He scanned her body. There was blood everywhere. Whether it belonged to bear or empress, Steven couldn't tell. His eyes snagged on her hand, held tight to her abdomen.

Those were guts. Steven tried not to throw up. "I hope you didn't have a belly button piercing."

Adira huffed and grimaced. "Don't make me laugh."

Above the crackle of fire, Steven swore he heard rotors. He reached for Adira's bloodied hand and squeezed.

"They're here," he said, smiling despite the pain and innards Adira seemed to be holding in. She squeezed back and pulled him close enough that he could feel her breath on his face.

"It's not going to be the same— after this. He's going to wipe my memory again," Adira whispered. Steven put a hand to her face, brushing a thumb over her cheek.

"What are you talking about?"

Lights flashed over the hills, rotors growing louder.

"Ares knows." Her words were barely audible.

Steven shook his head. "How could you know that?"

Adira sucked in a breath, her fingers tightening on her stomach. A helicopter descended in Steven's peripherals, wind whipping.

"Adira, please—"

"All I will remember is I am Adira Theron, Empress of Nyrland, servant and daughter of Ares Valeryn," she said, her voice distant. Medics rushed from the helicopter, a second helicopter descending behind Steven.

"I will not remember you," she said, her fingers loosening.

"No," Steven said.

The word was lost in the sound of the medical team swarming, hands grasping underneath his shoulders.

"No," he said again, pulling free. They grabbed hold again, Steven's feet dragging. "Don't let him, Adira."

She closed her eyes as medics placed her on a gurney.

"Adira," Steven called, his feet kicking, pain flaring and stars dancing. "Adira!" A third set of hands wrapped around his middle. Steven gasped as fingers pressed into his open wound, blinding pain seizing him. Darkness blurred at the edges of his vision.

She was being carried away, the rescue team rushing and clamoring under flashing light.

A man screamed, a gunshot went off. In the flashing light, Steven swore he saw something stalking beside Adira's helicopter.

Something in Steven's chest restricted. *"Adira."* A needle bit his shoulder and the world blurred to black.

20

Steven awoke to a pale blue ceiling, fat, white clouds painted across its expanse. Ivory crown molding, an unlit crystal chandelier.

A breeze flit through the open window, Steven breathing in the scent of dust and salt. He sat up, his body protesting with a dull resonance of pain. His side itched and caught on the fabric of his white cotton tee.

There was the pain.

He inhaled and tried to master it, blinking back the sunlight streaming in.

He was not alone here, someone in the bed across from his.

Adira had lived.

Steven slid from under his bedsheet, bracing himself on the bed frame. He whooshed out a breath as he waited for a wave of pain to subside, willing strength into his limbs.

He lifted the hem of his shirt to find a neat row of stitches. A survey of his forearms revealed a map of stitches there, as well.

Steven flexed his fingers. The movement was sore, but it seemed every nerve and tendon was intact.

A blessing amidst his many curses.

Steven limped to Adira's bed, bracing himself on the bed frame before taking another step. She was tucked on her side, her hands underneath her face, her hair a dark curtain on the pillow behind her.

A smattering of stitches peeked above Adira's collarbone, the rest disappearing beneath her shift.

Steven gingerly sat on the bed adjacent to hers, attempting to master the trembling in his body.

Whatever medications they had given him were either wearing off, or hadn't been strong enough to begin with.

"Adira?" he whispered. She didn't stir, her breath steady and slow.

With her unaided genetics, perhaps whatever drugs the medical staff had administered would last longer with her.

Adira had said she wouldn't remember him.

If Ares hadn't arrived yet, Steven could take her with him. Stop Ares from removing her memories and reshaping her into his weapon, his pawn.

Steven's fingers twitched and he resisted the urge to reach for her. Surely someone would catch him carrying her out.

His lips tightened. Adira was Ares' daughter. Surely the War Leader wouldn't let Steven get away with stealing her away.

Luther and Ares had to be dealt with first.

The prizefighter ran his hands down his face, a dull pain sharpening as he straightened.

Adira shifted, Steven stilling. The sheets crinkled as she settled, her legs drawn closer to herself.

She looked almost . . . cute.

He smiled. She would likely take his assessment as an insult.

She was dangerous, no matter how she looked.

He sighed through his nose, studying her stitches, her muscle-lined forearms and placid face.

Her memory was likely already wiped.

But if it wasn't . . .

He shook his head. With the high likelihood of one of them not surviving the Blood Challenges, Ares wiping Steven from her brain could be a mercy.

If he died, and she lived, she would have no one to mourn.

He needed to let her go. Just until the Blood Challenges were over and their enemies were dead. Adira would be free of grieving, control, and the threat of having her memory wiped again.

Yes. That would be best.

Steven rose to his feet, taking a tentative step toward the empress. He brushed a kiss over her forehead.

"I'll see you when it's over."

He did not look back as he left, promising himself it was better this way.

Even as something inside begged him otherwise.

⁂

Steven wandered several halls before voices filtered through an open door.

Carpeted floors in a hospital. Tyrnnth was ridiculous.

He paused as he recognized Luther Hawthorne's voice, the dictator himself.

The other voice was male, though Steven couldn't place who it belonged to. Their conversation was low enough Steven couldn't make out anything discernible. He drew closer, straining to hear.

Something piercing his back, a hand pressing over his mouth.

"You're not supposed to be awake."

Ire radiated in Natalia's pale eyes. Their mother's eyes. She dropped the dagger and pulled Steven away before releasing him. She walked backward and held a finger to her mouth, dagger flashing.

Steven rubbed his back as he nodded, finding a hole in his shirt. Natalia led him down a hall before blowing out a breath.

"I take it the pain meds weren't strong enough."

"I'll live," Steven said.

"You probably won't need anything soon anyways. I'm told

you're different than others. Have you heard the same?"

Steven brushed his palms on his pants. "No, I haven't."

A lie, but at least she wasn't looking at him.

Natalia didn't comment, breezing by rooms, paintings and gilded walls. Steven struggled to keep her pace until she cast a look over her shoulder and found him several feet behind.

"Jay and the others—" Steven began.

"Your War Leader has them. And yes, they're alive."

Steven blew out a breath.

Despite the odds stacked against them, Jay's plan had worked.

Steven nodded to the oil paintings lining the hall. "Your hospital is very decorative."

Natalia laughed under her breath. "This isn't a hospital, it's our home."

Steven surveyed the hall. "But the room I was in . . . "

"Our personal medical wing."

Steven halted, looking back. "Has Ares . . . "

"No," Natalia said, the word clipped.

Steven *could* get Adira out.

A hand settled on his shoulder, Steven turning toward his sister.

Her brows were drawn when she spoke, her voice low. "You don't know me, but trust me when I say Adira is a can of worms. It would be wise to leave her be."

"Is she safe?"

"You see the players on the table, Steven. There is no such thing as safe, at least for now. Adira knows that, and has chosen her actions accordingly. Do not fear for her."

Natalia dropped her hand and continued walking.

"And how do you know her so well?"

"It is my job to know. To read people." Natalia stopped once more, looking back at him. "Trust me when I say Adira chooses courage. Leave her be."

———∞———

Farran sat on the bottom step outside. Steven turned to thank Natalia to find the door already snicking shut.

Steven descended the steps, Farran turning his head, revealing a dullness to his eyes and hollows in his cheeks.

He rose. "Thank goodness you're alright, Steven."

The prizefighter reached the pavement, attempting to mask the pain coursing through his body. Farran took survey of Steven, his eyes snagging on the prizefighter's stitches.

"Luther and Natalia took care of you," the king said distantly. He shook his head, meeting Steven's gaze. "They truly don't trust Ares, either."

"I don't blame them. He ruins animals for fun."

Farran smiled weakly. "Right."

"What's wrong?"

The king looked skyward, at the street, everywhere but at Steven.

Farran drew a tight breath, finally looking at him.

"Everything."

———∞———

Tyrnnth had launched an attack on New Iberia's capital.

The warships circling had made land in the night, Evynmare becoming alight in fire. Tyrnnthian soldiers burned and slaughtered across a sixth of the capital before Farran's militia was able to stop it.

The king could barely recall it without taking pauses to stare out the plane window to gather himself.

Meanwhile, nearly half of Steven's country was under Tyrnnthian occupation, a draft pick missing amongst the chaos.

Steven scrubbed the scruff along his jaw. "All this happened in a week?"

Farran nodded, his gaze on the clouds below.

"We'll figure it out," Steven said, unsure of why he did. He hadn't a clue what to do about it.

Steven's job was to prepare for a single fight and hope his country could manage to survive long enough to see it.

He had yet to tell Farran about what Adira had shared; her heritage, history, motives—

Steven wasn't sure if he should even tell the king.

And Steven's own feelings for the empress— he supposed it didn't matter now.

He was to be wiped from her memory, her life to go on as if they had never crossed paths.

The thought made something in his chest sink.

Steven took a sharp breath, attempting to think of anything else.

War.

Everything else was petty by comparison, including Steven's situation regarding Adira Theron.

He needed to ask how Farran was doing. He had faced invasion, fought with his militia, attended search parties and burial ceremonies . . .

Steven forced himself to look up and say something, *anything*, but Farran spoke instead.

"There is something I must tell you." He clasped his hands on the table. The king's voice trembled as he breathed in. "I—"

Steven's phone rang. He let it, waiting for the king to continue.

Farran sighed. "That is going to be important."

He was right.

Steven rose and spent the next few minutes pacing as his country's War Leader fed Steven the same story Farran had shared, along with an update on Grace.

She was to spend a week in Calterra with the enemy's ally.

But Steven couldn't think past what Jaxin had said the moment before, the words repeating as he droned on.

Central was poised to fall, her soldiers tired and losing hope. And what Jaxin wouldn't say haunted Steven even more so.

He may be their only shot out of the war now.

———⚬⚬⚬———

A demarcation line snaked across the entirety of the Central Territories, the land pockmarked and charred south of it.

"Why do they burn everything?" Steven asked.

Farran looked up from his novel, though Steven hadn't heard him turn a page in the last ten minutes. "Tyrnnth believes burning renews the land."

"For who? He's killing everyone." Steven leaned back, scrubbing his face with his hands. "How did Ares get to his position of power?"

"Mr. Castellen, did you not finish your assigned reading materials?"

"Not all of us actually *enjoy* reading."

The corner of Farran's lip twitched. He opened his mouth to reply as the loudspeaker announced the flight path would cross over enemy-occupied territory.

Farran's brow furrowed as he set his book aside, searching the ground. "They took your western coast."

Steven shifted toward the end of his seat, taking in the dark portion of land reaching toward Vastlynd's border.

"We can take it back," Steven said.

"They must have come here after Evynmare," Farran said quietly.

As they passed over the coast, a spike of fear went through Steven. Between the swaths of smoke and poisoned air, a legion of Tyrnnthian warships sat.

Not a single Central warship remained.

21

Calterra was humid, hot and lush. The smell of tropical flowers stuffed up Grace's nose as she ran a hand over a fern leaning over the brick walkway.

When the eldest Calterran prince offered her a reward for her work on the rescue team, she'd said no.

Zakkai had insisted.

Now she was here for a week.

When the ex-slaves had piled into the helicopter, soaked and freezing, Grace had noted a fire in Zahara's eyes.

Grace liked her instantly.

Zakkai must have, as well, because when Zahara asked for solace in Calterra, the prince obliged.

The door shut, Grace turning as Zahara smiled, brushing her braids over a shoulder.

"There is much to see," she said.

It seemed Zahara had come alive after arriving here. Grace couldn't blame her; it seemed the rest of the world was cold, dark, or war-torn.

Within minutes, they began wandering with smoothies in hand.

The island of Maimawa sat within a Calterran bay, shores and reefs protecting the capital. Sloping up a hillside, houses and huts of every size nestled within palms and thick foliage. On the southern hillside, King Vincere's palace and vineyards sprawled.

Zahara had dared Grace to join her on a visit to Prince Zakkai's harem housing.

Grace had agreed, for whatever reason.

Sneak in, sneak out.

That was the plan.

Though the prince had been kind during the week they spent together rescuing people, Grace knew he couldn't be.

Anyone who *bought* people had to be wicked.

Grace hadn't realized her hands were shaking until Zahara set a hand on her wrist.

"What are you worried about?" Zahara asked. "The women are nice and the children won't bite. Well, hopefully."

Oh gosh, *children*. How many did Zakkai have at this point?

Grace figured she was about to find out.

They stopped outside the gates of the community.

The prince had an entire *village* dedicated to his women.

"He almost bought me once." Grace savored the shade of greens lining the sandy, brick road.

Zahara's eyes widened. "No way. And you— well, obviously it didn't happen."

"Fare— King Bardolph paid for my freedom."

Zahara made a thoughtful noise, sipping the last of her smoothie.

"That is some top tier lore," Zahara mused.

"I should start a list."

Zahara's brows shot up. "There's more?"

The gates opened for a ruby red car. One of the armed guards waved, his rifle glinting in sunlight.

"Girl, you look like you're about to pass out," Zahara said. "You sure you want to go?"

"Yes," Grace said. She brushed a strand of hair behind an ear before changing her mind and setting it loose. "I'm ready."

She was lying.

Grace walked forward, hoping she wasn't making a mistake visiting a prince's cage.

Zahara spoke to the guards, Grace able to translate almost all of the interaction in her head. The last part, she hadn't understood. The gates opened.

The first thing that struck her was the children.

They were everywhere.

Zahara greeted them in Calterran, as well as the women as they hung laundry or sat in the grass.

"Do you know them?" Grace asked. Zahara had extended family here, perhaps there were some unfortunate individuals amongst Zakkai's gated community.

"No, but give me enough time here, and I will." Zahara smiled at another villager. "Since we don't have contacts here, the women at the gate are asked if the visit is allowed. Women only, obviously. Men are forbidden to visit."

"Except Zakkai, I imagine."

Zahara nodded, waving at another stranger, her skin nearly the same beautiful, rich shade of chestnut.

"I should probably tell you everything," Zahara turned and grabbed Grace's hands.

"No need, Ms. Rutheme."

Zahara looked behind Grace and bowed low. "Your Highness."

This was bad.

This man collected women and stuffed them into this pretty, little village. Never mind everyone looked healthy, happy, even—

Grace was sure it was fake.

And all these kids? Those were all *his*.

Grace turned, exhaling through her nose. Zakkai was already smiling at her.

"What are you doing here?" Grace asked.

"What do you mean?" Zakkai raised a scarred brow. "I was summoned."

Grace's eyes narrowed before widening.

That's what she hadn't understood in Zahara's conversation?

Grace turned to find Zahara glancing over a shoulder, speed-walking away.

Maybe Zahara wasn't a very good friend.

Grace turned back to the prince, his smile not the comforting sort.

"I guess this means I'm your tour guide now."

Grace made it to the end of the tour before exploding.

They had seen terracotta homes painted in every shade of sea glass, bursting gardens, and shaded parks full of children, chickens, and women. A beach dotted with palms and edged in jungle. Flowers of every hue and shade of red, pink and orange.

It was a small utopia.

Grace was disgusted.

The prince had a private drive from his royal bedroom to the village, as well. She slowed and watched as he walked, leading them toward the palace. To Grace's left, ocean. To her right, dense jungle.

She knew she wasn't a strong swimmer, so escape would have to be made running through the jungle, if Zakkai insisted they continue this way.

She wasn't about to find out.

Grace planted her feet.

Zakkai strode a few paces before turning. "Yes?"

"I've seen enough."

Zakkai raised a brow, Grace holding back from snapping. When he looked at her like that, she felt young.

There was nearly a decade between them, maybe it was enough of an age gap for him to see her that way. She didn't particularly care.

"You didn't want to see the palace?"

Grace crossed her arms. "I want to leave."

Zakkai nodded, pursing his lips. "Okay."

"Okay."

Zakkai turned and kept walking. "Goodbye, then."

Grace narrowed her eyes at his broad back. "That's it?"

Zakkai didn't turn. A cloud swept over the sun, a breeze cooling her heated skin. She closed her eyes in the reprieve, breathing in salt and sweet flowers.

When she opened her eyes, Zakkai was watching her.

"You want to leave. I'm not going to stop you."

"But, all those women you *bought*— are they allowed to leave?" Grace stepped forward. "You invited me here, but why?"

"Really?"

"What did you expect me to think? You buy people and pen them. Even if they *look* happy, I'm not convinced they are."

She would know, in part. She had been a slave, even if it wasn't but for a few months.

Zakkai closed the distance between them, Grace's heart stuttering. She held a hand up, the prince halting.

"That's close enough."

He shook his head. "I thought you'd be different."

Grace's brows drew together. "How does my character have anything to do with yours?"

Zakkai's fiery eyes shifted to her hand, to the delicate band and beautiful, simple diamond on her finger. "You have King Bardolph's ear. You're in a position where you can change things."

"So?" She fisted her hands.

Zakkai sighed as he met her gaze. "The world is changing. We need more people like you, or who I thought you were."

She had nothing to say. Who had he thought she was, then?

"If you would just hear me out, I think you would find that you and I are not so different after all."

To her credit, Grace waited a moment before replying.

"Thank you for the tour, Your Highness."

169

She turned and walked away, heart thundering.

The prince's footsteps never followed, despite Grace listening for them.

22

Steven couldn't train as his body healed.

He did not like it.

His body still woke early, as if ready to go on a run that he couldn't take it on. Each day, Steven woke later. Each day, his wounds closed further.

And his body and mind weakened.

Steven nodded to Aubrel Bailey, Farran's Captain of the Guard, as the prizefighter joined him in the glass elevator.

"Which floor?" Aubrel asked.

Steven stuffed his hands into his sweatshirt pocket. "Seventh."

"His Majesty must like you." Aubrel pressed the button and stepped back, clasping his hands behind him.

Steven felt the world shift as they began to ascend.

The ninth floor was already selected.

"Another meeting?" Steven asked.

Aubrel nodded. "There are a lot of them these days."

They passed third floor.

"Does he think Tyrnnth will attack the castle?"

Aubrel's eyes flicked to the camera in the elevator.

Steven always forgot those things were everywhere. He looked at the floor and scuffed a shoe against the marble. "Never mind."

Aubrel offered a tight smile. "It's quite alright, Steven."

Captain Bailey had addressed Steven by name soon after the

prizefighter had moved to New Iberia.

Steven was ashamed to admit it had taken him much longer to remember the captain's name.

In the first two months, all of the guards appeared the same to Steven.

He knew it was not the case for Farran, and after the king and prizefighter grew from toleration to friendship, Steven began learning the guard's names.

And the staff's.

He adored the kitchen staff, and some part of him believed they might actually enjoy his company, too.

In an effort to learn more about the people around him, Steven had began playing chess with the guard in the barracks on afternoons he wasn't drop-dead tired or training.

"I'm sorry I'm still not used to politics," Steven offered.

"I wasn't either." Aubrel shrugged. "You get used to it."

The elevator pinged and opened to the seventh floor.

"Tell His Majesty I said hi," Steven said. "Best of luck."

Steven made to exit, the captain stopping the doors from shutting. "My men are up for some rematches, if you are."

Steven turned and smiled back at Captain Bailey. "I may take them up on that."

The captain nodded and stepped back, his hands clasped behind him once more. The elevator doors shut as Steven turned, dropping his smile.

He *wanted* to play chess with the guards. It was one of his favorite ways to kill time.

Why didn't he feel that way, though?

—⁂—

Farran was already rebuilding.

Steven wondered if it was too soon. The war wasn't over yet, and Tyrnnth could very well come back to finish the job.

During the few meals they managed to spend together, Steven hadn't brought it up.

When a week passed, and Grace's absence remained, Steven asked Farran for an update.

The king's eyes were wide as he looked from the dining room window back to Steven.

The king hadn't touched his food.

"Pardon?" he asked.

Steven took another bite. "I asked where Grace is. She's supposed to be here today."

Farran looked back to the window. "I know."

"So."

Farran frowned. "I mean, I know she's supposed to be here. I don't know why she isn't here yet."

"Well, she better show up soon."

Along with Grace's absence, Steven felt his brother's. A new hire to Jaxin Brown, the convict was sharing every detail of what he had seen and experienced with Ares.

It was still a month until Steven would see Jay.

"Cassius?" Farran asked.

"He'll want you to call him Jay."

"Why doesn't he use his given name?" Farran sipped his water. At least he was drinking.

"I don't know, I've never asked," Steven said. He set down his fork. "I can tell you're stressed about Grace, but you really don't need to worry—"

"Don't worry?" Farran rose in a smooth motion. "I am past worrying. I proposed to her, and now she is in our enemy ally's palace with a power-hungry, conniving prince."

"Well, when you put it that way, I guess that does sound bad."

Farran's shoulders dropped and he eased into his chair, staring at his cold plate of steak and potatoes.

"I apologize." The king ran a hand through his hair. "I think— I should file another report."

"We all stress." Steven shrugged. "Grace tells me when people lose it on you, it's more of a reflection of what's going on inside them than what the other person's done."

Farran offered a weak smile. "Well, then. It seems she is right again." The king rose with his untouched plate. "If you'll excuse me, I have work to attend to."

23

Grace sat in a lawn chair, breathing in the scent of florals. Waves crashed a below, frogs chittering.

It was a beautiful night.

And her last here.

Her week was over, and she was to leave at first light.

Zahara had proven to be an interesting . . . ally. She had insisted on selecting Grace's dress tonight, the piece simple and surprisingly modest.

When Grace had accused Zahara of sending for the prince at the village, Zahara hadn't denied it.

Zakkai also hadn't denied Grace's accusation of him buying women.

He hadn't said a thing.

No denial, no confirmation.

Grace kept track of such things.

People lied in half truths and quarter truths; whatever they believed would be easiest for their listener to swallow.

It was that sense that had her watching Farran when they were together; his body a little too tense, his eyes a little too shifty . . .

The young king was hiding something, and all it would take was one slip-up, one misstep, and his perfect, golden act would collapse.

If she was right.

She hoped she wasn't.

Grace didn't have time to think on it more as the door opened at the end of the roof.

The evening's meeting was the result of Grace finally answering Prince Zakkai's summons.

They'd talk.

Not for long, and only at the end of her trip.

Zakkai had stayed away, to Grace's surprise, and when they brought up the details of their talk, he had insisted they meet above his room.

She let loose a breath as Zakkai approached, smirking as usual.

"Ms. Fitzgerald, a pleasure," the prince said. As he neared, his eyes swept over her. "That's a pretty dress."

"Zahara has a good eye," Grace said. Zakkai sat in the lawn chair across from her.

The sight of two plastic chairs on the royal palace rooftop had set her laughing minutes before. Calterra's heir didn't seem to mind.

"Zahara will do well here," he said, leaning back. He smiled as Grace watched him, waiting. "You wanted to talk to me."

"You wanted to talk to *me,*" she corrected.

"You've adopted my eyebrow raise, that's cute."

Grace's brows narrowed in a look she hoped could be comparable to Adira's searing gazes. If Grace could even appear *half* as volatile as the empress, maybe Zakkai would leave her be.

The prince laughed and shook his head.

"That's not you," he said.

"You don't know me," Grace countered, ignoring the heat in her face. She despised that she reacted in such obvious ways.

Zakkai shrugged. "I know people like you."

"It's not the same."

"That's true." The prince's smile faded. He leaned forward, the motion causing a gold chain around his neck to shift, two rings clinking together.

As swiftly as they appeared, the prince tucked them away, leaning his elbows against his knees. "I'd love five minutes of your time."

"I think four sounds better."

Zakkai gave her a small smile. "I'll take four."

And then the prince told her the truth.

24

In the weeks following the Culling, Steven healed, leaving doctors astounded at his recovery.

They didn't know they were praising Ares' work.

Steven wouldn't look in the mirror as he stepped out of the shower. He dried his hair and slung a towel over his waist, his fingers tightening on the counter as he braced against it.

Adira. Her parents. Steven's mother. Max Fitzgerald— Steven would avenge them.

Ares would bleed.

He would die, and the world would breathe again.

Steven did not feel much else at all, other than that burning in his chest and the void that beckoned when his anger quieted.

His Blood Challenge was less than three months away.

He feared his rage would run out before he reached the pit, leaving him empty by the time he faced Luther.

Grace arrived a week *late*.

She had remained in Calterra to spy, to Jaxin's approval.

When Grace and Steven had met to catch up, she shared her experience on rescue team and her time in Calterra.

Memphis had survived.

Steven wasn't sure how Grace had managed to convince the eldest Calterran prince to save the rest of the contestants that survived long enough for aid to arrive.

Grace had been present when Jay, Sebastian and Zahara had been plucked from the sea. Everyone parted ways soon after that. Jay to Central with Jaxin, Sebastian to his homeland, and Zahara to her roots in Calterra.

With their enemy's allies.

Steven wasn't sure what he made of it.

When Grace spoke of Calterra when Farran was present, Steven tried and failed not to notice Farran's longing.

Grace did well to pretend not to notice.

Lacking the headspace to figure it out, Steven dismissed it and joined in pretending neither of them noticed Farran's despair.

The media frenzied over the swift end of Farran and Grace's engagement, just as the king had predicted.

Farran hadn't spoken, and neither had Grace, when she entered the study one afternoon to place the velvet ring box on his desk.

"I lived. Thank you," she said. Farran had merely nodded and looked down.

"Anytime, Ms. Fitzgerald."

Steven climbed into bed.

Healed enough to train, he had begun again. His muscles seemed to have forgotten his prior work, and the lack of meals during the Culling had eaten away at him.

It would take a lot of work to gain it back.

The thought had stayed with him the entirety of the day, the fire in his blood dimming.

His training partner was still unaccounted for. He'd heard rumors claiming the empress had returned home, ruling as though she had never left.

He wondered what her people made of her absence, her failed trade agreements, her Blood Challenge—

He didn't wonder long, sleep claiming him, even as the lights remained on.

Sometimes he dreamt of Jay getting shot again, sometimes he dreamt it was Adira taking the bullet.

More often, he dreamt he was in a lightless chamber, drowning or being stalked by a beast with scales and hate in its eyes.

As Steven awoke, chest-heaving and sweat coating his body, he closed his eyes and wondered how many times he could drown before facing Luther.

Steven *tried* to hold himself above the water, but he was growing tired. And it was everywhere, *everyday*—

Over and over and over again.

Again and again and again.

Steven drowned.

And nobody noticed.

A knock sounded at the door.

Steven groaned and rubbed his eyes, yet to rise from bed.

Although no one knew he was missing his morning runs, Farran and Grace had mentioned his lack of appearances at the dining hall.

Maybe today they would reprimand him for it.

Steven disentangled himself from the sheets, grabbing clothes off the floor to throw on.

The fabric hung looser than it had weeks ago.

Had it been weeks?

He opened his suite door to find Grace.

She smiled. "You owe me a coffee date."

"I'm sorry, I forgot," Steven said hoarsely. He stepped away,

Grace sweeping into his suite. He washed up in the bathroom.

The cold water did little to make him look more alive.

His eyes seemed more gray than blue today. He couldn't recall if they had always been that way, or if war had stolen the color from them.

He dried his face and exited, finding Grace thumbing through a pile of mail he hadn't noticed before.

"Fare brought these this morning. He said you were still asleep, though," Grace said. Steven joined her side.

"Snoop," he mumbled.

"Grab a coat, it's cold," Grace said, making for the door. Within minutes, they were out of the castle and on the road.

Though bright winter sun beamed overhead, Steven kept his hands in his pockets, his breath clouding. Grace mirrored him in a beige trench coat, a scarf wrapped around her neck.

Castle Hill's winding road was one of his favorite walks. He enjoyed the way sunbeams filtered through cedar branches and barren beech limbs, the view of the capital opening up through gaps in the wood.

Steven had grown fond of Farran's country. The thought of leaving weighed heavier than he imagined it would.

As the view opened up, sunlight glinted off the colorful roofs below, the city appearing as a handful of jewels.

Steven slowed until he stopped, a pang of guilt like a knife in his side. He would have slept through this if Grace hadn't awoken him.

What else had he missed these last few weeks?

Along with running, training had faded from his schedule.

He wasn't sure when the shift had occurred. It had happened so slowly, he hadn't noticed. He was just so *tired*.

Steven felt Grace's attention as he took in the sunlit, turquoise ocean, a breeze sending leaves skittering across the road.

"How are you?" she asked.

Steven inhaled, taking in the scent of crisp morning air. He felt better, somehow. Though not by much, he still couldn't deny it. He exhaled and looked at his friend and wished he hadn't.

He didn't want pity.

So he smiled. "I'm alright, Fitzgerald. Just tired."

A week passed before an aggressive knock sounded at Steven's door, followed by the sound of lock-picking.

Steven started out of bed, nearly hitting the floor as his foot caught in the duvet. He wrenched open a dresser drawer as the suite door opened.

"Just a second!" He yanked on a pair of pants, threw a shirt over his head and exited. His breathing steadied as he took in the broad back and dark hair. Jay turned and grinned.

"That lock was way too easy to pick," he drawled, crossing the room to wrap Steven in a hug. Jay stepped back and raised a dark brow. "I thought you'd be happy to see me. Are you ill?"

Steven huffed a laugh. "Want some coffee?"

"I'm good, I had some with G."

Steven ignored the dull stab of not being invited. The prizefighter shoved it away and stepped into the kitchen.

It was impossible not to feel Jay's eyes on him.

He would notice the mussed hair, sunken cheeks, the bruise-like hollows beneath Steven's eyes— not to mention the ill-fitted clothes.

Steven looked up to find his brother's arms crossed.

While Steven had wasted away, Jay had recovered.

Despite being a slave for months, the convict looked as though he had put on fifteen pounds and somehow managed to find enough sun to color his skin again.

"How's the new job?" Steven asked.

"Pays well." Jay prowled to the counter and claimed a bar stool. "Suits me that Jaxin's not afraid to work with a felon."

Steven dumped grounds in the coffeemaker and leaned against the counter at the wall.

"It probably helps that he knows *why* you went to jail," Steven said. "Jaxin knows of my . . . heritage? I don't know. He knows the truth. You're not a cold-blooded killer, you just did what you had to do."

"Who else knows?"

"King Ridgeway. Jaxin and him were the ones to—"

Jay raised a finger to his lips, his eyes searching the room. He leaned forward, elbows braced on the counter. He gestured to his eyes and ears, followed by a cutting motion.

Steven nodded, the dribble of coffee and its robust, bitter scent filling the space.

"How's Central?" Steven asked. "I was told Jaxin brought you to the front."

"He did. It's hell." Jay ran a tattooed hand down his neck. "I was at the line two days ago. We haven't been able to take back the west coast, and Ridgeway won't open his borders for supplies, refugees, *nothing.*"

Jay's eyes grew distant. "Our soldiers have lost hope. Jaxin says Tyrnnth has gotten too far in their heads."

"Is this new?"

Jay's eyes shuttered. "Ares released his leftovers from the Culling last week. Right onto the battlefield."

Steven's blood chilled as Jay went on. "It was dark, so they didn't see them until it was too late. The line . . . " He shook his head. "All the soldiers died and the next line fled."

Steven was glad to be leaning against something.

"You said Ares released the leftovers. Not Luther."

"It was on the news yesterday. Luther officially stepped down."

"What?"

Jay nodded. "Luther washed his hands in a bowl, claiming the blood was no longer on his hands. He's still sworn to be Tyrnnth's Blood Challenger, but Ares is in charge."

"So this is all for nothing?"

"No—"

"It sure sounds like it," Steven said, laughing. He wondered if Jay could hear the hysteria in his voice.

Jay's brows lowered. "It's not all for nothing. The war will end with Luther's death."

"How do you know?"

"Jaxin looked into it. Bardolph looked into it. We made sure."

Steven looked at his hands. "Nobody mentioned it to me."

"Can you figure why?"

Steven looked up, Jay shrugging as he leaned back.

"Now as much as I would have liked to come here just to chat, Jaxin sent me with a task."

Jay watched Steven a moment before continuing.

"He knows you're unwell."

Steven's grip tightened on the counter behind him. "Grace told you."

Jay flicked a crumb off the counter. "She sees through you. When I asked how you were doing . . . " Jay took a deep breath, exhaling before looking up.

"If you don't get your act together, Luther will kill you. You need to be strong. It isn't a choice anymore."

Steven's grip tightened and he could have sworn something cracked underneath.

"You look like you've stopped training and eating." Jay shook his head. "I don't know what you need to do to fix yourself, but you need to do it fast."

Steven needed time.

And his brother to leave.

"I'm not leaving until you're better," Jay pressed. "If my death was so motivating, I'm hoping I can be just as instrumental alive."

Steven flinched imperceptibly. He hadn't realized he had moved from the counter.

Jay rose. "Don't fall apart when it matters most. Adira isn't going to clean this mess up, *you* have to be strong enough for this."

Steven let his feet carry him to his room. The bedroom door shut. He leaned against it and waited for his brother to leave.

Instead, he heard footsteps approach and stop outside his door.

"Don't let them win now," Jay said. "Fight it."

No pity. No judgement. It was simple to Jay. He had already been through hell and back.

Steven closed his eyes.

"You are stronger than you think." Jay stepped away from the door, leaving Steven to wonder how dark it had been for his brother when he had discovered the sentiment for himself.

25

Steven dreamt of the front.

Halfway across a barren, pockmarked field, the scene shifted. Artillery rained, even as he now stood on Tybauch.

Instead of rolling hills and undulating grass, the ground beneath his feet was charred and littered with carnage. Smoke and rot stuffed up his nose, his eyes watering.

An explosion knocked the world sideways, Steven's knees hitting hot earth with a hiss.

It was hot.

Too hot, burning smoke filling his lungs and searing his skin.

As he tried to breathe, a hollow, cold laugh issued behind him. Steven knew that voice, despite years stretching between the last he had heard the man speak.

"Still as pathetic as I remember you."

Steven turned, anticipating to see the father Jay had murdered to keep Steven alive. Though instead of an aging version of Jay, Steven found four hyenas, still as death watching him back.

A shell exploded and Steven was thrown several feet, ringing filling his ears. He blinked back heat, light and darkness as a beast lunged. Steven caught it by the throat.

"Not this time," he whispered, and squeezed. The beast turned to ash and Steven rose to face the remaining three, knife in hand.

As fire danced and artillery assailed, he brought down his foes.

———⟨∞⟩———

"Morning, little prince," Jay greeted.

Steven made to slam the door in Jay's face as a shoe shot through the gap.

Jay pushed the door open and entered the suite. "A little bird told me you quit running. I'm going to take advantage of that and race you today."

The run was hell.

Jay could have smoked Steven, but had held back.

Despite Steven reprimanding him for it.

As they had approached the war-torn portion of Evynmare, dread piled in Steven's gut. Even from afar, he could see the destruction Tyrnnth had wrought, despite Farran's efforts to rebuild.

Jay hadn't questioned Steven when he turned down a road skirting the desolation.

When they reached the castle, a servant bore a message for Steven.

Bent over, his breath knives in his lungs, Steven watched as Jay grabbed the note and tore into it.

"Snoop," Steven breathed. Jay's eyes narrowed as he read, Steven shaking his head. "You know with your job with Jaxin, you could probably pay for a pair of glasses now."

"The king invited you to tea," Jay said, pursing his lips. "Did you say something about glasses? I don't need them."

Steven laughed under his breath, looking toward where the king usually parked his vintage, yellow pickup.

It had been awhile since he had spent time with Farran. The last time they had caught up had been weeks ago.

A pang of shame shot through Steven.

"Where is he?"

———— ∞ ————

Steven took a deep breath as he neared the cottage, a bite in the air as low clouds hung over the barren orchard.

He took in the white-washed paneling and paned windows. Farran had once told Steven the property had belonged to his mother's parents.

The couple had continued to grow and sell fruit, even after their daughter had married into the royal lineage.

Steven couldn't remember their names, though he saw their portrait every time he went up the stairs.

The porch creaked as he stepped up and knocked.

Footsteps issued before the door swung open, Farran standing at the threshold.

"You're always welcome to come in, Steven."

Steven kicked off his shoes. "I never know if an ex is here. I'd like to be safe than sorry."

Farran laughed under his breath. "You say things with such confidence, I fear people may start believing the things you say of me."

The king gathered a stack of papers as Steven propped his forearms on the back of a chair.

"Tea?" Farran asked, as if everything was normal and life wasn't falling apart.

Steven smiled and nodded. "I would like that."

———— ∞ ————

The sky had darkened by the time Farran bid Steven farewell.

It had been a pleasant day, and Steven had enjoyed the visit with his friend.

Everything had almost seemed normal.

They had caught up and fell into companionable silence, chatting every now and again. Kettles of water had been boiled, stroopwaffles and tea biscuits procured from the cabinet above the sink.

Farran had paperwork, and Steven had an *assigned studies* book he had never finished.

The king had huffed a laugh upon looking up and finding the novel in Steven's hands.

"I knew it," Farran murmured, sipping from his third cup of tea. He looked over his small-framed glasses perched on his nose, shaking his head. "I should have threatened you with a test."

"I don't think that would have worked. You should have seen my grades in school."

"Ah, but I'm sure you were good at sports, or perhaps had a remarkable personality. To make up for your lack, of course."

"Always so cordial, so kind." Steven raised his mug in mock toast. "To my lack."

For an afternoon, the burdens of war had momentarily lifted.

Steven turned down the king's offer for a ride back to the castle, deigning to stay the night at the cottage.

When he fell asleep, he did not dream.

───❈───

Crisp, winter air filled Steven's lungs as he stretched his legs.

A veil of fog drifted over the frost-laden fields, washed in pink from the awakening day.

"Look what you would have missed, brother." Jay leaned over to tie his shoes.

Steven smiled. "Yeah, I almost missed sleeping in and sparing my eyes from seeing your face this morning."

"I've been told I have a very nice face, thank you."

Steven rocked back and forth on the balls of his feet.

This would hurt. He should have kept training. Starting over after so long—

"Race ya," Jay breathed, taking off.

As the brothers ran, the sky turned, fog clearing as they raced through field and wood, along the coast and toward the capital.

It was beautiful, exhilarating.

Jay was *alive*.

Steven hadn't taken the time to appreciate that yet. His brother lived and breathed beside him, and it wasn't some figment of Steven's imagination.

Tendrils of chimney smoke rose from the city as they approached. When Steven didn't veer from the main road, Jay barreled onward.

Steven's pulse quickened as they ran through the marred streets.

Farran's beloved city, ransacked.

Though Steven didn't look close, his gaze managed to catch a shattered window in a familiar brick building.

Grace's favorite antique shop, owned by an elderly couple living in the apartment above.

Steven's throat constricted.

He hoped they had survived. He'd have to ask Grace.

When they passed the destruction, Steven loosed a breath. Jay glanced over a shoulder before joining his side.

"Use it as fuel for their destruction," Jay breathed.

26

Steven managed to hear the knock at the door despite the storm. He grabbed his knife from under his pillow, rain clattering against the window as a barrage of wind made the cottage groan.

It had to be nearly midnight.

Lightning struck, Steven's room filling with light, thunder rattling the frames on the wall.

He ran down the stairs, knife drawn.

Steven loosened his grip and opened the door. Grace nearly careened into him, a paper in his face.

"What is it?" he said. Grace shut the door and made for the living room, Steven following.

"We need to go." She drew a couch cushion back and procured a handgun.

"I didn't know there were guns here."

Grace looked up, brows drawn. "That's what you're choosing to focus on? Did you not read the paper?"

Steven grabbed the sheet from the coffee table. It was a manuscript of a conversation.

"What does it say?" Steven dropped the paper.

Grace strapped on a chest holster. "Farran's in trouble." She sheathed the gun and entered the kitchen.

"He's *been* in trouble," Steven said, leaning against the wall.

He straightened. "You mean now? What are you doing?"

Grace opened a drawer and pulled out an elastic band, hastily braiding her hair.

"Farran is meeting Ares tonight."

"Why didn't you lead with that?"

"Do you have a gun?"

"I—" Steven paced, a hand at his mouth before running upstairs.

Steven returned, Grace having finished her braid, the end snapping against the small of her back as she turned. Dressed in black, a gun strapped to her chest, she didn't resemble anything of the woman Steven had grown up with.

Perhaps he didn't resemble himself, either.

Steven ran his hands over the clothes he had found in Farran's closet. He had never seen the king dressed in an entirely black outfit.

Perhaps Steven had found Farran's funeral ensemble.

"I have a gun," Steven said, patting his holster. Grace looked him up and down and nodded once.

"Let's hope we won't need it."

———

Grace parked Farran's truck in a copse of trees.

Steven shielded his gun with a hand as they ran through sodden fields, his clothes already soaked through. Lightning lit the plain, thunder following.

They hadn't much time until the meeting began.

Grace had been doing more spying than Steven realized.

He wasn't sure if he should worry about it or not.

Grace crept atop a hill, Steven's shoulder brushing hers. Below, Steven noted a road and a swath of grass near the cliff's edge. A gathering of boulders.

"That's the spot?" Steven asked, checking his weapons.

Everything was soaked. He hoped his firearm would still work if he needed it.

"Ares requested it," Grace said under her breath, surveying the road. "We should cross after the next strike—"

Blinding light illuminated the road and cliffside.

Steven grabbed Grace's hand. *"Now."*

As thunder rumbled, they slid down the hill and raced across the road. Before the next strike, they jumped into the rocks. Though the fit was tight, Grace and Steven wedged themselves in.

Ares had picked a fine night for a meeting.

A pair of lights cut through darkness and downpour.

Steven shrunk as light passed over them, the car pulling alongside the road. A door opened and shut, followed by footsteps splashing in puddles on the road.

Grace sidled close, her shoulder pressing into his chest.

The stranger's footsteps squelched as they met grass and slowed. Steven dared a look over the rock.

A bolt of lightning lit up the planes of Farran's face, his gaze set toward the roiling, black ocean. Thunder barraged the cliffside, nearly covering the sound of another pair of footsteps approaching.

The sky alight, Steven watched Ares pass by, his eyes set and white hair plastered to his skull.

"Good evening, Your Majesty," Ares greeted. Farran turned, his overcoat open to reveal a three-piece suit. A meeting was a meeting to Farran, it seemed.

Grace gripped Steven's hand as Ares neared the king. Steven slid his free hand over his gun.

He should kill Ares now.

Between Farran, Grace, and Steven himself, Ares could be dead and tossed over the cliff in less than a minute.

His grip tightened, rain running from his brow into his eyes.

Grace squeezed his hand, drawing his attention. Her eyes flicked from his firearm to his face.

Not yet.

Steven's lips tightened, but he relaxed his grip.

This meeting could contain vital information.

Or prove Farran their enemy.

Though Steven was sure Faye was important, he couldn't let his country burn and bleed for one person.

He wasn't sure what that said about him.

"I'm surprised you showed," Ares said, sliding his hands into his pockets.

Farran angled his head, eyes dark. "I'm surprised you thought I had a choice."

Ares looked down, laughing once. "Touché."

A muscle feathered in Farran's jaw, his hair already a slick mess. "Don't waste my time, Ares."

The War Leader smiled. "Let's get to it then. But first things first, is this where you were to wed the girl, or bury her? I know you had hoped for both, but as you well know, she is a traitor."

Grace stilled, Steven replaying the words in his head.

Ares was playing another mind game.

"Why are we here," Farran said quietly, though not weakly.

Ares shrugged. "I am a reasonable man, and wanted to offer you a choice again."

Lightning painted the ocean off the coast, allowing Steven to watch the king's face fall. Thunder followed, the deluge opening further.

Steven blinked back fat drops as Ares stepped forward.

"You see, I have a problem, Farran. I was *this* close to having everything I needed to take out Central's east coast." Ares gave a pinching motion with his hand. "The only problem was . . . well, you know full well what the problem was."

Another strike revealed Farran's set jaw.

Ares smiled. "You always were a bad liar."

"I have neither confirmed nor denied anything."

"There's no need to," Ares said. "Your soldiers are dead

regardless, and replaced with my own. After the bullet holes were stitched shut, my men donned your uniforms."

Farran's fingers curled into fists as Ares paced.

"People trust that pretty flag on their arms, and now shipping slaves will be much easier, as my men actually listen to the orders I give them."

Steven stilled, Grace leaning into him.

"Your men's uniforms, as well as their bodies hanging from the barbed fences, gained us some footing in the war. Apart from that, they weren't worth much to me after you made them disobey my orders," Ares said. He stopped and regarded Farran. "Do you think my threats regarding your sister are empty? And what of your ex-lover? Surely you are not so dull to believe I wouldn't follow through with what I have said."

"To what end?" Farran breathed.

Ares let out a humorless laugh, resuming his pacing. "Until I finish what my great-grandfather started."

"What's the point?" Farran broke. "You think you're doing everyone a favor by conquering and killing everyone in your way? Do you not hear how idiotic that sounds? If anyone is dull, it's you."

Ares halted. "You think I'm dull? That's rich." He stepped closer to Farran, Steven pulling free his weapon. Ares looked skyward, laughing before loosening a sigh. "You house your greatest enemies, knowingly allow spies to share a bed with you, and claim *I'm* dull. You look foolish, Farran. Your parents would be ashamed of the man you've become."

Steven inhaled sharply as Farran whipped out a revolver, the barrel leveled at Ares' face.

The War Leader shook his head, though his smile remained. He raised his hands. "Shoot me."

Farran raised the weapon to Ares' pale forehead. "I will." He cocked the gun, the sound snapping Steven into reality.

Farran was going to kill Ares right here, right now.

Steven wasn't sure if Grace was breathing.

"No, you won't. And we both know it," Ares said, dropping his hands. "Unless you want your sister and Natalia dead, too, of course."

Farran's grip tightened, a flash of lightning revealing the war in his eyes. "I can't watch Central fall."

"Well, don't look," Ares said.

The king's eyes widened before settling. A flash of lightning, a glint of steel flashing as the gun shifted.

Farran pressed the barrel underneath his own jaw. Steven jarred forward, his breath catching. Grace let go of his hand.

Ares scoffed, turning on a heel. "Oh, please. There's no need for that. Just do what you're told."

"I won't," Farran said. "I've done enough."

"Not yet, not for me." Ares looked over a shoulder. "You will listen to me if you want to see Faye and Natalia again."

"I don't need to."

Ares halted. "I'll kill them if you kill yourself."

The threat was empty and Farran could hear it, too. Steven's blood ran cold as he watched his friend smile.

"Don't. Do. It," Ares bit out, his face contorting. "I *will* kill them."

Farran shook his head. "I am your puppet no longer."

A strike off the coast lit up the cliffside, alighting the rain and acceptance in the king's eyes.

"Don't look," Farran said.

And pulled the trigger.

27

A hand was over Steven's mouth before he could scream, the gun ripped from his hand.

Farran had shot himself.

"Don't make a sound," Grace whispered. Steven could barely hear her, his eyes widening as she stared him down, inches away.

He could trust her.

Couldn't he?

Ares had mentioned a traitor. Was it Grace?

Farran.

Steven pushed Grace off and looked over the rock. Farran's body lay in the grass, Ares making his way across the road.

Ares.

Now. Steven needed to end it *now.*

Steven made to move, Grace shoving him into the rock.

"Don't move," she hissed.

He stared her down as he listened to a car door open and shut, an engine start. He shook his head at her, but she wouldn't let go, something hard and unyielding in her eyes.

Headlights lit up the water-logged road and disappeared around the bend.

Ares was gone.

"What the hell, Grace? I could have had him!"

"If you killed him now, others would die."

"Yeah, instead—" Steven couldn't finish the sentence, the words dying on his tongue. He was up and out of the rocks, water splashing underfoot. He fell to his knees before Farran's body.

"Steven." Grace's footsteps sloshed at Steven's back. A hand gripped his wrist and he screamed.

"Farran?" Steven tried, willing his eyes to adjust.

The king nodded slowly, not a spot of blood on him. His eyes focused behind Steven.

"You moved the bullet in my revolver," Farran breathed. Steven looked over a shoulder at Grace.

"Why didn't you tell me?" Steven seethed. "I thought he was *dead.*"

"I was supposed to be," Farran offered.

"You, shut up," Steven snapped. "That was the stupidest thing you've ever done."

"It really wasn't," Farran said. "Grace—"

"No," Steven interrupted. "I am not done. What was the shot I heard?"

Farran sighed. "Ares took my advice and turned away. When my gun didn't go off, hers did. I played dead."

"Some warning would have been great."

"Well, I didn't think I'd be trailed, or my weapon tampered with," Farran said tiredly, closing his eyes.

"I hate you guys. You, especially. Never do that again," Steven snarled. Farran opened his eyes and looked at him, looked at Grace.

"I will do my best." Farran took Steven's outstretched hand.

Despite the darkness, Steven watched the king's legs shake as he rose. Steven sought Farran's discarded weapon next. He picked up the slick, cold metal as a clean smack broke the air behind him.

Steven whirled on a heel to find Farran's eyes on Grace's.

"Grace," Steven warned.

Undiluted rage shone in her eyes. "I *knew* you were lying."

"Faye is all I have left now," Farran said. "I have been fighting Ares, I promise."

Grace angled her head. "Liars make the best promises."

She didn't wait for his reply, disappearing into rain-drenched night.

Devastation crossed Farran's face, his body shaking.

Steven looked at the ground and pretended he hadn't seen what was left of his friend shatter in front of him.

"What's it like to be dead?" Steven asked, stirring a bowl of batter.

Farran pushed a stack of papers away and ran a hand through his hair.

"More stressful than I once considered." Farran watched Steven pour waffle batter into an iron. "What would you do if you were in my shoes?"

"Quitting probably isn't an acceptable choice?"

Farran shook his head slowly.

If Steven were Farran, and Ares and Luther thought him dead, he could run. Though, it wasn't the bravest choice, and the weight of what could have been would haunt him. Steven sighed through his nose.

"I would snipe them."

"Could you?"

Steven scoffed. "Yes."

Grace set a glass pourer onto the counter. "Why haven't you had them killed them yet?"

Farran slid his attention to Grace.

"I have tried. Many times," Farran said quietly. "In a last ditch effort to stop this war from ever beginning, I sent my Second over. Much like Luther's Second, she was my assassin and second-in-command."

Farran's gaze shifted to the wall. "She died. And I must admit, I quit trying so hard. She was— she was my best."

Emmaline Shrouder.

Steven remembered seeing her on the news at the eve of war, sitting in a coffee shop in an armchair across from Max Fitzgerald.

How the world had changed since then.

Farran inhaled. "When Tyrnnth murdered my family, most of my father's assassins had been killed. She had survived. The moment I became king, I made her my Second."

He raised a hand to his mouth. "Ares' executioner ended her life nearly a year ago. I still haven't a clue who he is, not that I would know what to do if I ever found him."

"How did she die?" Grace asked.

Farran met her eyes. "I didn't have anyone left for Ares, so I sent Emmaline." His voice wavered, but he went on. "They caught her."

Farran looked up at the ceiling and laughed, though Steven knew it had nothing to do with finding anything funny.

"My very best. It shouldn't have been possible." Farran inhaled sharply. "And then Ares' butcher located that Central Territorian fishing vessel.

"Before the crew sank with the boat, a chain was secured around— around her ankle. She remained on the warship until the weight of the vessel pulled her under."

That was the missing boat just before the war.

"I'm sorry," Steven said.

Farran smiled sadly, though he wouldn't look their way. "Everyone's sorry. I just wish there was something more I could do about it." His chair creaked as he rose. "But it seems I've done enough as it is."

"Where are you going?" Steven asked. Farran crossed the room to don an olive-green trench coat.

"Work. I have too much paperwork to be dead."

"Wait," Grace said. Farran halted, a hand on the knob.

"Yes?"

Grace looked at Steven before meeting Farran's eyes.

"Steven and I talked last night. We came up with a plan."

"If it doesn't involve putting a bullet through Ares' head, successfully, I must decline." Farran stepped out the door.

"It does."

The king paused. "Surely not."

"The only way you'd know is if you stuck around and ate breakfast with us," Steven said.

Farran watched from the doorway.

"I guess it wouldn't hurt to listen."

<hr />

Farran's truck hadn't started in the morning, Steven and his friends walking the dirt road back to the capital.

Despite the storm in the night, the sun shone against a blue sky, revealing a water-logged New Iberian countryside.

"What exactly did Ares mean when he said something about sharing beds?" Steven asked. "Grace, I know you're no traitor. I won't waste time asking. But the *beds*—"

"Truly, now? You're going to ask right now," Farran said, looking skyward. "Honestly, Steven, it is none of your business."

"You guys are my best friends. I know you guys had a thing, but last night it seemed Ares knew way more than I did."

"We didn't do anything," Grace said. Farran coughed.

"You're lying," Steven said.

She took a deep breath and looked toward the fields as they walked. "Okay, well— at first, Fare would invite me over for tea. Then we'd read together, and sometimes it got late . . . " Grace shook her head. "Eventually, I did stay the night."

"A few times," Farran said.

"Just sleeping," Grace insisted, casting the king an incredulous look.

Farran looked elsewhere.

"It's nothing like what Steven's thinking!" Grace said.

Steven halted. "That's it. Somebody tell me a straight story."

Grace looked from a tense, tight-lipped Farran to Steven.

"We've kissed, snuggled, whatever. Normal stuff," she said.

"Normal stuff," Steven mused.

"Yes," Farran said. "It was decided it would be best Grace and I remain friends. I had a moment of weakness at some point afterward, but—" The king scrubbed his face with his hands. "All of that is over now."

Steven opened his mouth to speak, but the king was already turned toward the castle and walking. "Pardon my haste, but we all have work to do."

A black limousine awaited at the castle.

Farran masked his anxiety, his shoulders and gait relaxing as they drew closer.

Jaxin Brown untwined his arms and stepped forward, his russet hair pulled up in a bun.

"Castellen, Fitzgerald, Your Majesty," Jaxin said. "Where have you all been?"

"Sleepovers aren't just for the young, Mr. Brown," Jay offered, breezing through the castle doors.

If anyone were to see through Steven, it would be Jay.

Perhaps it was another reason Jaxin had hired him.

"You were at the cottage?" Jay leaned against a pillar.

"Yeah." Steven halted before the men.

"And how was your night?" the War Leader asked.

"Fine, thank you." Farran nodded.

If Jaxin knew what Farran had done with the draftees, Jaxin would have every right to kill him, kingship or no.

But they had a plan.

Steven dared a glance at Grace, the portrait of ease.

As if she hadn't saved Farran's life last night and slapped him afterward.

As if she didn't know what he had done.

The smile she bore, the light in her eyes—

For some reason, it scared Steven.

"May I ask why you are here, War Leader?" Farran held his hands behind his back.

Jaxin jerked his chin toward Steven. "I came to borrow Castellen for a couple days."

"For whatever reason?"

"When my west coast was taken, my citizens fled for the northern border." Jaxin blew out a breath and looked at Steven, cold violence in his eyes. "King Ridgeway had them shot."

"Shot?" Steven wasn't sure if he said it out loud or not.

Jaxin looked toward the servants and visitors pausing.

"King Bardolph, perhaps you have a more ideal location for this sort of discussion?"

⁂

"I'm sorry, War Leader Brown, but I fail to see how Mr. Castellen is supposed to help with the conflict?" Farran leaned back in his chair, pulled to the circle of armchairs and couches in his study.

Steven was grateful to have somewhere to sit, his knees having grown weak after Jaxin revealed King Ridgeway's order to shoot Central Territorian refugees crossing his border.

Grace was pale beside Steven on the loveseat.

King Ridgeway's massacre was not the only bad news Jaxin had brought with him. It seemed fear was now running rampant through what remained of Central's soldiers and citizens, Ares' beasts set loose again.

The last thing Steven's people needed was Vastlynd putting

bullets in their foreheads.

Jaxin was speaking, but Steven had began staring at the wall. He didn't snap to until Farran spoke again.

"You truly think Steven will be able to talk your people down?" Farran asked, a hand propped underneath his chin.

"Yes," Jaxin said, leaning forward. "Steven is a symbol. There were eyes on him before the war, and since you two struck a deal, *all* eyes are on him now. My people are trusting him to end the war. I'm sure they'll listen to him."

"That's another matter we should touch on," Farran said, dropping his hand. "Steven has yet to finish the allotted time to complete citizenship, the duration of his stay being nearly perfect to achieve it before his Blood Challenge."

Steven reigned in a scoff, Jay barely concealing a smirk.

"Well, there's that." Jaxin crossed an ankle over his knee. "I guess I could revoke my ban and take him back."

Steven swore he could hear the specks of dust revolving around the room.

Farran leaned forward. "Revoking your ban now would cause a flood of Blood Challengers, another Culling, and unneeded, mass panic. Apart from that, we both know Steven is one of the only people qualified to successfully take Luther on. You would induce a bloodbath."

Jaxin watched the king with indifference. "Your Majesty, there won't be another Blood Challenge if Steven doesn't win. The Central Territories are not long for this world."

Steven's limbs felt cold.

"So I need him, just for a couple days, King Bardolph," Jaxin said, rising from his seat. "I need him to talk to my people. Calm them. Assure them."

"Assure them what?" Steven spoke finally.

"That they'll live," Jay answered. Steven looked to his brother, leaned back and watching calmly. "That you'll win and it'll be okay."

And what if I don't?

The convict smiled grimly, flexing his hands out.

"Someone has to give them hope," Jaxin said. "And right now, Steven is one of the only people who can do that."

<hr/>

As New Iberia disappeared behind a swath of clouds, Steven wondered what the hell he'd tell his people.

Steven's own father, King of Vastlynd, had approved the death of countless innocent men, women, children—

How was Steven supposed to tell what was left of Central it was going to be okay, when he wasn't sure he believed it himself?

A weight settled between his shoulders, and he let it drag him somewhere where he did not think at all.

28

Steven's flight landed in smoke-shrouded Central before taking off and heading north.

"Where are we going?" Steven asked. Jay leaned back in his seat, raising a brow.

"You actually bought our story?"

When Steven didn't answer, Jay laughed and ran his hands over his face. "You've spent too much time around that primping—"

"Where are we going."

The convict dropped his hands and leaned his elbows on the table between them. "We're going to Zephyr so you can talk some sense into your father."

Steven blinked. "When were you going to mention this?"

Jay pursed his lips. "Soon. Now, I guess."

Jaxin prowled forward, sliding a document across the table. "Here are some dialogue options that have worked with negotiating with King Ridgeway in the past."

Steven looked at the paper before looking up at the War Leader. "You want me to manipulate him."

"You are aware your father sanctioned the death of thousands of innocents."

Steven swallowed, nodding once.

Jaxin angled his head. "Are you not willing to save more of

them? Men, women, children. Shot. Tyrnnth's violence was at their heels, and they were so desperate to flee the enemy, a bullet to the forehead looked *appealing.*"

"I—"

"It shouldn't have happened!" Jaxin slammed a fist against the table. "Ridgeway claims he had to, or Ares would nullify the peace treaty and kill his daughter. But I'm in charge of Central now, and if Vastlynd doesn't stop murdering my people, I will make sure they are my enemy before this country burns. Is that understood?"

Steven glided up Vastlynd's palace steps, nightfall and the hood of his jacket obscuring his face from visitors streaming in and out.

He managed to reach the second floor before he was stopped.

"Sir, are you lost?" a guard asked.

"I need a smoke," Steven recited. "Starboard, midnight."

The guard narrowed his eyes, but nodded once, disappearing back down the stairs.

Steven went up six stories before stepping onto a balcony. Whilst the left side of the palace bore views of the capital below, the right offered views of night-darkened forest and snowcapped mountains.

Steven breathed in the chill air as he watched the silent, still landscape. The door at his back opened.

"Steven, why are you here?" King Ridgeway asked. Steven leaned against the balcony.

"I'm here as a courtesy," Steven said, the king bristling. "Jaxin is about to mark you as an enemy."

"Why would he do that?"

"You shot our people at the border."

King Ridgeway banded his arms over his chest. "I made it clear to War Leader Brown that I do not take refugees. Tyrnnth will slaughter Natalia if I do."

"Will they, though?" Steven asked. "As far as I can tell, Luther is infatuated with Natalia and has made her into his own personal weapon. I doubt the dictator of Tyrnnth would allow it."

"Ares is dictator now, and you know it."

"And Luther, his son. If Ares wants his son willing to fight the Blood Challenges for him, I doubt he'd kill off the only person Luther cares about. Wouldn't you do the same?"

King Ridgeway's face tightened. "I don't know who you think you are, but if you think you can march into my palace and tell *me* what to do—" Ridgeway threw up his hands. "I'm the *king!* And as far as everyone else knows, you're just Farran's sacrificial lamb."

Steven didn't move.

"Did you know they pity you? Here you are, training and competing for your Blood Challenge, and for what? I heard you fell apart after the Culling while Luther grew stronger."

King Ridgeway shook his head, taking a step forward. "He will kill you the second you step into that ring. I thought you'd be different."

"Likewise," Steven said.

"Oh, don't give me that." King Ridgeway waved a bejeweled hand. "And if I remember right, Jaxin and I asked you to spy for us, and you couldn't even do that. When was the last time you sent an update? It seems you only ever speak to Jaxin these days, and the one time you talk to your father, it's to ask something from him."

Steven slammed a fist onto the balcony, rock giving way and tumbling.

The king's jaw clenched, looking at the place where concrete had given way to flesh.

"New Iberia wouldn't take refugees, either," Steven said. "But King Bardolph lifted a statute to allow some, asking nothing in return."

King Ridgeway cocked his head, his mouth opening.

"My country is *burning.*" Steven pointed south. "And while my people are fleeing Ares' beasts and men, you're putting bullets in their heads."

"I am *not*—"

Steven laughed. "You might as well be."

He couldn't take another word. He was moving for the door before he could reconsider.

He had failed.

King Ridgeway would not take refugees, and that was that. Steven shook his head, his hand reaching for the knob.

"Stop."

Steven almost didn't. He paused and looked over a shoulder, finding a man standing on the balcony. Not a king, but a man.

Eric Ridgeway opened his mouth, shut it, turned away. He walked to the railing and leaned against it.

"How many is Bardolph taking?"

"One sixteenth of every city and town in New Iberia," Steven said. The king frowned. He sighed, head dropping.

"I'll match him." The king turned and began walking to the door.

Steven wasn't sure he heard correctly. "What?"

King Ridgeway leveled Steven with a stare. "When Ares finds out, I'll tell him I did it for Caradoc's son. That fool of a prince will get himself into more trouble than he can imagine if he goes on breaking traditions while the world maintains them."

"You knew Farran's parents?"

The king opened the door. "Dearly."

Eric made to step through the threshold, but shut the door. He leaned forward, his voice dropping. "Listen, son. If Ares knows you pose a threat to his plans, he will take out everyone and *everything* you hold dear. Caradoc and Marilyn were people who had posed such a threat. Now they're dead." Ridgeway looked skyward. "Farran is young, naïve. Ares hasn't needed to bother him. He may now. Just watch close, and try— try not to get close."

Steven's lips tightened.

"Ares finds Farran's stunt of taking you in for the Blood Challenge amusing. The moment Ares finds out there's more to all of this than it seems, he'll have you all finished.

"I gave him my daughter to keep my kingdom safe. Luther was kind, and I am grateful for that," Eric said, looking past Steven. "If you succeed, she will be free."

"Isn't that what you want?" Steven asked.

King Ridgeway cracked the door open.

"I don't know," he said. "She's happy. She may not be when her husband is dead and she comes home to find war on her doorstep."

"But the war ends with the Blood—"

"Central's war ends. Ours may just begin."

Steven opened his mouth, but Eric was already through the door.

"Goodnight, Steven."

The door shut. Steven exhaled, leaning against the wall.

It was too complicated.

He felt far from the beginning of the war, where he had simply been fodder for the front, declining a foreign king's offer to gain citizenship as a means to fight the dictator.

Now that king was Steven's dearest friend, Steven himself royalty, Grace set free, and Jay no longer a body in a trench.

Steven was grateful for the second chances, the friends.

But he had so much more to lose now.

29

Grace watched Farran run a hand through his golden hair, his body tense.

"It'll work," she said, resisting the urge to grab his arm. Shake him. Stop him from worrying.

The king was usually too deep in his mind to completely register her words in moments like this.

Farran picked a head of wheat as they walked and began picking at it. Grace let her eyes graze over the barren fields and wintering vineyards.

His country was beautiful, even in a season of rest.

Sometimes she wished they had met another time.

"How can you be so certain, Grace," Farran said, tossing the head of wheat to the ground, their steps scuffing against loose rock on the dirt road.

Grace chewed her lip before looking up, finding Farran's gaze on the ground. "I don't know. It *has* to work, so it will."

Farran smiled at that. "I see."

"Steven's getting in today," she offered.

It had been three days. Though she hadn't heard from Steven, Jay had called her.

Things had worked out, somehow.

King Ridgeway would slyly, very quietly, allow refugees into his neutral, northern country.

Though the king wouldn't announce anything, it would be fairly obvious when Centrallians weren't shot the second they passed over the border.

Grace wasn't sure how it had came about, as the men had left to talk people *down* from escaping.

She was relieved some of her people would find safe haven.

"Do you think Ares knows you're alive yet?" Grace asked. Farran looked up, his eyes narrowing in the sunshine.

"I'm sure he does." Farran turned his gaze on her, hazel eyes bright in the sunlight.

He had striking eyes.

She would never tell him.

He didn't need anymore encouragement to pursue her. This walk was enough, as it was.

She didn't want to continue to break his heart, though she knew it wouldn't entirely be her fault.

"I think he's waiting for my next move," he went on.

"Then I guess we'll see his reaction soon."

"I suppose," Farran said, a grim smile on his face as he looked at her. He stopped, Grace following suit. He took her hands in his.

"Grace, promise me one thing," Farran said quietly, looking down at their hands. "If this all goes to hell, I want— I need you to . . . "

He looked up, blinking. He laughed and looked down at her with a sad smile. He let her hands fall away.

"I want you to be happy, love." Farran's eyes showed an emotion Grace pretended he didn't feel for her. "Can you promise me that, if it all falls apart?"

Grace wasn't sure what to say, so she didn't say anything. Instead, she smiled at her friend, the man who had been willing to buy her freedom, no matter what it would have cost him.

The king who had been nothing but kind to her.

She hadn't apologized for slapping him, nor snapping when

she learned of what he had done.

It was unforgivable.

But as war dragged on, Grace was realizing there were more sides to everyone being revealed.

Even herself.

Each day was a gift. Each *moment*.

Life was too short now.

Grace's eyes felt hot, Farran blurring.

Perhaps she would forgive him.

She could die any day, and he could, too.

A stammering apology fell from her lips as she embraced him. Farran wrapped his arms around her, encircling her completely.

"No, Grace," he said. "You don't apologize for that. What I did can never happen again."

A few moments passed, the only sound Farran's breath and heartbeat. A rustle of stalks of wheat dancing.

"You didn't answer my question," he said quietly. "Can you promise me?"

"Only if you promise the same," she said into his chest. When Farran didn't reply, Grace knew they were thinking the same thing.

There were no point in promises in this world.

War guaranteed nothing.

Happiness, of all the things Farran wanted for her, seemed the least likely to survive what was to come.

Now, hope— hope was hardy.

Hope could survive war.

But Farran knew Grace was already holding onto it, and it would not be taken from her.

30

The summit arrived.

With the Blood Challenges a month away, it was a good time as any to enact their plan.

Steven watched a spring storm wreak Evynmare in rain.

Sighing, he turned to find Farran's hands trembling on the glass he lifted to his lips. Whatever the king was drinking, it was hard.

The king turned from the darkened city, the light of his green banker's lamp casting his face in harsh contrast.

"This better work," Farran said.

Ares had learned of the summit Farran was hosting, and had immediately sent the king a script. Farran had already practiced the words, easing the tremor in his voice.

He wouldn't chance losing his sister, which was what Ares had threatened him with.

Again.

Steven plopped into a chair, Farran perched at the edge of his desk.

"Grace is ready," the prizefighter said.

Farran nodded, knocking back the rest of his drink. "Yes, she's told me, as well." His hazel eyes slid from the flames dancing in the fireplace along the wall to Steven. "And are you ready, Mr. Castellen?"

Steven felt a pang of guilt at hearing Farran utter his last name.

He had yet to tell Farran who he was. If they were such close friends, should he have told him by now?

Steven gave a tight smile. "As ready as I can be."

Farran reached for the bottle on his desk, Steven grabbing it first. He brought the glass to his eyes to read the label.

The king had already drank quite a bit, and that had been since Steven had seated himself in the study.

"We've got to be on top of it tomorrow." Steven lowered the bottle onto the desk. "You don't want to drink too much of that, I would know."

Steven's father had been a drunk half the time, and Jay as well, before prison. Mulling it over, Steven realized he hadn't seen Jay drink since. Perhaps he had given it up.

Steven would be glad for it. Jay looked like their father when he was drunk.

Farran pushed the bottle to Steven. "Then please take it away."

Steven didn't say a word as he did, Farran's attention shifting to the rain-berated capital.

"If something happens tomorrow, I want you and Grace gone," Farran said distantly. "Do you understand me, Castellen? I want you both *out.*"

Farran's eyes slid to him.

Steven nodded. "Yes, Your Majesty."

Farran smiled and shook his head. "Don't lie to me."

Steven sighed and rose, bottle in hand. "Get some sleep. We'll see you in the morning."

Farran didn't say more as Steven exited.

The guests arrived an hour before the event, milling about the entryway. Tables had been set, stacked high with decadent meats, pastries and pies.

The smell would have made Steven's mouth water if he hadn't stuffed himself beforehand.

When the castle's head cook had exited the kitchen hall, finding Steven with a plateful of food, she had chided him for eating before the king.

Between the mouthfuls of food, she hadn't been able to discern Steven would be *sharing* his food with the king himself.

But Farran hadn't eaten. It seemed his nerves would gnaw on him instead.

Steven leaned against the stair banister as he surveyed the space, accepting a wineglass from a passing server.

"Lots of guests," Farran said, taking a sip from his glass. Steven noted a tremor in the king's elegant, scarred hands.

"Yes," Steven said distantly, catching Grace in the crowd.

She was dressed in a soft green gown, the piece covered in delicate, pressed flowers. She looked lovely, her golden-brown hair falling from her shoulders in loose waves, her eyes alight.

Grace caught Steven's gaze and made her way to him.

"Quite the party, Your Majesty." Grace curtsied, offering Farran a smile.

"Never enough occasion to dress up anymore," Farran replied, though his words seemed strained. Someone approached the king, drawing his attention away.

"You look beautiful," Steven said.

Grace flashed a smile. "And you clean up well."

Steven shrugged. "Thanks."

"The media beckons. Care to join, Ms. Fitzgerald?" Farran offered an arm, Grace lacing hers through.

Steven watched them disappear into the crowd, people parting as they made their way to the doors.

"What an attractive pair of love birds."

Steven's pulse quickened as he turned toward the icy, edged voice.

Ares leaned against the second level banister, giving Steven a viper's grin.

"Good evening, Castellen," Ares said, descending the steps to stand at his side. The War Leader was dressed in a charcoal, three-piece suit. Upon the handkerchief in his pocket, a small embroidery shown.

"What's the cloud mean?" Steven asked, despite himself.

Ares looked down, his chin bunching beneath his pale, angular face.

He straightened. "Tyrnnth is the storm to wash away everyone's mess. Nobody is a fan of the rain, but all would die without it."

Steven resisted the urge to roll his eyes and finished his wine.

"Nice and dramatic," Steven mused. "How do you bear the weight of saving the world for such an ungrateful populace?"

Ares smiled, taking in the gathering crowd. "At least we don't lie about who we are and what we do."

Steven masked his expression as Ares looked at him.

It was an effort of will to resist the urge to take a fistful of Ares' white hair and slam his face into the banister.

Steven smiled.

"At least you have that going for you."

Ares smiled back. "Enjoy the party, Steven." He whistled some off-kilter tune as he descended the steps.

Steven could spot Luther a mile away, the man taller and broader than everyone around him. Natalia was at his side, clad in a glittering gray dress, cascading, sheer sleeves brushing her shoulders.

Luther smiled at something someone said, turning to smile at Natalia, a hand around her waist.

Too human.

Way too human.

Steven turned away just as Luther Hawthorne brushed a kiss atop his wife's brow.

Steven meandered amongst the crowd long enough to figure

the assassin's ward was elsewhere.

After wandering several halls, Steven found Faye seated in a bay window lining the garden. The rest of the small library was empty, a fireplace guttering against the wall.

Steven halted, watching the young woman take in the night-darkened view. She wore a dress the color of mulled cider, her long, pale hair loose.

She appeared content to miss the party and stare at the rain instead.

If the fate of the war didn't rest in the next few hours, Steven would have been inclined to join her.

A Tyrnnthian guard stood beside the wall, his eyes promising violence if Steven so much as breathed wrong.

Faye slid her gaze to Steven, pale green eyes sparking. For a few moments, Steven watched her watch him back, rain pelting the window.

"Good evening," Steven said. "King Bardolph inquires to see if you are enjoying the party?"

"You may tell him I am."

"He will be pleased to hear that," Steven replied. He strode to an empty hall and pressed his earpiece. "Widowfinch located."

They hadn't been certain Ares would bring Faye, but knowing her presence would show Farran what he stood to lose— Steven was not surprised.

He and his friends had planned on it.

───────

Steven chatted with guests while Farran finished with the media. The king returned, Grace already dismissed and somewhere in the crowd.

Farran placed a hand on Steven's shoulder. "It's time."

As they strode through the crowd, Steven noted no lack of attention snagging on New Iberia's king.

Admiration, respect—

Farran, dressed in his finery, a crown atop his golden hair; he did appear ever the good king. Beloved by his people, trusted by his allies.

Steven wondered how they would look at the king if they knew what he had done.

The throne room doors opened and the crowd followed.

Gold-encrusted columns sloped into a fine, filagreed ceiling, crystal chandeliers hung high. Floor-to-ceiling windows lined the sprawling room, appearing as mirrors. At the end of the room, a throne sat before a carved wall of ivory wolves.

White wolves represented the Bardolph crest. Though the creatures had never roamed New Iberia, Farran's ancestors had originated from a land where they had.

Steven halted at the foot of the dais as Farran ascended the steps. He stopped before his throne, a shadow passing over his eyes.

He blinked and it was gone.

Farran gracefully took his seat, his eyes passing over the crowd. The room was already full of chatter, bodies, and flashing cameras.

Steven shifted and tapped the device in his ear.

A gasp, and Grace materialized out of the crowd.

Wine spilled the bodice of her dress, her eyebrows drawn and eyes glistening. Steven tried not to smile.

"Ms. Grace, do you have a drinking problem?"

"It's not funny," she pleaded. Farran rose to come to her side, a portion of the room quieting.

He drew her hands into his. "What happened, love?"

"It was an accident, I think."

Farran sighed, looking across the room. Tears threatened to fall from Grace's honey-brown eyes.

Her four years of drama club were paying off.

Farran turned to Steven. "Castellen, would you please take

Grace to my room. I have her dresses in my armoire."

Steven dipped his head. "Yes, Your Majesty."

Farran gave Grace a small smile, though Steven swore he saw something almost . . . despondent, in his eyes. Grace didn't look away.

Farran lifted a hand to her cheek and kissed her forehead. She stilled until he pulled away, brushing a thumb over her cheek.

"I can't wait for you, love. But do take your time, if you must."

Farran dropped his hand and strode up the dais.

———

The King of New Iberia began his speech as Grace and Steven entered the entry hall, the throne room doors shutting behind them.

The placating, envious, and pitying glances Grace had received while they exited proved their act had appeared genuine enough.

Everyone thought Grace was Farran's current woman, and someone had tried to sabotage her outfit for the night.

Steven ushered her to the glass elevator and pressed the button for the top floor. As they climbed, the glittering capital shrank beneath them.

"I'm sorry about your dress. It's not like every other girl didn't have their chance before you showed up," Steven said, well aware of the camera in the elevator.

If Ares was here, who knew what was compromised.

"It's okay." Grace looked skyward. "I don't know if I want to go back anyways. Those girls are just so mean—"

They hit the top floor, the doors opening.

"I'm sure His Majesty won't mind if you don't come back."

Because they wouldn't.

Steven and Grace walked to the king's suite, the hall windows reflecting their blurred opposites beside them.

There were no cameras here. Steven looked at Grace from the

corner of his eye.

"So what was that?"

"What was what."

"C'mon, G. You know what I'm talking about. He wasn't supposed to kiss you, or touch your face and stuff."

Was Grace walking faster?

"It was nothing. It wasn't supposed to happen," she said. "It wasn't part of the script."

"I did notice that." Steven reached for the suite key. "Are you okay?"

Grace rolled her shoulders, halting at the door. "Yes."

"Liar."

"Please unlock the door, we're on a clock."

Steven sighed and obeyed, Grace sweeping in. He changed in the dim light, Grace having shut herself in the bathroom to do the same.

"How do you expect me to tell the truth, if you don't?" Steven called. He pulled a covering over his face, leaving only his eyes visible.

The bathroom door opened, Grace standing beside an open hatch, a narrow spiral staircase descending into darkness. Dread coiled in Steven's stomach, dust stuffing up his nose as he neared.

"If it helps, I don't even know the truth right now," Grace said.

"Fair enough, but—"

"After you, Steven."

He smiled and descended. "Me first. For the spiderwebs, I imagine. Tell my story."

Grace shut the hatch door behind them. "Chivalry isn't dead."

"No, but it's next."

31

Steven opened a door, coming face to face with the castle catacombs. Dark stone and mortar made up the walls, dust motes swirling in their flashlight beams.

Even Farran hadn't been sure the last time the catacombs had been used. Judging from the stale air, it had been awhile. As Steven walked, he could have sworn the darkness beyond the cell bars seemed to reach out.

"I'm glad I moved to an apartment," Grace muttered at his back. "This place lives underneath you."

"It doesn't live. It's a place. It exists."

"Whatever. It's there."

Steven climbed a staircase and opened the grate at the top, entering the vault floor. Bright lights lined a marble floor, steel doors lining a corridor.

Steven had yet to ask what Farran housed here.

They swept up another set of stairs before reaching the ground floor. Steven was grateful to see a familiar hallway, though his heart rate remained at a steady sprint.

"How much time?" he whispered, pressing into an alcove. Grace sidled closer, checking her watch.

Farran's watch.

They were both thieves and liars tonight.

It had been Grace's idea— New Iberia had a grudge against a gang living in a country they had waged war against years ago.

"It just might work," Farran had breathed, holding a hand to his mouth as he looked out the window. When he had looked at Grace, admiration and something more in his eyes, she adverted her gaze.

Steven hadn't missed her hands wringing.

Nearly all of the affection tonight had been an act.

Somehow.

But then again— Steven had decided he wasn't the best judge of character, considering he had managed to somehow grow fond of Ares' adopted *daughter.*

Steven shook his head, shaking Adira from his thoughts.

She couldn't be an option until Ares was dead.

But that was the plan tonight.

Kill the dictator.

They could do it as soon as—

"Faye is still in the west wing hall lining the garden," Grace whispered. "We have five minutes."

"Starting when?"

The lights shut off.

"Now," Grace breathed.

They began running.

32

Farran held their interest.

Ares remained, Luther remained.

Natalia, too.

Which was the most important, as she was an assassin.

How far they'd come from the naïve adolescents they'd been in Vastlynd. Since then, the world had changed, ended, and began again.

Farran did not want to lose it once more.

So he continued to speak, even as each word from his lips had been written by Ares himself. Tyrnnth's War Leader smiled, as if he had won.

Farran smiled back, because he knew Ares was wrong.

The king kept his gaze away from the ceiling grate in the back of the room, where one of his assassins waited.

Sloane Vickenger, the best sharpshooter from Farran's father's wars.

He had come out of retirement for this.

He wouldn't miss. He never had.

So Farran kept a smile on his face as he spewed Ares' propaganda, even as heads turned and murmurs stirred.

It wouldn't matter soon. Faye would be safe in ten minutes.

And Ares would be dead.

33

Men and women bearing Scalbearer uniforms raced by, tipping vases and placing art on the floor.

Quietly, as they couldn't be caught.

Not yet.

With the lights out, Faye's guard had placed himself beside her, his gun drawn and ready.

It didn't make a difference. Even in shifting firelight, Steven's aim was true. The guard was down in a moment, a bullet through his knee. Grace kicked his weapon aside and kneeled as Steven approached Faye, her eyes widening as she watched Grace zip-tie her guard's hands.

Faye tensed, the fire dancing in her eyes. "Who are you?"

"The good guys. We're getting you out," Steven said. He dropped to his knees before Faye, pulling down his mask.

"Ares will kill you both," she said.

"He's welcome to try." Steven outstretched a hand to the princess.

"We don't have time," Grace said, zip-tying a pair of closet doors shut. She had already finished with the guard.

Faye looked at Steven's scarred, callused hand before meeting his eyes. She swallowed and set her hand in his.

Steven loosed a breath.

"We're going to have to run," he said. Faye nodded.

The room filled with red light, Grace's eyes snapping to Steven.

"That wasn't supposed to happen," she whispered. "We disabled the emergency lights."

"If you're going to do this, you have to do it now," Faye said, meeting Steven's eyes. "Ares brought his executioner."

The man responsible for Farran's Second's murder.

Steven tugged Grace and Faye from the alcove.

"If Ares' butcher is here, I need you—" Steven began.

"I'll get to the throne room," Grace said.

"No," Steven said. They were nearly to the end of the hall now. "We maintain order until Faye's chip is cut. I want you safe somewhere."

Chips. That was how Ares could guarantee another's death when his own life ended.

Steven let go of Grace's hand.

"I'll see you soon, G," he promised. Grace nodded and continued onward, Steven turning down another hall. He opened an artwork-laden door, ushering Faye in before closing the door behind him.

Not trusting Ares not to know where the safe rooms were, Farran had come up with the idea of making some of the common closets makeshift safe rooms.

Steven pulled a cord, dim light filling the space.

"I need you to lie on your stomach," Steven said, grabbing the med kit. He turned to find her watching him, brows drawn.

Steven stepped closer. "I need to cut that thing out of your neck so you don't die the second Ares does."

Faye looked at the kit before looking at him. She slowly lied down, her eyes on his. "You'll need to get it far from here after, the device recognizes when it is free of a body."

"Not a problem." Steven knelt and procured a knife. "This is going to hurt." He offered a bit of leather. The princess looked at it and shook her head.

"Have it your way." Steven set it aside and poised his knife above her neck. "I'm sorry," he breathed, and began.

Faye flinched once, and never again.

By the time Steven was done, he found the device no larger than a thumbnail. He handed Faye a bit of cotton to hold against her wound. and made quick work of sealing the chip.

Steven uncovered the cage behind him, Faye starting.

"That bird will explode."

Steven set the pigeon on its back, tying the sealed tube to its leg, feeling Faye's eyes on him as sweat ran down his neck.

How much time had passed? Surely they were running out of it.

"It's just a pigeon." Steven finished the knot and pulled a loose stone from the wall. He pushed the bird free, a clap of wings sounding on the other side. "I made sure the knot was loose. There will be no exploding birds on your behalf."

Steven pressed a finger to the device in his ear. "Widowfinch ready. Execute order two."

A double click sounded, the most Farran could do.

"Widowfinch?" Faye said slowly. "That's a terrible codename."

"Not my first choice, but your brother said it was your nickname growing up. Don't you remember?"

Faye's brows drew together, but Steven's mind shifted to important matters. The next move of the plan relied on Sloane.

Steven leaned against the wall and tapped his fingers against the floor. He had wanted to be the one to end Ares' life, but Farran had insisted on hiring his retired Head of Assassins for the kill shot.

Steven hoped the old man could still aim true.

As for Steven, he was to wait for three knocks, and then run.

Not nearly as enticing as pulling the trigger on a psychopathic murderer and tyrant.

Faye shifted, drawing his attention.

"Does it hurt?" Steven asked. Faye's lips tightened, Steven

sighing and beckoning with a hand. "Come here."

When Faye didn't move, Steven held up a needle and thread, shaking them for emphasis.

"This will help."

"No, thanks."

"We're going to be running soon. Come here."

Faye crawled over and pulled her long hair aside, the smell of pear and jasmine wafting.

"How old are you?" he asked, readying the needle and thread.

"Seventeen for the next three hours."

"You don't seem very excited to be escaping Tyrnnth for your eighteenth birthday." He squinted and hovered over the wound with his needle.

He wished the light was just a bit brighter.

Faye shifted and brushed his thigh. Steven hissed and clamped a hand on her shoulder. "Don't move. I'm about to start."

Steven released her shoulder and began to work, Faye as stoic as she had been before.

"I heard there's a cancelled wedding tomorrow," Steven said quietly, working as quickly as he could without injuring her.

"You haven't succeeded yet."

"Who was the lucky guy?"

"Destry. One of Luther's favorite generals," Faye said. She winced and Steven slowed. "He's twenty-seven."

"Hm."

"I think he loves me."

Steven paused his work to dab the wound. "What else can you tell me about him?"

Faye exhaled. "He's busy."

No doubt.

Steven finished stitching, dabbing a cotton round to his work.

"Are you ready to run?"

The bulb went out overhead.

"The executioner found us," she whispered, her breath on his neck. "You need to go. Tyrnnth won't kill me."

Steven stood and offered a hand. "We're leaving together."

Never mind that someone was supposed to have arrived by now.

Perhaps they were dead.

"Follow me," Steven breathed, opening the door to the hall bathed in deep red. His heart rate picked up as his mind slowed.

His gun was slick in his palm.

If he ran, claws and teeth would follow him.

Faye squeezed his hand. "If you're going to go, you need do it now."

Steven inhaled sharply. "Right."

They ran, the wallpaper and carpet blurring around them.

They reached the entryway as Steven heard a blade scraping across the floor, the sound everywhere at once. They sprinted for the doors, Steven letting go of Faye's hand to slam into them.

"They're barricaded," he breathed. "We'll have to go another way."

He grabbed Faye's hand and sprinted for the east wing.

Steven's feet hit something solid-yet-not, Faye gasping as she tripped.

In his mad sprint, Steven had missed the carnage.

The men and women Farran had hired were dead.

Steven's heart couldn't beat any faster.

He pulled Faye forward, taking routes he hoped Ares' executioner wasn't privy to.

Steven silenced his footfalls as he entered a tiled bathroom. When Faye struggled to keep quiet, Steven swept her into his arms.

Upon reaching the far stall, he opened a hidden door and ushered Faye inside. He followed and locked the door behind them.

Red light glowed from the bulb on the short ceiling.

Steven crouched beside the hatch and stuck his fingers into the lip. He heaved, adjusted his grip. Nothing. He shifted and tried the other side.

Faye joined.

Steven grit his teeth, muscles and tendons straining—

Faye's nails broke with a click and hiss of breath. The princess drew her hands to herself, Steven releasing his grip.

Steven raised a finger to his earpiece and tapped three times.

A signal to communicate their situation was dire.

Steven hoped Farran and Sloane had succeeded on their end.

A few moments passed, Steven's earpiece silent.

Perhaps Farran was busy controlling the panicked room, chaos ensuing from Ares' body hitting the floor.

Steven slid against the wall with a sigh.

They were trapped with an assassin on their trail.

Steven cursed and pinched the bridge of his nose. "I'm sorry."

He wasn't sure exactly what he was sorry for. The botched escape, the faulty hatch door—

He knew she was shaking, so he leaned forward and pulled her in. She nestled into him.

"You are afraid," she said quietly. His brows knotted together and he felt her smile against his chest. "And now you are embarrassed."

He drew back. "How would you know that?"

Faye shifted her hair to reveal a tattoo curling along her hairline.

White checkered squares.

Like the animals on Tybauch.

Faye dropped her hand. "Ares gave me this. It allows me to read other people's emotions."

Steven shook his head against the wall, Faye's smile disappearing. "Now you're angry."

Steven's lips thinned. "I'm angry you were experimented on by a psychopath who thinks he has a right to everyone's lives. My brother went under his knife, too."

"What did he do to him?"

"I don't know."

Faye bit her lip, looking down. "He must be strong. Ares doesn't bother with the ones that aren't."

Jay was in the throne room tonight. If things had gone terribly wrong—

Steven groaned, running his hands over his face. Gently, they were pulled away, revealing Faye's strange eyes.

"Is there another way out of here?"

Steven shook his head. "I figure we'll stay until the executioner shows, I shoot him, and we find out what happened to everyone else."

Faye nodded once, settling against him again.

Steven breathed in her scent, savoring the warmth and pressure of her body against his.

Her breath picked up, fingers digging just a fraction.

Steven swallowed.

"We should try the hatch again," he murmured. Faye peeled away, looking at him.

And then at his lips.

Steven looked away.

"You're a Blood Challenger," she said.

"Yes."

Faye's brows rose. "It breaks Tyrnnthian Code to kill sworn Blood Challengers."

"Would this stop Ares' butcher?"

Faye rested her head on her knees. "It should."

"Well, if I miss my shot, I'll mention it."

Steven knelt before the hatch, his thigh pressing against Faye's, heat coursing through him. It was an effort to focus, digging his fingers inside the stone lip and heaving *up*—

He needed to get Faye out. If they ran into Ares' butcher, Steven didn't know if he could manage to keep himself and the princess alive.

He didn't trust anyone anymore.

Pain radiated up his fingers and arms.

He needed to find Jay. Steven's brother was alive and Steven would not lose him again.

Grace. Had she made it somewhere safe before the executioner had slaughtered everyone?

With Farran's secrets and lies, the radio silence— was the king alive, or bleeding out on the floor?

Farran had trusted Steven to take care of his sister.

Steven had failed.

Ares would take her back, and she would wed a some random, likely psychotic, general for her eighteenth birthday.

Sweat stung his eyes, red hot tension and pain weaving its way in every nerve of his body.

"Steven." Faye gripped his face in her slim hands. "Stop. There may be another way."

He retracted his fingers, blood dripping from his fingernails.

"There's a chance Ares won't take me if . . . " Faye shook her head, looking up. "Tyrnnth is very strict. Destry won't want me if I'm not—"

Steven's brows furrowed as the princess dropped her hands and held her face in them.

After a few moments, his eyes widened.

Steven cursed. "Oh, hell no. I can't."

"I don't *want* you to. We would just have to make it look like we . . . did." Faye shook her head. "If we're convincing enough, the wedding will be called off. Ares has no other reason to bring me back."

"Why haven't you done this before? If it's that simple, you could have escaped a long time ago."

"Ares told me he'd kill Farran if I stepped out of line."

With Steven's status as Blood Challenger potentially guaranteeing his life and Faye's chip removed—

"Will it work?"

"I don't know."

Those were the odds they were left with. Judging from the silence in Steven's earpiece . . .

He had to assume the worst.

Ares was alive, waiting for his general's fiancé.

"Okay." Steven swallowed, surveying the princess. After a moment, he carefully pushed a strap off her shoulder.

"There we go," he said, settling back.

She held her face in her hands before peeking through her fingers. "Really? With your history, I'm surprised you— oh, never mind."

"I don't do stuff like that."

"Well, that's good, I guess. Here, let me—" Faye's cheeks flushed as she reached for his hair. She threaded her fingers through and mussed his hair. He allowed his head to fall back an inch as he watched her.

Faye slipped her hands to his chest, Steven wondering if she sensed the shift in his breathing.

"Easy enough," he said. He attempted to muss her hair. He winced as he drew his hand back.

It looked the same.

"That's not going to cut it," she whispered.

Steven lifted her chin with a finger, her gaze settling on his lips. "And what will?"

Faye's lips were on his. She tasted like honeydew, bright and sweet.

She deepened the kiss.

He hadn't meant to draw her into his lap, but there she was, arms around his neck.

Grace had been Steven's only girlfriend once, a lifetime ago.

They had kissed once, but it had been nothing like this.

He had never done *this* before. Max Fitzgerald had strongly advised Steven to keep away from the women who attempted to lure him.

"Save it for your wife, Castellen," Max had told him, shaking his head as other fighters walked by, transient women on their arms.

"What's wrong with having a girlfriend?" Steven had pressed. Max's lips thinned, his no-nonsense gaze assessing the prizefighter.

"Well, nothing. As long as you treat her like she could be someone else's wife someday. Kid, at your age, there are high chances of that."

Max had said it with enough heart and conviction . . . Steven could still see his crossed arms and hear the good intentions in every syllable.

The prizefighter hadn't forgotten the words since.

They were in his head *now*, even as he ran his hands down Faye's back as if she were a meal and he was starving.

He was not treating the princess of New Iberia as if she were someone else's wife.

And this was Farran's *sister*.

Steven cursed, pulling away. Faye had freed the button of his pants.

"Faye, I don't—" he rasped. "I think we look convincing enough."

"I—" She drew back, shutting her eyes tight. "I'm sorry."

How long had they been in here?

Steven couldn't tell if it had been seconds, minutes, hours.

He shifted toward the door.

"What are you doing?" Faye asked.

"I'm going to find out what happened."

"But the executioner—"

"I'll deal with him," Steven said. "You're safest here. If it goes south, you wait until the military arrives."

Faye nodded. "I'll be fine. Save my brother."

"Let's hope I won't need to." Steven opened the door and crawled out. Straightening, his heart stopped dead in his chest, ice replacing the blood in his veins.

Bathed in red light, a figure leaned against the wall, a long, black scythe strapped over a shoulder, blood on the arc of metal.

"Having fun with the princess?" Ares' butcher drawled, his voice distorted by the mask over his face. With the hood, the man's face was shadowed. He stepped from the wall, pulling the scythe free in a smooth motion. "Before her wedding day, nonetheless."

Steven leveled his gun at the executioner's head.

"By law, you can't kill me. I am a sworn Blood Challenger," Steven said, his hand steady.

The executioner's laugh was hollow as he pulled back the hood, a curtain of dark hair spilling. "Likewise."

The mask pulled away, Steven knew her face as well as the scars on the backs of his hands.

"Adira," Steven breathed, his gun dropping a fraction.

The empress whipped her scythe, his gun skittering. She crossed the stall in a stride, a gloved hand wrapping around his throat as she slammed him into the wall, her blade angled for a killing blow.

"You're coming with me," she said, her voice edged in steel.

Steven could hear it then.

Ares had not removed Steven from her mind.

No stranger would look at him with such ire and *disgust* unless they had stumbled upon something like this.

Adira had been standing there for awhile.

"You said Ares would remove me from your memories. Like we had never met," Steven breathed.

Adira smiled, and it was a cruel, beautiful thing.

"He did. But for some reason, I fought back and chose to remember." Adira shoved Steven out the stall.

"Come out, Your Highness," Adira crooned. Faye did, Adira shoving her forward, too. Faye didn't make a sound, even as blood shone through her dress.

Adira's uniform included sharpened, iron nails.

The blunt end of her weapon pushed Steven forward, Faye stumbling beside him. He resisted the urge to steady her, knowing Adira was as unpredictable as she was cruel.

Steven swallowed and hoped and *hoped*, that against all odds, Farran's end of the plan had gone smoothly.

34

Everything had gone to hell.

In one moment, Farran was addressing the crowd, in the next, Grace was being dragged across the throne room floor. The entryway was lit in blood-red emergency lighting beyond the doors as they slammed shut, a lock bolting in place.

The crowd shied from the blood-stained assassin and her prey, revealing Natalia's fist wrapped around Grace's hair.

Farran found he couldn't breathe.

He hadn't realized it until he took a step forward and nearly felt his knees give out.

He masked his features into neutrality. Authority.

He was King of New Iberia.

Farran swallowed, his mouth dry, taking in the situation and weighing the odds.

Grace was covered in blood, though he couldn't say how much was her own. The crimson from her split lip and nose were certainly hers.

Farran shut off the mic pinned to his chest.

"Natalia, explain yourself," he demanded.

The assassin did no such thing, warning flashing in her crystalline eyes as she dropped Grace's limp body before the dais, turning to take a spot against the wall.

"Ares, what is the meaning of this?" Farran demanded.

Guests shrank back as Ares made his way forward.

"Your Majesty, don't you know I could ask the same of you?" Ares said, the corner of his lip lifting.

Everything happened within the span of a heartbeat.

The grate in the ceiling fell, carnage in its wake.

Shouting, screaming, fists banging on the windows.

Farran's heart stopped and started and stopped.

He looked to his guards just in time to watch blades driven through their chests. Aubrel looked down, as if he could make sense of the steel between his ribs. Farran wanted to scream, but he could not. His Captain of the Guard met his gaze.

"I'm sorry, Your Majesty," Aubrel tried to say. Farran opened his mouth, but no sound followed.

It's okay. It's not your fault. Don't be sorry, please.

Ares snapped his fingers and every blade pulled back, Farran flinching as the movement wrenched Aubrel's body backward. He swayed on his feet while the rest of the guard fell.

But when he did fall, something snapped in Farran.

He leveled his gun at Ares.

Now. He had to pull the trigger *now.*

Faye's chip was cut.

He could do it.

But the other life tied to his actions—

Farran looked at Natalia. The assassin raised her chin.

Despite what she had done to Grace, Natalia could have killed her, and she hadn't.

"Your Majesty," Ares said, drawing closer. "I believe you've talked past your script. If you're not careful, some may start to believe you love to hear the sound of your own voice. Everyone else does, so why not?"

Farran tore his eyes from Natalia.

She was going to die, and it would be his fault.

"Aren't you interested in what I have to say at all?" Ares

gestured to himself, brows rising.

Now.

Sloane was dead. Aubrel was dead.

"Not really," Farran said, his finger squeezing.

Three beeps sounded in his earpiece, Farran stilling. Relief flooded him, the feeling dissipating as soon as he remembered what it meant.

Steven was in grave danger.

"Aren't you going to answer that?" Ares asked, cocking his head.

Panic, swift and sure, swept through Farran.

Ares sighed. "Natalia, you're being negligent. *Do it.*"

An inhale of breath, and—

There was a blade imbedded in Farran's forearm, his mouth opening with no sound to follow. His gun dropped to the floor and he fell to his knees.

The knife was clean *through* his forearm. He hadn't been injured like this since his father's war, the pain stealing the breath from his lungs.

He was going to die today.

"This was clever," Ares said, gesturing to the room. He continued speaking, but Farran's attention was on Grace, a mere yard before the dais.

At least she was breathing.

Farran's blood soaked the ivory carpet and he wondered how long it would take for him to lose consciousness. He bit back a wince as he shifted, a wave of pain shooting up his arm.

Grace needed help. Though Natalia hadn't killed her, the assassin was still expected to maim like a servant of Tyrnnth.

Ares would order her to do far worse before the end. And the end—

That was what Farran feared the most.

Perhaps they would all die tonight, and that would be it.

"Grace," Farran beckoned. She lifted her head and looked at

him, pain dulling her eyes. She shook her head weakly.

It was over.

And just when Farran thought it couldn't get any worse, the throne room doors opened to reveal Ares' executioner.

Emmaline's murderer now bore Steven and Faye.

35

Steven wasn't sure where to look first.

There were dead guards all over the floor, replaced by armed strangers. To Steven's right, blood and carnage—

That was *Sloane*. Bile rose in Steven's throat and he turned his attention to the end of the room.

Ares stood before the dais, a viper's smile on his face.

Farran was on the floor, a blade *through* his forearm.

The king's face paled, his eyes wide as he took in the sight of Steven and Faye, Ares' butcher at their back.

Adira had pulled the mask up and drawn her hood, making her unrecognizable again. Steven wasn't sure why she bothered.

Grace was collapsed before the dais, her head rising to look over a shoulder. Blood dripped from her mouth and nose, but from how she looked, Steven knew there were injuries he couldn't see.

Steven knew death would be a reprieve for the rest of the evening and was half-tempted to turn on Adira just to end his misery.

Still, he kept walking.

For his friends.

"Mr. Castellen, I'm glad you could finally join us. Where have you been?" Ares' eyes drifted to Faye as they approached, the humor disappearing from his face. His lips tightened.

"Executioner, speak," he demanded. Adira shoved Steven and Faye to the side of the dais.

Adira angled her head, studying Steven, her eyes just visible above her mask and beneath her hood. Whatever her attire was made of seemed to absorb light, the material blacker than a moonless night.

The cut of her suit hid every curve, embossed feathers covering the surface. Steven ran his eyes up and down, narrowing them as he met her gaze.

She was a stranger, a killer. Nothing remained of the empress and friend he had known before.

Adira turned away.

"I found them in an escape room with a faulty door," Adira said, her voice distorted. Ares' jaw clenched as he approached, studying Steven and Faye.

"What the hell did you do to General Chevalier's fiancé?"

Steven had never seen Ares truly mad. The prizefighter raised his chin, interlacing his fingers with Faye's. Ares sneered, his eyes meeting Steven's.

"Fix your pants, Castellen. You look foolish."

Steven's face heated, his jaw clenching. Ares turned away and Steven subtly fixed his button, wondering if the room could see the flush on his face and neck.

Wondered what Jay made of it, Farran—

Steven looked to the king, still knelt and bleeding on the floor. Farran and Grace watched with wide eyes, the king's jaw slack, his eyes searching his sister.

Oh, Steven and Faye's illusion had worked *too* well.

Steven willed his friends to read the truth in his eyes, but they wouldn't look at him.

"Well, now that everyone's here, let's get this over with," Ares said.

Ares picked the microphone off Farran's chest, clapping his hands once as he took in his captive audience.

"It seemed some Scalbearers visited tonight," Ares said. "Not to worry, though. My executioner took care of them. If you have a weak stomach, I advise you to look away from the gates when you depart."

Steven resisted the urge to stir.

A glance toward the king showed devastation in and out of his eyes in a blink. Past the king's shoulder, that was Aubrel, blood staining his pressed uniform.

Steven couldn't begin to imagine what Farran was feeling.

His sister, seduced. His Captain of the Guard, dead.

A longtime, family-friend, in pieces.

His heart, bleeding three feet out of reach.

Not to mention Farran was bleeding himself, a six-inch blade pierced halfway through his forearm.

Judging from where Natalia stood beside the dais, she had been the one to deal the blow.

Faye squeezed Steven's hand and he returned it, ignoring Adira tensing behind them.

He refused to look at her.

"Get the hell out," Farran snarled, his body shaking.

Ares angled his head. "Not before I've said my piece."

In one moment, Farran was staring down Ares.

In the next, the king had pulled the knife from his forearm, the weapon at the War Leader's throat.

Before Steven could open his mouth, Natalia had a blade imbedded in the king's shoulder. Farran cried out as he stumbled, his crown rolling.

Screams pierced the room, fists and chairs hammered the windows.

Ares strode up the dais, taking in the scene.

"I would like your attention, please. I am not finished." Ares clasped his hands behind his back.

Dark blood shone through Farran's suit jacket, his jaw clenched.

Weapons rose amongst the crowd, the room quieting.

"That's better." Ares smiled blandly. "To those who don't know me, I am Ares Valeryn, Grand Leader and War Leader of Tyrnnth." He waited a moment, bouncing between his heels and toes before continuing. "I am also King Bardolph's speech writer tonight."

Steven held his breath as the room began to murmur.

"Peace is my goal, as you heard tonight." Ares placed a hand on his chest. "Many of you may not see the full scope of my impact, but the generations to come will."

Ares slowly paced the dais, halting near its edge to meet Steven's gaze. "And they will be thanking me."

A tremor wracked Faye's body, Steven tightening his hand. The War Leader missed nothing, his eyes snapping to the movement. He grimaced and turned to the room, fists clenched behind his back.

"I will finish the work my family began generations ago," Ares said. "The gas at the beginning of the war is only toxic to people. The environment, however, will revive."

Steven watched as Farran's chest rose and fell, violence in his eyes. While the prizefighter had been watching the War Leader, he hadn't noticed Farran had managed to pull the blade from his shoulder.

It was gripped in his bloodied hand, his jaw set as he watched Ares' back. Steven adverted his eyes, not wishing to draw Ares' attention to the king.

Surely Natalia watched him, anyways. And surely Farran knew that. Steven scanned the room to find Luther Hawthorne was no longer among them.

"I am offering a fresh start. A better world. The Central

Territories are just the beginning," Ares went on. "I believe I've said enough about me. There is someone else to thank in the room tonight."

Grace reached for Farran.

Steven's stomach dropped as Ares approached the king, Farran's knife hidden.

Ares dropped to a knee and reached into a pocket. "Your Majesty, it would appear you're missing something *here.*"

Farran cried out as Ares stabbed a knife into the king's wound.

Steven jerked forward, finding Adira's scythe at his throat. When he turned his burning gaze to her, she jerked her and pressed further.

Farran pressed a hand to his shoulder and panted through his teeth, his eyes aflame.

"Not going to give up yet?" Ares said. "I doubt your aim is much to brag about now, anyways."

"You have ten seconds," Jaxin drawled. The Central Territorian War Leader stood before the crowd, arms banded over his chest.

"Generous as always, Mr. Brown," Ares replied. Jaxin ground his jaw as Ares gestured to Farran and smiled. "Ladies and gentlemen, meet my newest ally, His Majesty, Farran Bardolph, King of New Iberia."

36

Murmurs and cries rose from the crowd. Farran tried and failed to rise, bracing a hand to the carpet.

"I am, very clearly, not your ally," Farran ground out.

"Five seconds," Jaxin said to Ares.

"I'll make it clear to you." Ares lifted a brow. "If it weren't for King Bardolph, I wouldn't have three fully stocked mines. I have so many slaves, I've began sending them to Tyservn."

Steven's blood chilled as he remembered what Adira had told him a lifetime ago— the fumes on Tyservn killed non-locals so quickly, Ares had ruled foreign slaves sent to the mines to avoid the waste.

It seemed Ares did not care anymore.

"What do you mean." Jaxin was deathly quiet.

"I have your draftees, Mr. Brown! And half your country in my palm, not to mention nearly both your coasts."

"You claim such wild things," Farran said.

"Is it true?" Jaxin asked.

Farran's eyes guttered, his mouth opening before closing.

The truth. Farran needed to tell the truth.

He blinked twice. "I—"

"It's nothing to be ashamed of, Your Majesty. It would have been a difficult decision for anyone," Ares said. "Even more so for a man of honor and loyalty, such as yourself."

Farran's face contorted as he procured the hidden dagger and threw it.

The knife stuck in the wall beside Ares' neck. The War Leader kept his gaze on the king, smirking.

"Ah, dear Farran," Ares said. "Almost, but not enough. I'm sure you're used to that by now."

The king lunged.

"No," Steven shouted, but it was too late.

Natalia had a blade in Farran's thigh and he stumbled, falling to his knees before Ares.

Steven's chest was tight as he could do nothing but watch. He barely registered Adira's scythe pressed to his neck.

"What do you think? Is he guilty?" Ares asked the crowd. "None of you know where your people went. I do. New Iberia was in charge of transportation, following King Bardolph's orders. His Majesty's Second has been dead for a year now, your king left unchecked during your most vulnerable time as a country."

Murmurs rose and Ares regarded the room.

"Well, there you have it." Ares clapped his hands and descended the dais. A pale-faced Farran seethed behind him, his chest rising and falling, hair askew.

"Where's your proof," Jaxin ground out. Ares paused before him.

"All in here, Mr. Brown." Ares reached into his suit jacket before handing Jaxin a folder.

"Where's Luther?" Steven asked. The words hung in the air, the room quieting. Ares turned toward Steven, his lips tightening into a sad smile.

"Concerned for your competition? How considerate," Ares said. "Luther is outside stringing bodies on the gate."

Steven narrowed his eyes, but Ares turned away. He looked down and adjusted his leather gloves before taking in the room. "I guess I've said everything I need to . . . "

Ares' gaze paused on **Grace**.

"About the girl," he **said** distantly, his eyes tracking Grace as she cleared the final step to Farran. "I am not sure what you do in your country, but Natalia caught her sneaking around dressed as one of your enemies. While the others were killed, my son's assassin spared this one. I believe a traitor careless enough to find themselves caught should not be allowed to live comfortably after."

"The hell are you talking about?" Jay demanded. Jaxin placed a hand on the convict's chest.

"No," Farran said. "You can't do that, she is my—"

"Zakkai!" Ares called.

Steven hadn't even noticed him amongst the crowd, but there he was, stalking forward.

"Yes, Grand Leader Valeryn."

Ares jerked his chin. "Your turn."

Steven took a step, Adira's scythe biting his skin.

He needed to fight for **Grace**, protect her, do *something*.

Anything.

But Steven did not. He **did** nothing but feel his lungs constrict and heart race as he watched Grace's hands ripped from Farran's face.

Did nothing as Zakkai wrenched her away.

Farran roared, Grace's legs kicking, her scream cracking something in Steven.

Blood slid down Steven's throat as Adira pressed her weapon. Zakkai dragged Grace out the doors, the bolt echoing through the room.

Steven looked toward **Ares** to find him watching back.

"I will kill you," Steven promised.

The scythe cut deeper. How far would Adira go?

Steven almost wanted to test her limit.

Part of him hoped she didn't have one.

Ares angled his head, smiling.

"You can try," Ares said. His smile disappeared as he opened his suit jacket. "Oh, one more thing."

Ares pulled a handgun free. "Thanks to you, Steven, I don't have a use for these anymore."

It happened in less than a second.

A bullet for Natalia.

A bullet for Faye.

***

There was blood on Steven's face, his neck.

People rushed for the doors, now open wide.

Steven could barely hear the chaos over the ringing in his head.

His sister was dead, her body collapsed on the floor.

Steven was vaguely aware he was on his knees, a hand settling on his thigh and squeezing weakly.

He looked to the side.

Faye's eyes were half-lidded, her breath rasping.

Alive. She was still *alive*. Steven blinked back the haze, his body shaking as he rose and picked her up off the floor.

Steven watched as a mob descended on Farran, the prizefighter swaying before righting himself.

"You're bleeding," Faye whispered, her eyes on his neck. She slumped in his arms.

"Jay!" Steven screamed, his voice nearly unrecognizable. He could feel something hot and sticky running down his neck as he searched the crowd. Jay appeared, shoving toward him.

"Save Farran. Please," Steven begged.

Jay's brows knit together. "Who's going to save you?"

"Myself." Steven was moving. He ran for the medical wing until the walls began to warp and cave in around him. In his next breath, everything went black.

37

There was a vice around Farran's chest.

All he needed was for someone to tighten it enough for his bones to break and heart to burst. Death would be a mercy, and he knew he was a coward for craving it.

Curses and insults were screamed over him and his body broke under boot and fist.

He couldn't help the sound that came out of his mouth as his rib cracked under the barrage.

He was a traitor, a liar, a thief.

There was blood filling in his mouth, but he couldn't turn his face to spit it out.

Perhaps he would drown.

A shout, and the mob scattered.

Farran turned and spat as the pair of boots moved from the sides of his face. His body shook as he tried to rise, blood spurting from his shoulder, forearm, thigh—

A broken noise escaped his throat and he collapsed. He looked to where Grace had been moments before.

Zakkai had taken her.

Ares had ordered it.

Nobody had stopped them.

Farran tried to rise again, his vision blurring.

"Easy there, Your Majesty." Steven's brother. Farran met the man's cobalt gaze. "Medics are coming. It'll be alright."

Farran laughed.

He laughed and laughed and laughed, his head dropping to the carpet soaked with his own blood.

People lied at the most inconvenient times. Did they know one could see through it? That when someone lied, they gave it away with their eyes?

"Is my sister alive?" Farran asked, his eyes shut.

He'd endure that lie. He waited for Jay to give it to him.

But Jay never did.

38

Jay watched Jaxin pace before the hospital room window, running his hands through his hair.

It was a wonder the War Leader still had hair.

Jay and his coworkers were taking bets on when Jaxin would bald, having ripped it all out from his job.

It was well past two in the morning.

Farran and Faye were still undergoing surgery.

Steven had since been patched up, sedated and moved to his room on the seventh floor.

Jay shook his head, a muscle feathering in his jaw.

Steven had a lot of nerve showing up like that.

Really, what the hell?

And Farran had a *sister?*

Jay now understood how Ares had been able to force Farran's hand, if Ares' claims were true. Jay wasn't sure he could have allowed Steven to die, even to save an entire country.

The king wasn't a bad man. But Jay had decided he wasn't a very good one, either.

Farran had lied to them.

Jay hung his head into his hands.

Jaxin Brown would have Farran killed.

Steven would live. He had to, for the Blood Challenge. If Jay's brother managed to survive the ordeal, life would never be the same.

Even if Tyrnnth was full of sadists, Faye had been betrothed to another man. For Steven to step in and—

Jay shook his head, hands splaying over his thighs.

He had spent the evening taking bodies off the gates.

Nobody had asked him to, but he didn't want Steven to try and do it before Farran woke.

Despite the countless times Jay had washed his hands since, there was still blood underneath his fingernails.

39

Farran woke in his bed, hazy morning light on the ceiling.

Yesterday could have been dismissed as a nightmare if not for the dressings on his body. One on his shoulder, another on his forearm. Underneath the sheet, another around his thigh.

He wriggled his fingers. Sore, but functioning.

Natalia always knew where to hurt someone without harming them for life.

She was dead.

Farran wondered if he should have felt more for her loss, but found he couldn't feel much at all, as if reality hadn't truly up to him yet.

He was shirtless, and he did not feel steady.

"Welcome back to the land of the living, Your Majesty."

Farran started and sat up, finding Jaxin Brown at his kitchen table, though the War Leader wouldn't look his way.

Farran inhaled. "Is my sister alive?"

"Yes."

A knot loosened in Farran's chest.

"You have two options, Your Majesty," Jaxin said, his eyes on the knife in his hand. "You can either pay the debt now, or pay it enduring what my people went through."

Jaxin's eyes flicked up. "It's your choice." He stuck his blade into the table. "So what will it be?"

Farran sighed. One option was considerably easier.

The knife was sharp and Farran would be dead in minutes, at worst. But in one of Tyrnnth's mines . . .

Ares had not been honest with Farran about the amount of people he had shipped over.

Now they were to aid their enemy until their bodies gave out.

Because of Farran.

Because he had been *weak*.

Farran dragged his eyes to Jaxin, loosening a breath. "I must suffer as they did."

"Good." Jaxin plucked the knife and rose, striding for the door.

"On one condition."

Jaxin stopped at the door.

"I want Grace Fitzgerald safe. Allow me a week to see to it before I'm sent to the mines."

"As long as you're dead in the following, I don't care."

The War Leader took his leave and Farran settled onto his bed, eyes shut.

A week was too long. A day, too much. An hour—

With Zakkai, anything more than a minute . . .

Farran wasn't sure when he began crying.

40

Steven's bedroom door was open.

He watched as his brother perused his kitchen, cooking something. The coffee pot bubbled, a fry pan hissed. Jay looked up and shook his head.

"I knew if I made coffee and bacon, you'd wake up."

Steven fell back and covered his face with a pillow.

"You're so predictable sometimes," Jay went on, his voice muffled. Steven pressed the pillow further.

"Except—" Jay's voice was closer now. Steven hissed as the pillow was plucked away from his face. " . . . when you decide to rut around with Farran's sister. And what the hell for? A dude fell through the ceiling, all the guards got *impaled*, and Farran and Grace—"

"We didn't do anything," Steven cut in, his voice hoarse. "Faye said if we made it look like we did, Ares wouldn't take her back."

"Yeah. Instead he shot her."

Steven shrugged. "Yeah, but she wasn't wrong, though."

"Do you hear yourself?"

Jay dropped the pillow to the floor and dragged the duvet off Steven's bed as he walked out. Steven sighed at the ceiling.

"It's time to face the day, brother," Jay said.

Steven met Jaxin in the dining hall.

"Afternoon," Steven greeted, Jay breezing through the door behind him. Jaxin nodded toward the convict before meeting Steven's gaze.

"Afternoon," Jaxin drawled.

Steven took the seat across the War Leader, Jay seating beside his brother.

Hollows had formed underneath Jaxin's eyes, his russet hair dull and tied at the nape of his neck. Though still dressed as sharp as he had been the night before, Central's War Leader looked tired.

"King Bardolph has decided to pay the life debt he owes," he said. Steven withheld the urge to look at Jay, who hadn't mentioned it.

"And His Majesty chose well." Jaxin leaned back. "I am here to ask what you think you deserve, Steven?"

Jay tensed.

"I pay the price when my time comes," Steven said. He wasn't sure what Jaxin knew.

Did he know Steven had withheld information?

Maybe Grace had cracked.

Maybe Farran had.

It didn't matter now.

"How could you so willingly betray your homeland?" Jaxin was on his feet, hands braced on the table.

"Ares was supposed to die last night. Luther would rule just fine without him," Steven said. "Farran would have been alright the moment we had his sister—"

"But Ares knew what you were doing a mile away, and had planned on it," Jaxin cut in, his eyes dark. "You were predictable, foolish."

Steven tapped his fingers along the table.

He should leave.

Certainly Jaxin had nothing more to say to him.

The prizefighter rose, Jaxin's eyes simmering.

"You have nothing to say?" Jaxin demanded.

No wonder Jaxin and Jay got along so well.

"Not particularly," Steven replied, tucking his chair back into the table. Nothing he would say would change Jaxin's mind, and he was too tired to try and prove himself.

He had failed in many ways, but hadn't in others.

Of course he would try to free his best friend's sister, ensuring his friend could no longer be used as the enemy's puppet.

If Steven and his friends had succeeded, New Iberia could have continued to offer aid. Central needed anything they could get.

Steven doubted Jaxin would agree with a thing he said.

Jay shifted to look at Steven. "I was hoping to talk before I go. About Grace."

"Yes," Steven said distantly. "We should."

"Haven't you done enough?" Jaxin seated himself. He crossed his arms over his chest and leaned back. "I would leave her be. I can assure you, she will be well cared for."

Steven braced his hands on the table. "I saw Zakkai drag her out as she screamed and kicked. I'm sure you can find it in you to see why I don't agree."

Jaxin shrugged. "At least she'll get what she deserves."

Steven moved before he could think, over and across the dining table, his fingers wrapping around Jaxin's inked throat.

The War Leader kicked Steven off, both of them tumbling to the floor. Steven pinned Jaxin and landed two blows before Jay pried him off.

Jaxin cursed as he rose, wiping blood from his face as he watched Steven.

Jaxin nodded to Jay. "I've had enough. Let's go."

Jay released Steven, pausing to brush a piece of lint off his shoulder. Jay took a step back, regarded Steven, and turned toward

Jaxin.

The convict's fist connected with Jaxin's jaw, the War Leader nearly knocked off his feet. Jaxin straightened after a string of curses, eyes narrowed as he studied Jay.

His nostrils flared, both freely bleeding now.

"And what the hell was that for, Castellen?"

Jay lifted his chin. "If you talk about Grace like that again, I won't hold back next time."

The War Leader ran a hand along his jaw before nodding. He made his way to the door. "Your services are no longer required, Cassius."

The door shut with a resounding click.

Jay turned to Steven. "That kind of felt nice."

"To punch your boss in the face?"

Jay smiled. "Grace would have wanted it that way."

Steven laughed. "In what world?"

"You tried to choke him," Jay noted.

"I guess I did."

⁂

Steven found himself at Farran's study doors, pulling at the locked knobs. After a couple minutes, he was at the king's suite door.

The door opened to reveal Farran in an untucked shirt, a sling, and a crutch propped underneath his good shoulder.

Steven took in the bruises on Farran's face before pasting on a bland smile. "How are you?"

If this was what the king's face looked like, his body was likely a topography map of contusions.

Farran's own people had done this.

"What you see is a good representation of how I feel." The king tried to smile. "Please, come in, Steven."

Farran's suite was a bedroom, a small walled kitchen to the

right, and a bathroom with a hidden personal escape.

To the left, a four-poster bed took up a fourth of the room, bedecked in ivory and cobalt.

"How patriotic," Steven said.

"It's traditional." Farran ran a hand down his neck. "Though my room is not. I picked this one out myself."

Steven walked to the wall of windows, velvet curtains neatly tucked and tied between each.

"I think I prefer your style in the cottage."

"As do I," Farran said distantly. Steven turned to find the king staring at the ocean. He blinked, meeting Steven's gaze. "Would you like to see the best part."

The king approached a large painting next to the bed. He held the frame's edge and pulled, revealing a brightly-lit room. The king disappeared into it, Steven following.

The small space was surrounded by curving windows, save for the bedroom wall, which housed a stocked bookshelf.

"Now I know where Grace was every time I couldn't find her in the castle," Steven muttered. "She probably stayed the night just to watch the stars."

"Sometimes, yes."

Grace. Steven's mind replayed her being wrenched away and dragged across the floor.

Your turn, Ares had said.

Farran leaned against the bookshelf.

"She must be rescued," he said quietly. "Zakkai is rumored to be as unpleasant as his father."

Steven let loose a breath and crossed his arms, looking northeast.

Adira's homeland lay nearly three thousand miles from them.

Steven could have sworn it felt farther today.

He hadn't told anyone Adira was Ares' executioner. He wasn't sure why. When Faye recovered, perhaps she would reveal it.

Steven vowed to tell Farran if she didn't. Sometime.

They had different things to discuss now.

Steven turned to find Farran seated, his head in his hands.

"Jaxin spared you," Steven said.

"Yes," Farran said. "He gave me a choice this morning; die then and there, or die in Tyrnnth's mines. To suffer as his people did."

"You're going to the mines."

Farran looked up, his eyes shadowed. "I don't really have a choice."

"You can make a difference here. You can't make a difference in the mines. You'll work and then you'll die."

"I believe that is the point, Steven." Farran sighed. "Besides, I am no longer worthy of my crown, my people. I did not know— didn't know how many people I had sent away."

Farran rubbed his face with his hands.

Steven frowned. "Well, we would have fallen by now if you hadn't stepped in. If you apologize, maybe—"

"I've done enough," Farran said sharply, dropping his hands. "My people will soon hear of what I have done and have me cast aside."

The ire in the king's eyes— it was not for Steven.

It was towards the king himself.

Farran looked down. "If I leave of my own accord, I can at least keep a shred of dignity."

A knock sounded at the door.

The king shouldered his crutch and made for his bedroom, Steven following. Farran opened the door and Steven smiled at the familiar faces on the other side.

"Jay . . . and friend," Farran said slowly. "How might I help you gentlemen?"

Sebastian grinned beside Jay. "An honor, Your Majesty. Hi, Steven."

Jay smirked and angled his head. "I hope you're both ready to continue your law-breaking streaks."

———

Steven was grateful Jay had been fired.

The convict had sent for Sebastian, claiming they needed a fisherman's expertise for Grace's rescue.

They had a week until Farran sacrificed himself to Tyrnnth's mines.

Jay was doing his best to convince Farran otherwise, sharing his experience behind enemy lines.

Steven hadn't realized the extent of his brother's torture.

Before the mines, Tyrnnth had cut him open and poked and prodded, the experiments never including pain medication. Some days Jay woke without a voice, having lost it screaming the day before.

Sometimes Ares removed Jay's memories only for them to come back in his nightmares.

It made Steven sick.

"Why did he experiment on you, specifically? I was told you had nearly died at the front," Farran said.

Jay shrugged. "I can breathe their poison. Ares must have figured I was a new breed to experiment on."

"Like Steven."

Jay nodded. "Yeah, he can breathe it, too."

Farran's brows drew together and he opened his mouth to speak, but Jay went on.

"There were times I was not . . . myself. I think Ares is developing a way to capture someone's body." Jay flexed his fingers in and out. "I had a dream last night. I could hear his voice in my head, and my body moved of *his* accord. Not mine."

"That happened here?" Farran asked.

Jay shook his head and met the king's gaze. "No, in my dream. I was underground again."

"I see," Farran said, his jaw tense. He relaxed a fraction and studied Jay, as if looking for something. "And despite all this, Ares let you go."

Jay smiled. "Only when I was as good as dead. I don't think Ares expected me to remember, let alone live."

"Dalmar found him first," Sebastian said, shifting on the edge of the bed. "He brought him to Zahara and she patched him up. I distracted the guards so they wouldn't—" Sebastian shook his head. "It was a mess, but he lived."

"Mind control," the king said quietly, as if to himself. "Ares is far more twisted than I gave him credit for."

"He's been semi-successful with altering memories," Jay said. "Even if it hadn't worked on me, I know it's— I know there are records where it's worked for years."

Steven brushed a hand over the wound on his throat.

It would scar.

A match to his entire experience with the empress.

Jay's attention snagged on Steven's fingers before he could slip his hand into his pocket.

"How are you faring, Your Majesty?" Sebastian asked.

Steven ignored the question in Jay's eyes and instead looked toward Farran as he ran a hand over his thigh.

"Stitched and healing. Thank you, Mr. O'Malley. Nothing important was severed."

"That's because Natalia has good aim," Jay said.

Farran sighed through his nose, his eyes on the ceiling. "Let's start fresh tomorrow, gentlemen. I am quite tired."

⁂

Steven woke to his suite walls bathed in gold.

He had been thinking of Adira before drifting off.

And Faye, Grace, Farran, Luther, the war . . .

Steven ran his hands down his face.

If Ares could infiltrate someone's mind and body—

This all needed to end before it went too far.

Lying on the floor wasn't going to fix anything, just like sleeping his life away hadn't dissipated the darkness within himself.

Some days were better than others.

He still fought the oily murk that threatened to drown him.

Though it was getting easier, he couldn't afford what even that was costing him anymore.

Steven shut his eyes and relived what happened with Adira.

Ares' executioner and butcher.

What had she done over the years serving him?

Had she done it willingly?

His heart constricted.

She did not care for him. Though she had fought Ares' mind manipulations to remember—

She had found him with Faye.

Steven groaned, dropping his hands to the floor.

What a mess.

He was nothing to Adira, and it was best this way. He was important to others. To himself.

His love life was the least of his worries.

He needed to *focus.*

Steven sat up, soaking in the last rich, golden rays before the sun dipped into the ocean.

"Sic itur ad astra," he murmured, claiming it again.

Ares would not take it from him.

Though Ares had gifted Steven strength, his mother dying for it, he had earned it for himself, too. He had worked and bled for years.

And Max Fitzgerald had honed Steven into a weapon, molding and shaping him into the man he was today.

The sun had fully set by the time Steven opened his eyes.

He would not be undone again, tossed and thrown—

No, he would toss and throe, and yield no longer.

Steven made for the rooftop training area.

Stars wheeling, his breath clouded as he struck the punching bag with fist and foot, his breathing in rhythm to an unheard song.

Time ebbed and flowed, hours passing as his blood and body sang to that song.

No more. No more. No more.

No more dead friends. No more feeling helpless.

He would have the upper hand when it was time to play the game again. He would be in control of his body, his mind.

A weapon to be honed and ready when it came time to end it all.

Steven paused, sweating and shaking, as dawn appeared. His breath ragged and throat parched, he welcomed the burning. He approached the railing to lean against it, watching as New Iberia's capital began to glow in golden morning light.

He was another day closer to the war's end, and the world he knew with it.

41

Steven, Jay, Farran and Sebastian sat at a table in Farran's room, pouring over plans.

The king had set out a platter of butter biscuits and tea, while Jay had brought a coffee pot. Steaming cups of liquids and papers littered the workspace.

Steven went over the Calterran castle blueprints once more.

While Steven's plan had been brash, Jay's had been complex. Farran's, too careful. Sebastian's, incomplete. Between the four of them, they had come up with something decent.

Now they needed to eliminate chances of things going wrong, as well as solutions for if it went awry anyways.

Steven picked up his mug, forgetting he had emptied it.

Jay rose. "I'm out, too. Want more?"

Steven frowned. "I've already had two."

Jay grabbed his mug.

Farran lowered a paper, blowing out a breath as he pinched the bridge of his nose. Steven's gaze flicked over the title.

Prince Zakkai's Harem Residence

The prince had an entire *village* for them.

Steven wondered if anyone else noticed the king's hands shaking.

"The princess is not ready for guests."

Steven drummed his fingers on the nurse's station, hoping his eyes could wring out a different answer from the woman.

He dropped his hands. "But Marge, Faye is—"

"My sister, and *off-limits* to you."

Steven whirled. "When'd you learn to walk so quiet?"

A shadow passed over Farran's eyes as he stepped forward, a muscle working in his jaw. He directed his attention to the nurse.

"I'd like to see my sister, Miss Marge."

Marge bowed swiftly and straightened. "As I've told Mr. Castellen, the princess is not ready for guests, Your Majesty."

Farran raised a brow. "Even her own brother?"

Marge looked between the men. "Let me ask."

Farran turned on Steven, jutting a finger into his chest. *"You."*

Steven held his hands up. "I recommend talking to your sister first before assuming anything."

Two seconds passed before Farran's eyes softened. He dropped his finger. "It was her idea, wasn't it? Tyrnnthians won't— *oh,* that makes sense."

"So glad you could figure that one out on your own," Steven said, earning a withering look from the king.

"Fare?"

Farran whirled. "Matching slings!" He set his crutch into motion, leaving Steven to watch from a distance.

The king took Faye's face in his hands and carefully embraced her.

No one noticed Steven slip away.

Half a week of planning, training and running, and Steven found himself on a plane with his comrades. They landed on a trade port island southeast of New Iberia before walking to the harbor.

The sky and sea wore similar shades of deep violet, the clouds and waves painted in a way that Steven couldn't stop staring.

And Jay couldn't shut up about it.

"It's getting darker. Now it's getting *more* colorful. Sebastian, do you see this? Someone take a photo. Farran, you have a phone on you. You should take a photo."

"Where is your phone, Mr. Castellen?" Farran asked.

Jay walked backward, raising a dark brow. "Oh, I have it. It just sucks. With your budget, I'm sure you have a nicer camera."

Farran sighed and paused, procuring his phone from a pocket.

Steven's eyes went wide as it flew from the king's grasp and went straight into the water.

Farran stood with his hand frozen mid-motion, watching the ripples in the water.

"Oh," he said.

Sebastian unbuttoned his flannel. "You've got to be kidding me, lads." He dove, Farran unable to stop him. When Sebastian resurfaced, he climbed out of the water and dropped the phone into Farran's palm. "Rice. We'll put it in rice."

"Thank you, Sebastian," Farran said quietly.

The Hymnlynder shook his wet hair and resumed walking, his shoes squelching with every step.

It wasn't long before Jay pointed out a Calterran fishing vessel and the men boarded. Sebastian started up the engine as Farran, Steven and Jay settled.

Steven freshened up in the bathroom before finding Farran and Jay in the bunk room. Jay was already in his cot with the curtain pulled closed, Farran neatly arranging his own bed.

Jay's backpack, tossed. Farran's rucksack, carefully set aside.

Steven smiled and approached, setting his backpack beside Jay's.

His smile didn't last. He surveyed the threadbare blanket and pillow in the bunk above Jay's. A small porthole sat in the wall, the mattress completely surrounded by dark wood.

A casket.

"Are you claustrophobic, Steven?"

The prizefighter turned to find Farran watching him from his bunk, his head propped up on a hand. The boat rocked and swayed, Sebastian bringing them into open ocean.

With the movement and engine noise, at least he would fall asleep quickly.

"No, I—" Steven's mind flashed to the bunks in the trenches, wood creaking as artillery bombarded them.

Steven loosed a breath. "I guess I've never lived on a boat."

"I see."

"You?"

Farran nodded slowly. "I spent a few weeks on a warship circling Iniqua."

"You never talk about your time at war."

"Neither do you."

Fair enough. Steven nodded at the floor, pulling the light cord before taking the step to crawl into his bunk.

"Steven."

The prizefighter paused, his eyes adjusting to the dark. Farran's brows were drawn.

"I know we spoke earlier, but I need clarity," Farran said, his voice low. "You didn't, in fact, sleep with my sister?"

"I did not. She said if we made it look like it happened, Ares wouldn't bring her back to marry someone."

Farran watched Steven for a moment before nodding. "Thank you."

Never mind they hadn't been *entirely* innocent. Though Steven was sure that conversation never needed to happen.

Steven crept into his bunk and fell into a deep sleep.

The first full day at sea went as planned.

The men were left unbothered by Tyrnnthian war ships with the Calterran flag waving at the mast, though more appeared as they drew closer to Central. By nightfall, Steven was sweating.

Tyrnnth was everywhere.

Steven tried not to think about it, averting his gaze from their hulking shadows as he tidied and coiled lines.

Jay had pulled strings for Grace's rescue mission. When Steven had inquired about his brother's connections, Jay had merely told Steven not to worry about it.

Jay had made many friends in prison.

While nearly all of them had died on the front, the families knew who he was. Jay had been the one to write them on how their sons and daughters had fought so well, for so long.

Even when they hadn't a choice in the matter.

Steven was shocked Jay had been able to work with Jaxin, the very man who had ordered all the inmates to be sent to the front at the start of war.

"Do you think we're too late?" Steven asked, stars blazing overhead, their light reflecting off the waves.

He wasn't even sure what he was asking. Too late for Grace? Or too late to save what remained of his country?

Farran's brows drew together. "I hope not."

Grace had been gone half a week.

"What did Grace . . . " Dare Steven ask? Though half the question was already out his mouth, the last moment between Grace and Farran seemed too intimate to discuss.

Farran wouldn't look away from the stars.

"She told me she loved me."

"Really?"

An arm slid over Steven's shoulder, twin to the other settling around the king's.

"Can you blame her? He's handsome, tall, rich—"

"Jay," Steven warned.

The convict gazed upward. " . . . has war-hero status . . . drinks tea, reads books—" Jay made a face. "I think he's everything on her list, plus some."

Jay was kind not to mention Farran's faults.

Which were now many.

"I certainly couldn't make the list," Steven muttered.

"Me neither." Jay dropped his arms. "But you were her boyfriend for a week."

"Only to be labeled 'ex-boyfriend' whenever it suits her best."

A small smile graced Farran's lips. "Thank you, Mr. Castellen."

"Please, it's Jay." The convict stepped away. "And trust me, everyone's thinking it anyways."

———

Sebastian docked the boat, Steven and Jay tying off. Dressed in work pants, oil-stained shirts and tank tops, the men gained only a few glances upon hitting Calterra's slums, orange street lights flickering between the canopy of palms and tropical trees lining the dirt road.

Once inside the inn, Steven breathed easier.

So far, so good.

"You didn't practice your accents," Jay muttered, the room key jangling as he unlocked the door. Steven followed him into the small room, tossing his pack to the floorboards.

Farran stood in the doorway, lips pursed. Jay noticed.

He smiled. "Sebastian won't bite."

Farran's lips tightened, but he smiled and turned. Steven shook his head at his brother.

Jay shrugged. "He's so polite. It makes me want to be mean to him."

"What is wrong with you?" Steven slapped his arm, looking down to find a bug corpse.

Since leaving the coast, the air had become hotter and heavier.

The bugs were new. Perhaps standing in one place summoned them.

"It's hot as hell in here," Jay said, digging into his pack. He slapped his neck.

"Imagine it during the day." Steven grimaced at the holes in the window screen. "Will it be boiling or bugs?"

Jay looked at the useless screen. "Surprise me."

The men converged in the Castellen brother's room, going over the plan for the following night, bug bites and new ink on their skin by the end of it. Sebastian and Farran departed sometime well after midnight.

"Feels like we're little kids again," Steven said quietly, his voice nearly lost in the chorus of insects buzzing and frogs chirping outside.

"Tell me about it." Jay shifted. "If only Mother could see us now."

Steven smiled. A thought began to gnaw and he frowned at the slice of streetlight leaking through the curtains.

"Did you ever meet him?" Steven asked.

Jay nodded. "I did."

Steven propped his head on a hand. "Did he tell you he was my father?"

Jay was quiet a moment. "Yes. He was the one to assign me with my . . . responsibilities."

"To kill anyone with the information."

"Close enough." Jay gave Steven a small smile. "He said you would be hunted if people found out."

"Why didn't he take me with him?"

Steven could have spent the rest of his adolescence in King Ridgeway's palace. Instead, he had spent it in a spare room in Grace's manor. With Jay incarcerated, their mother dead, Harrin killed— it was either that or the orphanage.

Though Steven could have turned into an entirely different person. Without Max's training, guidance and discipline—

The man had loved Steven like a son.

Max was the closest thing Steven had to a father, and would ever, he assumed, after watching Eric Ridgeway's character unfold.

"I don't know," Jay said, smiling at the ceiling. "If Eric had taken you, you would have missed out on getting caught kissing Grace on the couch, and—"

"Ah hell, don't bring that up." Steven covered his face with his hands. "I should have let Farran kick you out."

"Oh please." Jay laughed. "I would like to see him try."

"So confident, as always." Steven dropped his hands. "We'll arrange a fight when we get back."

42

Intricate buzzes, whistles and calls filtered through the open window, a breeze blowing the curtain aside to reveal a hazy, pink sky.

Steven slowly rose and slipped out the door, Jay still clutching a pillow to his chest.

The man's back was covered in tattoos. A pair of circling tigers in the center, latin phrases on his left shoulder, roman numerals on his right. A pair of daggers. Coordinates.

Jay had boasted of his prison tattoos to Adira once. Steven now understood why.

The exit beside Steven's room led to a metal spiral staircase. As he opened the door, birdsong and the scent of florals greeted him, cool air kissing his skin.

Bright, flowering trees lined the gated backyard below. Steven leaned over the rail, taking in the scent, breeze, and small honey-colored birds flitting about.

At the top of the stairs, he found himself on a flat rooftop strewn with potted plants, a laundry rack set in the corner. He grabbed a chair and propped it to face the ocean.

Birds dressed in red congregated in the backyard, their calls joining the sound of the town waking up.

Steven had thought they had been in the slums last night.

Seeing it now, it was simply a neighborhood. Fishermen headed to the dock as the clatter of pots and pans worked their way through open windows. A warm sun appeared over the water, bathing rooftops in gold and alighting the sails of boats preparing to leave the harbor.

The war seemed far from here.

For a few minutes more, Steven pretended he didn't know better.

Zahara arrived with breakfast.

The men had since found Steven on the roof, propping chairs in a semi-circle to join him.

Jay wrapped Zahara in a hug and pulled back. "You didn't."

"You literally asked." Zahara smiled and handed him the bags. When she caught sight of Farran, her eyes widened. "Who's this?"

"Oh my gosh, she doesn't recognize you," Steven said under his breath, turning to Farran. With the king's worn work pants, stained top, sling and crutch, every fading bruise on display, it shouldn't have surprised Steven.

"Zahara," Sebastian whispered. Zahara smiled at her friend, frowning as he, undoubtedly, mouthed something behind his raised hand.

Her eyes flared, dropping to a knee. "Your Majesty, I apologize I—"

"Oh, no. Please don't," Farran said. "It's quite alright. I am not supposed to look like myself, and am no longer King of New Iberia anyways."

"What?" Zahara squeaked, looking up. Jay offered a hand, the woman taking it. "Did someone try to kill you."

Farran smiled. "They're not quite finished yet, but yes."

"But—"

"A story for another time," Jay said, pulling a chair forward.

"Okay," Zahara said, seating herself. "Are you . . . okay?"

Farran smiled. "Yes, just fine. Thank you."

"Well, good. I'm glad, Your Majesty." Zahara smoothed her skirt and looked at Jay. "Are you guys sure you want to pull this sort of stunt? I am nearly one hundred percent certain that girl is *fine.*"

Jay draped an arm over the back of her chair and imitated a buzzer noise, looking into her eyes. "Wrong. She is not *fine*. What makes you say that?"

Zahara shrugged. "I see her everyday."

"We need her back," Steven pressed. "Jay told us you could help."

"I can," Zahara said slowly. "If you know her on a level I don't, and need her away from Calterra, I can help."

⸎

Steven and Jay, dressed as servants, slipped into the Calterran palace as the shift changed for the evening.

They followed the staff toward the hearty scent of roasted chicken and spices emanating from the kitchen. Heads down, they prepared cheese and wine. Steven looked up from under the brim of his hat to watch Jay wipe sweat from his brow.

The convict had covered his arms in a long-sleeved shirt, makeup slathered over his hand tattoos. His eyes met Steven's as he continued arranging the tray.

Steven pretended to grab the bottle of wine he had already smuggled in.

With the flurry, no one gave the men a second glance as they departed, walking down the rich, orange-carpeted halls, sunset light bathing the palace in tangerine hues.

Where's the brute? Steven texted Sebastian.

He's walking the coast, heading your way. Grace is with him.

Sebastian manned a rowboat along the palace, taking tabs of

everything. With boats everywhere in the bay, no one would take note of the extra fisherman.

Jay knocked before slipping into the eldest prince's quarters, Steven on his heels. The suite jutted over the water, offering a view of the dusky, tropical sea, Calterra's mainland in the distance. To Steven's right, a kitchen. To his left, a bedroom.

They swept into the bedroom, Jay setting the tray and wine on the bed while Steven unlocked a window, laying a coil of rope behind a curtain. A translucent line dropped to the water, attached to the rope.

With the dying light their only witness, the brothers exited.

Cheese in the trap, Steven texted.

Somebody shouted in Calterran.

Steven and Jay turned to find a finely dressed man with tan skin and thinning hair approach, his brows drawn. Jay replied in Calterran, Steven remembering to dip his head under the brim of his hat.

The man grabbed Steven's shirt, drawing the prizefighter's gaze. The Calterran's eyes widened. "Centrallian. You are *assassins.*"

Steven knocked the man out, his body collapsing.

"Quick, find a closet," Jay said.

We may have a problem, Steven texted.

Steven sent a photo of the man stuffed in a closet, the stranger's hair and clothes askew.

Is he dead? Farran asked.

KO'd. Steven looked up and shared a look with his brother, their strides quickening.

They were on borrowed time.

———— ❦ ————

Jay handled curious servants with smooth, practiced lies.

The brothers claimed to be new hires, requested to join the event for the experience and extra hands.

The Head of Servants was absent this particular night due to the use of another connection Jay had utilized. Mild food poisoning, he had claimed.

An open-air wall surrounded the Calterran throne room. Past the beams, the scent of exotic flowers and crash of waves wended their way in. Steven cast a glance to the darkened view as he set plates along a table.

Sebastian would be ferrying Farran and himself to the prince's bedroom soon. Despite the king's injuries, he had insisted, claiming he had done much more in much worse conditions before.

Steven believed it. He wasn't sure he could have handled the beating Farran took the night of the summit the way the king had. To pull a knife free and *use* it— let alone throw one within inches of an intended target.

Steven looked up to find Jay setting plates on the other side of his table, a sheen of sweat on his tan brow.

Another reason Sebastian hadn't been allowed inside; his skin and hair would have given him away immediately. With Steven's hair hidden by his cap, his skin was just within the requirements of not standing out *too* much.

And even then, Steven had still been caught.

With Jay's complexion, dark hair, and experience speaking Calterran, he was the most important asset tonight.

A clock chimed, Steven joining the servants along the wall. Back straight and chin high, he watched as the great doors opened.

The King of Calterra was the first to walk in.

Saber Vincere.

The man looked as though he had been handsome once, cruelty and bitterness hardening his face. His lips were a thin line as he surveyed the room, his muscled arms on display in a sleeveless tunic.

There were rumors the king hadn't risen to power honestly, but had schemed and manipulated his way there.

King Vincere sat on his throne, twin carved boas poised above his head.

The king's sons filed in, each appearing vastly different from the last, confirming Steven's suspicions on whether or not each had been borne of different women.

Zakkai appeared. With his size, mane of hair, the way he carried himself— while the other sons were princes, Zakkai already appeared a king.

He was also the only prince with a woman on his arm.

Grace.

Dressed in a form-fitted, orange dress, she walked at the prince's side. A pair of gold chain earrings glittered beneath her pinned hair, her face tan and rosy, the apples of her cheeks brushed in gold dust.

As she ascended the dais, Steven's breath caught.

Grace had two eagles tattooed down her back. Talons interlaced, twining and twisting as they fell from the sky— one outlined in red, the other in black.

The golden eagle was Zakkai's personal crest.

It hadn't been a full week, and she was already branded as his *property*. It was an effort of will for Steven to appear unbothered, but he couldn't give into his anger yet.

He unknit his fists and exhaled.

Jay brushed Steven's shoulder, Steven directing his gaze to the woman strolling along the line of servants.

"Let me do the talking," Jay breathed.

The woman reached him, looking Jay up and down. With a nod, the woman stepped before Steven.

He would be the one to worry about, with the media's coverage on him.

The woman's eyes narrowed as she spoke in her native tongue.

Jay replied. The woman snapped at Steven, jerking her chin before resuming her survey.

"What did she say?" Steven whispered. Jay leaned forward, his hands folded before him.

"She says you should have been at the piano by now."

Steven cursed under his breath.

"You knocked out their pianist," Jay said, his eyes darting to the woman as she cast a glance over her shoulder. "You can play. Now *go.*"

Jay shoved Steven, the prizefighter stumbling to catch his balance and straighten his clothes.

Steven would throttle his brother later.

The prizefighter pulled his cap lower. Even with the piano tucked against the wall, the chances of him being recognized were much higher now.

Zakkai, Memphis and Grace all knew who he was.

There was a violinist beside the piano, her dark eyes snapping up as Steven took a seat at the bench.

Though her voice was lovely, Steven had no idea what she was saying. The woman's brows knit together as Steven offered an attempt at an apology.

"You are not Luis," she bit out, each word accented.

"He's sick," Steven lied. He shifted his gaze to Zakkai, now seated in a throne beside his father. Grace settled onto the prince's lap.

Steven was glad Farran was elsewhere.

He set his fingers over the keys, savoring the cool, crisp touch.

"I don't know your music. I'll follow your lead."

"You don't know the music?" she hissed, looking toward the line of royals. She muttered something in Calterran. "Follow, foreigner."

Steven nodded and steadied his breathing. He glanced at Grace, noting her drawn gaze, the prince's broad hand around her waist.

The violinist raised her chin and drew her bow and began to lay the foundation of the piece. Steven closed his eyes.

Grace was trapped. Bound to her enemy.

Steven set his fingers into motion and accompanied the violinist, their instruments dancing in sound until the song dissolved, the piece seamless.

Steven opened his eyes to find the violinist lowering her instrument, dipping her chin before looking at the dais.

The room was full.

"Greetings, subjects and guests," King Vincere said, his voice like an edged blade. "Tonight, we celebrate the rebirth of our kingdom at hand."

The king's voice faded as Steven peered from under his cap to watch the prince and Grace. She appeared physically healthy and strong— more so than when Steven had last seen her.

Maybe it was the fruit and sunshine.

The king talked about Calterra's alliance with Tyrnnth before wrapping up his speech with a toast to his heir, who was now master of another concubine. Zakkai smiled as the crowd raised their glasses and cheered, Steven's blood roaring.

He nearly missed the violinist readying for the next piece. Steven's fingers trembled as he poised them over the keys.

Grace would be safe soon.

The violinist's chin raised as she looked down her nose. She drew her bow and Steven followed.

Servants bustled in and out, courses of food served and replaced. Clinks of silverware, conversation, and crashing waves filled the spaces between songs.

Steven spared glances toward his target throughout the evening, even giving Memphis a once-over. The seventh son of Calterra had healed, his clothes tailored for his missing appendage.

Steven was glad.

Memphis had stood up to his father's alliance in his own way, and managed to survive the ordeal.

Maybe Steven could hire Natalia—

Steven nearly missed the note.

Though Natalia could have put Memphis on the throne, Ares

had killed her.

And though that line of thinking was wrong, the thought still passed through Steven's head.

Grace had always told him unwanted thoughts did not need to stay. Whenever she experienced thoughts she didn't want, she balled them up as a wad of paper and tossed them into a trash can, where the paper went up in flames as she spun in her mental office chair.

When Steven had laughed outright, she had shrugged and claimed it worked for her.

But Steven did not smash his thought into a paper ball. He held it and looked at it, as if it were a bird that had hit the window and died.

After an hour, Zakkai and Grace threaded through the crowd.

Steven jolted as a hand met his shoulder.

"The pianist is awake," Jay whispered. Steven glanced past Jay, a man storming for them.

Steven had given the man a black eye.

"Luis?" The violinist's head whipped, ponytail swinging. Her eyes narrowed. "You said he was sick."

"Sorry." Steven nearly knocked the bench over as he rose.

Jay tugged him into the crowd, the violinist left to finish the piece alone.

Steven fell into step beside his brother as they entered the servant's passage.

"I can't believe—" Jay began. He shut his mouth as they passed another servant.

They began sprinting.

Steven halted before the servant's access door to the prince's quarters.

Jay checked his phone. "It's empty. Good luck."

Steven shoved the door open. Sebastian was already hidden in the coat closet beside the suite door, Jay to remain in the servant's passage.

Steven crossed the space and entered the bedroom. As he slipped into the bedroom closet, he raised his brows at Farran. A sheen of sweat shone on the king's forehead as he nodded, exhaling.

Steven's heart hammered as he gingerly shut the closet door as the suite door opened, sandals kicking off in the entryway. Steven closed his eyes and calmed his breathing. Feet padded on the tile floor. A click, and a glow filled the bedroom.

Farran and Steven leaned toward the slats in the closet door, watching as Zakkai stalked across the room, Grace disappearing into the bathroom. A faucet started as the door was half shut.

The prince's expression was unreadable as he stood at the window, arms banded across his chest.

Steven hadn't taken into consideration the threat of Zakkai's ability to smell. Between Farran's cologne, and Steven's unsavory fragrance from the heat, he hoped the closet door would be enough to keep the prince from detecting them.

Grace entered the room, drawing Zakkai's attention.

Farran tensed, surely taking in what Steven already noted.

She was not afraid. She had let her hair loose and dressed herself in an oversized band tee, not at all concerned with the threat across the room.

"They left us wine and cheese," she mused. Zakkai followed her gaze, grunting by way of response. Grace perched on the edge of the bed, raising the bottle to read the label. "Good wine, too."

Zakkai neared the bed and sat across from her.

As soon as they drank, it would be lights out. And if they didn't drink . . . that was why all the men were nearby.

"How are you?" she asked, uncorking the bottle.

"Alright. You?" The prince's words were a low rumble.

Grace shrugged, earning a small smile from the prince. She

filled the wine glasses, eyes adverted as the prince watched her.

Zakkai cleared his throat. "I'm sorry about— y'know." The prince made a gesture with his hands and slapped his thighs. Grace huffed and shook her head.

Farran went still.

Why was she smiling? Zahara must broken her word and let Grace in on the plan, despite Jay asking her not to.

Steven fought the urge to wipe his sweating palms against his clothes. Grace held the glasses of wine and rose.

Zakkai tracked her until she was beside him, offering a glass.

"To the end of the world," she said. Zakkai lifted his glass, though his eyes remained on Grace's.

"And to its beginning again in the morning."

Steven's attention flickered to movement in the corner of his vision. Farran's hands trembled, his scar-flecked fingers curled into fists.

"Is it worth it?" Grace whispered. Zakkai's brows furrowed, Steven noting a scar cutting through one of them.

"It will be." Zakkai leaned his forehead against hers.

And she let him.

Steven wasn't sure Farran was breathing.

After more wine and a few bites of cheese, the prince and Grace's voices grew quiet.

Zakkai rubbed broad hands down his face, looking blearily at Grace. "I was going to walk you home, but I don't know if I'll make it. My brother can—"

"It's alright." Grace waved a hand. "I'll stay."

The prince sighed. "Okay." He shifted back onto the bed and smacked the spot next to him.

Steven looked at the floor as Grace willingly lied beside their enemy's ally.

It was too hot and stuffy in the closet and Steven was eager for them to pass out. And then— and then what?

Grace was fine.

She looked at Zakkai as he ran his fingers through her hair.

"Does it bother you? To pretend?" she murmured.

"No. I don't care what people think of me." The prince's words were low. Her eyes fell closed as she leaned into his touch.

"Grace." Zakkai dropped his hand and tugged her into his arms, his eyes closed.

"Hm?"

"You pretend so well, sometimes I think I might be your next act," Zakkai whispered, each word quieter than the last.

Grace was already asleep.

Steven dared a glance at Farran. The king blinked, a tear on his cheek, though his face was hard, a muscle feathering in his jaw.

Ares' words came back to Steven.

Almost, but not enough. I'm sure you're used to that by now.

Ares had known about this, somehow.

Zakkai and Grace's breathing slowed and deepened, the sedative taking a firm hold. Outside the window, the view was near black.

It would be easy to sneak Grace to Sebastian's boat now.

The only problem was, now Steven couldn't wake her to find out if she wanted to go.

And what she had said . . .

"She played me a fool," Farran whispered. "She spent two weeks, no, *three* counting the rescue team— with him, and hadn't been the same since. And when Ares gave her away, she . . . " Farran shook his head, his lips tightening.

Steven lighted a hand on Farran's shoulder to find he was shaking.

The king had really fallen for her.

Steven looked at the floor. "We don't know for sure."

Farran stepped away, covering his face with his hands.

"I do, though. I really do."

Jay texted and asked what the hold up was. Steven looked at Farran, the king appearing as though he was still trying to piece himself together.

"Do we take her?" Steven asked quietly.

Farran exhaled and shook his head, closing his eyes.

"I don't know," he breathed. "I don't— wow, what a mess. Steven, I have to go to the mines anyways. Do what you think is best."

Zahara had mentioned Grace had been happy here.

Steven had no idea she had meant it, but the evidence was on the other side of the door. He watched his childhood friend sleep in his enemy's arms and knew she couldn't know they had tried to rescue her.

Farran knew where he stood, and where he may have stood for awhile.

"Alright," Steven said, exhaling. "Let's go."

"What the hell happened?" Jay demanded, his voice a hoarse whisper as their strides ate up the inn's hallway. Sebastian kept a few paces back.

Steven slung his bag over a shoulder. "I told you."

Farran was already at the boat, warming the engine for their departure.

Steven hadn't blamed the king for wanting the distance.

The moment Sebastian had mentioned the task, Farran had volunteered, likely seeing the fisherman's offer for what it truly was: the gift of distance from Jay, who hadn't ceased to hound them.

The New Iberian king had sat on the floor of the prince's closet for several minutes before departing, leaving Zakkai and Grace unaware they had ever been there.

Steven let the men know their mission was called off; Grace was safe, and her extraction would cause more harm than help.

He had not mentioned she may have orchestrated things to go

this way. Not yet.

Jay had been furious.

When the men had met on the street afterward, Jay had nearly knocked Steven to the ground.

"What the hell are you thinking!"

The convict's snarl echoed in Steven's head, even now.

The prizefighter hadn't deigned to explain at the time, noting Farran's distant gaze.

Northeast, towards Tyrnnth.

Steven's shoes scuffed against the dirt road outside the inn. Jay grasped his brother's shoulder.

"You said you'd tell me," Jay pushed.

Steven turned and lowered his voice. "She may not be as innocent as we thought."

"What do you mean?" Jay raised a brow. The prizefighter shrugged him off and kept walking. Perhaps he had said too much already.

"I don't think she'd willingly leave," he added quickly.

"That's not my Grace."

"Mine either," Steven snapped.

"Boss, if I may," Sebastian offered. "He's telling the truth. I heard everything from the coat closet."

"I still don't believe it," Jay said, though the fight was gone from his voice. "We could have at least left a note. Hell, I could call her now—"

"No." Steven halted. Jay had his phone ready, challenge in his dark, cobalt eyes. People along the street watched. Steven lowered his voice as he glanced at shadows. "Jay, you have to trust me. She can't know we were here."

"I want to know why."

Of course he did.

Steven sighed and rolled his eyes. "She might have played Farran. Played all of us. Zakkai isn't a punishment." Steven kept his voice low. "They spent three weeks together, and she wasn't the same when she came back. Now she's willingly wearing his t-shirt to bed, oh, and willingly sleeping in his bed with him. They're buddies, probably more. She wouldn't want to know we overheard what she said tonight, and she *won't* know."

Jay's brows drew together and he slowly pocketed his phone. He looked at Sebastian, the fisherman offering a nod.

"Thank you," Jay said, "for the truth."

When they reached the boat, the engine was purring and ready to go, the king already in his cot with the curtain drawn.

43

Farran awoke before the sun gilded Evynmare in gold, before dawn painted the sky pink.

He had to.

Farran hated goodbyes.

Steven awoke early to run, so the king rose before then.

Goodbyes were permanent. If nothing was said, perhaps all would be well, and he would see his friends again. Though the king doubted it, his grip tightening on the briefcase at his side.

He was thankful for the time he had been given.

His sister was free, Steven was strong, Grace was happy.

It was more than he could have hoped for.

Farran crossed the castle entryway, turning once to look up at the filagreed ceiling and carved columns, the sweeping grand stairs.

His family had lived and ruled for two centuries, reigning with loyalty and honor. The king himself had grown here as a boy, racing up those steps with his mother, his father watching from the glass elevator as he waited, a broad smile on his handsome face.

Farran inhaled sharply. His hands trembled, but he did not know how to stop it.

His council would take care of his country, appointing a proper leader as soon as Farran left to settle his debt and pay for his crimes.

Murder.

Farran had orchestrated a way for innocent men and women to work and die for their own enemy.

He bit his lip, his brows furrowing as he looked skyward.

Maybe he deserved every bit of torture that had come his way. Deserved to have his heart ripped out just before his death sentence.

Grace Fitzgerald had looked at the Calterran prince the same way she had once looked at *him*.

Farran rubbed his face with a spare hand.

Yes, perhaps he deserved it. Whatever torture would come next would be mild compared to everything he had felt watching Grace with the prince.

She was in love with him.

Farran blew out a breath and turned from his home, the servants having already swung open the grand doors, carved with a pack of ivory wolves.

The proud, brave Bardolph crest.

Farran had dishonored it.

Though, he was alone, the pack having died the day his family had been slaughtered by Tyrnnth in these halls.

With his truck at the cottage, the limousine undergoing repairs, Farran found it ironic to find the royal hearse waiting for him.

He did not look back as he entered the vehicle, closing his eyes as they pulled out the castle drive for the king's very last time.

As the briefcase pressed into his thighs, he reminded himself that Tyrnnth's mines would be a wasteland by the time he was done with them.

His last contribution, the last chapter in his story.

He hoped it would be enough of an apology to the country he had damned. Though Farran was sure the friend whom it belonged to would never forgive him.

But Farran was beyond forgiveness.

44

The kitchen staff were quiet when Steven and Jay greeted them.

Before the men had parted ways the night before, Steven had promised Farran tea at the shooting range.

The prizefighter figured the king would want something to take his aggression out on. Though Farran seemed to prefer archaic swordplay, Steven hadn't taken up the king's offers to teach him yet.

Maybe that would be better.

He would have to ask and if Farran preferred that instead.

Steven looked over a shoulder at his brother, wondering if he could sense whatever was in the air, too. Though his eyes were sharp, he only offered a shrug.

The morning run was brutal, swift.

Running the usual haunt backwards, Steven spotted Farran's yellow pickup at the cottage as they crested the hill south of the orchard.

"I'll see you later," Steven called, gravel skittering as he slowed. The convict grunted and continued on.

Steven wiped sweat from his brow, cool spring air whipping

threadbare clouds across a pale, awakening sky.

He stretched his arms above his head as he neared, the porch creaking with each step. He knocked before letting himself in, taken aback by the silence to greet him.

The lack of warmth, the absence of the scent of freshly steeped tea.

No whisper of pages and pleasant 'good-mornings.'

"Farran," Steven called, shutting the door behind him.

It was early. If the king had stayed the night, there was potential he could still be asleep, especially after their week of—

Steven's legs weakened and he reached for the stair banister.

Farran's week was up.

But he couldn't leave without saying goodbye.

He wouldn't—

There was a letter on the table. Steven stumbled forward and tore into the envelope before grabbing the keys on the counter.

Dust plumed behind the truck as Steven went over the words Farran had written.

He was going to the mines this morning.

Steven might just catch him.

He pressed the gas pedal further, the smell of burnt rubber filling the cab. Steven rolled down the windows, his eyes narrowing against the wind assailing him. He crested the hill leading toward the airport just in time to see a sleek aircraft rise over the horizon line.

"No." Steven slammed a fist against the wheel.

He hadn't realized he'd stopped. But the truck was still, stalks of wheat whispering as Steven watched the clouds swallow the jet whole.

—⁂—

Steven took his time on the drive back.

His Blood Challenge was a week away.

Farran could survive a week in the mines.

He had to.

As long as Steven's countrymen didn't figure out who Farran was, he would live.

Steven's knuckles were white on the wheel.

A small, sick part of him whispered Farran deserved it.

No.

Steven took the thought and chucked it so hard, the trash bin in his mind nearly fell over, flames enveloping the thought before leaving it ash on the wind.

Farran would survive.

The legal consequences of his actions could come later.

He had left Steven his truck if he didn't survive the mines, his will included in the envelope.

Farran hadn't changed a word in it, despite Steven sneaking into his office months ago to get a peek at it. Despite the lack of trust Steven had shown, the king hadn't withheld a thing away he had wanted to give him.

The cottage, the unholy sum of money, his clothes—

Steven's vision blurred.

He had never revealed to Farran who he truly was, Crown Prince and heir of Vastlynd.

What kind of best friend didn't share something like that?

Steven pressed the heel of his hand into his eye. He needed to train more. *Needed* to be ready.

Because if he lost, Farran and every person in the largest slave mine in Tyrnnth would die.

If Steven couldn't end the war, Farran would cripple the enemy in the only way he could now.

45

Grace ducked further into the tub.

Even with the opaque glass shades drawn, Grace could make out the colorful shapes of boats sailing on the other side of the open-air bathroom.

Could they see her?

She didn't know, she didn't like it.

"Someone could murder you very easily in here," Grace called, scrubbing her hair. She grabbed a pitcher and poured out the suds.

"It didn't work the first time," Zakkai drawled from the bedroom. Grace stilled before leaning toward the slats, as if she could see the water directly beneath.

"Wait, really?" she asked.

Footsteps approached, Grace slinking into the tub. Zakkai knocked on the wall.

"Can we talk?"

Grace held her arms around her knees.

Not that it would hide anything.

She was in a bathing suit surrounded by bubbles.

"Now?" Grace asked.

Zakkai laughed under his breath. "That's the idea."

"Sure," Grace said, ushering more bubbles to herself. Zakkai stepped onto the porch and reigned in a smile.

"Grace," he started.

"Prince."

"Why are you wearing a bathing suit?" He was taking pains not to laugh.

"We're not married," Grace said matter-of-factly.

It was true. While she was technically the prince's concubine, she didn't intend to play the part.

Zakkai took a seat in the folding chair along the wall, leaning back.

His curls were tighter than her waves, the color burnished bronze at his scalp, sun-bleached at his chest.

She loved his hair.

She would never tell him.

The prince drew his hands behind his head.

"We could be, if you wanted." Zakkai winked. Grace rolled her eyes and looked toward the ocean, turning the slats to see clearer. Terns and gulls circled the massive bay, the mass of Calterra hazy across the water.

Zakkai meant his offer.

But Grace was too busy to get married, and had no intention of ruling an entire continent, even beside him.

Despite whatever— they had between them.

She wasn't sure what it was yet.

"You wanted to talk," Grace recalled, turning to him. Zakkai's eyes were considering as he watched her. He dropped his hands and leaned forward, elbows braced on his knees.

"I need you to know something about me."

"More secrets?"

"Not the good kind."

Grace blinked.

It would be hard to beat Farran's secrets.

The New Iberian king would have never breathed a word of the men and women he had sold to keep his sister safe, if not for Grace catching him.

The war could have been lost with Farran's hand in it, and no one would have known.

Grace nodded. "Okay."

Zakkai's lips thinned. "After my father took the throne, he made it mandatory for each of his sons to prove themselves. A different test for each."

The prince's eyes became shadowed, but he didn't break his gaze.

"I murdered three cousins," he said, so very, very quietly. When Grace merely watched back, he straightened. "My father's Calterra is not the one I grew up with. This war, this alliance— this would have never happened under my grandfather's rule."

Zakkai watched boats drift by for a few moments. "I wanted to talk to you because I think you may be able to help me."

"How?"

The prince frowned. "My father allowed me in the war room with him. Tyrnnth plans to launch an all-out assault soon."

Grace straightened, a hand raised to her throat. "What?"

"They're gathering up the rest of our young men. *My* men. I don't think my father realizes how badly this could end for everyone. If Vastlynd allies with Central, we'll be wiped out. If Vastlynd doesn't, and Central's wiped off the map, then . . . " Zakkai sighed and scrubbed his face with scarred, broad hands. "I just have a bad feeling about it. About Ares. I need another plan if this all goes wrong."

"How am I supposed to help?"

"You're going to hate it."

"Oh."

"I'm just being honest." Zakkai met her gaze. "If you agree to this, I have to trust you to go through with it."

Grace inclined her head. "If I wanted to run, I already would have."

46

Steven was seated at Farran's breakfast table, a bottle of liquor between him and the door, when Faye Bardolph slipped in.

"He didn't tell you either," he said. Faye shook her head. She approached, Steven taking in her ivory three-piece suit.

"Council meeting?" he asked.

"Endless council meetings. I'm going back in ten."

Steven grimaced. He gestured to the bottle. "I'm not drinking. Just thinking about it. I can't technically offer you any, sorry. Despite being princess, you're still too young for it."

"It's alright." Faye took the seat across from Steven.

He gave her a thin-lipped nod, drumming his fingers along the table once before rising.

"You don't have to leave," she said.

"I know." Steven smiled. "But I should."

He withdrew into the kitchen to hide Farran's alcohol. Faye's voice followed him.

"What happened on the trip?"

Steven returned and leaned against the kitchen threshold. "Why?"

Faye shook her head. "When Farran left, he was hopeful. Even after everything."

"His week was up." Steven pushed off the wall and made for

the door. "If you'll excuse me, I have to go."

"Steven."

"Yes?" He turned to find Faye had stood.

"The council decided it's next ruler."

Steven tensed. "Who?"

Faye smiled as if she had no way of hiding it. "It's me."

Steven braced himself on the chair beside the door.

"Congratulations." He smiled and hoped she wouldn't read into his emotions. "I'm—"

"It's alright. I know what everyone is thinking," Faye said. "I can translate their feelings well enough."

Steven shut his mouth.

"Everyone will learn in time that I have New Iberia's best interest in mind," she went on. "For now, I'm sure the council is placing bets on whether I live through the year or not."

Steven took a step forward. "Faye—"

The young queen shook her head. "I don't want you to lie to me."

He stilled. Nodded. Almost forgot to bow. "I— I'll see you later, Your Majesty. Congratulations."

Steven vacated, running a hand down his neck as he walked away.

Faye was Queen of New Iberia. At eighteen.

And she was right.

Everyone would be anticipating her demise.

Steven made it to the glass elevator and cursed inwardly. He had forgotten to ask how she was doing. With her brother shipped away, Natalia dead—

Steven needed to leave anyways.

It was probably best not to grow attached when either of them was likely to die within the year.

"I'm leaving," Steven said. Jay threw a trash bag to the floor, dusting off his hands as Steven shut Grace's door.

"And where exactly are you going, brother?" Jay grabbed a jar of pickles, scrunched his face, put them back.

"Nyrland."

Jay groaned and picked up another jar. "This crush with the empress has gone on long enough. You could have anyone you want, why must you choose the psychopath?"

Steven shut one of the fridge doors. Jay looked tired, shutting the other door to cross his arms and lean against the counter.

"Why Nyrland."

"I need Farran out of the mines."

Jay's eyes narrowed. "It's just a week. He's been through worse, I'm sure. Have you ever seen his back?"

Steven's brows furrowed. "No? He— when did you see his back?"

"Changing on the boat. That's not the point. The dude's back is *wrecked*. Your man's been through it. He'll be fine."

"Well I don't want him to go through it any more. Aren't you his friend? Why would you want him to suffer?"

"It's part of life. Okay, fine. I'm joking. Don't look at me like that." Jay ran a tattooed hand down his neck. "Please go on with your plan."

"Adira has access to everything," Steven said. "I want to hire her to get Farran out."

Jay snorted. "With what money?"

Steven shrugged. "Farran left some."

"You do realize he has to *die* before you can touch that, right?"

"I know." Steven sighed through his nose. "We'll figure that out after he's rescued."

Jay braced a hand under his jaw. "I think I see clear enough. You want to bribe an empress who has everything. And oh— that's *right*. She's Ares' brainwashed daughter and will probably keep you captive for him. Or kill you. This is a great idea."

"She doesn't have everything."

It was a moment before the light in Jay's eyes winked out.

"You can't tell her you're Ridgeway's heir."

Steven shook his head. "I can't let him die. He's the only friend I have. Apart from you, of course, but—"

"But I'm your brother, and we're family." Jay snatched the trash bag, shouldering past Steven. "I have things to do. Maybe I'm too busy to hear your suicide mission. Did you ever consider that, Steven? That maybe we're our own main characters in our stories?"

Jay opened the door and looked back. "Or do you still only think of yourself these days?"

"I am sacrificing myself in a week," Steven ground out. "Is that not selfless enough for you?"

Jay watched him, a muscle in his jaw feathering before he pointed an accusatory finger.

"No," Jay said, simple and plain. "You signed up for that because you thought everyone was dead and you didn't want to live anymore."

Steven kept his mouth shut.

"Though," Jay said, dropping his hand, "I'll be honest and say I don't know what it means to you now."

He turned away, paused, and turned back.

"Steven, do you want Farran back because he makes your life easier, or because you actually care for him?"

Steven took a step back. "I— why would you ask me that? Of course I care about him."

"Well, good." Jay said quietly. "I was just making sure."

Steven left before Jay could return.

47

Compared to the crisp, dry cold of Vastlynd, Nyrland's southern archipelago was covered in fog-laden rainforest. Silt-stained river water mixed with the ocean as the jet passed further into Adira's territory.

Steven and Jay vacated the airport and stood at the road.

"It's colder than I thought." The convict dropped his pack to pull a sweatshirt free.

"*South Illynoma Prison.*" Steven laughed. "You've got to be kidding."

"This guarantees I get a ride every time." Jay winked and raised a thumb, flashing his broad smile at a car.

"They drove faster," Steven choked. "Oh, here comes another. Try it again, Jay. Bigger smile, more thumbs."

Steven couldn't remember the last time he had laughed so hard as when the approaching minivan swerved into the other lane as it passed.

"Never change," Steven said.

———⚭———

Forests blurred as the taxi sped onward. A great lake, peppered with waterfowl. A rock pit—

Farran would have entered the mine by now, if Ares had decided not to cut him open first.

If Steven's hypothesis was correct, the War Leader wouldn't bother with the king.

Farran was just like everyone else.

Though, Ares had experimented on Faye . . .

Steven hoped Adira would agree to his plan.

He knew she was Ares' butcher; perhaps promising to keep his mouth shut could buy Farran's safety.

Steven had run the idea by Faye before leaving New Iberia. She had agreed she'd keep her mouth shut if there was a chance Farran could be saved.

So here Steven was, his brother still unaware of who Adira truly was.

"What if she holds you hostage?" Jay asked under his breath. Steven dragged his gaze from the view.

"She won't."

"Or so you think."

The driver took a call, Jay leaning in. "She's not the woman you spent the Culling with."

"I have to try something."

"It's only a week." Jay shrugged and leaned back.

"It was only a few minutes when I lost you."

Jay's lips thinned as he looked out the window, the capital longhouse coming into view. The vehicle pulled to a stop and Jay paid the driver as Steven steadied his breathing.

The smell of low-tide and cry of gulls filled the air as Steven opened his door, street lights flicking on. Jay joined his side as the cab pulled away.

Red, black and dark green paint depicted ravens and wolves across the carved building, the style reminiscent of Jaxin's tattoo.

Nyrland traditional art.

"Do you know what Jaxin's tattoo is?" Steven asked, pausing before the door. Jay stuffed his hands into his sweatshirt pocket and shrugged, his hood already drawn over his head.

"Yeah, thunderbirds."

"Oh." Steven lifted his brows.

"Yeah, real neat. Are you stalling? I don't mind."

Steven pushed the door open, a waft of cedar brushing his senses. He approached the reception desk and leaned against it, a woman with olive skin and dark eyes looking up at him.

"Good evening, miss," Steven said. "I was wondering if I could have an audience with Empress Theron."

The woman clasped her hands together. "You think you can just walk in here and see the Empress?"

"I'm a friend."

"Very funny, sir. What message would you like to leave?"

Steven leaned forward. "I really, truly need to see her in person."

"And why is that?"

Steven's blood iced over. He turned to find Ares, glacial eyes sparking as he slid his hands into his pockets.

"Welcome to Nyrland." Ares sketched a bow. "I apologize to say the empress is currently elsewhere."

Steven cursed under his breath, looking over a shoulder.

Jay was gone.

"Your brother is fine," Ares said, picking his nails. "Insurance. You can have him back as soon as our meeting is over."

"Alive." Steven stepped forward. "He will be alive and unharmed when he is returned to me."

Ares smiled. "Of course. If you will, please follow me."

Steven followed Ares down a hall, wondering how his knife would feel going through the War Leader's back.

They turned into a dark-wooded office, a guard shutting the door behind them. Ares rounded a desk, bracing his pale hands against its surface.

"Please, have a seat." Ares motioned to the chair across from him as he took his own. Steven shrugged off his coat and hung it beside the door. He made his way across the dim room, pausing beside a chair. The War Leader pulled out a cigarette and struck a match.

That explained the low gravel in the War Leader's voice.

"I doubt Adira would want you smoking in her office," Steven said.

Ares took a drag. "Ah, yes," he said, his lips a thin line. "She doesn't like the smoking. Says it'll kill me sooner than I need to die. Thankfully, this is my office. And I don't care. Please, take a seat. You're making me anxious standing there like that."

Steven's brows furrowed as he eased into the seat, surveying the space. Amber lights hung throughout the room. An antique, stained glass lamp stood guard beside an armchair. Bookshelves lined the walls, save the one to Steven's left, which instead housed paned windows overlooking a night-darkened sea.

"What can I help you with?" Ares asked.

Steven scoffed. Ares smiled in a way that made Steven reconsider his response.

Ares had Jay somewhere. Steven needed to stay civil.

He leaned back. "Did you raise Empress Theron?"

"That's a long story, I'm afraid," Ares said, smoke escaping his mouth. "In short, yes. I killed Adira's parents and raised her after. Her parents, Emperor and Empress at the time, had been part of a group of leaders running the world into the ground." He shrugged. "You know what I stand for already."

Steven grit his teeth, Ares' eyes crinkling in amusement.

"I'm just answering your question, Steven." Ares' face sobered. "I gathered Nyrland's potential heirs and set them against each other on Tybauch, promising the winner rule of Nyrland. Adira lived, the others did not. She proved herself cunning, deadly, and clever."

Steven cast a glance around the room.

Ares laughed once. "Don't worry, I won't kill you." He leaned back. "No one would believe you anyways."

"You really set *children* against each other to crown the survivor your puppet?" Steven's nails dug into leather.

Ares nodded. "Something like that, yes."

"You're *sick.*"

"Well, that's enough about me," Ares said. He took a drag. "Did you know your mother was born and raised Tyrnnthian?"

Ares leaned forward. "And before you deny it, let me confirm that I do, in fact, know this to be true. Evelin Peters was my secretary, and she and my wife were very good friends."

"That's madness," Steven said. "She was a baker her entire life in that little town you've already burned by now."

Ares smiled, tapping his cigarette.

"That's a lovely story," he said quietly, raising his dark brows. "She made it up herself."

"What the hell does that mean?"

"I'm sorry you have to hear this from someone you detest, but it seems I'm one of the only people telling the truth around here." Ares shrugged. "Evelin didn't want to remember who she was, what she had done. Her heritage, history; she asked me to remove it all and replace it with her own narrative, so I did."

Steven was shaking his head, as if he could stop Ares from wriggling the lies into his mind. "That's not true."

Ares angled his head. "And what is so wrong with being Tyrnnthian?"

When Steven didn't reply, Ares went on.

"Your mother was a good friend of my beloved's, and thus, mine as well. Since you're here, I want to take this opportunity to apologize for Evelin's death."

"*No.*" Steven was on his feet, hands braced against the desk. "You don't get to apologize. She suffered for *years*. Nothing you say could cover that suffering, that loss."

A part of Steven balked at the cold death in Ares' eyes.

"You think I don't know that already?"

Steven ground his jaw and pushed off the desk. He made it to the door before Ares spoke again.

"Your mother did not trust the Vastlynd king." Ares had risen from his chair. "Don't you find it strange Eric Ridgeway started coming around after your mother's memories were reconstructed?"

Steven turned and met Ares' gaze. "If Jay isn't out there, unharmed and whole, I will come back in here, and I will kill you."

"I keep my word, Steven." Ares' eyes sharpened. "Even your closest friends cannot claim the same."

"Go to hell," Steven said, his voice low. He grabbed his coat and slipped from the room.

He found Jay in the parking lot. Unharmed. Whole.

Ares could have destroyed Steven, and yet he hadn't. Steven brushed the thought aside and surveyed the street.

"You alright?" Jay asked.

"I'm going to kill him."

"You could have, you know." Jay's long legs matched Steven's pace. "What did he want?"

Ares' words echoed in Steven's mind.

"He just wanted to hear himself talk."

When they arrived to an inn, Steven procured the unfamiliar scrap of paper he had been toying with from his coat pocket. His blood chilled as he noted the elegant script.

I know you came to barter for Bardolph's life, but I am afraid, with my absence from Tyrnnth, I cannot guarantee that for you.

Jay was at Steven's side as the plane touched down in Vastlynd, the prizefighter's mind still entangled with what Ares had revealed.

Nothing made sense.

Their mother couldn't have been best friends with Ares' wife, let alone been born and raised Tyrnnthian.

Perhaps Ares was attempting to drive Steven insane before facing Luther. Though, the War Leader could have achieved as much taking Jay's life, and he hadn't.

Another part of Steven believed Ares; recalling gaps in the stories his mother told, her gaze growing distant at times.

All Steven knew for certain was his endeavor to save Farran had failed, and all he had managed to bring back with him from Nyrland was confusion and repulsion.

Tyrnnthian.

Steven couldn't be.

48

Farran knew he was to die the moment he appeared.

It was fitting, he supposed, to die at the hand of the same person who had murdered Emmaline.

Ares' executioner was dressed in black, a scythe strapped over his armored shoulder.

Farran stilled, the pickaxe heavy in his hands.

He had lost much of his strength today. He couldn't recall if he had eaten two or three days ago. His body was leaden, his head wracked with a pounding, relentless headache.

Though the slaves knew the king was in the mines, they hadn't been able to identify him with the ash and dust obscuring his face and coating his hair.

Farran had a new tattoo.

He hated it.

They didn't have names here, they had numbers. His was *79779,* a column of numbers down the back of his bicep.

He had new scars, too.

The first day upon arriving, slaves were whipped thirty times. Farran had been told it was to weed out the weak.

He was shocked Tyrnnth had become so twisted. If he ever became king again, he would see to it that every slave was freed and every overseer was wiped from the face of the planet.

The executioner raised his chin. He saw through the grime.

Against the scythe and the executioner's reputation . . . even with all of Farran's training and experience, he was a dead man.

The king released his pickaxe, a hollow clink echoing off the walls.

"Times up, Your Majesty," the executioner said, his blade swinging free. The man began to make his way toward Farran.

"Why."

"I take no chances."

Farran's hand tightened on the object in his right hand; too small to note while Farran had held the pickaxe in the other.

If Farran was to die, he would take Ares' butcher out with him.

As well as the entire mine.

Bombs, as well as weapons of war deemed too destructive, were illegal to possess, let alone use. Ares' great grandfather had made it so with a treaty that had ushered the world into a mess of power struggles and wars.

Despite this, the Bardolph family had hid some, just in case.

Farran's honor was stripped already.

With everything that had happened over the last few days, he truly had nothing left to lose.

He needed his switch. Not wanting to risk accidentally setting it off, he thought it best to keep it at his cot.

It did not seem best now.

Farran would need to pass his opponent before even attempting to grab it.

He could no longer wait for the Blood Challenges.

"Let's go," the executioner said, shoving Farran to turn him around.

Farran laughed out loud. "You're going to parade your prized hog before you slaughter him?"

"You laugh when you're full of fear, Your Majesty."

There. *There* it was.

The cadence. That *tone*.

The way Steven had looked at the masked killer in the throne room . . .

Something cold and calm sluiced through Farran's veins. "Tell me something I don't know, Empress."

Farran knocked the scythe from Adira as he pivoted, shoving a shard of rock for her throat. Blood shone, her body slamming into the rock wall.

An announcement echoed through the hall, Farran entering the crowd of slaves heading toward the assembly hall. He shoved through, sorry and not sorry, but mostly hopelessly desperate, above it all.

There were too many people heading in the opposite direction.

When the screaming began, Farran knew Adira was on her way.

He made it down a level, sweat running down his back and coating his palms—

Another level. And another.

The sole of his shoe tore off as he collided into a wall in an attempt to take the corner. He was vaguely aware of pain in his foot and blood on his face.

All three of Natalia's stab wounds hurt.

Everything hurt these days.

His mind caught up enough to think.

Adira.

Adira was Ares' executioner, his *butcher.*

Instead of crushing waves, it would be the weight of a mountain for Emmaline's murderer.

And Farran himself.

It likely wouldn't feel like anything at all.

There was his door.

Farran threw himself into the doorway and into the empty bunk room. He flipped up his thin mattress, reaching into the crevice.

It was empty.

Farran ran his hands along the stone, along the floor. Perhaps he had sent it flying when he moved the mattress.

"I imagine this is yours?"

Farran looked up to find Adira, the mask pulled away.

"You were going to murder three thousand people because you thought it was the right thing to do," Adira said, her voice low. "How does that make you any different than Ares?"

"I— I don't know."

She pocketed the device. Angled her head. "Do you know why Grace chose the other prince over you?"

"No, I do not." Farran's eyes caught on her bloody neck. How was she still functioning?

Adira smiled. "She chose him because while you appear perfect on the outside, your heart rots of cowardice."

Farran shook his head, wincing as the pain in his head multiplied.

"No, I think not," he said. "Zakkai buys women and uses them. I'd hardly consider him perfect."

"That's what he wants you to think. He is courageous enough to bear the appearance of a villain while he is anything but."

Farran opened and closed his mouth. "What do you mean?"

Adira pulled her scythe free. "Will I have to knock you out, or will you play nice this time?"

"Why tell me at all?" Farran breathed.

Adira angled her head. "You're about to die, Farran Bardolph. The least I could do was offer you the truth."

Adira, indistinguishable again, led Farran up the raised platform before the long, cavernous dining hall. The breath left Farran's body as he took in three thousand bodies and six thousand eyes, hanging lights flaring bright.

He squinted as lights pointed toward the platform, blinding him.

The crowd's chatter died to murmurs.

Adira positioned Farran at the front of the platform before standing beside him.

He did not see the bucket of water. A guard doused Farran and he gasped, unable to stop the shiver as his rag-worn clothes were soaked.

He was going to be wet, cold, and humiliated when Adira severed his head from his body.

He had it coming, the king supposed. He had given Tyrnnth thousands of lives for one.

They were yet to recognize him for who he was.

What he was.

Adira scrubbed his face with a cloth, Farran resisting the urge to shove her off the ledge.

He could.

But it wouldn't be a very becoming end for either party.

Adira pulled away, cries and curses rising.

As noise and light and disarray flooded his senses, he backed into a quiet corner of his mind.

This was usually where Grace was.

She was not here anymore.

No, Grace was in another man's bed. Content, happy—

Farran had fallen so thoroughly in love with her, he hadn't stopped to wonder if she could play his feelings to her advantage.

He wasn't sure how she had done it.

She was sunshine on his skin, hours under the stars, fresh-cut flowers, unrelenting *hope*—

How could she?

Farran ground his jaw as reality began to draw him back.

Grace had made her choice, and Farran was not it.

Whether or not she manipulated him did not matter. Nothing mattered. His blood would be spilled across these wooden planks within the next few minutes, and a part of the king was glad for it.

"Slaves of Slauvebach," Adira announced, her voice not her

own. "Allow me the honor of introducing the man who sold you to Tyrnnth. Those of you searching for the New Iberian King, search no more."

Farran blinked at the curses and claims against him.

He would not pity himself. He had made a choice, and though it would cost him everything, his sister would live because of it. Farran raised his chin.

"What shall we do with him?" Ares' executioner went on. The frenzied crowd grew louder.

Traitor.

Betrayer.

Murderer.

Farran's knees buckled as a chant rose above the others.

Kill him.

This was it, then. He refused to lower his chin, even as trembling overtook him, cold water seeping into his bones.

"Get it over with, Ad—"

There was a blade at his throat, Farran managing to smile as he looked into Adira's eyes, just barely visible.

"Don't," she breathed.

"Or what. You'll kill me?" Farran murmured.

Her scythe cut stubble he couldn't shave anymore.

A thought jarred him, his knees nearly gave out.

"He needs to know who you are," Farran breathed, the sound nearly lost to the impatient crowd. Rocks hit the platform, one nailing him in the thigh.

Farran hissed, avoiding crying out.

"He already does," Adira crooned.

"What?"

Adira looked to the crowd, addressing them. "Did you decide? Kill him?"

The crowd roared.

A nightmare. At any moment, Farran might wake.

Steven already knew who she was?

What she was?

"That's not true—"

"Shall it be at the end of my scythe," Adira went on, her black blade glinting. "Or, at the end of your pick axe?"

The crowd cried their answer, Adira turning toward him.

His quick, clean death was denied.

"He knows?" Farran asked. He could barely hear himself.

Adira pulled down her mask as she drew near. "Goodbye, Farran."

"Wait—"

The blunt end of her scythe rammed into his back, and Farran went over the edge of the platform.

49

Jay was intent on throwing Steven a celebration before his Blood Challenge.

As Jay prepared, Steven strolled through Zephyr. Bright, winter sun reflected off the snow-covered capital, snow flurries built up against the edges of the road.

A beautiful day for the eve of the war's end.

If Steven succeeded, he would see his friend soon.

Farran and Steven's countrymen would be free, Central's borders would bounce back, and they could all begin rebuilding what was left of their country, their lives.

Steven's world before the war had been perfect, and he hadn't a clue until he had lost it all. Though, if not for the war, he would have never found out who he truly was, and he would have never met Farran.

Steven would have never known his limits.

He stopped and pulled the scarf away his mouth. Even in the cold, the heat of the sun kissed his skin.

"Is it safe for you to wander by yourself, Your Majesty?" He turned to find Faye behind him, as he had been suspecting for the last two blocks. She smiled slightly.

"What gave me away?" Faye said. "Obviously I wasn't trained well enough."

"You had to show up eventually, and your frame is . . . memorable."

"You're telling me I'm short and predictable."

Steven winced. "Jeez, well when you put it that way— should I be afraid?"

Faye smiled. "Not yet."

"Oh, good." Steven offered his arm, Faye intertwining hers.

She was his date to the party tonight, though not entirely for his own benefit. She had connections to make, and Steven enjoyed having someone to dance with.

A symbiotic relationship.

It seemed to be a theme for them.

They walked in silence for minutes, cars buzzing by, small whorls of snow drifts lifting to dance in their wake.

Zephyr was such a typical ski town, Steven found it humorous. White-walled chalets with dark trim, little porches with little doors. Dark-wooded buildings with red shutters.

To think Steven would bear the weight of not one of these cities, but hundreds more, as well as thousands of towns and villages . . .

It was a bit much.

Especially when Ares still lived and breathed somewhere on the same planet.

"Have you heard from— what's his name?" Steven looked down at the Queen of New Iberia.

"Destry. And no, I haven't heard from him."

Steven breathed in the crisp, cold air before exhaling. "He'll probably stay away now that you're Queen."

"Let's hope."

Steven stopped at the intersection. "Apart from Luther, does Ares have any more kids?"

Faye's eyes flashed before meeting his. "Any more kids?"

"Yeah," Steven said, raising a brow. "Am I killing Luther just to find another Luther-a-like in his place?"

Faye sighed and shook her head at the ground. "No, I don't think so." She looked up, eyes narrowing as she looked over the winter-bright street. "Ares never— he was loyal to his wife."

The stoplight turned, Steven and Faye crossing with other bundled strangers.

Did they not pay enough attention to the news not to know who walked amongst them? Perhaps the scarves and hats were enough to allow them ambiguity.

"Does Tyrnnth do concubines like Calterra?"

"Och, *do concubines*. I hate that," Faye said from under her scarf, brows drawing together. "No. Tyrnnth is strict. No *doing* before you're married."

They took a turn into an open park, tall evergreens and firs dotting a path winding toward a frozen lake. Despite the cold, the park was lively with Vastlynders. Some had dogs on leashes. Others bore hot drinks.

Life was almost normal here, if not for the war just south of them.

Chickadees called and flit from a nearby hemlock, reminding Steven of hunting birds with Jay.

The memory was nearly a decade old.

If he were to shoot a chickadee now, he would be arrested.

Were there still chickadees in the woods behind their old trailer? Ares had claimed the gas was beneficial to the environment, but surely the wildlife couldn't handle it, if humans couldn't.

Faye had halted at the lake edge, Steven brought back to the present.

There were ice skaters everywhere. Some huddled around burn barrels to warm their hands, others glided across the glass surface of the lake. Steven exhaled and looked at Faye, wondering what she was thinking of.

Did this sight make her yearn for normalcy as much as it did him?

"Do you ice skate, Your Majesty?" he asked, instead.

Faye raised her chin above her scarf. "No, I don't."

"Do you want to?"

The last he had ice skated had been with Grace and Max during a fight tour in northeastern Central.

He was likely terrible at it now.

Not that he'd ever been great at it.

Voices rose and Steven looked up to find people nearing, phones raised. New Iberia's Blood Challenger and new Queen had finally been identified, and it was time to go.

———

Faye's jaw dropped as they entered the decorated ballroom, turning on a heel to raise a pale brow at Steven.

"Do you know how expensive it is to rent this?"

"Only the best for my brother." Jay sketched a bow.

"We'll see you after your meetings," Steven said, watching as Faye's eyes shifted to something behind him. "I hope they go well."

Faye grabbed his hands and squeezed before breezing out the door. Jay's expression was wary.

"What is it?" Steven asked.

Jay watched Faye retreat. "Nothing. She's just a little odd. I'm sure I'll figure her out soon."

Steven huffed a laugh under his breath. "And why does everyone need figuring out?"

Jay met Steven's gaze. "In prison, you don't trust every face that smiles back at you."

———

Jay raised a toast and the party ensued.

Steven sipped from his glass, Jay's laughter booming beside

him. Steven remembered to put a smile on his face, though his eyes focused on nothing and nowhere.

Gowns and suits blurred, voices floated and the scent of roasted meat and hearty vegetables filled his senses. He leaned on a column. The wallpaper was red and gold, white-half-wall panelling coming up from the crimson marble floor—

This was where Steven had seen Adira for the first time. His drink jostled as someone bumped into him.

It felt like an eternity had passed since then.

It had only been several months.

So much had changed. Lives had been lost, and even himself—

"Steven," Jay said, jarring him. The prizefighter looked at him.

Jay's smile fell. "I was wondering if this would be too much."

"No, this is great, Jay." Steven leaned against the table beside him. "I was just thinking of—"

"Everything."

"You know me so well." Steven looked at Jay's polished, black dress shoes. "I should know you better."

Steven hadn't even asked about Zahara yet.

"We'll have plenty of time to fix that later," Jay said, shrugging as he sipped from a straw. He set his drink onto the table and pointed. "Look what the cat dragged in. Do you think her bodyguard will let me keep her?"

Steven followed Jay's line of sight.

Zakkai, Grace and Zahara entered, the room quieting. Steven tried and failed not to hear their murmurs.

The king's fiancé, already with another man—

"Jay," Steven began.

"It's *Grace*. Of course I'm going to invite her. I didn't intend for beefcakes to show—"

"Beefcakes?"

"—and Zahara showing up is a bonus."

The Calterrans wove through the crowd, the prince a head and a half taller than everyone else.

Steven downed his glass and strode to meet them.

Zakkai saw Steven first, the prince smiling in a way that wasn't friendly. "Castellen, good to see you," he drawled. Grace whirled.

"You're here," Steven said.

"You." Grace's voice was low enough that he knew no one else could hear her next words. "How dare you spy on me."

"We were going to rescue you. It wasn't— well, I guess it technically was spying." Steven ran a hand down his neck. "We left because you were fine."

"I assured her it could have been much worse," Zakkai said.

"That's nice."

Grace grabbed Steven's arm. "Why?"

"Why rescue you?" Steven dropped his voice. "You were *screaming* when he dragged you out. We had to."

Zakkai turned toward Zahara as Grace's voice dropped further.

"No, I mean . . . how did you know I was okay?"

Steven studied her, his mind going back to the prince's shirt she wore, her ease around him— the way she allowed him to hold her.

"There were a few factors," Steven whispered.

"Was he there?"

Steven swallowed and looked away. People were watching. Grace gripped his arm harder.

"Was. He. There."

Steven met her gaze. "Yes."

Her face crumpled. "He went to the mines after."

Steven held her face in his hands. "That will *never* be your fault. He had a debt to pay, and that was how he chose to pay it."

His lips thinned as he wiped a tear away with a thumb. "You know how it works, G. He wanted to make sure you were okay before he left. We all did." He loosed a breath. "You were, so we left you. Then Farran went off to do what he had planned to all along."

"You should have talked to me, so I could explain."

"Another day," Steven said quietly, but not weakly. "He'll live, Grace. He'll walk out with everyone else."

Grace nodded once, Steven pulling her into his arms.

She exhaled before letting go. "I hate this war, I hate these politics, and I hate him for leaving like that."

"Me too." Steven offered a tentative smile as she ran the back of her hands under her eyes. She raised her chin, meeting his eyes.

"He'll be okay," she said.

Steven had always envied Grace's ability to rise up after every problem life threw her way. Even with war, her parent's deaths . . .

She had never ceased to rise up every time, never allowing bitterness to fester, as Steven did.

"If Jay can survive months down there, Farran can handle a week," Steven assured.

"Right." Grace managed a smile.

"Food," Jay said, materializing out of the crowd. He pointed at a plate in his hand. "Yours. This is your food. Hi, Grace. You're in trouble and we need to talk."

"Hi, Jay," Grace said. "You are also in trouble. We will talk."

"Good." Jay winked at Zakkai and dragged Steven away.

After a plate of savory meat and grilled asparagus, Steven danced with Grace. Faye returned and Steven danced with her until Jay slapped him on the shoulder, Steven faltering mid-dance.

"Yes?" Steven said. Jay jerked his chin, Steven following his line of sight. Faye's hand tightened on Steven's waist.

Dressed in black silk, a diadem atop her head, Adira Theron had arrived.

Jay crossed his arms as the empress slipped through the crowd. Steven looked at Faye, the new Queen of New Iberia, and only other person who knew who Adira was.

What she was.

A liar. A two-faced, murdering—

Faye ran her hand up Steven's chest. "Find me when you're done."

When Steven looked at Adira, she was tracking the queen. Adira locked onto his gaze.

"She's not worth your time," Jay muttered.

Steven would give it, anyways. Just a piece. He wove through dancing bodies until she was before him.

"You're late," he said.

"That can happen when you're not invited."

He smiled. "Touché. Care to dance?"

Adira smirked at his outstretched hand. "I suppose."

She took his hand and stepped forward, her calluses scraping against his own.

"I tried to find you," Steven said. "You weren't home."

Adira nearly faltered. "You went to Nyrland."

Steven nodded, his eyes intent. "I did."

They swept into the next song, the piece slower than the last.

"In Nyrland, what did you find instead?" Adira asked.

"Nothing important." He blew a breath out his nose, watching Adira look him up and down, her eyes sparking.

"Why did you want to find me?"

"It doesn't—" Steven halted, his eyes caught on a jagged line across Adira's throat. A near fatal wound, makeup pasted on in an attempt to hide it.

The room blurred as the world continued to exist beyond them.

"What happened?" Steven ran his thumb over the wound.

It had not been a clean cut, and would scar.

"This shouldn't have happened," he said quietly, his eyes meeting Adira's. "You're a Blood Challenger. It's against the law to kill you."

"I'm not dead," she said, eyes narrowing. He felt her swallow under his hand, his thumb still against her throat.

"Who did this?" Steven whispered.

"No one," she snapped.

He caught her jaw as she pulled away. "Please don't lie to me."

If her alliance with Ares had fallen through and she was fleeing him—

His brows drew together. "Are you safe?"

Shadows flickered in and out of her eyes before she pulled away.

"I shouldn't have come."

"Wait—" Steven made to grab her wrist, the empress twisting out of his grasp.

"I'll see you tomorrow."

Adira didn't wait for his reply as she disappeared into the crowd.

Steven stood in place, weighing the merits of pursuit. Just as he stepped forward, a scream cleaved the air.

Steven turned to find Grace dropped to the floor. He was moving, eyes searching for an enemy. All the guest's eyes were wide as they did the same, already beginning to panic.

Grace clutched her chest as if she had been shot, though there was no blood. Steven's feet slowed as the world fell away. She was fine.

But between her sobs and screams . . .

Someone was dead.

Because that was the sound someone made when they found out.

50

An alarm blared, people racing by Steven.

Zakkai drew Grace into his lap, his eyes promising death as he scanned the room. Jaxin's jaw was clenched.

Steven's brother wove through the crowd, eyes blazing. He halted a foot away. "Where is she."

"Who?" Steven's voice sounded hollow.

Jay grabbed Steven's shoulders, shaking him. *"Adira."*

Grace doubled over in Zakkai's arms.

"Where did she go?" Jay demanded.

Steven drew his eyes to his brother. "Why."

"You know why!"

"I don't know what you're talking about."

This wasn't happening. It couldn't be. The alarm droning on in the background was his phone alarm.

He would wake any second now.

Steven discerned what the crowd was saying.

The king, the king is dead!

"Is my father—" Steven began, but Jay was already turned away, joining Zakkai and Jaxin. Guns and knives were drawn as the hunting party ran through the doors.

Steven already knew the answer anyways.

He barely recalled walking to Grace, nor the sensation of his knees hitting the marble floor.

Grace was crying. Steven couldn't recall if he was, as well.

As the crowd fled, he pulled her into his arms.

"He's dead," Grace said. "He's dead and it's my fault."

"No, it's not," he whispered. "It's really not."

Steven ran his hand over Grace's hair, his eyes glued to the wall.

He remained that way until Zakkai came back, lighting a hand on his back. Steven removed his arms from Grace, allowing Zakkai to gather her up in his own.

She had passed out minutes or hours ago, after muttering the same thing over and over again.

It's my fault.

Steven hadn't been able to convince her otherwise.

<hr />

A pale, awakening sky mocked him. At some point, servants had brought and left Steven tea. It was cold now.

Steven supposed he should have thanked them, or replied when they asked if he needed anything.

The only thing he needed was time to slow until it reversed, so Steven could stop everything from turning into this nightmare.

Steven was alive and Farran wasn't.

Everyone refused to tell him what happened. All he knew was that Farran was dead the day before the Blood Challenges.

Jay opened Steven's door and slipped in. The convict's face was grim as he ran his eyes over his brother.

"'How are you' is a stupid question, but I have to ask it anyways."

Steven ran his hands down his face, his legs stretched out before the armchair. He had been sitting for hours, watching the sky shift in his tower room.

His room.

Despite the ire and displeasure the king had shown Steven during their last interaction, the king had given him his own residence in the palace. Steven was sure it was only because he was the king's heir, and nothing more.

"I want to know," Steven said. Jay nodded, chewing on a lip as he stared at the ornate, round rug on the floor.

"Look, it really isn't—"

"Please."

Adira couldn't kill Farran and show up to the party. Not without bearing an inkling of guilt or—

Steven's breath caught. Her wound.

If Farran had been attacked, he wouldn't go down without a fight.

Jay sat in the chair opposite of Steven and procured something from his pocket. "I have your phone."

"I figured."

Jay swallowed. "Are you sure?"

"Yes." Steven had never seen tears in his brother's eyes, but there they were. Steven looked away.

Metal slipped into Steven's palm.

The first thing Steven saw was a body hung from a rafter, skin marred with gashes, bruises, and— Farran was missing his right hand. Steven's own began to shake as he doubled over.

"Adira told them," Jay said quietly. Steven heard Jay rise and walk to the window. "She told them who he was, and then she pushed him."

The deep, dark gashes, those were from pick axes. Steven was shaking his head, unable to look away.

He had done this.

This wouldn't have happened if not for his ignorant, foolish plan to keep Farran on their side when Steven should have let him go.

Now Farran was dead, his body nearly unrecognizable.

His death hadn't been clean, and likely hadn't been quick.

The room spun. Jay turned from the window and braced a knee on the floor, picking up Steven's phone.

He must have dropped it.

"Don't do it alone," Jay said. "We didn't talk when I shot our dad. I think it's good to talk. Stuffing never did us any good before."

"How do we know Adira did this?"

Jay scrolled and turned the screen.

"I had wondered if she was Ares' butcher at the summit. It was the way she walked and looked at you, if that makes sense. See the blood here? It matches the wound across her neck she tried to hide."

"Who else knows?" Steven asked, his voice hoarse.

Jay stood. "I don't know if they believe me yet, but I told Jaxin and Prince Zakkai. They tried to help me find her after the party."

"And were you successful?" Steven dragged his eyes up.

"No," Jay said plainly.

Adira had hidden behind her mask when she sent Farran to die, three thousand ready to deal in revenge.

"I bet Ares made her do it," Steven breathed. "You talked about mind control before we tried to rescue Grace."

Jay shook his head. "No, Steven. You have to be in close range. Ares was in Nyrland when this happened."

"Maybe he made progress!"

Jay raised a brow. "You need to let her go, brother. There was a reason Ares sent her to New Iberia as part of the payment for Grace's freedom. Have you ever considered that?"

Steven scoffed. "She was owed a favor, and Ares guaranteed her a chance at trade agreements."

He wasn't sure why he was defending her.

Maybe he just wanted to hear his brother agree that Adira wasn't the reason Farran had been slaughtered so mercilessly.

It was fake.

She wasn't herself.

Jay met Steven's gaze, and the prizefighter looked away, jaw clenching as he took in the mountain range encompassing them.

"Just think about it," Jay said. "It didn't make sense, and nobody had clear answers. It's a bit odd to send an empress for trade agreements."

Jay rose and headed for the door, pausing at the threshold.

Steven's gaze remained on the peaks, holding on long enough for Jay to leave.

After the door shut, Steven's body curled inward and he allowed himself fall apart.

"I'm attending his funeral," Steven said by way of greeting, his bag slung over a shoulder. Jay stepped out of the way as Steven swept down the stairs.

"You can't. The Blood Challenges happen on the Crow Moon and Tyrnnth is strict as hell," Jay countered.

Steven halted, Jay nearly running into him.

"I will not fight until Farran is buried in New Iberia. The funeral is tomorrow, and Luther is going to have to wait."

Jay's lips thinned. He looked down and nodded. "Okay."

"Okay," Steven repeated.

"It won't hurt to try."

Steven's knees weakened, but he held himself upright.

This was real.

It shouldn't be real.

"Right." Steven turned and descended the stairs.

He had meant to walk right out of Ridgeway's palace, but was called from an open doorway. Grace ran and wrapped her arms around him.

"Where are you going?" she asked, stepping away.

"New Iberia."

"You should eat before you go," Grace offered, glancing at Jay.

Steven entered a breakfast nook. There were bowls of fruit, pastries, a kettle of tea— Steven lurched as he approached, watching steam rise from the mugs.

Would it be like this from now on? Would the things that reminded him of his friend tug at the thread holding him together until he unraveled completely?

Worn books, oil paintings, half-tended orchards, fresh peaches and tea. Not to mention Castle Hill and New Iberia itself.

Steven would be gutted everywhere he went.

Steven took the seat beside Grace, Jay joining Zahara's side. Zakkai stood at the window, a thin gold chain between his fingers as he gazed down at the valley.

"There's pancakes, grapes—" Jay began.

Jaxin burst through the door. "I'll have her head on a *pike.*"

"Good morning to you, too, War Leader Brown," Jay said. "Would you like some breakfast? Or perhaps another attempt at being a normal, civil human being?"

Jaxin dropped a newspaper onto the table, glasses rattling. "You were right. Adira is Ares' executioner. The cut on her throat matched. Her height. Her shoe size."

"What does this mean for you?" Jay asked.

"It means we should have killed her when we had the chance." Jaxin ran his hands through his hair. "But now we won't have to."

"Why?" Steven asked.

"Well, if she has the first Blood Challenge tomorrow, Luther will."

"Why did she do it?" Grace asked.

"I don't know," Jaxin said. "Adira had nothing to gain from butchering Farran like that."

"She's rebelling," Zakkai said, turning towards them. "Farran could have been a bartering tool for Ares."

"Or he could use him," Jay said. "Ares could turn Farran into a puppet and have New Iberia in his palm."

"What are you talking about?" Zakkai stepped forward. Jay

picked up a grape and studied it.

"I was Ares' guinea pig for— oh, I don't know how long." He shrugged. "He's finding a way to control a body with his own mind."

"Bull." Zakkai's eyes narrowed. "That's not possible."

"Hey," Steven said, looking between Jay and the prince. "When did we decide to trust the son of our enemy's ally?"

Jay shut his mouth, looking to Jaxin.

"Because," Grace said, "he isn't our enemy."

Zakkai did not own a harem.

The village? They were women he had bought, rescued, and set free. The prince visited the world's darkest places and spent fortunes freeing the enslaved. The heir also sent assassins when he was finished with particularly nasty dealers.

Steven no longer wondered how Grace had grown fond of the foreign prince. Zakkai's only response to Steven's apology was a request to remain discreet about it.

Jaxin checked his watch. "Mr. Castellen, if you want to go to the funeral, we need to leave now."

"Ares is allowing it?" Steven asked.

"No, he's not. Luther is."

The funeral was set on the cliffside Farran had made bargains with Ares, the grave overlooking the ocean. A gust shoved Steven's hair from his brow as he watched waves crash below an open, dusky sky.

Farran was dead.

Soldiers lowered an oak casket into the earth, Farran's broken body inside, a folded New Iberian flag atop its surface.

Shots rang as the military honored Farran's past career as a soldier, as well as his prior seat as king.

There should have been more in attendance.

But with what Farran, what *Steven* had done . . .

Steven had beat a man.

Upon hearing the stranger slew insults at Steven's best friend, the prizefighter hadn't stopped himself. Jay had tore Steven away before he could break more than the man's nose.

After the priest finished, the first shovelful of dirt fell.

Farran was dead.

Steven would never forgive himself for causing it, nor forgive Farran for leaving without saying goodbye.

Steven remained after everyone else had left, watching flowers wilt.

He hadn't had much to say. His knees hit the dirt before Farran's grave and all his words were lost under the weight of his new reality.

Tyrnnth and his Blood Challenge would come tomorrow, but for now, it was just Steven and his friend six feet under.

"If this goes poorly, I may see you soon," Steven whispered.

Steven wasn't sure how much time slipped away before Jay approached the king's headstone and laid a hand upon it, his eyes dark.

"Denique sine onere," Jay said quietly. Steven recognized the words, his brother having uttered them when one of his own had fallen at the front.

"Finally, without burden," Steven translated, a cold wind snapping up, the stars winking overhead.

Jay offered a hand. "Let's go, brother."

51

Tyrnnth was encompassed in smoke.

As Steven stepped off the plane, inhaling a lungful of smog, he understood why Tyrnnthians were built different.

Why he might be built different, from more than one cause.

Jaxin strapped a gas mask over his face and narrowed his eyes at the city. Jay crinkled his nose. Within fifteen minutes, they were through the airport and in a dark vehicle.

"You alright?" Jay asked.

Steven faced his brother as the door shut. "Yeah."

He would be alright as soon as the war was over and Farran was avenged.

Nobody else spoke during the drive through the capital. Soon enough, they arrived at the hotel Steven had stayed in before the Culling.

Alone in his room, the crash of waves tugged something within Steven's chest. He leaned against the shut door and breathed.

The woman he had known was dead, someone new in her place.

A faceless murderer, *Farran's* murderer.

The last time Steven had stood in this room, Farran had been alive, Steven himself oblivious to Adira's true allegiance.

Things were so different now.

No matter what happened next, at least Jay would make it out. Steven could hold onto that.

He loosed a breath and stepped from the door. A year of earning citizenship, training, and surviving, and Steven had arrived.

He couldn't have done it without Farran, and the offer he had extended that day in the infirmary. He had been the one to see Steven's potential.

While Steven had still been broken, the king had faith in him.

It was soon time to prove him right.

Even as Steven screamed, slaves tore into his friend, raised pick axes shining with blood. Steven wriggled through a gap in the crowd.

He could have pulled Farran away, had Steven been there a moment sooner.

Instead, Steven arrived just in time to watch a pick axe strike clear through Farran's throat.

A knock jolted Steven awake. Grabbing his knife, he stalked to the door. A glance through the peephole revealed Jay.

"I'm alright," Steven called, opening the door. Jay had his firearm drawn. He peered past Steven before meeting his eyes.

"It didn't sound like it. You were screaming."

"It was just a bad dream."

Jay blew out a breath and holstered his weapon. Though the concealed firearm was illegal in Tyrnnth, Jay had insisted. When Steven had argued against it, Jay claimed if he were caught, Tyrnnth was free to throw the charge on his pristine track record.

"That must have been one hell of a bad dream," Jay said. He turned as Jaxin strode down the hall.

"Time to go," Jaxin said. He frowned. "Steven, you're the face of the free world tonight. Please make it look like you care."

The coliseum was packed to the point of standing room only for miles outside the structure.

Steven tried not to think about it.

He entered a side door as the sky turned apricot, the sun headed for the ocean beyond the city. Having parted ways with Jay, Steven felt unsteady.

Jaxin led the prizefighter through stone halls until reaching a columned room lit with high windows.

"Steven," Jaxin said. The prizefighter turned from the washroom.

"Yes?"

Jaxin stepped forward and handed a dark bundle of fabric into Steven's hands. "This is from Bardolph."

Steven's brows furrowed. "What is it?"

"He referred to them as *fighting leathers*. Whatever the hell that means. It'll be more protective than what you have."

Jaxin took a call in the other room as Steven dressed.

The prizefighter ran his eyes over the fitted, flexible suit. The material covered all but his feet, hands and face, Steven donning shoes made of a similar material.

A gift from Farran.

A subtle embellishment adorned the black surface, so faint Steven hadn't noticed at first. He turned in the faint light.

Wolves. Fighting and twisting around each other.

Whilst the Bardolph family crest featured white wolves, Ridgeway's crest honored wolves with darkest fur.

But Steven had never told Farran the truth.

The prizefighter looked at his reflection once more.

Surely the embossed wolves were an ode to New Iberia and Steven's newfound citizenship, and not the country he was to inherit.

Steven exited the washroom as Jaxin pocketed his phone.

"That's quite the suit," Jaxin said, regarding him.

"It is." Steven ran his hands over the material. "What was the call about?"

Jaxin ran a hand down his neck. "Nothing I can discuss here." A glance to the open doorway.

Steven nodded. "So what now?"

Jaxin lifted a dark brow. "Now, you win. If you don't . . . well, you won't be alive to see what happens if you don't."

The War Leader cast a glance over a shoulder before entering the washroom, turning the water on full before jerking his chin.

Steven followed, Jaxin shutting the door.

"Tyrnnth amassed their largest host outside the demarcation line with the intention to sprint as soon as the Blood Challenges begin," Jaxin said, his voice low. "Did Adira or Ares mention why?"

Steven shook his head. "No. Maybe if they take over the country before the Blood Challenges end, or before Luther dies, they can keep it?"

"That's how it works, yes." Jaxin worked his jaw. "But they would have tried this already, if that were the case."

"Maybe they didn't have enough men yet."

"Perhaps." Jaxin narrowed his eyes. "Don't die tonight."

"I'll try."

A roar rumbled through stone, Jaxin shutting off the water to exit the washroom. Guards stood at the doorway, ready to drag Steven to his fate.

The guards stepped back as Jaxin snapped at them in Tyrnnthian, deigning to lead Steven himself.

Jaxin led Steven to a darkened tunnel, the noise much louder. Steven stared toward the light at the end.

He was shaking. That wasn't good.

Jaxin dropped a hand on Steven's shoulder, drawing his attention.

"Sic itur ad astra, Steven Ridgeway."

Steven swallowed and nodded once, Jaxin dropping his hand to leave. When the door shut, the prizefighter turned toward the only direction left for him to go. He walked to the edge and stopped before the light, remaining hidden in shadow.

The crowd was deafening, the air thick with sick, sweet poison. A loudspeaker blared in Tyrnnthian, and afterward, in Centrallian.

"We welcome our first contestant for tonight's Blood Challenges," the announcer spoke, "Steven Castellen, citizen of New Iberia."

Steven forced himself into the light, the crowd roaring under a deep orange sky.

The noise of over fifty thousand people was assaulting.

He halted at the center of the pit, dust crunching underfoot.

"And our second contestant for the evening, Her Majesty, Adira Theron, Empress of Nyrland."

Screams and whistles rose from the crowd, Adira's presence like a brewing storm at Steven's back. A wave of anger hit him so suddenly, it was an effort of will to unclench his fists.

She had killed his friend.

Really and truly.

How had he even been able to *attempt* defending her the day after Farran's body had been found hanging? Pieces missing, the king's body marred beyond—

Dust swirled as Adira stopped at Steven's side.

He would not look at her. He did not trust himself not to wring her neck. If fate would have it, she would go first and he wouldn't have to.

The empress' feet shifted, her chin lifting.

The gate at the other end of the pit opened, their beast of an opponent stalking forward.

"Luther Hawthorne, prior Grand Leader of Tyrnnth."

Steven clasped his hands before him as the ex-dictator approached, a smile on his broad-planed, pale face.

He had lost weight since Steven had last seen him, at odds with his gait and smile, the violence in his eyes.

Had Natalia's death destroyed him?

Luther hadn't been in the room when Ares shot her. Perhaps Ares had convinced his son that Steven had killed her.

An announcement declared pit weapons to be decided.

Steven's pulse quickened as dying rays stained the clouds blazing, red-orange. Ares rolled dice on his raised dais and smiled at the crowd.

Then he looked at Steven, something glinting in his eyes.

"Pit weapons shall be bones from the mines."

No doubt, Ares was trying to unnerve Steven. Men dressed in red cloaks entered the pit, tossing bones to the ground as a poison-laden, dry wind snapped through.

Steven didn't look close.

At least none of the bones belonged to Farran.

"Heads or tails, Empress?" Luther asked, his eyes sharp.

Had Ares drugged his soft-hearted son, or had Ares mastered his ability to control a body?

A chill went down Steven's spine.

"Tails," Adira said. Steven finally looked at her.

Her suit was exactly like his, though hers bore an embellishment of ravens, the material the same dark jade of her eyes.

"Is that from Farran?" Steven breathed.

Adira looked at him and nodded.

"And you wear it despite what you did to him."

He couldn't look away, even as the coin was tossed.

She didn't balk under the weight of his gaze.

"Tails," Ares announced, the crowd roaring.

Adira would be first, then.

"I hope he rips you to pieces," Steven said, unable to look away. He turned and strode from the pit.

—⊗—

Steven entered the darkened hall, footsteps following behind him.

"What do you want." He didn't bother to turn around.

"Steven, listen to me," Adira said. The prizefighter stopped, Adira nearly colliding into him.

"Why did you kill him?" Steven barely got the words out without his voice breaking. If one of them was to die, he might as well ask.

Adira stared at him. "I didn't."

Steven stepped toward her. "What?"

A moment passed. Two more.

He could have sworn her eyes held an emotion he hadn't seen before. He angled his head.

"What do you mean, Adira."

She blinked. Her face became sharp and her eyes darkened. She stepped back.

"If I remember right, the crowd did."

Steven blew out a sharp breath. "You—"

"There's something you need to know about me, Steven," the empress cut in. "I am not who you think I am."

Steven attempted to swallow the bile in his throat.

She had killed Farran and felt no shame about it.

"I don't care who you are. Not anymore," Steven whispered. "You can go to hell, for all I care."

Adira didn't break her gaze. "Already there."

Despite the challenge in her eyes, her words were hollow.

She turned and left him in the hall, Steven watching her until her silhouette was bathed in dying light, the crowd frenzying as the first Blood Challenger entered the pit.

52

Steven and Jay sat in the front row as Jaxin met Ares at the dais.

Adira's Blood Challenge began with the blast of a horn, the empress and ex-dictator circling.

Adira was the first to advance, quick as a viper.

But Luther was quicker.

Steven turned away as the ex-dictator nailed her in the jaw.

Jay exclaimed something incoherent, his attention on his phone.

"Tyrnnth is launching a massive attack."

"I heard," Steven yelled over the crowd.

"How did you know?"

Steven looked back toward the pit, his heart dropping as Luther landed a blow to Adira's face, her stomach—

She shifted away, rage in her eyes, blood dripping from her mouth, a rivulet from her nose.

They circled again, the empress stooping to pick up a bone. She cracked it over a knee, snapping it in half. She raised either end, now razor-sharp.

Steven shifted to the edge of the bench, his legs bouncing.

She could kill Luther with a quick maneuver now. With her experience with swordsmanship, and her smaller, lither build, she could do it.

Luther lunged, Adira veering away.

Too fast. Whatever was in the dictator's system, paired with Ares' genetic manipulations, Luther was too quick.

Jay bumped into Steven. "Look."

Steven dragged his eyes to the map on Jay's phone.

"This is all that's left." He pointed toward the strip of land beneath Vastlynd.

Tyrnnth had already advanced exponentially.

Adira snarled and Steven looked up in time to watch her wrestle free of Luther's grip, her shoulder out of socket.

Her eyes blazed as she backed away. A cry, shove, and her shoulder was back in place.

Luther crouched, the crowd roaring as he rose with a lengthy bone.

He paused to snap it in half.

The crowd frenzied as he approached the empress.

53

Zakkai wiped blood and sweat from his brow, Calterrans and Tyrnnthians falling around him.

The Centrallians fell faster, beaten down in body and in mind. Their final push had started well, but had began to fall apart when Tyrnnth had put a new machine to the test.

Ares had built something to disrupt a bullet's structural integrity, and it had worked.

The rest of the war was to be fought with blade, fist and staff.

And beast.

The rest of Ares' experiments had been unleashed, breaking up Central's front line.

Tyrnnth was too lost in the battle to notice Zakkai and his men never aimed to kill.

And they had fallen behind, which had never happened before.

Zakkai raised his chin, regarding his men.

Thousands of Calterrans stretched behind Tyrnnth's line now, everything going as he and Grace had planned. He hoped she could pull off her end of the plan, or else his would never come to pass.

Cloud-shrouded mountains shone on the other side of the valley.

Vastlynd's border.

Between where the prince stood, and where he could make out a swath of evergreens; that was all that remained of Grace's once-great nation.

Zakkai flipped his knife-tipped spear to the blunt end and knocked a Centrallian soldier unconscious, turning to deal a blow to another soldier's stomach.

He was always targeted on the battlefield, as if ending him would be some sort of trophy kill.

It never worked out for the opposing army.

Zakkai swung his staff, a soldier falling to the bloodied mud.

Not dead. For the future of his world, for Grace— he would spare any he could.

Until the call was made and Calterra could make up for their mistakes and Zakkai's father's sins.

It was only a matter of time now.

54

Grace's palms were sweating.

She patted the frizzy strands of hair escaping the smooth mass of it over her shoulder.

The dress she had donned showed every curve and hollow of her body, her tanned, freckled skin on display.

She would never dress like this on her own.

But tonight, her body was a weapon.

Hanameel finished Grace's makeup, stepping back to regard her work. She was nearly Grace's mother's age, if her mother had lived.

Grace offered a smile and thanked her in Calterran.

The woman gripped Grace's hands and blinked twice.

"Be careful," Hanameel whispered.

But careful wasn't something Grace could afford to be anymore.

She squeezed Hanameel's hands and rose.

Exhaling, Grace took off her ring and threaded it onto the chain around her neck, dropping it into her dress.

She could barely feel Zakkai on the other side of it now, the distance between them wearing their connection thin.

But she felt his tug.

It was time.

"I will see you soon, friend," Grace said in Calterran. Hanameel nodded once, her black, graying hair dipping.

Grace strode out the the prince's chamber door and into the palace halls. She flinched as the door shut, sealing her to a fate she never asked for.

Grace raised her chin and strode forward.

For her friends, she would not falter.

55

A dark cloud opened above the coliseum, the rain lit up like liquid fire as the sun set.

The sight would have been beautiful, if not for the bloodbath below.

The pit floor turned to mud within moments.

Steven shouted, despite himself, despite everything Adira was, as Luther drew back an arm to throw a bone.

The empress ducked.

As Adira pivoted from the second strike, her foot slipped. She screamed, Steven rising to his feet as she fell.

A bone had struck her above the knee.

Steven's heart hammered as Luther approached. Adira raised her chin and clenched her jaw. She weakly lifted a bone shard.

Without landing a single blow, she would lose.

Nyrland's Empress, brought down within minutes.

Luther picked up a bone and broke it. When he neared, Adira lashed out with a snarl. He struck her shard away and dropped to his knees, shoving a bone beneath her collarbone. Steven lunged forward as she screamed.

Jay was shouting, but Steven couldn't decipher him above the crowd and the roaring in his head.

Luther let Adira go, allowing her to crawl away. He rose and took his time closing the distance, Tyrnnthians raising a chant.

Luther picked up a broken bone.

This was not a quick, clean death, this was a torture session.

Steven shut his eyes. He now understood why Jaxin had banned Centrallians from watching and participating in Blood Challenges.

Luther never lost, and made a spectacle of ending a life.

Steven opened his eyes to find Jay shouting before him, rain sliding down his face.

But Steven was no longer at the coliseum, watching Adira crawl from slow, merciless death.

He was in cobblestone streets, Adira's eyes alight. With her at the orchestra. Feeling her warmth radiate beside him as she curled against him her under a pelt.

Beside her on a New Iberian cliffside above a crushing blue sea, gulls crying overhead as sun shone in her hair, her smile unrestrained as she threw her arms out.

She was going to die today.

Luther caught and pinned Adira again.

"No," Steven breathed. Luther raised the bone, the fight gone from Adira's eyes. She had never plead for anything, but Steven lurched forward as she did. Jay shoved him back.

"Let her go," Jay shouted.

But Steven couldn't.

He shoved Jay and gripped the chainlink fence as Luther rammed the bone beneath Adira's other collarbone.

Cold metal bit Steven's fingers, Jay cursing at his back.

A hand wrapped around his ankle as Luther pulled the bone free, Adira screaming as her blood ran.

Steven looked down to find Jaxin.

"This was her choice!"

"And this is mine." Steven kicked Jaxin, the War Leader cursing as Steven shot over the fence.

He could have sworn he heard Adira scream *at* him.

Just one word, desperate and pleading.

No.

When Steven hit the ground, the breath shot out of his lungs, cold mud soaking his suit.

When Steven could draw breath, every inhale was monumental effort. He groaned as he attempted to draw the strength to move.

He turned his head to find Adira across the pit, her eyes locked on his. She shook her head, blood dripping from her face, a pool of crimson beneath her.

She spoke, but Steven heard nothing over the crowd.

"I was wondering when you'd show," Luther said. He dropped the bone he had been torturing Adira with and began stalking toward Steven.

56

Zakkai pulled his knife-tipped staff from the man at his feet, the soldier's scream blending with the rest.

The man's wounds would heal, Zakkai told himself.

He hoped.

It was hard not to aim to kill when he was trained to do so.

The border of Vastlynd drew closer.

Savea Emarani raced toward him. Zakkai halted as the young spy reached his side and doubled over.

"Why aren't you at the border, Emarani."

"Your Highness," Savea rasped. "There are— Tyrnnthian gas tanks at the border."

"There are gas tanks everywhere."

Zakkai watched the front draw further away, leaving him behind his men.

"They're *full.* Did General Chevalier mention them?" Savea asked.

"No. He didn't." Zakkai stuck his staff into the ground, working through the information. "They're going to wipe us out, too."

"Your Highness, Master Kamaka says if we retreat now, we may be able to outrun it before—"

"Tell Kamaka to order the spies to disable any tanks they can.

The rest of us will take care of the Tyrnnthians."

"But, Your Highness—"

"Running is not an option. We're in the valley now, we don't have time to run," Zakkai said. "We may as well die giving it all. Do you hear me, Emarani?"

Savea nodded before sprinting into smoke.

Zakkai made for the front, stepping over bodies and ignoring the pleading soldiers and the sounds of the dying around him.

"Hurry, Grace. Now."

The ring the prince wore communicated with the bearer of the matching gold band.

He hoped Grace could hear him across two thousand miles.

Zakkai sprinted until he was once again leading his men. He shouted above the din of war, rallying them.

He swung his spear, knocking two Centrallians out in one blow, his eye on the border.

They were getting close.

57

Grace wandered the halls, Zakkai's thoughts resounding in her mind, the ring shifting against her chest with each step.

It seemed Tyrnnth had never intended on sharing the Central Territories with Calterra.

While Prince Zakkai had laid a trap for Tyrnnth, Ares was already planning to wipe out his ally as soon as they were no longer useful to him.

Grace's hands clenched into fists before she released them. She couldn't let her thoughts show.

Zakkai was waiting on her.

The coil of dread in her stomach tightened.

She turned down a window-lined hall, pushing past the fear.

It was stormy today. Waves berated the shore as clouds raced to cover the sun.

She nearly collided with Memphis. He drew back, catching her elbow with a hand.

The seventh prince was kind, his eyes always somber. His brows drew together as he surveyed her.

"What are you doing out here?" He looked down the hall. "You know it's not safe without a guard."

"I can take care of myself," Grace assured. Zakkai hadn't told his brother the plan.

He should have.

Footsteps approached, Memphis stilling.

She shook him off. "Goodbye, Memphis. I'll be fine."

"Grace, *please.*"

King Vincere rounded the corner, Grace's heart galloping faster.

"Boy, step away from your brother's concubine."

Memphis stepped back, but remained at Grace's side as the king ate the distance between them.

Grace's heavily-shadowed eyes dropped to the floor as she curtsied. She watched Memphis' feet shift.

"Zakkai always had the prettiest ones," King Vincere said, a chill snaking down Grace's spine. He turned to his son. "Out, boy."

Memphis opened his mouth.

"Are you as deaf as you are useless?" the king snapped. Memphis ground his jaw, pausing before turning away.

Grace listened to Memphis retreat, wishing he hadn't, but knowing he must.

She smiled at the king. "I've been looking for you."

58

The gray of Luther's eyes— shadow, dust, death. His fighting leathers matched, mud spitting up with each step toward Steven.

The prizefighter rose, attempting to master the pain.

Luther cocked his head as he halted. "It's too late to save her."

"You're going to bleed for what you've done." Steven didn't recognize his own voice.

"You should be thanking me," Luther said. "There was a debt to pay for Farran Bardolph's life, and I had nearly paid it."

"He wouldn't want it this way." Steven rolled his neck, adrenaline covering the pain with each step forward.

"He wouldn't want you here, that's for sure. Though he wouldn't mind Adira's demise. Did you hear how your king screamed? How he begged? The pick axes were blunt, the slave's nails sharp—"

Steven snarled, his steps stronger. "Enough talking."

"Agreed." Luther dropped into a defensive position.

With the sky blood-red above, Steven launched, his body unfocused with rage. Luther feinted and knocked Steven to the ground.

"*Roll,*" Jay roared.

Steven did. Luther's boot came down and Steven stumbled upright.

He glanced to Adira as he backed away. She was still breathing. He regarded the sky, raindrops ruby red in the setting sun.

Blood Challengers never survived past sunset.

Steven glanced to the dais to find Ares lounged on his throne, watching intently. Steven turned in time to duck out of Luther's strike, the prizefighter thrusting an elbow for the man's back.

Luther grunted and pivoted.

Steven anticipated it, crouching and sweeping a leg. Luther fell hard, snarling. Within a breadth of a moment, the ex-dictator was on his feet again, teeth gritted and fists swinging.

Luther landed a blow, pain exploding in Steven's jaw. Iron and heat filled his mouth. He spat blood before blocking Luther's next strike.

"Did you know Ares shot Natalia?" Steven said, his voice hoarse. "I'm sure he told you I did, but I've never had reason to hurt her."

"You killed her to try and break me," Luther countered.

"I would never do that."

Luther blinked, his body stilling before he shook his head, snarling as he advanced again. Steven danced out of the way, blinding lights flaring above.

"*Steven!*" Adira's voice startled him.

Luther landed a blow to Steven's ribs.

The air left Steven's body as he slammed into concrete. He hadn't realized he had backed so far—

Luther smiled as he shot out a hand, wrapping his fingers around Steven's throat. Steven clawed at Luther's hand as he pushed Steven up the wall. The ex-dictator leaned in.

"Ares may have pulled the trigger, but Natalia is dead because of you," Luther said. "If you hadn't convinced Ridgeway to disobey my father—"

"No." Steven could barely get the word out. "She would have done the same, and you know it."

Luther's fingers squeezed as a familiar voice screamed above all the others.

Jay would watch Steven die the way Harrin had intended that day in the trailer ten years ago. But this time, Jay could do nothing to save his brother.

Luther's eyes narrowed as his hold tightened, his eyes piercing.

Steven couldn't breathe. He struggled and clawed, but it was not enough. His vision blurred and his lungs burned. Blood shone under his fingernails, but Luther held fast.

Luther grit his teeth as his other hand joined and *squeezed*. Steven tried to gasp, but no air came.

He would die soon.

And then Adira would.

And Jay—

He would live.

Farran was already dead. But Jay would live, and Grace would live. With Jaxin and Zakkai, they could find a way to end the war.

The thought had Steven relaxing, his bloodied hands falling away.

The world would be fine without him.

It had to be.

Luther smiled at whatever he saw in Steven's eyes.

59

Zakkai could make out the branches of the trees along Vastlynd's border. On either side of the prince, Tyrnnth pushed the last of Central's army to the brink.

Zakkai tripped, his staff catching the mangled, bloodied earth.

He had taken a hit to the shoulder. After he had withdrawn the knife, the enemy soldier ran.

Enemy was an interesting word right now.

Zakkai was still waiting for Grace to make the call.

A hiss issued from the border. He shoved a Centrallian aside and stepped away to listen.

The sound was growing, seeming to come from the west to the east.

Tyrnnth was opening their gas tanks.

"We're dead," Zakkai said to Grace. *"I'm making the call."*

What was there to lose now? He had tried to be honorable, as only a king could command their army to switch sides.

But if he was to die anyways—

"I can't wait for you, Grace. I'm sorry."

"What did you say, Zakkai?"

There she was. He smiled, grateful to hear her voice one more time.

"NOW," Zakkai roared, the command carrying over the din of

war, and the screaming of dying men, the keening of hound and beast.

Staffs turned on Tyrnnthian backs, and Calterra's heir watched as Tyrnnthian blood shed, death looming as greenish, yellow fog began to cover the field.

He roared and raised his staff, joining his men in one last fight.

60

"You were looking for me?" Saber Vincere looked Grace up and down.

Grace tucked a strand of hair behind an ear. "I was told you could tell me where His Highness, Prince Zakkai, was."

"He didn't tell you?" the king mused. "Your prince is at the front."

Grace raised a brow. "Your own heir?"

Saber smiled, drawing close enough for her to smell albacore on his breath. "One is not worried about heirs if he has *seven.*"

Grace masked her grimace with a coy smile and attempted to steady her hands. This man held no value for his own children, even his favored heir.

Saber placed a hand on Grace's hip, the other settling on her waist.

"You are worried for him. No wonder you are his favorite right now. If he passes in war, which is a great honor, I can take care of you." Saber smiled. "Besides, I do believe you would look best at a king's side, not a prince's."

"I think you may be right," Grace said. Dare she lean in? She was supposed to.

She didn't have to.

Despite everything screaming in her not to, she allowed Saber to pull her close. When he put his mouth on hers, Grace shoved down her disgust, the red-hot rage in her veins.

This is wrong.

How often had this man done this to women that hadn't wanted this? If Zakkai was right, too often.

Saber Vincere was not allowed in Zakkai's village.

The death Grace offered the king was far more merciful than men like him deserved.

She was going to throw up.

Zakkai spoke at the edge of her mind, though her own thoughts were too loud to hear him.

"What did you say, Zakkai?"

Saber Vincere's eyes flared wide.

Grace pulled back and angled her head. "Is something wrong?"

"You're—" Saber inhaled and choked.

Grace spat onto the floor. "Poisonous."

Saber stumbled back onto the rug, looking up at her as he shook his head. "You think you can kill me that easily?"

"Yes," she whispered. "I know I can."

The king's eyes went wide before his face contorted. "How *dare* you, you insolent, little—"

And then he was spitting and snarling.

She hadn't wanted to kill him. Zakkai had claimed it necessary.

Grace stepped back, surprised to find someone at her back. She turned to find Memphis, his grip slackening on the dagger in his hand.

"What is going on?" he asked quietly.

"It's done," Grace said to Zakkai.

"Don't just stand there boy, *save me,*" the king screamed, foam flying, a hand wrapped around his throat.

"I don't think I can," Memphis said, stepping back as the foam turned blood-red.

"Zakkai? Make the call. It's done. It's over."

"Dagger, boy. Give it to me," Saber begged.

Grace turned away as Memphis dropped his dagger to the floor.

"Zakkai?"

In the reflection of the darkening windows, Grace watched the king draw the dagger across his own throat.

Grace had completed her end of the plan, but it was too late.

Her knees hit the floor and the shaking in her body doubled.

The bond between her and the prince was silent.

And Zakkai was dead.

61

Despite Steven's body shutting down, he heard Jay's roar.

"Don't let him win now! Fight it, Steven!"

Luther grinned, veins in his forehead bulging as he pressed Steven into the wall. Something in the prizefighter's spine popped.

This was not Luther Hawthorne, the man who had shown kindness to a sold princess.

The man who had chosen to undermine his own father's decisions, even when there was little room to do so.

Steven looked toward the dais and noted a faraway expression on Ares' face. Luther angled his head.

"That's right, Steven."

Steven narrowed his eyes in one last act of defiance, the edges of his vision blackening.

One last push of breath through his lips.

"You're next, Ares."

Steven shot his fingers into Luther's open eye.

The crowd roared as an inhuman sound tore from Luther's throat, Steven falling to the mud. He heaved in a rattling breath, attempting to rally the strength to move.

After his second attempt to rise, he made it to his feet.

Pain tore through his side as his legs pumped, each breath like razors in his throat, his lungs.

He fell to his knees before Adira, paling as he noted the gouges and blood. He ran shaking hands over her before cupping her face with a hand.

"Adira." He shook her. "Hold on, it's almost over."

"Get out," she breathed, her eyes dull with pain.

"What?" Steven rasped.

"You need to—"

Adira screamed, a bone now imbedded in her shoulder. Steven whirled to find Luther approaching, a dark, bloody socket where his eye had once been.

"Sorry, I missed," Luther ground out.

Steven rose, grasping a bone shard as he did.

"I won't do it again," the ex-dictator promised. *Ares* promised, through Luther's mouth.

Steven stepped away from the empress.

Adira inhaled. "Get out before—"

"Shut up, girl," Luther snapped, striding across the pit as Steven continued to back away.

"I didn't meant to gouge out your eye," Steven said.

Luther snarled, the sound more animal than human.

"If you think this looks bad, imagine loosing both." Luther twisted a bone between his fingers. "You won't have to soon. You'll *know* what it'll feel like."

Steven wiped the rain from his brow, shifting his hair aside.

Fear would get him killed, so he shoved it aside for something else.

Something calm, confident.

Courage.

He breathed deep, his back hitting the wall.

"Nowhere to go," Luther said, his face and teeth bloodied. He raised the bone as Steven raised his chin.

"Likewise," Steven said.

Luther lunged with a roar, bone outstretched.

Steven turned and kicked off the wall, his foot connecting with

Luther's jaw. Steven fell with Luther, mud spraying. Something cracked, but Steven forced his body to move. As Luther made to rise, Steven pivoted atop him.

The prizefighter shoved the bone shard deep, Luther's scream cleaving the air.

Steven leaned down. "That was for Adira." He pulled the shard free, blood spilling. He shoved Luther down as he made to rise.

"And this is for my country."

Steven drove the bone buried beneath Luther's other collarbone, his ears ringing as Luther screamed louder.

Luther's remaining eye snapped to Steven's, pain and fear replacing the cold and cruelty.

"Don't," Luther breathed. His body shook as he closed his eye. "If you kill me, the war will not end."

Steven leaned in. "You and I both know that is not how a Blood Challenge works."

The crowd grew louder, repeating something in Tyrnnthian.

Steven blocked them out, along with Jay's voice.

"Let me throw you out," Luther said, blood dribbling from his mouth. Steven pressed the point of the bone into Luther's chest, angled between the ribs and above his heart.

"You'll carve my eyes out if I let you go," Steven said.

Luther shook his head weakly. "I give my word that I will not harm you, Steven."

Steven shook his head, raindrops falling from his hair.

"But you will," he said. "Ares is using you."

"There's nothing left to use. It's over." Luther coughed blood, his body shaking. "I can try to stand, and you could reach the fence from my back. That may work before—"

"Before I have a chance to end the war?" Steven shook his head. He drew a breath, preparing for the killing blow.

He had ended lives on the front.

This felt far worse than pulling a trigger.

Steven raised the bone, rain sliding down its point.

"I loved Natalia . . . very much," Luther said quietly. "I will see her soon, so I am not afraid."

Steven was vaguely aware he was shaking his head.

"I beg of you Steven, do not kill me. Not like this."

Steven inhaled. "I'm sorry."

"Please—" Luther gasped as Steven lodged the bone between his ribs. The prizefighter stumbled back as the ex-dictator grasped for life.

Natalia's husband. Steven's brother-in-law.

Ares' scapegoat.

The war was ending before Steven's eyes, and all he could think about was how *wrong* it felt to end his enemy's life.

Luther looked up at the sky, his breath rattling as blood escaped his mouth. The crowd had grown silent by the time Luther's hands fell away from his chest.

Steven tried to remember how to breathe.

Luther was dead.

Steven's bloodied hands shook as he reached forward and shut Luther's remaining eye, unable to leave him staring into endless rain.

He rose, Luther's parting words like a lead weight in his chest.

Luther was dead.

The war was over.

62

Zakkai's heart slowed as poison flooded his bloodstream, each breath more taxing than the last.

Saw blades had made their way down his throat, his lungs burning.

The prince gasped, body lurching upright.

He threw up blood.

Grace was speaking to him. He could barely hear her, as he had taken his ring off and placed it over his heart, hoping she wouldn't feel his life slip away.

She didn't need to know how painfully slow it was.

Grace had completed her task, and Zakkai's father was dead, the cause all his own.

Saber Vincere could no longer harm anyone, and Zakkai Mililani was King of Calterra now.

He would die with dishonor, as his father had still been breathing when the prince had made the call.

There hadn't been enough time to wait.

Zakkai retched, the soldiers nearest to him already still and silent.

Soon, he promised himself, thudding back to the ground.

Death would claim him, and he would see his mother.

His cousins.

Then he could apologize to them for being the reason they had left the world too soon.

Grace would be fine. His death would not break her.

Not as she currently broke him.

She told him she loved him. Over and over again.

As if she thought him already dead.

Zakkai sighed, his hands shaking as he went against his own order, slipping the ring on one last time.

He could have sworn he saw stars in the black sky beyond the haze of smoke, beyond the carnage around him.

"Zakkai?"

He smiled as he felt Grace's hope, her joy, the weight of what she had said before settling like a blanket, tucking him in for a long sleep.

She loved him. It was enough.

The poison would not allow him his life back, despite how bright his future looked.

Zakkai blinked slow.

"Goodbye, Grace." He closed his eyes. *"I am sorry I could not rule by your side."*

"No. Please—" Grace reached for him, but he was already gone.

"Long live the queen." With what little remained of his strength, Zakkai slipped off his ring.

63

The crowd watched as Steven limped to Adira.

I loved Natalia . . . very much.

Steven's knees hit crimson-stained mud.

I will see her soon, so I am not afraid.

Steven had murdered his sister's husband, as much a monster as the man on the dais.

He moved the wet strands of hair from Adira's face. Though her breathing was whet and rasping, and her face pale, she was still alive.

"It's over," he said.

"You shouldn't . . . have jumped in," Adira breathed.

"He was going to kill you."

Adira looked at him. "And you should have let him."

The deluge began to lift as Ares approached, stopping just before Adira.

Steven lifted his gaze. "It's over."

He set a hand on Adira, as if he could stop Ares from taking her. If he could control Luther, she could be next.

Despite everything, Steven hated to admit he needed her.

He didn't need her near him, he just needed to know she was alive, somewhere in this wretched world of his.

Ares' face was hard to read as he watched back, his eyes lifting to something behind Steven.

Splashing echoed through the pit, Steven glancing over a shoulder to find Jay sprinting, face bloodless.

Jay slid to a stop and crouched, his voice dropping. "Let's go."

"We need to take—"

"Oh, for the love of all that is still good in this world! Leave her!" Jay pulled Steven up with him, the prizefighter shaking him off.

"I *can't*."

"The whispers are true, Cassius," Ares said.

"What whispers?" Steven looked at Ares.

The War Leader smiled sadly. "Some say it's your loss."

"What the hell does that mean?" Steven stepped forward.

Ares gestured toward Luther's body. "Most would call what they witnessed tonight murder."

Steven shook his head. "No, I won." Steven pointed a finger at the empress. "And I managed to save your daughter, too. You can't claim the same. Why haven't you called for medics yet? She *needs* help."

Ares angled his head. "You dishonored Empress Theron by interrupting her Blood Challenge and killing her opponent in cold blood. I believe I heard my son begging for his life before you slaughtered him."

Steven flinched. "Luther is dead. The war is over," he pressed. Jay set a hand on his shoulder.

"Steven—" Jay began.

"The war is *not* over. It shall resume as soon as the mourning period is complete," Ares said, clasping his hands behind his back.

Jay tightened his grip, though Steven wouldn't move. He wasn't entirely sure he could, each breath tighter than the last.

"No one's going to agree to that," Steven said, his voice low.

"They don't have to agree." Ares shrugged. "It's going to happen anyways."

Something agonizing passed in and out of Ares eyes as he

glanced over to Luther's body.

Something red hot entered Steven's veins at the sight.

"You have no right to look at him like that," Steven spat. "You made him do this, you don't have the capability to feel—"

Ares was in Steven's face in a heartbeat.

"You. Don't. Have. A. Clue," Ares snarled, "what I am capable of."

Steven's eyes blazed as Ares stepped back, dusting off his suit jacket. He snapped his fingers, medics appearing.

"I'm going with her," Steven declared.

"No," Adira said, her voice strained.

"Why?" Steven asked, resisting the urge to kneel beside her.

"Because you can't," she snapped, her eyes pained. For a moment, Steven could have sworn there was something else in them.

Adira looked away. Medics swarmed, blocking Steven's view. When he could see her again, she was on a stretcher, her blood dripping as she was lifted off the ground.

"Adira," Steven said. "Please look at me."

"Goodbye, Steven," she said. She wouldn't look at him.

Steven hadn't registered Ares had been speaking.

"You should listen to her," Ares said, watching the stretcher move toward the gate. "Adira was the one to come up with the plan to overthrow Luther, proving to me she has what it takes to rule free of . . . influence."

Steven wasn't quite sure what he was hearing, watching as Ares' eyes tracked another stretcher take the field, the bearers in no rush to retrieve the body collapsed at the wall.

"Don't play games with me, Ares," Steven warned.

Ares laughed under his breath, shaking his head as he met Steven's gaze. "I have so much fun without them, what makes you think I need them?"

Steven ground his jaw as Ares looked skyward.

"I'll give you the truth, and you can decide when you want to believe it." He met Steven's eyes. "Deal?"

Ares took Steven's silence as acquiescence to continue.

"We all knew you would be Luther's undoing."

Adira made it to the gate as four medics struggled to lift Luther's body.

"I set the board for the Culling to take place in an attempt to take you out. Adira knew better, and thought smarter." Ares watched a medic slip as they set Luther down. "She knew you'd jump in today, and had planned on it."

Steven looked toward the darkened gate, his breath coming in fast.

This was Ares' cruelest manipulation yet. Why had Steven allowed himself to listen to this?

"Brilliant, isn't she?" Ares stepped back. "You jumped in, killed Luther, and she lived. The war goes on."

"Steven," Jay murmured.

"You're lying," Steven rasped.

"What do I have to gain by lying to you?" Ares turned on a heel. "I nearly have everything I need now. If not for Saber's son, I would have it all."

Zakkai had managed to save something to fight and bleed over, if the war was to go on.

But it couldn't.

Steven moved, slamming into Ares' back. They fell to the ground and rolled, Ares pinning Steven with a blade at his throat.

"Oh, don't be so predictable, Castellen," Ares ground out, cold metal pressing until Steven's blood ran.

"I'll kill you," Steven promised.

Ares leaned in. "I suggest you try harder next time." He flipped the knife and rose. Steven watched Ares exit until Jay offered a hand.

The crowd was silent as Steven and Jay crossed the pit, medics looking their way as they attempted to bear the weight of Luther's body.

64

From the moment Steven arrived to the Central Territories, people cursed him.

Citizens lined the street and shouted as they drove by.

Bodyguards, armed to the teeth, escorted Steven and Jay into Capital Hall and to the President's conference room.

Steven would have been torn to pieces, if not.

Advisors and council members lining the table exited, but not before casting vicious glances Steven's way.

Jaxin gestured toward the long table, the President's eyes hard as he regarded Steven and his brother.

"President Vanzena, let me introduce you to Steven Castellen, as well as his brother, Cassius Castellen," Jaxin said, taking a seat beside the president.

"Let's get this over with," President Vanzena said, two lines forming on between his brows. "My schedule is quite full today."

Steven was banned from Central.

The President had chastised Steven for not following protocol, orders, and for allowing the daughter of their enemy to seduce him.

If Steven had still been a Central Territorian citizen, President Vanzena assured Steven the consequences would have been much worse.

Steven would never forget Jay's reaction.

"Ban me too, then. I did even less than Steven," Jay said, his knuckles white on the armrest as he leaned forward. "I just sat on my ass and watched."

The president banned Jay, too.

After the meeting, Jaxin followed Jay and Steven out. The War Leader apologized for the meeting's outcome.

Steven was beyond caring.

He had expected burning rage and smothering shame— but found he couldn't feel anything at all.

Farran was dead.

The war wasn't over.

And everything had been for nothing at all.

65

Grace would find him.

Rain poured as evening darkened the field before her. Embers burned, sparks flying underfoot with each step.

Nobody had stopped her as she tore through the airport, running, running, running—

The field would take days to cover.

Grace searched charred bodies until darkness, her knees dropping as she held her head in her hands. The scent of burning flesh had since stuffed up her nose and choked her senses.

The rain had since rendered her flashlight useless.

Death was everywhere, in everything, a nightmare in which when she screamed, no noise followed. When she sobbed, there were no tears.

Grace had called his name until her voice gave out.

A drowning rain fell with force, dimming the scattered fires, her body shaking as a cold so thorough soaked her bones.

The poisonous fog had blown away.

She would have came regardless.

Grace lifted her face to the battlefield.

Zakkai was out there.

Though after hours of searching the other bodies . . .

Only bones would remain, Zakkai's gold ring smelted.

A broken sound made its way out of her body.

After minutes or hours, a blanket fell over her shoulders, familiar arms and a familiar scent wrapping around her, lifting her up.

"C'mere, G," Jay said, drawing her close. "Let's go home."

66

Steven's bag thudded to the gravel drive as he looked at Farran's night-darkened cottage.

Someone needed to tend the orchard now that the king was dead.

Steven ran a hand over Farran's truck— the prizefighter's truck now, the metal glinting in starlight.

He did not want it.

Everything would remind him of his friend, and inexplicably lead Steven to remember the woman who had manipulated him.

Jaxin had shown Steven the evidence pieced together.

Everything Ares claimed had been true.

Adira had pulled strings in the background and cast herself as someone else entirely.

She Ares' butcher and executioner.

The woman at the concert? *That* had been the act.

Each glimpse of *her* had been the lie.

Despite the President's ban, Jay had stayed in Central to find Grace.

Zakkai's body had yet to be identified, though Steven was sure it had been consumed in the fire that followed the end of the war, leaving what was left of Central's hard-won land desolate.

Steven looked toward the darkened windows, yet to muster the courage to go inside yet.

It would smell like tea, candles, dust and books.

He wasn't sure he was ready for it.

After watching constellations wheel overhead, his breath clouding in the night air, a thought seemed to whisper from the starlight.

If it is not good, then it is not the end yet.

Steven closed his eyes, a breeze picking up from the fields, kissing his brow.

He couldn't recall if he had seen the quote typed on a scrap of paper tucked in Grace's mirror or on a piece of paper set in Farran's windowsill.

Perhaps Max had said, Steven having forgotten it until he needed it most.

But there the words were, a light in the darkness.

Nothing was good.

Not one thing.

Steven opened his eyes, a burning star cutting across the glittering expanse. Bright for a moment before fading to black.

Steven's breath rattled as he inhaled.

He was a murderer. Luther's blood was on Steven's hands, the arcs of his fingernails still crimson.

It was never supposed to end this way.

"But it is not the end yet," Steven promised.

EPILOGUE

"I am Edwin Mulrennen, son of Ivor Mulrennen, eighth light keeper of Einerech Bay."

It was always the first thought Edwin woke with.

The lighthouse keeper brought a cup of coffee to his mouth, tentatively sipping the hot, bitter liquid. He swallowed, his lips thinning as he took in the brewing storm on the horizon.

He would have to depart soon.

Edwin downed the rest of his mug, something about the smell and taste reminding him of something familiar and lost to him, all at the same time.

It likely had to do with the head injury he had suffered weeks ago.

Somehow, he had fallen down the lighthouse stairs.

Edwin turned to find his wife folding laundry on the kitchen table.

Their home was small, offering just enough space for a bed, kitchen, table, and living room. Bookcases, framed paintings, and cabinets lined the wall space that wasn't occupied by a window.

For Edwin, it was home one day out of the week, inclement weather not allowing him to stay long.

The fronts coming off the southeastern coast of Hymnlynd were a different breed, the fisherman trusting Edwin to warn them to keep off the rocks when the sea grew dark and tumultuous.

"I must go, darling," Edwin said. He crossed the room and planted a kiss on his wife's hair. "I will see you soon."

Leah's arms wrapped around his torso and squeezed, her muscles always surprising him. Though she was pale and lithe, her fine hair like sunlit copper, Edwin had seen her complete thirty pull-ups the other night.

While he had slept.

He wasn't sure why she waited for him sleep, but she rooted around the house at all hours of the night.

"Stay safe," Leah said, drawing back.

"You, as well." Edwin sighed, looking into her crystalline, cold eyes. "You can come with, if you would like."

He had offered before. Many times.

Leah smiled and wrung her hands. "I have to meet the fisherman."

Edwin stepped back with a smile. "Right."

"Someday."

"Someday," he echoed.

He gathered his rucksack as the storm drew closer, the grass outside their home undulating in the wind.

White caps shown under a bright, afternoon sun, clouds coming from the west soon to cover its brilliant light.

"I'll see you in a week."

Judging from the storm report, it could be two.

But Leah already knew that.

Edwin turned on a heel, a hand on the doorknob.

A knock sounded, the light keeper's brows going up.

"It seems we have one here now." Edwin opened the door to find a young, shorter man on the other side, his face pale and heavily freckled. A fisherman, judging from the wool sweater and twill pants.

"Those stairs nearly killed me," the man said in the typical brusque accent around these parts. He continued to dust off the grass seeds clinging to his pants. "I'm looking to moor in your bay until the storm passes. Do you folks need food, water?"

"You are more than welcome to moor, and no thank you," Edwin said, offering a small smile.

The fisherman looked up with a start, his brows drawing together. Leah approached Edwin's back as the stranger set a hand to his throat.

"No," he breathed, stepping back. "Farran?"

Edwin angled his head. "Pardon?"

"Oh," Leah said. "Though my Edwin is quite handsome, you're mistaken, lad."

The fisherman's red brows drew together as he looked from Edwin to his wife. "I surely must be."

The man took off his cap and bowed once. "Apologies, I could have sworn you looked like somebody I once knew."

"It's quite alright," Edwin said. He offered a sad smile, placing his cap back on. "I'll be— I'll be on my way, then. I'll leave as soon as the storm passes. Thank you."

The stranger left, casting a glance over his shoulder before heading down to the bay.

"Interesting fellow," Edwin said, looking to his wife. Her lips were twisted in a frown, her eyes unreadable.

Leah looked up and smiled. "Aren't they all?"

"I suppose." Edwin grabbed his wool coat from the rack before pausing in the open doorway, the wind grabbing at his hair and clothes. "I love you, darling."

Leah was already turned away, her hands in the sink. Over the water running, she must not have heard him.

Edwin departed, wind blasting up the cliffside to blow his hair from his brow, his knit sweater and wool layers keeping him warm.

"Farran," Edwin murmured to himself, the wind carrying the sound of it away from him. Ivory-feathered gulls soared overhead, crying in the last rays of sunlight.

Farran.

Why was it so familiar, yet unknown?

Sometimes Edwin dreamt of another world.

A world where there was a honey-brown eyed woman, magnetic and warm, yet incapable of reaching, with roses on her cheeks and doves in her hands.

Sometimes he dreamt of a man who fought with scarred fists and smiled with his eyes, sometimes of a dark-haired man with art on his skin and cunning on his tongue.

Edwin could have sworn the name had come from *that* world, those dreams the light keeper fought to remember each time he woke.

Perhaps he would write a book about it all.

He had plenty of time to in the lighthouse.

Edwin shook his head as he reached the bottom step, wading through grass to hoist his rowboat over a shoulder.

This was always the most difficult part.

The pain in his shoulder flared, Edwin gritting his teeth. As he bore weight on his other leg, pain seized him.

His breath was labored by the time he dropped the boat near the water's edge, and he took a moment to pull himself back together.

He wasn't sure how he managed to wound himself so thoroughly on that fall.

Leah said it had to have been the errant nails sticking from the wooden boards.

Edwin looked up and watched the growing waves slosh over the rock upon which his lighthouse sat.

He needed to go.

Edwin pushed the boat into the water and hopped in gracelessly. As he rowed across the bay, he drew close enough to the fisherman's vessel to read the name on the bow.

Lady Creidne Áine

The wood boat was beautifully crafted, bearing a solid hull and thoughtfully managed rigging. The stranger Edwin met earlier most assuredly took pride in his work.

As if summoning him, the pale, red-haired man stepped out onto the aft deck and raised a hand in greeting.

The light keeper returned it, smiling even as clouds darkened the sun and his boat pulled back as he halted his efforts for but a moment.

The fisherman almost looked as though he was going to call out. Edwin waited a moment, just in case, but the fisherman stepped back. He looked toward the island and entered his boat once more.

Edwin needed to get going anyways.

He fought each wave and white cap as he neared the lighthouse, the shadowed waves painted a deep, dark cobalt. His muscles burned, sweat coating his brow, neck and back, but he soon reached the rock and hefted his boat in.

Edwin sprinted up the steps lining the lighthouse walls, fighting the weakness in his body. Though the visitor had delayed him, he arrived in time.

Nobody would be lost today.

"Farran," the light keeper whispered to himself as he lit his beacon, lighting up his perfect, dark corner of the world.

It would keep him awake tonight, wondering.

Who was he?

ACKNOWLEDGEMENT

Dearest reader, thank you for taking the time to read my novel! I hope you enjoyed the story and fell in love with the characters and their world.

I have encountered many who have encouraged me on this journey, but there have been a few who have went the extra mile, and I would like to take the time to thank them.

My husband is one who has gone *several* miles. To my partner in life, thank you for your support, encouragement, and assurance. Thank you for bearing with me, funding my writer's diet of confections and caffeine, and dealing with my night owl tendencies. I appreciate you. Thank you for the work of your hands and heart— thank you for everything.

To my family, thank you for your reassurance and patience, for your excitement. Even as attempts to write this novel fell through over the years, you continued to spur me on. Thank you for listening when I rambled, and for smiling, even when I spoke for far too long.

I have a friend with hazel eyes and joy so contagious, I find it difficult not recall a memory of her where she doesn't bear a bright smile. Despite the miles apart, she continued to cheer me on. Thank you, G, for setting time aside to catch edits and spend time with my characters. Thank you for your genuineness and heart, and for your honesty. You are amazing.

I have a friend who lives in a land with endless sunshine in the summer and overbearing darkness in the winter. She is beyond wonderful, and I love her dearly. P, thank you so much for your steady, authentic encouragement and investment in this story. Thank you for your excitement, your willingness to help, and for being you. This process was made so much brighter by you.

To the friend in whom I share so much in common with, including title of ex-roomie: thank you for your authenticity, support, and wisdom. I will never forget our first conversation being about this book (unless I do forget) on the ferry all those years ago. I can only hope I have been such a good of friend as you are to me. You are a blessing and inspiration to me.

To Kyles (reader; don't worry, this is most assuredly a code name), thank you for being my reading buddy for life. Ours is my most beloved book club of all. Thank you for your support and encouragement from day one. Thank you for being willing to read an entire rough draft, years ago, when it well and truly sucked. I hope this version is better, and if it is not; please tell me, that I may throw myself off the nearest cliff. I digress. Anyways, thank you. My world is a million times brighter with you in it, even with the distance between. I love you so much.

There are so many to thank. A terrible, wonderful amount. As I sit here and remember each person and blessing in my life, I can scarcely believe I have been so fortunate.

To the Texans who poured time and love into my life, throughout many stages and years, you all made such an impact on me. I fear the version of me I would have been without you all. I love and miss you all terribly, and think of you far more often than I reach out.

To my teachers, you must know I still talk about every one of you. You were amazing, and quite frankly, the best. Thank you for investing your time and energy into your work and students. It made a very positive impact on me, and I am so grateful.

To my English teachers in particular, your encouragement and guidance was especially appreciated. To one English teacher, more particular now— I'm not sure if you remember reading one of my assignments senior year, where a particular character's name may have aligned with this novel's, but I must admit, your encouragement may have been part of the catalyst for me to pursue this dream.

Thank you for giving me hope. I have carried it with me since.

To my beta readers, thank you for taking the time to read my story. Thank you for your insight, encouragement, support, and excitement.

To the people who smiled and offered their support upon hearing about this endeavor, this acknowledgment is for you, too. I never forgot.

And to every reader, thank you, thank you, *thank you* for taking the time to get to know these characters that are so near and dear to me, and to read their story.

I am so grateful, for all of you.

ABOUT THE AUTHOR

Linnea K. Warren hails from the state of Alaska.
Wife to a hard-working carpenter, mother of two wonderful
children, she spends many nap times and nights writing. She loves
traveling, coffee, driving with insensibly loud music, and spending
time with her friends, family, and Jesus.

Made in United States
Troutdale, OR
02/16/2025

28826732R00239